TAMARA BURKE

BROKEN WITH STAINS

NOUVEAU SOUL PUBLISHING

NOUVEAU SOUL PUBLISHING

BROKEN WITH STAINS

Copyright © 2011 by Tamara Burke

Cover photo by Larysa Dodz

Cover design by Tamara Burke

ISBN: 978-0615511252

First Nouveau Soul Publishing paperback printing: July 2011

10 9 8 7 6 5 4 3 2 1

Printed in the United States of America

2

"Do not give what is holy to the dogs; nor cast your pearls before swine, lest they trample them under their feet, and turn and tear you in pieces."

Matthew 7:6

ACKNOWLEDGEMENTS

THE LORD

Never do I want to continue my journey without giving You the praises You are due. This book couldn't have been completed without You. Your Word is what inspired me to write.

CAROLYN BURKE

To my mommy, I love you and thank you for being a listening ear for all of my fears and cares. I appreciate every single word of encouragement you've given. You are strength and light and God's supreme gift to me.

DEBORAH RICHARDS

Aunt Debbie, you saved me from myself with that sharp eye of yours. Those 2 a.m. sessions were worth every minute of missed sleep. I Love you and thank you so much for reviewing and giving the honest opinion I can always count on you for. Your help meant everything to me!

BENJAMIN MCKISSICK

Thank you a million times for helping me with everything from computer issues to everyday drama in my world. You've always been there for me, I have so much love and respect for you.

KIT LAU

Reviewer extraordinaire! Thank you for churning out reviews quicker than quick. Your help has been phenomenal and I appreciate your honesty too.

1 noelle

"**Y**ou rotten bastard . . ." Forget words – Noelle took her three inch red sandal and threw it at the back of her boyfriend's head. Blinded by her rage, she unfortunately missed her target. But when the shoe whizzed past his dome by a mere half inch, he turned around with wide, startled eyes. That was all she needed. The other foot came off and she didn't hesitate to take it and aim for his sockets - whichever one was lucky enough to get hit first.

"What the hell are you doing?" he yelled, wincing from the heel imprint left on his forehead. Her aim needed work.

She huffed out her frustration. "I was trying to draw blood, jackass." Now as mad as Noelle was, she was still knowledgeable about the pending situation. She watched Christopher's six foot three, two hundred and fifty-two pound frame walking her way and knew he could most likely snap her neck in two with very little pressure applied. With those facts in mind, she also knew that she should either, A: run for her life, or B: run for her life. She was prepared to do just that. But just one glance at the crazy-haired, chunky girl trembling in the corner. One glance at the tire-like roll spilling over her naked waist, was all it took to make the blood in Noelle's veins boil over her limit.

"Oh my God - Chris what is she doing?" the girl yelled while struggling to keep the paisley sheets around her body. Squeezing herself into the corner of the wall, she watched Noelle's movements, saying, in an attempt to escape the wrath, "You told me you didn't have a girlfriend, Chris!"

Noelle's eyes made a quick sweep to the left and then over to her right. She spotted just what she needed on the bureau beside her. Picking up the plastic container of darts in one quick motion, she threw them at Chris, one by one, like she

—
5

TAMARA BURKE

was pitching for the Yankees.

It was two years ago, on their very first date, Chris had taught her how to throw darts. Now after months of practice, she was practically an expert.

One in his shoulder. One in his chest. One in his arm. The other three she aimed straight below his waist. He was quick though and blocked two of the darts before they could reach their intended target. The third little stunner landed in his upper left thigh.

His stunned plaything screamed for bloody murder, which only helped to make Noelle more upset. "Shut the hell up you dumb broad. Your ass is next," she said as she raised the couple darts that were left.

Unfortunately, it didn't happen.

Chris' room mate, Troy, flew through the door.

"What the fu . . ." He looked at Chris removing darts from his body, and then turned to look at Noelle. "Are you serious? Talk to me – just calm down. Chill for a minute!" he said reaching for her hands.

She pushed him away. "No! Don't say nothing to me right now. You knew he been seeing her behind my back. Don't try to act like you didn't."

Chris lunged towards Noelle, but Troy held him back.

"Yo man, chill. Both of you, chill."

With hands on hips, Noelle grilled Troy up and down. "You knew about this, didn't you?" The question was only to see if he would lie to her face.

"Nobody told me nothing," the girl hollered from the corner. "I wasn't -"

Noelle charged after her, reaching halfway across the room, before Troy pulled her back. Shrugging and twisting out of his grip, she pushed him backward, and yelled in his face. "We're supposed to be cool and you couldn't tell me? Not even a hint or something, Troy?"

"I'm not in this, Noelle."

"I'm not trying to hear that. You coulda told me something. I gotta come find out like this?" Chris jumped bad from his spot by the bed, "Nobody told you to barge up in my apartment without calling."

"You gave me a key, stupid," she spat.

"You a crazy bitch - you know that?" Chris huffed out. Noelle cocked her head back. *Oh hell to the no,* she thought to herself, looking his dart-riddled body up and down.

"Bitch?!"

She grabbed the green ceramic mug from the same desk that held the darts. Obviously Chris had learned his lesson because he turned his back to her and ducked just as she began to throw it at him. The cup grazed his ear and crash-landed by crumpled clothes on the floor.

"Stop breaking my shi -"

"I'll break whatever I want," Noelle shouted, "and I'm going to break her face too."

She tried again to get at the scared girl. Troy bear-hugged her, dragging her backward towards the door.

"Troy if you don't let me go - "

He cautiously released her and placed his hands firmly on her shoulders.

"Noelle, come let's go outside and talk," Troy urged.

"Talk about what?" She took a couple steps toward Chris as Troy followed close behind. "Two years. Two years I wasted with you. You were supposed to hold me down Chris and I come find you between another bitch's legs? I had nothing but love for you, gave you everything, and this is how you turn around and do me?"

Noelle was thoroughly disgusted. All the good times, all of her commitment, all the days and nights falling deeper in love were all for nothing. It amounted to nothing more than a waste of time and energy. Even more so, because she'd given him a second chance.

"If you wanted your freedom, you coulda been a man and just told me. Remember, you came back for me when we broke up the first time. You should've just let me be. You dragged me into this. It was all you. Why didn't you just leave me alone?"

As much as she wanted to kill Chris at the moment, looking at him made her think of all the times they'd shared dreams, plans, and bright hopes for their future together. The end was here. An ending that she never imagined would take place. This cheater before her wasn't the guy that she could one day see herself marrying. He was a fraud. Not the one who'd brought her food when she was hungry, helped her study when she had a big test, massaged her feet when she'd had a long day, washed her hair just because he wanted to. He wasn't the one who bought her ten dozen red roses on her birthday. Not the one who said he loved her time and time again.

"I took you back because I thought you'd changed. Thought you realized what you were missing. But you got me – I definitely see it now – you ain't nothing more than a dirty, lying bastard!"

2 sienna

"Thank you, Jesus!" Sienna plopped down on her brand new king-sized bed. Inhaling the comforting scent of her newly washed laundry, she was happy she'd finally gotten it over with. The past week had slipped by in a blur. Today was her best chance to steal two hours for her seven loads. She lay there promising herself, even if it killed her, she'd find time and never let her laundry get this out of control again.

Her lids felt heavy. Still, as sleep tugged at her eyes, she wondered what Marcus was up to right now. *Working hard probably.* She admired her man's work ethic. Too bad lately he'd taken on extra at the architectural firm. Their quality time had been cut back significantly. She missed seeing him more often, but refused to be the nagging girlfriend who didn't understand. Before long, she went from thinking about Marcus to contemplating strawberries, papaya, and pears.

She inhaled tropical breezes and could almost taste the kiwi and watermelons dancing on her tongue. Sienna licked at the different flavors. Devouring and savoring the juices, she bit into the fruits harder until her eyes slowly fluttered open. Confused, she rolled her tongue around her dry mouth and tasted nothing but a thin coating. Sienna looked around at the mint green walls of her bedroom.

Great, I fell asleep.

Her head fell back onto the massive pile of clothes. Sienna was scared to get up and check the time, terrified to see how many hours she'd unconsciously let slip by. Instead, she laid there. Checked her watch which said three-thirty.

Only five more minutes.

Her five minutes came and went as she slowly slipped back into sleep.

TAMARA BURKE

What? Where's that . . . where's that ringing coming from? She shot up in the bed, remembering she needed to be at the studio for Eve's portfolio shoot. Marni might smile and sigh if she was late. But Eve would flat out kill her. She hustled to the cordless phone by the large flat screen TV. The cable box read four-thirty. It had to be Eve calling to curse her out. Another unanswered ring and the voice mail would pick up. Sienna stubbed her pinkie toe on the foot of the bed in a mad dash to get to the phone.

Reeling from the pain, she grabbed it from the receiver and answered, "I'll be right there."

Silence greeted her on the other end.

"Helllooo?"

"Yes . . . umm . . . Sienna, right?"

The syrupy voice definitely didn't belong to her friend.

"Yes, who's this?"

"You don't know me."

Sienna sighed over the silver phone. Tiredness was still in her bones and she was not in the mood for games.

"Help me to know you. Who is this?"

"My name's Nonda."

Nope. Nobody she remotely knew.

"And what can I do for you . . . Nonda?"

The woman cleared her throat.

"Nothing much, really. You're pretty much in the dark about everything."

Sienna could hear the smugness in her voice as she continued.

"I was calling to shed some light in *your* world. I'm doing a little something for *you.*"

Sienna arched a perfectly sculpted eyebrow.

"And how so?"

"We . . . how should I say it . . . we share someone very special in common. I'm not calling because I mind sharing.

BROKEN WITH STAINS

Only problem is, things have changed in a very major way."

"Look . . . Nonda. I don't have time for this -"

"Relax. We need to clear some things up, so it's in your best interest to let me speak."

"Well, what are you saying then?"

Sienna listened with baited breath.

"Marcus," Nonda breathed out.

Sienna walked over to her bedroom window with a hand placed over her speeding heart.

"Marcus? What does Marcus have to do with you calling me? Is he okay?"

"Oh, he's more than fine. But it's my son I'm worried about."

"I don't understand. What does your son have to do with Marcus?"

"Everything. My son is number one. And nobody comes before him," she laughed into the phone. "Let me just break it down for you real quick. I peeped you a couple times and you're cute or whatever. But it doesn't make a difference, 'cause being cute don't mean a damn thing. Basically, because I look better than you. Especially, since your man's been spending his spare time with me. Oh, and mainly because I'm his baby mama. I ain't seen Marcus in about a week, but he probably just mad 'cause I told him I was gonna call you. "

Sienna looked at the telephone not sure whether she should drop it, throw it, or hang it up. Alarms were going off all around her. Centering herself, she took a breath, and decided this girl had to be telling a lie.

"And you expect me to believe you?"

"You're probably too dumb to. You've been in the dark so long, I wouldn't be surprised if you didn't. But for your info, we have a son who's a month and a half. I think it's best you tell Marcus to start dropping off my child support payments.

Matter-of-fact, let him know I'm about two seconds from running his pockets in court."

Sienna's heart was dropping at the speed of light. Her pulse raced off the charts. For a second she thought she might still be dreaming. But it wasn't tropical breezes floating by. This time around, the air smelled of pure shit. She ran a shaky hand through her closely cropped hair. Cleared the spit that had started to form at the back of her throat.

"I . . . I don't know who you are or what bull you're talking about, but I think it's best that you leave me and Marcus alone."

"No, sweetie. You can run your mouth with me all you want, but it's your man that needs the leash. Trust, he stays running back to me for more. I just thought I'd call and let you know the deal, so you'd know where you stood. You're the fool. I'm the baby mama and I'll always be in his life. And to keep it really funky, you can have him when you want 'cause he ain't all that to begin with. He just better make sure he brings me my money."

"And how do I know what you're saying isn't a lie?"

"How do you know it is?" Nonda countered.

For the first time, Sienna ran out of words in response. Thoughts ran back and forth and around in circles going haywire through her head. She didn't want to believe the words coming through the telephone. Didn't want the tears to start flowing, this new drama to disturb her life.

The only reply she could come up with was, "How'd you get my number?"

Nonda let out a short high-pitched laugh on her end.

"Don't you think that's a little irrelevant at the moment?"

Sienna wasn't going to believe a word unless she had proof.

"For all I know, you could be making this whole thing

up."

"But you know I'm not."

"Well I have only your word to go by, so as far as I'm concerned you're a lying trick!"

Click.

Sienna's trembling, sweaty hand stuck firmly to the receiver after the call's abrupt ending.

I know this can not be happening again. Not another female with more drama. Wait until I get to that fool, I'm gonna shove my foot so far up his . . .

BRIIIINNNNGGGG!

She looked at the phone. What if it was Nonda again? What could she say to her after she'd just hung up in the girl's ear and called her out her name?

She swallowed her nerves, refusing to be scared to pick up the phone in her own home.

"You - "

"Trick, where you at?" Eve hollered into the phone.

"I . . . I'm at home."

"Duh. I know that. I remember dialing your home number just five seconds ago. I mean, where your head at? It's almost five o'clock. Meeting was at four, hon."

"Eve, um . . . I don't know if I'm still gonna make it. I – uh . . . "

"Stop it," Eve said, cutting her off. "Get your butt over here right now."

Sienna couldn't find an excuse quick enough. "I . . ."

"Uh-uh-uh. Save it. See you in a few."

Now it was Sienna's turn to hear the dial tone. Eve had spoken and Sienna knew if she didn't show up, she'd never hear the end of it.

With the little energy she had left, Sienna sucked it up, calmed herself, and wiped her eyes.

* * *

"The queen has entered the building. Now we may all die."

"Quit it," Marni warned Eve.

The studio was all brick and open space. About as cold as an ice box too. Sienna plopped down in one of the makeup chairs and threw her shades on the counter in front of her.

"Okay, Attitude. Wassup with you?" Eve asked, leaning forward to apply concealer to the woman's face. Her jet black lace-front wig, sat perfectly on top of her head in a pony tail that grazed the side of her square jaw. She was armed and dangerous with her makeup tools, clearly, ready for battle.

Every shade of foundation, blush, lipstick, and liner was at her fingertips - she was ready to paint some face. But in order to do that, the atmosphere had to be conducive to her creativity. And right about now, Ms. Pouty Face was jacking it all up.

"I'm good. Just do me," was Sienna's stoic reply. She was in no mood to be quizzed by either of her two best friends.

Marni fiddled with her long copper and pink dreads, pensively watching Sienna's face through the mirror. Sienna knew she was fixing her mouth to say something. They were always aware when she had issues and never failed to take part in the tug-of-war to drag it out of her.

"Mama, what's wrong?" Marni asked, tilting her head to the side.

"Marni, not you too. I'm one hundred percent good to go. Just not trying to be in here all day. These cramps are kicking my butt."

Eve intently applied pressed powder to the face of the only other model there besides Sienna and Marni.

"Cramps my behind. You knew I only rented the studio for four hours. Tryna wrap up these looks for the portfolio and you over here trippin'. I know you're doing me a favor, but damn. Now I have to rush." Eve cut her eyes in Sienna's direction. "I'm almost finished with Ketra and then I'll do you next. If you weren't the last person to get here, I would've done you first. Luisa already done came and went."

"Yeah, I know. Sorry, I'm late. Like I said, these cramps got the best of me at the last minute."

Eve looked at her friend sideways, lips twisted, exposing her doubt.

"That look on your face doesn't say 'My stomach's about to send me to my grave'. It looks more like it's saying, 'In a minute I'm about to send someone to a grave'."

Sienna grunted.

It was clear Marni agreed with her friend. She walked behind Sienna's chair and placed comforting arms around her. "You look like you need a hug."

Sienna refused to admit it, but was grateful for the warm hug Marni was intuitive enough to give. It was exactly what she needed. Marcus would get dealt with later, but until he did, every inch of her would be tight.

Marni squeezed tighter. "We know you Sea. Ever since you thought it was still cute to rock baby hair down the side of your face. Don't play yourself and act like we can't read you by now. Before Eve puts one fake lash on your eye, I wanna know wassup."

Eve dropped her blush brush in her tool bag, puckered her lips, and trained her eyes on Sienna.

"And I'll get the popcorn ready in a second, 'cause I can't wait to hear what Marcus-The-Screw-Up did now."

* * *

Click. Click. Click, click, click.

"Beautiful! Move your face up, just a bit hon. There we

go."

Jean, the rail-thin photographer from Belize, snapped away in his endeavor to capture Eve's art with perfection. Ketra was up at the moment.

Naturally she was a very pretty girl, but Eve's expert work took her a notch beyond breathtaking. After a couple more shots, it would be Sienna's turn, though she still wasn't up to it.

Without a doubt, Eve had done an amazing job on her face as well. The bright oranges and reds made Sienna's warm brown skin glow like lava slipping down an erupting volcano. But Sienna didn't feel like being beautiful. She felt like getting ugly with the man she'd spent the last three years of her life with.

Sienna stroked her temples after she'd finished retelling the story to her two friends. Eve was in the midst of painting her face a frenzy of red. Just a minute ago, she'd only saw red because of the last-minute call from Nonda, but now it was all over her face too.

"And you'll still stay with his crusty butt. You shoulda dismissed his behind donkey years ago. Went and picked you up another Daniel," Eve stated as she rolled her eyes for the hundredth time.

"Don't even take it there. Marcus is nothing like your horrid ex. He could never be a dog like that."

Eve glowered in Sienna's direction. "So young. So stupid."

"I'm older than you Eve. You're calling me young?"

"Yes. And don't forget naïve too."

Sienna turned her attention to Marni who sat quietly monitoring her two friends.

"Marni, do you really think Marcus is anything like Daniel?"

"I don't know, Sea. I'm saying – can't put nothing

against these men out here."

Eve snickered at the comment. "Don't baby her. Speak truth. Every man - including her man - got some Daniel in him. I'm just telling you now, don't act like you're all crazy surprised when Marcus dogs you worse than Daniel did me."

Sienna tried her best to fight the feeling in her heart. "I don't know that this girl is telling the truth."

Eve and Marni exchanged looks. Eve's saying: I'm so going to cut her. Marni's saying: Leave it alone.

"I'm sure she's lying," Sienna persisted.

Eve began flapping her arms in the air.

"If she's lying, I'm flying." She let her arms fall to her sides. "Wake the hell up Sea. Your man's triflin'."

Sienna curled a short piece of her deep chocolate hair with a finger.

"I know he's made some mistakes in the past. But, I . . . I . . . I just don't want to believe he hasn't learned from those mistakes."

"Girl, I don't wanna believe he'd do this to you either," Marni cut in, "but his track record speaks for itself. We can't stop you from making your own decisions. You're grown. You're gonna do what you want. It's your right to. But aren't you tired of stressing over Marcus yet? You don't need the extra baggage in your life."

"Amen to that," Eve shouted as she added some finishing touches to Sienna's eye shadow. "Like my daddy used to always say, cut the cancer before it spreads."

Sienna kept her mouth shut. A migraine began its slow churn, working its way through her brain.

Marni was right. She didn't need this added stress in her life, but she was too scared to let him go. Figured after three long and strong years of history, there was something worth holding on to. And besides, it wasn't always a headache with him. There were Friday evenings watching flicks while slurping on Bailey's and vanilla ice cream. He never forgot the little things, like flowers delivered to her school at the moments she least expected. And life was always freaking amazing when they found the time to make a getaway to someplace like Mexico or Bermuda.

Those times were special. Their bond was formed and solidified through all the little nicks and cracks along the way. How could she possibly give up on what they'd built? Even saw why a woman like Nonda would go to such extremes to lie and try to tear it all down.

There was no way she'd throw it all away over a silly phone call. Sure knowing Nonda was out there made her nerves tingle a little. That's all it was though, a tingle. Until she had cold hard evidence, she wouldn't make a move.

3 joy

"You can't be serious."

Joy rolled her eyes at the loser beside her and proceeded to step out of the black Range Rover.

"Hold up, hold up." He quickly grabbed her wrist before she could get the door completely open. "I'm talking to you and you're just going to walk away like that?"

Joy screwed her face, five seconds away from punching him in the mouth. "I told you the deal. Now you wanna talk about you catchin' feelings?"

His face gave him away instantly. *Look at him*, she thought. *About to cry like a little girl.* He stared straight ahead, trying to think of what he could say next to keep Joy in his life. There was no doubt she was a tough broad and saying one wrong word could make a bad situation worse. He popped a few knuckles and ran a hand over his low cut. His stainless steel watch felt like ice against her skin as he gently took her hand and commenced to caressing her fingers.

"Joy . . . baby . . . I'm saying . . . you know I been trying to put you on that wifey status for a minute and some change. I give you everything you want. Here with you whenever I can get away. Real talk – I see you having my kids one day and all that. How you just gonna walk away from what we have?" Could it be that he was mentally challenged? Joy, yanked her hand back and rolled her eyes, unimpressed. The average chick might've wet her panties after lapping up his game, but Joy was hardly amused. He could have saved himself. All he had to do was let her step out of the jeep, but since he wanted to get his feelings hurt, Joy was happy to oblige.

"Yaz, let me keep it real with you: I wouldn't be your wife even if you paid me to." She watched his face hit the floor and used it as motivation to crush him swift and proper.

"Furthermore, I'll be damned if I had even half a kid by your dumb ass. Not in this life or the next. How are you going to sit up here talking about wifing me up when you go home to your bitch at night, lying about where you been all day? I'm supposed to wait 'til you get rid of 'ole girl so I can step up in her predicament? You must be bugging if you think you mean more to me than that chedda in your pockets."

His bottom lip touched his chin. Speechless, he studied her, waiting for the signal that said she was joking. Without question, Joy gladly took it as an opportunity to continue.

"Don't come at me like you on that brand new shit. From the very beginning you knew how it was going down. Yeah, you gave me what I wanted when I wanted it, but it ain't like you ain't get nothing in return."

She opened the door again and put a stilettoed foot on the concrete before facing him once more.

"You were cool for a minute before you started tripping. But, you need to stop worrying about me and start worrying about your chick and what she was probably doing all them times you was banging me. I'm good. I got a arsenal of dudes lined up to take care of me. And they know not to come with this shit." She slammed the door and walked towards her building with her middle finger in the air. Stepping inside the cool, clean elevator she decided she wouldn't let Yaz's foolishness spoil her evening now that she had to find another source of cash flow.

The arsenal of dudes didn't exist. Once she milked them for what they were worth, they were of little use and discharged just like the meathead she'd left by the curb. Yaz was actually a straggler. She'd been doing just fine taking care of herself with the seven hundred and fifty thousand her grandmother unexpectedly left when she passed away. Over the past year, the money evaporated at a heady pace. But now the well had run dry.

Five months ago, Joy only had ten thousand left after

purchasing her treasured chinchilla. Yaz's dough paid her rent while she ripped through the stores every chance she could get. She hadn't checked her bank statements in over four months. Yet, there was no doubt she had close to nothing left. Why did he have to get nauseating at a time like this? A clingy man was one thing she wouldn't tolerate under any circumstances.

She was knocking on broke's door and knew she'd have to think of something quick. *It's all good, I'll be alright,* she told herself as the elevator made its way to the ninth floor. *He needs me more than I need him.* She laughed out loud remembering the embarrassment on his face when she'd said her final word and exited the car.

Joy O'Brien didn't do commitments. Wasn't her fault if he'd thought himself invincible to the golden rule.

* * *

The unmistakable aroma of spaghetti and meatballs rushed Joy's nose as she stepped through the apartment's front door. Clanging pots and pans could be heard even above the sound system riding on blast. She prayed Poochie wasn't tearing her kitchen apart. She'd given her friend access to the apartment as an emergency type of thing, but somehow Poochie always found herself tangled up in Joy's fridge, getting comfortable with the food she never managed to purchase.

More recently, a love affair with spaghetti and meatballs had begun. If it was left up to Poochie she'd eat it for breakfast, lunch, and dinner. And if Joy could remember correctly, she had eaten it for all three a time or two.

Joy danced her way to the kitchen. Poochie spun away from the stove and turned to see her in the entranceway.

"How many times do I have to tell you, you ain't I-talian?" Joy teased.

"I am. I just have one of them really deep tans you

don't know nothing about," Poochie quipped, sprinkling
Parmesan cheese on her plate. "And I should body you like I'm
Gotti reincarnated 'cause your cell phone been driving me
crazy, ringing nonstop. That's why I got the music so loud. You
need to stop leaving your cell phone home."

"Excuse you. You need to stop eating my damn food,"
she shot back. "And I never leave my cell home. This time, I
just forgot it. How's my baby Ja'Nya?"

Joy walked back into the living room, turned
the stereo's volume down, and picked up her phone
from the glass-covered side table she'd left it on this morning.

"Bad," Poochie said following behind. "Tell me why
my daughter thinks she's slick. Four years-old and trying to use
her brains on me. I caught her in my mother's bedroom by
herself the other day cutting up the phone bill with scissors,
talking 'bout, 'I was trying to make a snowflake'. I snatched the
scissors out her hands and said, 'No, you was trying to cut up
the freaking phone bill.' "

Joy laughed and put the phone to her ear. "I should
give her my bills so she could cut them up too."

She listened to the automated voice tell her how many
calls she'd missed.

"Twenty messages? Who the hell was calling me? The
whole United States?"

"Nah. Not just them. Africa and Japan too," Poochie
said, stuffing her face as she sat on the sofa and flipped on the
cable.

Joy listened to the abundance of messages. Some of
them were from the same people who felt they had to leave
three or more at a time. She hated that with a passion.
Annoying as it was, she could deal with it and move on. It was
the last message, from the one person she least expected, that
made her want to snap the phone in two.

"What does this trick want?" She didn't want to hear
from the one person who'd made her childhood a living hell.

BROKEN WITH STAINS

Most days Joy forgot the serial idiot even existed. She could feel her anger rising as she listened to the woman's sardonic voice.

"Answer your phone sometimes. I know you live to ignore me, but at least you can't say I never tried. Anyway, just got back from Brazil with Tom. In case it crossed your mind - which I highly doubt - that's where I've been for the past week. I meant to tell you before, but it completely slipped my mind. Now, as for the reason I'm calling, I have some things I need to get in order because time is of the essence. I'm going over the guest list. Let me know if you're coming to the wedding or not. The wedding planner needs confirmation now, which means, I don't have time to waste. Give me a call so I'll know what to do."

Abruptly, the message ended on that note. Joy sucked her teeth as hard as she could and turned to the hungry girl with noodles hanging from her mouth.

"Poochie, that's my word - you gonna see me on the ten o'clock news when I bust a cap right in Blue's throat."

She had to be crazy. Now she was back from Brazil with her white millionaire and Joy was supposed to drop everything and call her back? No. And she wasn't going to the shitty wedding either. Blue could wait for a response until her hair turned gray.

Joy thought Yaz had taken the crown - the only person lame enough to leave a bad taste in her mouth for the rest of the day. But now, retard number two had swiftly taken his spot. If only her mother would just disappear for good. If only she'd never have to hear her voice again.

4 paul

Over and over and over again. Paul's daughter wouldn't stop banging on the wooden bedroom door until he let her in.

"Alright, alright. I'm coming," he yelled, hoping that would calm her relentless fist.

Paul wrapped his hand around the gold knob and pulled, but the door wouldn't budge. He shook his head, *Great the door jammed again.* Paul wiped his slick palms on his pants and tried a second time. His effort failed to work and the girl started her pounding again.

"Hold your horses. The door's stuck. Can't you see I'm trying to get it open?" Unfortunately, it wasn't enough to deter her.

He ran over to his bedside table, opened the single draw, and pulled out a screw driver. Hurriedly, he made his way back to the narrow door, trying unsuccessfully to unscrew the knob. Paul persisted, but the stubborn screw wouldn't turn as he desperately tried to twist it. Stuck or not, the delay only made her grow more impatient. The door shook violently as she put more force into each knock.

At a loss for what to do next, Paul began to speak to the door.

"Come on, I don't got time for this."

He reached out with hoping fingers, turned the knob, and smiled to himself when it opened. *Go figure,* he mused. "I don't know what -" His words dissipated when he stepped through the door and saw no one standing there. *She couldn't have left that fast.* He moved further into the long, silent hall and looked expectantly to the left.

"Where are you? I got the door open."

Paul turned the other way and took a few steps down

the hall to see if she might've rounded the corner. Still, there wasn't a trace. Only her vanilla scent brushing against his nose.

"Well ain't that some bull," he mumbled to himself, stepping back into the room.

Paul's eyes felt strained in the bedroom's darkened interior. It was bad enough he could barely see since he didn't have his glasses on. He remembered leaving them on the windowsill a few minutes ago, when he'd peeked out the window to let the sun wash over his face.

Putting them on, he opened the semi-sheer curtains Camilla picked out when she re-decorated for the summer. The rays warmed every inch of his body as he bathed in the heat it produced. Paul didn't want to pull himself away though he knew it was time to get a move on. His clients would be at the studio waiting – something he tried to avoid at all costs. It was a crime to show up late - that had always been his way of thinking. Primarily because, money needed to be made and bills didn't pay themselves. With that in mind, he turned away from the window. His heart almost stopped in his chest when he turned around and saw her standing by his bed. The thudding against his ribs was as loud as a pounding bass.

"You're quiet as a mouse, huh? I didn't hear you come in."

Paul's eyes traveled from the crown of her head to the pearls on the strapped shoes. He was amazed at how she seemed to glimmer before his very eyes. The delicate yellow chiffon of her strapless dress shimmered intensely as the sun's light enveloped the room.

Paul wasn't sure if his eyes were playing tricks on him, but her caramel skin somehow transformed to a creamy brown and then back to its original color. He almost reached out and touched the soft, dark hair that lay against her shoulders. But as soon as the thought crossed his mind, instead she reached out to him.

"Here." She took a step forward, extending a camera

towards him. "Take my picture daddy."

He took the camera and looked through its lens. Focusing and refocusing, he made sure to capture all her glory. Paul faintly smelled something like smoke, but disregarded it to concentrate on the person before him.

His index finger sat on the trigger while she readily revealed her pearly whites.

"Just like that," he said as he snapped a number of frames. Unable to take anymore shots, he walked over to her to hand the camera back since there was no more film left.

Paul looked at his baby girl who'd transformed into a woman overnight. Shaking his head, he couldn't help but reveal his pride. "Look at my pretty, pretty princess. My baby doll is all grown up now. I'm sorry I couldn't - " His words were cut short as he went soaring through the air.

It was a mystery what he'd tripped on, but the next place he found himself, was on his knees at her feet. Paul looked back to see the cause of his fall and saw his other daughter dressed completely in red.

"Get up daddy and take my picture." The rhinestones on her bold dress twinkled as she stretched a different camera towards him. Paul was shaken by how she appeared behind him like that. Couldn't recall seeing her enter the room. Wondered why there were little reams of smoke swirling out from under her dress.

"I really need to get these glasses checked out," he said to himself. It was the only excuse he could think of.

He reached out to take the camera from her slim hand. But, before he could get hold of it, he was shoved hard from behind and fell to the floor once again. Paul turned quickly and saw his middle daughter dressed in a black leather dress. She smiled brightly and shoved a camera at him.

"Quick, daddy - take my picture."

He paused for a second, not understanding why he kept getting hit every time he turned around. Paul was as hesitant as a mouse at a cat convention, but not wanting to disappoint, he reached to take her camera. He barely had it in his hand before it blew up into a ball of fire.

"Nooooo," Paul cried out, scrambling to get up on his feet.

His body shot forward when an unknown object hit against the back of his head. He didn't even have time to recover. Before he knew what was going on, he was being pushed, kicked, punched, and pinched by a multitude of young women who surrounded him.

They were all yelling at him. All wanted their picture taken.

"Daddy, take my picture now."

"Daddy, you should have taken my picture already."

"Daddy, what's taking you so long to take my picture?"

"Daddy, don't you want to take my picture?"

"Daddy, I need my picture taken before you leave."

Paul tried in vain to grant their frantic wishes, but under the circumstances it was impossible. He was attacked every time he attempted to get to his feet and now the carpet had caught on fire too. The flames were rising higher, threatening to engulf all three of his girls.

His desire to help turned to panic as he yelled, "I want to, but the fire's out of control!"

He could still feel the rough hands jerking and pulling at his body.

"Paul, Paul - it's okay, baby. It's just a dream."

Shaken out of his nightmare, he opened his eyes to see Camilla staring down at him.

"Dreams back again, huh? It's okay - it's just a dream. Let me get you some water."

Camilla returned shortly, walking slowly back into the moonlit room. She turned on the lamp above the bed, eased herself back down, and pulled the sheets from around his chest. His wife leaned into him and planted a tender kiss on his cheek as she rubbed his back.

"I thought they'd stopped, 'cause it's been a while," Paul said.

He gulped down half the glass of water, some dribbling down the sides of his mouth onto the front of his shirt.

"You need to face them Paul," she said using her hand to wipe the water that had gotten away.

He scratched his chin and leaned back to rest his throbbing head on the headboard. "In the dream, I did face them. It was just like before. They were -"

"That's not what I mean Paul." She turned to look him squarely in his eyes. "I mean face your children. Obviously these dreams are not going away. And they won't go away for good if you won't stop running from them. I've kept my tongue for long enough, because I felt in time you'd realize it on your own. But now . . . it's getting to the point where you're going to have to do something. I think it's time you see your daughters."

"Can't imagine them wanting to see me. Been years since I disappeared. How am I supposed to go about it all now?"

"You're their father."

"Not much of one. And just 'cause I am, don't mean they're gonna accept me for it."

She took the cup of water from his hands and placed it on the nightstand beside her. Moving closer to him, Camilla placed a soft hand in his. When he turned his face towards her, she kissed his lips sweetly, and received a smile in return.

"Baby you know I love you, don't you?"

He nodded his head, knowingly.

"Good, because I'd want you to know that as I'm strangling you next time for waking me out of my sleep." They both laughed at that visual. "Not only are you losing sleep over this, Paul, but I am too. I'm not trying to force you to do anything; I know taking this step isn't that easy for you. But, it's time, honey. Once and for all, it's time to just do it. Think on that for me."

Paul sighed and looked at the time. Three thirty-five a.m. and counting. He knew his wife was right, but translating that knowledge into action was something different in itself.

"What if they want nothing to do with me?"

"What if they do?" she countered.

True thing, he thought.

Camilla was not about to simply let him wiggle away from his dreams this time. She knew the only way he'd have peace was to find his daughters and try to be a part of their future. The past was gone and he could never change the fact that he'd missed out on a chunk of their lives. He could never hear first words, see them off to their first day of school, or see beautiful young women in prom dresses gliding off to a waiting limo. That didn't mean there was no hope left. New memories were waiting to be created. She wanted him to realize that he could see his daughters face to face. Who knew what one meeting could bring about?

"Take a risk. Just close your eyes and leap. Think how much those three girls are worth it," she said, massaging his fingers with her own. "You're strong enough to do it. Even if you don't feel it, you have to believe that strength is there."

She reached up and turned off the lamp. Settling back underneath his arm, she told him, "You are a good man, Paul. Despite what occurred back then, I married a wonderful, intelligent man seven years ago. And you're still the same man today. But that man has been running long enough. Kick that fear in the behind and go find your daughters. They probably need you just as much as you need them."

5 noelle

Noelle's mother floated from room to room like a ghost. From her place at the round kitchen table, she watched as the tall, washed out woman with her head down moved without a sound.

The peaches in the bowl before Noelle sat untouched. It had always been her favorite thing to eat, only now, she didn't feel like eating much of anything lately. The food her mother brought home from Soul Divine's last night was still wrapped up in the foil container sitting in the refrigerator.

She dipped her spoon into the fruit and twirled it about. The figure dressed in a white t-shirt and white sweatpants moved into the kitchen. Turning on the pipe, she rinsed her hands. Noelle was used to the ritual. The obsessive compulsive procedure her mother indulged in: thirty seconds of warm water running over her hands at least three times every hour.

She pushed the peaches to the side and stuck her finger in the tiny hole of the plastic tablecloth decorated with cherries.

"Why make the hole bigger Noelle? I bought that with hard-earned money."

Noelle stopped fiddling with it and covered the hole with the bowl.

"Did you take a look in that microwave?" her mother asked. "Filthy. Don't ever be scared to go over it with a rag."

Picking up the fruit, Noelle sighed, and walked over to the garbage can.

"Why waste the fruit, Noelle?"

She let the lid slam with a bang and looked at her mother.

"Ma, I paid for it, not you."

The woman scrubbed the inside of the microwave with a worn rag. "Fair enough. Just a shame to see it go to waste."

BROKEN WITH STAINS

Noelle placed the bowl in the sink and tried to make an exit before her mother could aggravate her any further.

"Come here," she said, placing the rag in the sink. Noelle stopped in her tracks, turned, and waited for her mother to finish her ritual again.

"I need you to look out for the plumber. He's coming to look at that pipe upstairs in the bathroom."

"Well, is he coming soon? I have to run over to Aunt Rinni's to pick something up." Noelle answered.

"Any minute now."

"What are you still doing here anyway? Thought you had to be at work by two?"

"Today's Friday. I switched my schedule to three."

"I forgot Aunt Rinni wanted me to ask you if she could borrow your crock pot. Hers broke. Oh, and she wanted to borrow your green dress with the gold buttons on it too."

"Rinelda can go scratch her behind."

"I'll tell her that's a no." Noelle turned to leave.

"Come here," her mother called after her.

She blew through her nose. The will to go forward was lacking already, stopping and starting was only making it worse.

"You been moping around here since last week."

Noelle shrugged her shoulders.

"That's all you got to say?"

"I'm just stressed."

"What that boy do to make you so stressed?"

She was stunned at her mother's ability to discern the reason behind her mood. Chris had yet to be a topic discussed between the two of them. She barely looked at him when he used to come around. When had she ever shown interest in anything that had to do with Noelle's love life?

"Who said it had anything to do with Chris?"

"What else could it be? I wasn't born yesterday."

Noelle pulled at her ponytail.

"I heard you crying in your room last night. You should

know better. No boy is worth all that."

The heat rose through her face. What was her mother talking about? Sharon Caldwell never talked about boys. She wouldn't even talk about Noelle's father who disappeared years ago. There was never a sit-down about the birds and the bees. Never a question about any of her past boyfriends. So why all of a sudden did she seem to care?

"It's nothing you'd understand."

"I'm sure I understand more than you think," she said, removing plates from the dish basket and putting them in the overhead cabinet.

Noelle wished she could find out what her mother meant by that, but knew Sharon would in the end, turn around and avoid digging any deeper. That was her steelo, just like the perpetual washing of invisible germs from her hands.

"Thanks for the food in the fridge. I'll eat it later."

Her mother put the last cup on a short shelf and closed the small doors.

"Don't let me see that food anywhere near that garbage."

"From the fridge to my stomach is where it'll go. I'll listen out for the plumber." She slowly trooped past the table, bunching the tablecloth after dragging her fingers across the top.

"Study your books and forget about men," Noelle heard Sharon say as she reached the bottom of the hallway steps. "They ain't worth half the trouble they stir up. Be glad the bum isn't in your life anymore."

* * *

His beard was beaded against the leathery skin of his face. Noelle recoiled as soon as she smelled the rank breath accompanied with, "You a pretty little thang. Yes you are. What's your name again?"

BROKEN WITH STAINS

The plumber's eyes darted to Noelle's chest. Bile rose in her stomach as she watched him stick a finger up his nose, unabashedly flicking a booger.

"Your wedding ring needs polishing," she said.

"Oh," he snorted, waving his hand to sweep away the observation. "Too busy for all that. But you 'sho got some nice eyes."

"Thanks," she muttered.

Noelle stepped onto her front porch while the man spoke to her back. Pulling the cap further over her eyes, she ignored the plumber's attempt to flirt with her and closed the front door. She plodded down the concrete steps, then jumped into her navy blue Neon. Backing out of the driveway, she looked over at the deplorable man. *Some nerve*, she ruminated. If Noelle had five million dollars to spare, she would've placed a bet on it, convinced, that would be Chris in twenty more years. The usual fifteen minute drive was taking longer than usual. Chris consumed her thoughts at every turn she took. She tried to remember all the things she had planned on her calendar. Websites needed to be finished. Papers for Marketing, English, and PR had to be turned in within the next two weeks. There was stuff on her plate, but it failed to block out the picture of Chris in bed with another girl. The image haunting her like a demon that refused to go away.

She turned the music up as far as it could go. Maybe that would make it easier to block out the events of last week. She passed East 180th street and made a left past the corner store where she was first approached by Chris. His white tank enhanced the fact that he was no stranger to a gym. Later on, she thanked Aunt Rinni for sending her on a last minute errand to the store. Noelle daydreamed about Chris' white teeth and inviting smile. The small dimple in his chin and the way his eyebrows were bushy, but suited his face just fine. Thought about the large tattoo on his thick brown arm and fantasized about having her named etched somewhere near one day.

That was then. Now, as she drove up the narrow street, Noelle could body slam Aunt Rinni for craving pork grinds two years ago. If her aunt had taken the bottles of water Noelle came to drop off and been content enough to let her go about her business, she wouldn't be in the disaster she was in right now.

Snapping out of the blame game, Noelle crushed the brake petal with her foot. Close call, after noticing at the last minute she was about to breeze past the stop sign. The last thing she needed was a ticket. She looked to the right to see if a cop was coming down the one way street. The coast was clear of any squad cars, but a ticket might've been better considering the fact that the person she locked eyes with was not someone she wanted to see at that moment either.

Chris watched her from his stance next to the curb. Suddenly, she felt the urge to twist the wheel of her car around and ram the vehicle into his body. He took a step back up on the sidewalk still gazing at her behind the wheel. Noelle basked in a lovely vision of the impact sending him flying through the living room window of one of the houses nearby. But that vision was cut short by a blaring horn from the van behind her.

She continued down the street before sneaking a peek in her rearview mirror. Chris stood still in between the streets, wistfully looking at her drive away.

* * *

"Good. You're here. See the excitement on my face? Can't wait for you to take this big ass package out my doorway."

Noelle looked at her aunt and smiled. Rinni's face was plastered in a dark green mud mask. One bony hand realxed inside the pocket of her favorite hot pink house pants with the bleach stains on the butt. Her other hand patted the bleached blonde head twined in a rainbow of rollers. Noelle inhaled the smoke that wafted from a Newport perched comfortably between her red lips. Aunt Rinni without her red lipstick was like rice without the white. Didn't matter that she was in the house, she'd tell you in a flash: "You don't like it, stay home." It was hard to believe that her mother and Rinelda Bass were sisters born only a year apart.

"Sorry I took so long to pick it up," Noelle said.

Rinni blew a trail of smoke in the air and kicked the large cardboard box. "Mmmhmm. What's in there anyway?" she asked.

Noelle had anticipated that question, nosey as Rinni was.

"A play set for my godchild. I didn't want it sent straight to his house because it's for his birthday. And since I'm in and out all day and go to school, Ma's hours vary - I didn't want to get it delivered to mine."

"I see. I was wondering why you didn't get it sent to Chris' house since you see him more often. But his momma told me you two ain't together no more."

It completely slipped her mind that Aunt Rinni and Chris' mother, Geraldine, were friends. The questions were sure to come tumbling in now. Noelle watched her aunt lean against the coat closet – arms and feet crossed – as if she was waiting for an explanation.

Noelle bent down and lifted to feel the weight of the box. She would have to drag it to the car as soon as possible in order to avoid any further interrogation. "No we aren't together anymore, but thanks so much for holding my package for me."

"So I guess that means you're trying to tell me to mind my business."

"Aunt Ri -"

"No-no," Rinni cut in. "It's okay, sweetie. I know when I'm getting the brush off."

"Aunt Rinni, I'm not trying to brush you off."

"Tell me anything."

"It's just that I have to get Ma's stuff from the cleaners before they close," Noelle lied through her teeth. She looked at her watch anyway. "They close at seven and it's already six fifteen, so I need to catch them before it's too late."

She twisted her lips up at her niece. "Whatever." Noelle was about to explain herself out the door, when the bell rang. Looking through the peephole, she wished she'd delayed picking up the set for one more day. Chris' mother stood there. Why did she have the feeling that Geraldine showing up was no coincidence? She might as well have been a pig at a roast. Now, they could both take turns grilling her to death.

"Hi gorgeous," Geraldine said as she stepped through the door. Chris and his mother were practically twins. Noelle studied the short woman. She could see his almond-shaped eyes and long eyelashes, his dimpled-chin and his big head. They even smiled the same.

"How are you, Ms. G?"

"I'm fine sweetheart," she said kissing Noelle's cheek. "You smell wonderful. What's that?"

"Rimmel."

Rinni lazily detached herself from the closet door.

"Never mind some dang cologne. It's about time you got here. I was a minute and a half away from passing out with hunger," she said, taking a bag of Chinese food from Geraldine's hand.

Geraldine put a hand on her hip. "Well excuse me for not running a few red lights and driving one hundred miles per hour." She turned to Noelle. "Your aunt's a trip."

Noelle chuckled at the truth and proceeded to open the front door.

"I'll see you soon, Ms. G. I need to get to the cleaners before they close."

"She telling you that lie too?" Rinni yelled from the kitchen.

BROKEN WITH STAINS

Geraldine rolled her eyes at the comment. "It's okay. I won't bombard you with questions about what happened between you and my son. Believe me, I want to. But I don't want to keep you."

"Go 'head – bombard her. She won't tell me nothing," Rinni continued.

Here we go, Noelle thought. Once Aunt Rinni got started on something there was no stopping her.

"One minute they together and the next they're not. These young people . . . I don't know. Just the other day they were over here, together, in my back yard inhaling my barbecue chicken, licking every bit of sauce off their grubby little fingers. Now here she is – as single as a dollar bill – don't want to tell me why they broke up. But it's okay Ms. Noelle. Your 'ole aunt don't gotta know a thing. She'll *be* alright."

Noelle pushed the door wide open, held it with her foot, and pulled the heavy box through it.

"I know you will, Aunt Rinni. You'll definitely be alright."

Noelle hoped she would be too.

6 sienna

"It's two o'clock in the morning, Marcus. I told you to leave me alone. What part of 'leave me alone' don't you understand?"

Instead of answering, he stood there, begging with his eyes. Sienna's patience was running on empty. "You've wasted enough of my time. Waking me up at two in the morning to waste some more of it really isn't helping your cause."

He moved himself closer to the crack in the door.

"Sunshine, you know I love you and I'm sorry. I know that girl told you some nonsense, but that's all it is . . . nonsense."

She folded her arms across her chest and sighed heavily. "I don't like drama. You know this."

"I know and I apologize for her. She's just some chick from my past that can't leave well enough alone." Sienna laughed and shook her head in disbelief.

"Oh, you apologize? She's just some chick from your past?"

"Yes and I do apologize."

"I see. Well, do me a favor and keep your useless apologies to yourself, because all you've been doing is complicating my life. She called me not once, not twice, but three times, Marcus."

Sienna didn't know why she even bothered to open her front door. His pitiful mug made her sick. It was time to call it a night. Pushing the door, she tried to shut him out. He stopped it with his foot before it hit him in the face.

"Sea, just let me in so we can talk. I know you're upset and everything, but we should discuss this. You can't just up and believe everything you hear." He sighed as if she was sapping the last of his strength. "All I'm asking is that we be adults – just sit and talk with me."

Sienna held her breath, giving herself a chance to calm down. "I've done enough talking with you."

"Sunshine," he started as he put his hand between the sliver of space that separated them. "Let me come inside and talk to you. I don't want anyone with their ear pressed to their door listening to our conversation."

"Might be a bit late for that since you decided to come here acting like you've lost your mind."

Irritation rose on his face as he took a step back to lean his shoulder against the wall. "Look – whatever. Doesn't matter one way or the other. All I'm saying is, at least hear me out. You haven't even given me that opportunity. I'm apologizing for the unnecessary drama. And if possible . . . I want to show you how sorry I am."

It was time to throw up the barbecue chips and ginger ale she'd stuffed herself with for dinner. She was in awe of his audacity to stand in her doorway trying to seduce her with puppy dog eyes and a lame "I want to show you how sorry I am."

"You know what? You're right. You are sorry." She put her muscle in it when she slammed the door in his face.

Three hours until sunrise and she was stomping back to her bedroom pissed off. She wasn't going through it one more time. Marcus always had an excuse, always came with the same tired mess. And she always went right back to him. Things never changed. This time around would be different.. It was obvious Marcus' intent was to make her lose the little sanity she had left. She'd hold on to it if she had to fight until her last breath.

She reached over to the alarm clock on her nightstand, making sure it was set to wake her up at seven. Sienna hoped she'd be able to head off to the gym in the morning. Didn't look like it would happen since Marcus would be on her restless mind for the next few hours.

She slipped between her rose-printed sheets, which instantly warmed her from the chill of the air-conditioned bedroom. Sienna's eyes closed and then opened in a flash when the fervent knocking resumed at her front door. She clenched her fists at her sides.

Marcus stopped after a few long seconds, but a minute later he began to call her name, becoming louder each time she heard his voice through the thin doors.

"Sienna! Sienna! Open the damn door!"

She bit her bottom lip and punched the large mattress. In the morning, she would try to ignore the evil stares from the early risers who shared the fifth floor. Pushing herself from the bed, Sienna made her way to the front door and stood with hands on her delicately curved hips.

"So you're really going to stand out there and make a complete fool of yourself?"

"Can you open the door, please?" he asked, defiant.

"Marcus, go home."

"I'll bang some more if you really want me to."

"Don't be childish just to spite me. You're twenty-seven years-old. Grow up."

"And you're twenty-four, so you're not too far behind. Be mature enough to have an adult conversation with your man face-to-face and not through a damn door. Now let's stop this, Sienna. Open up. I want to talk to you."

Her strategy wasn't working. He was supposed to go away. Resisting him only forced him to try harder. The way things were going, sleep was illusive at best. Above it all, she needed her neighbors not to kill her.

It was a no-win situation. She didn't want to do it, but her choices were slim. Sienna slowly opened the door and let him walk in.

He made his way over to the plush burgundy sofa and sat down, sliding off his tan boots.

"No need to get comfortable," Sienna eyed him, folding

her arms. "Make this short and sweet. I have to get up early."

He patted the sofa next to him. "Sit."

She looked blankly. "Talk."

"My girlfriend can't sit next to me?"

"At this point, I don't think it's necessary to claim me as your girlfriend."

He smiled. "So you're trying to say we aren't together anymore?"

"I thought I made that clear last night?"

"Sea, that's not the first time you've claimed we weren't together anymore."

"Well this time I mean it. I don't have room for your crap anymore."

"So, if I'm full of crap, why'd you let me in?"

Sienna closed her eyes and counted to three. "You're running out of time. Say what you have to say and get out."

"I wouldn't have had to make all that noise if you let me in the first time."

She could see that Marcus took pleasure in grating her last nerve.

"Okay, you basically came over here to say nothing. Leave."

"You know, I hate when you get real bitchy like this."

"Out!" she yelled, opening the door. Marcus stretched his sexy, toned frame and took his time getting to his feet. He strolled over to where she stood, removed her hand from the knob, and closed the door. Aggressively, his rough fingers gripped her behind. Sienna smacked them away and used her elbow to shove him backward.

"See this is why I didn't want to let you in. Sex doesn't fix everything, Marcus."

"Well then what do I have to do to show you I'm sorry?"

"Nothing," she said, with an intense anger surging through her system. "Since we've been together I've gotten nothing from you except lies on top of lies. This last episode is the final straw. How do you expect me to look over the fact that another woman's calling my home telling me she has a child with you? You heard the message she left and you still haven't explained how she got my number."

"She's lying."

"I wish I could believe that. I simply can't do it anymore. I can't believe she just woke up one morning and said 'today I feel like telling Sienna I have a child by her man'. She has to be telling the truth."

"That could be anybody's baby."

"So why would she choose you? You must've been sleeping with her for her to pick up the phone and call me. Are you going to keep denying nothing was going on between you two?"

"She's the past."

Sienna looked at Marcus and read the lies written all over his face. It was always someone from "the past". She was tired. Mentally tired and frustrated from similar incidents that had popped up over the course of three years. Before Nonda, it was the numbers in his pocket. The calls he wouldn't answer in front of her. The woman he claimed was his god-sister, she'd encountered leaving his apartment. The flattened tires on her car with 'Your man's a whore' written on the windshield. The disappearing for a week. The ex-girlfriend who wouldn't stop blowing up his phone. The other ex-girlfriend who called and threatened her for two months straight. In hindsight, she swore if she could do it all over again, she would have left Marcus in the Starbucks where she'd first laid eyes on him on a rainy September night.

"Marcus, I don't even care about an explanation from you right now."

"But -"

"It's time for you to go," Sienna fumed, knowing he didn't understand the mental torment he'd put her through.

BROKEN WITH STAINS

"How much more of this do you think I can take?"

He opened his arms and looked at her as if she were hallucinating. "How much of what? You blow everything out of proportion. There's no trust, so if anything, I should be asking how much more you think *I* can take. You think you have everything all figured out, but you don't. I'm here right now because I love you. If I didn't love you and want to be with just you, I'd be home in bed."

Normally, she would have re-evaluated the situation and concluded that she was indeed taking things a little overboard. It would've been at this moment that she pushed her intuition and doubt to the back burner and melted into his arms.

But right now, she wasn't feeling normal.

"Three years. I've given you my love, my trust, and all of my heart. Even after those times you've shaken my faith in you, I decided to keep giving you the benefit-of-the-doubt. Letting go of my own hurt and disappointment, just to keep giving you the best of me. And what have you done with all I gave? You've taken every bit of it for granted."

Her lip trembled as she shook her head at the man she'd loved until it hurt.

"You say you love me, but you only care about yourself."

He stepped towards her. "Sienna, you can't believe -"

"Don't interrupt me, Marcus. You'll listen to what I have to say for a change. I've been giving you everything and you know it. That's my fault. It's my fault for wasting my love on a man who only loves himself. I won't do it anymore. I'm tired. I'm spent. I've been giving and giving and giving. And I don't have anything left," she said as her voice wavered. "You had your chance to speak, now do us both a favor: walk out of that door and do not come back."

7 joy

"**Y**o."

"Good afternoon – Joy?" the man's smooth baritone voice answered.

She brought the bottle of Smirnoff to her mouth and took a swallow before asking, "Who's this?"

The sound of jazz trumpets died down in the background as he answered securely, "The love of your life."

Joy took a long gulp of the drink once more as she walked over to her open apartment window.

"I'm about to introduce you to the click since you wanna be difficult."

"You don't have to be that cold," he laughed into the phone.

"Well who is this?" she demanded, eyeing the Bronx streets below like a hawk, staking out its prey.

"It's Luce."

"Luce who? The name means nothing to me."

Air filled the line as she waited for his reply and he left her hanging on.

"Lucien Warren. Dark skin. Excuse me – dark chocolate. Six feet. Sexy smile. From Blaze Saturday night. You danced with me for about three songs and then you gave me your number."

A bell went off. She'd left that night, drunk out of her mind, she and Poochie, holding each other up.

"Oooooh. Now I remember you and your chocolatey self." His roaring laugh filled Joy's head piece as she vaguely recalled him whispering naughty things against her ear two nights ago on the dance floor.

"Yeah, well I'm glad you remember, because I couldn't forget you in that stellar getup you had on."

BROKEN WITH STAINS

"Stellar? Where you from? Try sick. My outfit was sick that night."

"It was all that and more. Couldn't get you and that dress out of my mind if I tried." Joy shook her head at his poor attempt to make her feel good. "Like you really remember every tiny detail," she said taking the long white envelope from her back pocket. "I'm sure you noticed fifty other dresses and collected twenty other numbers that night."

"Maybe a couple," he laughed. "But I had my eye on you first and foremost. That black lace you had yourself wrapped in definitely had heads turning. Don't act like you didn't notice. The Gucci heels were a nice touch too. There were some bad pieces in there, but you were the baddest by far. I can appreciate a woman who knows how to sell her attributes in a classy way. That's why I had to get to know you better."

Sell her attributes? Joy had to smile at this fool.

"So you know your Gucci heels, huh?" she asked, spreading the white sheets of paper out before her.

"Of course. That's half my closet."

"I'm hoping the heels ain't." He laughed, while Joy faked hers. The bank statement glared back at her, mocking and bold in black ink. Her remaining balance read four hundred and fifty-two dollars, ninety five cents. Nothing to smile about at all. That wouldn't cover even half of next month's rent. "A sense of humor. I love that. We'll have a good time together. What are you doing in an hour?"

She swallowed the lump in her throat and kept her answer light.

"I'll be lounging. I was about to warm up some left over spaghetti before you called. My friend makes truckloads of this shit every week."

"Throw the leftovers away, go get dressed, and let me take you out for some real food." Seven hundred and fifty thousand down to less than five hundred in only a year? Joy blinked, hoping she was being deceived and somehow the numbers on the page would turn out to be a hoax. There was no way she could go back to hopping from one friend's couch to another. Poochie was out of the question. She had a four year-old that she could barely support with a lousy bartender's paycheck and tips while contributing to more than half her mother's rent. Her only other option wasn't much of an option at all. She'd beg and grovel on the street before she asked her mother for one red cent.

"I think I'll take you up on that. Been in the house all day, I need to get out."

"Sounds good. Got money in my pockets. Sun's shining bright. A beautiful woman's letting me take her to lunch. This must be my lucky day."

"You got that right," she responded, gripping the papers in her hand and plotting how to turn lunch into a four-course meal.

8 paul

The congregation was awash with tears. Any other Sunday, one might be caught dozing. Another might find the time to take a quick break or two to use the restroom. Even the smallest children were abnormally still. Pastor Fisher's reverberating message, hit a cord in those young and old.

It had been seven years since Paul first met most of the people who sat around him. It was then that he'd decided enough was enough. There had to be more to life than depression and that nagging empty feeling. Nothing else seemed to be helping. The partying. The drinking. The excessive womanizing. Paul made the first mature decision since becoming a man, giving all of it up when Camilla came into his world and showed him something could be done. There was no need to stay miserable in his sin. She told him of a man named Jesus. And though hesitant at first, Paul eventually grew thirsty to learn more. He was still thirsting almost a decade later. But now Camilla was no longer the woman whose cart he'd accidentally crashed into at the grocery store. She was his wife, the rock he'd been blessed to encounter. The one who was beside him as the congregation roared all around them.

Paul sat in the midst of it all, wondering if God had spoken a word to the man at the podium on his behalf. Driving to church this morning with Camilla studying him in silence, he'd tried to hide his downcast mood. The heaviness had grown steadily since the last dream about his daughters. Now, the Pastor's words were eating away at his conscience. It all seemed to be solely directed towards him.

Camilla folded her cotton handkerchief and dabbed the corners of her eyes. Paul looked over at his wife and viewed the change that had begun to take over. She was headed to that place. That place where she let it all go and let God's warm embrace milk the tears from her soul.

"All because we do not carry everything to God in prayer the song says. Everything to God. Not a piece, not a part. Everything. He's able to fix in less than a second, what we've been trying to fix for years." The congregation moaned in agreement as Pastor Fisher continued. "Jesus understands all that you're going through. Trust Him. He became like you so that you would come to Him. He experienced pain just like you. Remember Gethsemane? Remember Jesus Himself fell on His face and pleaded with His Father. Matthew 26:39 tells us that he prayed, saying 'O my Father, if it be possible, let this cup pass from me: nevertheless not as I will, but as thou wilt.' He needed help too. But what did Jesus do about it? He prayed."

Paul felt Camilla's fingers wrap around his and squeeze. Her head was down and the tears flowed freely. He knew she had her own burdens that were too heavy for her to bear alone. He clutched her hand, feeling the diamonds of the engagement ring pressing into his thumb. Camilla's grip was strong as she held on and let out a small sob.

"Don't ever think there's anything too great for God to handle. All He wants is for you to come to Him with what you got. All of what you have. Come to Him with your heavy heart. Come to him with whatever hurts. Too many bills, not enough money. That's nothing He can't solve. They're giving you a hard time on the job. That's nothing He can't solve. Depression's got you in a choke hold and you feel all alone. That's nothing He can't solve. You're having problems with your children and you don't know what to do anymore. Guess what? That's nothing my God can't solve."

His eyes connected with the Pastor as he paused to meditate on his words. Paul believed God could help him overcome the struggles he'd been trying to handle on his own, yet questioned whether he ever really placed it in His hands to do the job that needed to get done. The truth fought with the fallacy he preferred to use in order to cover up his conviction. He could lie to himself and say yes, his complete trust was in the Lord. But deep down, he couldn't deny that the real answer was that he didn't know how to let go.

"There's only one twist to getting the Provider to help you out," the Pastor continued. "He wants you to pray and then lay it down in His hands. Ya'll don't hear me out there." Moans and shouts rang out from the benches, shaking up the weary-hearted in agreement. "I said, He wants you to get on your knees, lay on your back, or stand up on your feet and pray any time the need hits you. It really doesn't matter. But my Lord says to give it all to Him however you want to do it. He wants to be your refuge and your strength. Your very present help in times of trouble. Hallelujah!"

Hands flew up in praise all around the church. Paul raised a hand in the air giving honor to God. Reaching out to grasp at the only One who could make him strong enough to do something about the three little girls he'd left behind.

He'd tried to approach God on the subject before. If there was a bright side to his bleak situation, Paul just couldn't see it. Truth was, the shame consumed him after years of allowing the guilt to fester in his heart. He wanted a break through. Wanted God to rid him of the painful consequences of his actions, but it was hard to let go of the things he'd done.

His throat was still dry from the dream two nights ago. The unshakeable dream that resurrected itself after a month of lying dormant. Years of running from his demons and now God was pushing him to take action? Did it mean he had to do something this instant? Fifty years he'd lived on this earth and for forty-one of them, the ducking and dodging had become his way of life except where Camilla was concerned.

"Step out on faith and believe that everything will be all right", Camilla always said. But he didn't want to face the chance that all three of his daughters might hate him. Didn't want to see exactly how much he'd hurt them. Knew what it was like to not have a father around. Paul remembered the tragedy that took his own father from his life those many years ago. It was a memory he forced himself not to think about right now.

"You see, saints," Pastor Fisher hollered from the pulpit. "We block our own path to the blessings God has in store for us. We don't trust Him enough. But just think for a minute. At this very moment, He's giving you the air you're using to breathe. He woke you up this morning in your right mind. You don't do those things by yourself. So if The Provider does all those things for you on a daily basis without fail, that's your assurance that no matter what the situation, you really can't lose when you cast on Him all your cares."

He hadn't done that yet. Not completely, if he wanted to be totally honest with the man he was today. The inevitable was pressing his back against a wall. Paul had to go forth, relinquishing his fears into the hands of the One who could make him whole. There was no other way around it.

9 noelle

"**H**ap-py Birth-day toooo yoooouuuu!" The crowd of four year-olds burst into applause and a ton of noise.

"Auntie Noe, Auntie Noe, I want the first piece," the little man of the hour said as he jumped up and down.

Noelle kissed her godson, Charlie, on his cute button nose.

"Of course you get the first piece. You're my little birthday boy."

He took the slice of cake from her and used his small hands to shove the chocolate layers into his mouth.

"Fanku Onfi Noe," he smiled before walking off to devour the rest.

Eager kids salivated as they swarmed her, waiting for a plate of their own. She managed to serve half of the sugar-addicted party bunch before she felt fingers pinching her waist. It was Candace, who slipped an arm around her hips and leaned in close.

"Don't look now, but your ex-man just rolled in."

Noelle's heart dropped to her big toe. A wave of emotions took over, rocking the minute stability she'd been able to muster just recently.

"What the hell is he doing here?"

"CJ, I guess. It wasn't me. You know I wouldn't do that to you."

Cutting cake could wait. *Should I act nonchalant? Casually slip out the door? Hide in the bathroom?* She was flustered, but was determined not to let it show. Noelle placed the cake knife in Candace's hand and headed to the kitchen to wash away the icing on her fingers. The coast was clear. Her thoughts scattered every which-way as she headed to the fridge, forgetting why she was in there to begin with. *Wash my hands,* she reminded herself. Noelle moved to the sink and lathered the crusted blue confection off with dishwashing liquid. She heard the voices before she saw them enter into the small space.

Chris, Troy, and Candace's boyfriend, CJ, rounded the corner clutching Heinekens in their hands. The booming voices came to a halt when they saw her stone-faced and mute. Noelle turned off the pipe, not caring about the soap suds sliding down her wrist. She reached above the sink, grabbed a paper towel, and concentrated on her escape.

She glimpsed Chris in his red striped polo. Lingering anger, bubbled at the bottom of her gut. There was a bad taste in her mouth as the man-whore stood with his chest erect. Adding fuel to the fire, he stared, challenging her to look as she came his way.

You're in a kitchen full of knives, Noelle. Move fast.

"Hey, um, Noelle . . . your hair, it's nice," CJ offered in an attempt to break the tension. "What you do? Add a brighter color or something?" Now was not the time for casual conversation. Her hands were itching for round two.

"Thanks," Noelle quickly answered. "I did a little something."

"Well it looks good," CJ replied, still feeling a need to speak.

He was taking it too far now. "Thanks. I'm gonna go keep an eye on some of these crazy kids," she said and hustled out the doorway.

Noelle exhaled a huge breath, unaware she'd been holding it in. She bee-lined it to the brick house's front entrance and plopped down on the concrete steps. *Don't do it, don't do it, don't do it.* She let her head fall into her lap and shut her lids tight to hold back the tears.

Just then, a soft hand rested on the back of her neck. "Sugar, are you okay?"

BROKEN WITH STAINS

Noelle acknowledged her bestfriend's mother, "Yeah, I'm alright, Mimi."

Hope's sweet, caring nature remained the same today, unchanging from what Noelle had become accustomed to ever since she was seven years-old with cornrows and scabbed knees. Noelle had not only gained her bestfriend, Candace, on her first day of second grade at PS 6 Elementary School, she had also been blessed with a second mom, the loving woman she'd always referred to as Mimi.

"You sure? You don't look like everything's okay. Sitting out here like your head's too heavy to hold up."

Noelle gave up a half smile. "I'm fine. Really."

"Not buying it," Hope said, taking a seat. "Be honest with me . . . what's wrong with my baby?"

She didn't want to revisit the hurt she'd been trying to keep at bay. The incident was on Noelle's tongue each day since it happened. It was all she talked about with Candace, who did her best to comfort her through the tears.

Looking into Hope's face, it was obvious the woman would wait however long she had to until the truth came out. The subtle wrinkles on her round face coupled with a faint gleam of sadness, now made sense to Noelle. It spoke volumes. Revealed the gentle woman had experienced her own share of a similar hurt before.

Noelle opened her mouth to speak, but nothing came out. Hope rubbed circles in her back until she could find the appropriate words.

"Mimi . . . he hurt me so bad," she uttered, choking up. Noelle waited for Hope to say something. Instead, she sat patiently, waiting for Noelle to finish.

"Last week, I walked in on Chris having sex with some girl. And I'm so messed up, I don't know what to do. I loved him so much. Wanted to be with him so much. And all along, he was dogging me out behind my back."

Hope shook her head in disgust, though her face lacked

surprise.

"Baby, I know it's a tough pill to swallow."

Noelle laughed out loud as she wiped the falling wetness from her eyes. "It's more than a tough pill to swallow. It's more like trying to swallow the whole bottle. Every day I think to myself . . . how am I supposed to get over this?"

Hope stroked the empty space on her ring finger as if conjuring up old memories.

"Men do these things all the time, never stopping to think about the lives they rip apart in the process. Sorry you had to experience this, Noelle. Hurts my heart to see you have to go through it," she comforted, looking down at the unadorned finger. "It's really a shame that he couldn't appreciate you for the beautiful young woman you are. It may take a while, but you'll get past this. All that love you got in your heart will overcome the hurt you're feeling today. Know that."

Noelle looked across the street at a couple in front of their home. Two young children - a girl and a boy – resembled mini versions of their parents. As the two kids ran towards the back of the house, the couple shared a playful moment. With his woman's back turned, the average-built man playfully smacked her on the butt. She jumped forward in exaggerated pain and then turned around, flinging herself on his back. He squirmed in his plaid shorts as she punched him in the shoulder. The woman laughed wildly when he charged towards the back of the two-story house, piggy-backing her the entire way until they disappeared around the corner.

Noelle's sadness plunged to a new low. That was supposed to be her life with Chris, built on a bond that was unbreakable and everlasting. Hope watched Noelle's mood decline further. She placed her hand on the hunched back and commenced to rubbing circles again.

"I threw darts at him Mimi."

She stopped rubbing. "You did what?"

"He had some darts on the desk in his room and I just

picked them up and started aiming. I wanted to hurt him as much as he hurt me."

She smirked. "My goodness, girl. Did you get him good?" They both laughed at the thought.

"He was pretty good at dodging them, but he got darted up a couple times. Troy came in and saved him and the girl."

"Troy was there?"

"He walked in on me and Chris arguing. He wasn't there when I first came. But, I guess he got home soon after, heard the commotion, and stopped me from killing them both."

"So what did he say?" Hope asked.

"Troy?"

"No, Chris."

"Not one word of apology," Noelle said as her nostrils flared. "From the time I walked in on them, the closest thing I got to an apology was when he jumped up and said, 'Oh shit! Noelle, it ain't nothing. Don't even trip.' "

Hope looked at Noelle in disbelief. "That's what he said? You're kidding me, right?"

"No - I'm not. After that, I just blacked out. Throwing stuff at him, going crazy. I was mad as hell. And then on top of it, he had the nerve to call me a crazy bitch."

Hope closed her eyes at that one.

"He acted like he was about to hit me before Troy made him chill out. But I promise you, if he had put one finger on me, there would've been some furniture moving up in there."

"My, my, my. Let's just thank God it didn't get to that point."

The two entwined bodies played through Noelle's mind in a continuous loop. Water blurred her eyes as she looked over at Hope. She took Noelle's hand and put it on the left side of her chest, above her heart.

"What do you feel right there?"

Noelle paused before replying. "I feel my heart beating."

"Exactly. Smile, baby. That's the bright side to all of this mess," Hope said, releasing Noelle's hand. "Your heart's still beating which means you've survived the reality of the situation. He's a liar. A cheat. And he's clearly not for you. Realizing that has only made you a stronger woman. You can take that to the bank because you're talking to someone who knows."

The tears were fighting to make an entrance. Noelle didn't want them to win right now.

"I still love him so much, Mimi. But, I feel like killing his stupid self at the same time. I want him to explain because I don't understand how he could do this to me. Guys always complain about girls these days just after their money and having ten different kids by ten different men, but that wasn't me. I'm in school. I run my own business on the side. I never begged him for anything. Never cheated on him or lied. Now, I can't even sleep at night because it just hurts so bad. Don't I even deserve an explanation?"

"Noelle, what explanation do you want? Because whichever one it is, he can't give it to you. That's why he hasn't been able to face you. He know she's wrong. And he knows there's nothing he can do to explain his behavior away. Don't stop your heart from healing by waiting for an explanation."

The big burst of laughter coming from the house across the street suddenly caught their attention. The couple and children emerged from the back of the house running, screaming, and laughing in the midst of a water fight. The playful family soaked each other with large water guns. So caught up in their water and excitement, they didn't notice that everyone on the street had stopped to watch.

In a fit of excitement, the man's wife and kids turned their guns on him until he decided to surrender. He wiped his soaked face with his wet t-shirt and threw his hands up in the air yelling, "Somebody call the cops. Call the cops somebody - they're soaking me to death." Noelle and Hope couldn't help but giggle at his humorous pleas.

That was the future Noelle had pictured for herself for as long as she could remember - a joyful marriage with beautiful children soaking up life. Smiling at the sunshine that swept over her just then, she briefly prickled with a feeling that the dream was still attainable. She was only twenty-one years old, and though Chris had caused the light in her eyes to diminish somewhat, she realized her life wasn't over yet. There was time to bring it back to life.

"I know I'll heal," she said turning her attention back to Hope. "I don't know how I'll get there. But you're right, my heart's not completely dead."

Hope continued to stare across the street. "That's right. See how happy that woman looks?"

Noelle nodded.

"Well guess what? I was the nurse who comforted her when she came to my hospital nine years ago and found out her husband died in a car accident. Dead on arrival before she was even notified."

Noelle watched the family go inside their home, drenched from top-to-bottom with smiles on their faces as they shut their front door.

Hope peered down at her ringless finger, "Maybe she does have a faint ache in her heart, but look what God can do."

10 sienna

Why did I become a teacher? Sienna yawned and pondered the question inspired by the rowdy teens she'd dealt with today. *No. Scratch that. What possessed me to become a high school teacher?* Sienna knew the exhaustion had settled in once these thoughts started to take residence in her head.

Using her red pen to make the appropriate corrections on one of her student's test papers, she put to rest the numerous events of the day.

Wrong.

She marked an X next to the first question on the test sheet.

Wrong.

She marked an X next to the second question on the test sheet.

And wrong.

She marked an X next to the third question on the test sheet.

Sienna double-checked the name written at the top of the paper.

Tandi Black. Why am I not surprised? Maybe if you showed up more often and quit the loud-talking, gum-popping, and stink attitude whenever you do manage to step into my class, you might actually learn something. Today not only had she dealt with Tandi, but dozens more students just like her. Wednesdays were when the students began to shake off the Monday morning slump. Hump day was the official start of papers thrown across the classroom, trivial arguments, class clowns, and whining.

She was drained.

And though her mind had wandered from the papers she needed to finish for tomorrow, the only thought she truly wanted to focus on was how good her body would feel soaking in a lavender-scented bubble bath.

With that vision in mind, she collected the test papers that lay on her desk, swallowed the last of her lukewarm coffee, put on her khaki jacket, and left the class room.

Good riddance.

She'd squeeze in grading the rest of the papers somewhere between a microwave dinner and the eleven o'clock news.

Sienna listened to her new Pradas click down the hallway. Click-by-click, she became increasingly wracked with guilt. A guilty pleasure for Prada shoes filled her with shame. It was a crazy craving, considering her teaching salary. But how was she supposed to pass up these black beauties when she walked into Saks two days ago? Shouldn't have been in there in the first place, but she needed the retail therapy since she'd cried her eyes out all weekend.

Marcus never did give up. Sienna had done everything from ignoring his calls to hanging up on him and yet he still didn't seem to get the drift. On Sunday night she even called her mother to make sure she was doing the right thing. Annette Burgess confirmed that her daughter was a beautiful, educated, independent woman and should no longer subject herself to a relationship that had slowly become toxic. That was an answer Sienna expected. From day one, her mother had never acquired a taste for Marcus.

Sienna knew time would be what it took to remove thoughts of him from her mind. If she had to supplement a few sleepless nights with pocket-draining shopping sprees to fill up the void she felt, she'd do what was necessary.

She checked the Michele watch on her arm - a present Marcus had given her after one of his previous foul-ups. The thought of separating herself from it, put a faint mist behind her eyes. It would have to be given back to him if she was serious. All reminders of him had to be removed or destroyed, but she'd worry about that later. It was fifteen minutes after four and she needed to run over to Eve's to pick something up before her friend left for the theater where she did makeup at nights for the past two weeks. She hated rushing and thought about calling Eve to tell her she'd meet her at the spot.

Quickly, Sienna threw out the idea, remembering how far out of the way the theater was from her home.

Instead, she picked up her feet and hustled, choosing to use the students' rest room. She would lose time if she ran all the way upstairs to the ladies' room in the teachers lounge.

In her haste, she pushed open the peeling door to her right, not realizing she'd entered the boys bathroom until she was greeted by the large, stained urinals up against the wall. She turned on her heels ready to make a swift exit when she heard a loud slap and a scream.

Her body froze as she listened.

"How many times I gotta talk to you? You that stupid, I gotta speak twice?"

"I wasn't in -," the female never got a chance to finish her sentence. Another slap viciously sounded down on her.

Chills coursed through Sienna's spine. Slowly, she turned back around. Something had to done. That something? She racked her mind to figure out. In the mean time listened as the girl cried and her abuser continued.

"I'ma punch you right in your lip. You wanna make me look like a chump in front of dude? I'll murder you before I sit here and let you disrespect me like that. Thought I wouldn't find out? Well guess what?" His slap against her skin sounded even louder than the previous ones. Adrenaline pushed Sienna forward and around the corner. What she saw tore her apart.

"Get your hands off of her," she yelled. A fist was raised over his victim, ready to strike again. Tandi Black sat on the floor shielding her face as she awaited the next blow.

The enraged frown plastered across his face, unnerved Sienna. She didn't know what she should do next, but she wasn't about to let him hit the scared girl one more time.

BROKEN WITH STAINS

"Tandi, are you okay?!" she asked, looking down at her student shivering in fear. Tandi nodded her head, obviously in pain as she gingerly ran a hand over the side of her face.

Sienna turned back to the boy whose lips were clenched in a tight scowl. Spit sat in the corners of his mouth. His jaw muscles flexed each time his chest rose and fell.

"What's your name?" Sienna questioned.

Threatening fists formed as he puffed out his chest with his head held high. Asking again would be useless. Moving past him, Sienna hurried to the nearest porcelain sink, and knelt next to the girl who sat sobbing on the floor.

"What's his name?"

Tandi turned to look at him. Daggers shot back at her.

"I'm good Ms. Burgess. I just made him upset, that's all."

Sienna's face contorted into a look of confusion. She couldn't believe Tandi would take responsibility for a boy who'd just warned that he would murder her.

"No, it's not okay. I'm not going to just stand by and watch him beat you like you're some dog on the street. A dog doesn't even deserve to be treated this way. I want you to tell me his name."

Sienna wasn't prepared when Tandi jumped up, blood dribbling from her swollen lips. "Bitch, I said it's okay. Ain't none of your business what goes on between me and my man. Stay the hell out of my problems!"

Sienna took a step back. "Tandi -"

"You better not say nothing to nobody," she continued to scream. "He made a mistake and hit me - the whole world doesn't need to know."

Shock rocked the foundation of Sienna's comprehension. "Look at your face," she said, pointing to the dark scar forming around the outskirts of her mouth.

"Shut your ass up," the boy finally spewed out.

Sienna tensed. His fists were opening and closing.

Tandi was now standing partially behind her. She didn't know who might pounce first or if both would double-team her.

"If I didn't come in and stop him, it would have been worse," Sienna said turning to face Tandi. Her pulse raced out of control, still, she continued talking, choosing to take a chance on the girl who needed her help. "Take a look in the mirror before you sit here defending him. He doesn't care about you if he would do that to your face."

He took a step towards Tandi and screwed his face.

"You gonna sit here and listen to her? I don't even know why I mess with you. I thought you was better than these dumb broads out here, but you're just like the rest of them hoes."

Her bruised lips quivered. A new well of tears sprang forth from her eyes.

"You know I love you, Malik -" His eyes narrowed into tiny slits. Tandi instantly covered her mouth. Cover now blown, he stepped forward, but abruptly stopped himself before he reached his target.

"Look at you giving away my government. I should've known you were a snitch too. Just like a ho – can't be trusted."

He made a move towards the bathroom door.

"Wait!" Tandi screamed, running after him.

Sienna couldn't help herself. She reached out, pulled Tandi's shoulder, and said "Let him go. He's not worth it."

He was gone by the time she managed to shake herself free. She swung at her teacher through her tears. Sienna leaned back just in time to miss the impact of Tandi's right hook.

"See what you did?" she screamed. "I know how to handle him, but you messed everything up. Now he won't want me anymore."

With that, she grabbed her back pack from under the sink and ran out of the restroom.

Sienna's knees felt as if they would buckle. She looked

down as she tried to steady her feet. She didn't know what to do first. Should she cry or faint? The wobbly teacher knew she'd most likely do the latter when it set in that the test papers she'd been correcting were scattered all over the bathroom floor.

Foot prints marred the yellow sheets. Some were ripped and crumpled beyond repair. Defeat punctured the resolve she'd held onto only moments ago. Sienna didn't understand what had just happened. For a second, she forgot how to blink. She wanted to move, but couldn't; her brain needed to thaw.

It took effort, but somehow she found her way to the floor. Collecting the damaged papers, she unconsciously went through the motions. Such savage behavior by a man directed towards a woman was something Sienna had never encountered before. Never imagined it was something she'd one day get caught in the middle of. And it was happening to Tandi? How would she get her student to see she didn't have to put up with her boyfriend's abuse?

Sienna shifted and attempted to steady herself on the dirty, tiled floor. Her moist palms slipped off the sheets. She gained her balance, proceeding slower on her second try. The random X's on the test papers seemed to become larger and more frequent. Sienna's eyes narrowed in on the marks. The hairs on the back of her neck rose at the same time her heart skipped a beat.

She stopped gathering the tests and gaped at the sight that made her throat constrict. It wasn't her felt-tip red pen covering them with X's. The sheets were buried under something more detrimental. A little darker. Something much more distorted. Sienna dropped the blood-splattered chaos. All around her the stains were blindly spread out across the sheets. They were the final marks of correction. Clear and steadfast. Signed permanently by Tandi.

11 joy

She waited for him at the train station three blocks away from her apartment. He was cool, but she wasn't sure just yet that she wanted him showing up unexpectedly to her crib.

A few days ago, after scrapping the leftover spaghetti in favor of Frankie and Johnny's on Bronxdale, she reassured herself that she could reach the pot of gold at the end of the rainbow if she handled her business the way she always did. Joy went over her three unfailing rules to success: Build him up. Bed him down. And bullshit him every step of the way.

The train rumbled out of the station above her, heading towards Manhattan just as she spotted Luce's shiny red S-Class Benz. The glistening rims lit up the street. Female gawkers, openly admired the stylish ride, craning their necks to see the man behind the wheel. He made his way over to where Joy stood acting bored by the whole thing.

Drool, suckers. Watch the queen take her seat on the throne, she inwardly smiled.

Luce's aviator sunglasses covered most of his face. Joy appreciated how scrumptious he looked, though it wasn't the most important thing. Nonchalance guided her every step. In reality, she was fully aware of all eyes on her, just the way she liked it.

She strutted up to the car in her gravity-defying pair of strappy gold heels, form-fitting Seven jeans, and a black baby-tee with the words "Woman on Top" beaming across it in bold gold studs. As she opened the door of the car and got in, she flung her long burgundy mane over her shoulder and sensually lowered herself into the comfortable leather seat. Looking good had never been a problem. Especially when it came to using it to her advantage.

He smiled his wickedly sexy smile. "What you trying to

do? Cause accidents out here?"

Joy winked at him and blew a kiss. Code for telling him to shut up and drive. Attempting to make her blush was like trying to get a four hundred pound man in a ballerina's leotard. It just wasn't going to happen.

"I have no control over who keeps their eyes on the road and who keeps their eyes on me," she said. "But anyway, I'm starving. Where are we going?"

He drove away from the curb. "I was thinking Mc Donald's."

Joy's face went blank. He might as well have said they'd be dining in the city dump. Luce laughed.

"Nah, I'm just messing with you, sexy. I thought we'd have a nice lunch at Cipriani's in the city. You cool with that?"

"That's fine with me. I've been there a couple times. I can dig the food."

"Yeah, I enjoy the food myself, but I haven't been there in a couple months so I thought it'd be nice to stop by."

Joy trailed her eyes along the length of his body, a million scandalous thoughts dancing through her mind. "I bet you enjoy a lot of nice things."

He stopped at a red light and caught her just as her roving eyes moved from the bulge between his legs and landed on his full lips.

"Look at them lips," she said, crossing her legs. "Where does a fine specimen like you come from?" Building the ego was something she did better than any other.

He looked her in the eyes, surprised by her boldness.

"Well, I'm originally from Brooklyn, but I lived in Queens for about three years before I started living between Brooklyn and Cali four years ago."

"A BK boy. I like that. Are you single or does your woman think you're with your boys right now?"

He smiled a slick, one-sided smile.

"You hit the jackpot, sweetie. I'm dolo. Been that way

for about two years."

Jackpot was exactly what she had in mind.

"That's very single, but I don't buy it, Mr. Rolex," Joy said nodding towards his wrist. "I can definitely see you pimpin'."

"So you're saying, right now you're willingly rolling with a pimp?"

"No. What I'm saying is, right now you're taking me to get something to eat like we agreed. That's what I'm saying Mr. . . . Mr. . . . Mr. Chocolate Balls."

They both fell out laughing. Joy didn't know where that came from, but she had to admit to herself that she'd suffered a loss for words. She didn't come across his type of smooth, dark skin every day. Luce's uncharacteristically handsome face had a compelling force behind it. So did his powerfully built arms and salaciously tempting lips.

Luce took her hand in his and brought it up to his moist mouth. He kissed the tip of each finger and said, "Keep talking like that and we might not make it to the city."

Joy loved a challenge.

She flipped her hand underneath his and brought his index finger to the tip of her tongue. Sucking it in down to his knuckle, she let her lips gradually rise over its length.

"As you can see, I'm hungry. But if you think this is anything, you'll bug out when I get to dessert."

* * *

Joy didn't reach home until seven a.m. the next morning. As promised, she had wanted to finish off dessert in between the sheets after their lunch at Cipriani's. The sooner she infiltrated his system, the better. To her surprise, Luce put part two of her plan on hold.

Their next stop was a bowling alley later that afternoon. Then a movie theater. And finally the Shark Bar for dinner. It was only then, after stuffing themselves with lobster and crab, that they retired at the Marriott, passing out on the hotel's inviting bed.

She scratched her head as she walked to the bathroom in her apartment. *No sex?*

Joy hadn't prepared herself for that. She couldn't help thinking about Luce's singing her to sleep the previous night. It was corny at first, but as he continued his rendition of Stevie Wonder's My Cherie Amor, she had to give him props - his voice wasn't as bad as it could've been.

He was okay. His company was different. It was weird not to experience a nightcap filled with weed smoke and bed-squeaking, but the three Benjamins he put in her hand at the end of the night, made Joy feel like it was something she could get used to.

Three hundred was just a start, she reminded herself. Not nearly enough to pay the balance of her rent. A twinge of disappointment passed over her. If she'd gotten to the 'bed him down' step of her plan, Luce probably would've added another couple hundred, maybe more.

He'd dropped her off in front of her building this morning. That meant she was feeling him sooner than she thought she would. *How'd I manage to let that happen*, she queried herself. Joy didn't even know what he did for a living yet, usually it took at least two weeks and a full interrogation, before her victims were privy to her place of residence. Until then, it was only hotels or their place, provided the girlfriend or wife was gone for the night. Luce was able to bypass that rule. Joy knew she had better get herself together.

She climbed into the steaming shower and scrubbed her curvaceous body. It was the one thing she gave Blue credit for – helping to create her beautiful face and delightful physique.

Joy let the warm, soothing water cascade down her five foot six inch caramel frame and for a brief moment thought about the man who created her other half. She promptly brushed that thought to the side. From very early on, Blue had punished her whenever she'd brought up the loser who was missing in action. Resentment was alive and kicking. She fumed at every recollection, memories piled high of the numerous times she'd been sent to bed without dinner any time she asked Blue about the man she shared DNA with.

It was hard to distinguish where the heat was coming from. Was it the hot water beating down on her or the anger burning in her stomach? She shoved her face under the cascading water. Let it rush down the contours of the face, that on many tear-filled nights, she yearned to find out who it resembled. He'd never come searching her out either. Joy lathered her face with cleansing liquid, wiping beyond the surface of her skin, and aiming for the memories too. Back when she was thirteen, she'd been doing the same in the shower when one of her mother's boyfriend's had slipped his hand behind the curtain and welcomed himself to a squeeze. "That you, Joy? My fault. I was trying to get to the soap," was his excuse. It was only the beginning of a situation that later spiraled out of control. But, it wasn't the beginning of the root of the problem: Blue had never been a real mother at all.

The liquor. The men. Staying out all night and leaving Joy alone. Forcing her daughter to fend for herself, Joy didn't know when her mother had become so "refined" in the midst of it all. There certainly wasn't always the white men with money and beachfront homes. Joy remembered the times only hazed black faces revolved through her bedroom door like it was the entrance to the bustling Macy's Herald Square.

She never felt like a priority in her mother's life. Couldn't count one time Blue ventured to check her homework. Before she went out for the night, Blue took the time to explain to her daughter why she'd get slapped if she touched the stove while she was gone, but never took a moment to divulge what the red spots on Joy's panties were all about. And where in the world was the mother to make sure she had a decent dinner to eat before she went to sleep at night? Hot dogs and bologna sandwiches didn't count. It had been three years since Joy had moved out on her own and she still hadn't seen her yet.

Joy rinsed the soap from her face in the same way she'd washed her hands of Blue at the age of thirteen. She let the water take her back to the grimy, enduring memory that wouldn't die. Joy clearly remembered the torturous six months she was forced to live through when Blue's newest boyfriend moved in. She couldn't forget the morning she woke up in the hospital screaming, arms aching, one eye swollen shut. But he wasn't there. It wasn't dark anymore. His filthy hands were no longer ravaging her underdeveloped body.

When her mother's boyfriend came to her room that night, she'd had a six inch knife waiting for him under her pillow. One touch and pure impulse took over. Joy swung with all her thirteen year-old might. Red rage replaced all fear. She blacked out after the first blow to his neck.

The white walls of the hospital room were the next thing she awakened to. Blue wasn't even by her side.

A lanky, white police officer came to speak with her later that day, pen and pad in hand. Everything after that was a blur now, mostly because she'd forced herself to forget.

Stabbing Blue's man to death marked the moment in time Joy lost every ounce of her innocence. What was left of it, after he'd stripped her of ninety-nine percent. Tears and all, Blue denied any knowledge of his late-night feasts between Joy's legs.

So convincing was the mother who was barely there, the doctors and the police believed her story of lies. "I had no idea. How could he do this to my baby? Can't believe I didn't see the signs," Blue sniffled. "She was acting up in school lately, but I didn't imagine this was the reason why."

Joy remembered listening to the foolishness in the hallway as she lay on her back in the stiff patient bed. Lies. All ridiculous lies. There was no hope whatsoever for the genuine article – the person who would love and protect Joy like only a mother could.

Since that point in her life, she'd never looked back to how things could've, would've, or should've been. Joy made her own way. Took care of herself and was very proud of that fact.

If men were going to use her it would never be against her will and it most definitely wouldn't be for free. Survival of the fittest. Didn't matter who got slaughtered in the process.

All she wanted was everything and if that was a problem, it was too bad for whoever was involved. There was always a victim who'd be willing to take his place. Joy wanted to get all she could. The money. The jewels. The trips. The good life. "Get" was her second language. "Take", her third.

She allowed the scathing water to cleanse her one more time and then turned off the pipe. Joy watched the remaining pool scuttle over her manicured feet and down the noisy drain. She'd work her magic and get what she wanted. Luce would be at her feet in no time too.

12 paul

The cool breeze drifted into the room hitting the hairs on the back of his neck. At first, Paul wasn't sure if it was from the chilly weather or if it was from the memory of the day before.

He clicked on the mouse and scrolled down the images on his computer. The lace. The flowers. The smiles. The champagne. It was all a blurred memory to him. He had been there. Capturing the essence of his surroundings was what he did best. A twinkle in the eye. A wayward dress. Even a solitary tear escaping down someone's cheek could warrant a snap shot in time. Paul was never unsuccessful at grasping a feeling - that's what made his phone ring off the hook. But today, as the sunlight faded against his spacious studio, Paul failed to remember actually seeing the intricate details that induced him to click away at his client's wedding.

Something had caused his focus to disappear into thin air. It caused a tearing away at the inner lining of his soul. A sour taste came to rest at the back of his throat, just like that something currently taking up residence in his mind. That something, though flesh, was more of a force than a human being. That something, once far removed, was now undeniably lodged under his skin. It was the one and only Rinelda Bass.

Rinni hadn't been anywhere in his foremost thoughts until she came into focus through his camera's lens. A slip changed his mind's functioning in less than three seconds. Paul aimed to please. It was in that aiming - the search for the photographs that would bring a smile to the newly weds' faces for years to come - he scanned the church benches full of family and friends during the singing of My Endless Love. His zoom landed on Regal Rinni - a name she'd been called for as long as he could remember.

TAMARA BURKE

Those red lips he'd never forget. She had cussed him out with them something fierce the last time he laid eyes on her. That was almost twenty years ago. The thought slapped him in the face at the same time his heart wedged inside his throat.

Rinni, the aunt of his second daughter Noelle, stared back at him through his lens. Yes, she saw him and had probably been seeing him since the moment she stepped into the building. Paul felt an urge to drop his camera and run. But he was never a man to run away from anything. Except for his children of course. He cut himself some slack because that was a delicate situation. Throughout the years, he'd persuaded himself that he hadn't been running, just tip-toeing around it. That was done now. As Rinelda looked through his exterior, a sneer swathed over her no-nonsense face, he knew his picture of truth was about to be discarded.

After closing the window to block out the unpleasantly cool air, Paul slowly leaned back in his comfy black leather chair that had always been there. It was old. Yet, the chair remained reliable, flexing and molding to accommodate him, something Regal Rinni never did. He chuckled at the thought. The thrift shop purchase had been made in Harlem around the same time he'd first met Sharon and her older sister Rinni. And while he worked on breaking in the brand new addition to his small studio, Rinni worked on breaking away at his ego.

He remembered the year that he'd become a father for the second time. Noelle made her entrance on February 8, 1986. The itch that never failed to make its appearance every time it was time for him to make a move, had already permeated halfway through his six foot three inch body.

While his woman, Sharon, preferred to grin and bear his distant treatment of both herself and their newborn, Rinni refused to close her eyes and ears to the fact that Paul was hurting her sister and innocent niece in such a way.

As the cigarette bounced up and down between the

vivid red lips, she'd told him straight out, "You better act like you got some God-given sense and take care of your woman and child. If you don't want to, that's your damn problem. You should've stayed in the studio instead of staying up inside my sister."

Paul dared not answer back. He was a lover, not a fighter at heart. The simple alternative was to walk away. And that's what he did, when she'd cornered him in the hallway after leaving the apartment she and her sister shared.

"She didn't make that precious baby all by herself," she said as he started down the flight of steps. "It's your responsibility too. So you better shake that shit off, whatever's got your balls gripped. You have a family you need to take care of."

The back of his eyeballs felt like they'd began vibrating. Paul didn't want to think about all those years ago. It was a place he never liked to visit; a bad time in his life when things were chopped and screwed and restlessness ruled his days. He'd known back then that Rinni's keen radar had honed in on his unsettled spirit from the very start. She was like a bloodhound in blonde hair and red lips with a cigarette smashed in between. The smell of fear was underneath her nose. It was the reason why she watched him with a fierceness. Her younger sister was vulnerable. Rinni was a fortress - she saw the wolf in Paul.

She didn't miss a beat at yesterday's wedding either, as Paul hoped she would once he fairly regained his concentration. After their first encounter, he tried to avoid her. The taking of pictures, the buzz of chatter, bulb flashes, clinking glasses, lens adjustments - they all ran together.

His goal was to keep himself in motion. He kept close to the bride and groom at all times and when he did give them space, he busied himself taking photos of the guests. Paul did his best to escape any confrontation. He whirled about, ducked, and dodged until finally, he turned around to see Rinni a mere inch away.

TAMARA BURKE

All five feet ten inches of her.

The thin, stern woman was a vision in black. Her brave blonde hair, grayed slightly around the edges. She was no more than fifty, like himself, yet she'd physically aged very little since he'd last seen her at her very youthful thirty. Paul wondered if she still smoked. Wondered if she'd ever changed her views against marriage. He was curious about whether she still snacked on chocolate-covered grass hoppers. Really wanted to know if she still hated him. "Here's her number." She thrust a pink piece of paper towards him. "You act like you got some God-given sense and reach out to that young lady. Your child. If you don't have a mind to, that's your problem. You've wasted far too many years being a coward. Stand up and be a man for once." With that, she left.

As he lifted the pink piece of paper from his desk, the coldness crept up his spine. Paul rose to close his window when he realized the cold couldn't be coming from that direction because he'd closed it a few minutes ago.

The spine-tingling sensation was familiar. Something he recalled experiencing the same moment he held Camilla's hand at the altar seven years ago, right before he said "I do".

The surreal feeling that commemorated the instant Paul opened up his heart wider than he'd ever done before. It unnerved him. The chains had been broken. Camilla brought about a change that unlocked the chambers of the heart Paul had made himself close off from those that entered his life throughout the years. The realization rendered him icy to the core while staring into her eyes as the reverend spoke.

Somehow, touching the pink piece of paper Rinni gave to him, had the power to do the same. Paul put it closer to his face. Seven digits and his daughter would be on the other line.

Sharon would kill him. He knew there were no ifs, ands, or buts about that.

He'd wait before he let his fingers dial the numbers in front of his eyes. Time felt hurried, like it was swiftly running away, but Paul told himself he wouldn't rush to knock on any doors just yet. He would plot his steps properly before he made a move once and for all.

Paul was going to make a move, once and for all. It was time to get a hold of the three lives he'd let slip away.

13 noelle

Taking the bus was the last thing Noelle wanted to do. But since someone had decided to throw a rock at her windshield - producing a crack the size of a lightening bolt - she had no other choice.

She rang the bell and hoisted the large Coach tote over her shoulder. The bus's back exit placed her right in front of an over-flowing garbage can. She waved the stench away and trudged up the sidewalk.

Noelle was miserable. Though it did wonders to strap in her small gut, her girdle felt too tight. She rubbed at her eyes, thanks to the pollen in the air that viciously made them itch. Her feet felt as if they could use some Epsom salt, the patent leather ballerina flats were made more for cute than for comfort. Thankfully, she could rest easy - Griggs' Auto was only five blocks away – her Neon was all patched up and waiting patiently. She forged ahead, quickly passing three young girls excitedly chatting away and an old man walking in a scandalous pair of biker shorts. Reaching the barber shop a block away from the garage, she breathed a sigh of relief at the miracle. Couldn't believe she managed to reach that far as much as her dogs were barking. Only one more street to conquer and she'd be at the garage, in her ride, and ready to zoom home.

Her feet weren't trying to hear it though.

Swearing she heard her corn-toe beg for mercy, she stopped in front of the barber shop's windows to rotate an aching foot. She shoved it back inside the evil shoe and almost lost her balance when it wouldn't cooperate. Her head turned towards the shop to see if anyone noticed her lack of grace. And that's when she saw him. He was standing sideways with his back partially to her, but there was no denying who it was.

Gray tee. Low fade. Brown skin. Broad shoulders. He gave another guy a pound with his fist and then turned to face Noelle.

She tugged at her ponytail and scratched the bridge of her nose.

Continuing up the street, she could feel the disappointment level out against the pressure of her belt.

Gray tee, low fade, brown skin, and broad shoulders, wasn't Chris in the least.

* * *

"Yeah, he'll be out in a sec." The balding man did all he could to show interest behind his lingering eyes.

"Thanks," Noelle said, looking at the square clock against the garage's far wall. Not only did she not have time for middle-aged men on Viagra, there was studying to do and a client's music website she had to get home to finish in time for tomorrow. She wanted to make this a quick stop. As far as she was concerned, a sec could turn into a full-blown hour. Luckily, the wait wasn't too long.

Noelle watched him come around the corner, his opened khaki mechanic's jumpsuit revealing an oil-stained white t-shirt underneath. Her usual mechanic, the shop's owner Griggs, had informed her he'd be out of town for a few days, but a new and very capable mechanic could replace the broken windshield on the car.

"Hi. Noelle, right?"

She nodded, too flustered to speak.

"I thought you'd pick it up sooner. I heard you left a message earlier," he said as she followed him out onto the street to the back of the garage.

"I couldn't make it 'til now."

They stopped in front of her car.

TAMARA BURKE

"Like new," he smiled, rapping his knuckles against the hood.

And who the heck does he think he is? Noelle took in his heart-warming smile. The new guy's rich cocoa skin had a dreamlike glow to it, despite the dirt and oil.

"Is it all good with you, Ms. Caldwell?"

His overwhelming presence was a blinding distraction. No man had the right to look that delectable. Black stains soiled the baggy jumpsuit, but he wore it like it was an Armani original. Even the smudge of fluid on his chin was disturbingly attractive. The diagonal scar above his right eyebrow looked edgy, yet perfect against his brown skin. And how long were his eyelashes anyway? He blinked and Noelle just knew they touched his high cheek bones. Cheek bones that were direct and prominent, but not too severe. His chest was well-defined from what she could see. No jumpsuit or t-shirt underneath could succeed in playing it down.

Noelle snapped out of it. *Feels like I just drank a glass of Hypnotic.* Gaining her composure, she moved to the front of the car to inspect the job. Griggs was on point about this guy. He hadn't given Noelle much information about him, but she was satisfied with the great job he'd done replacing her windshield. She saw him gazing at her from the corner of her eyes.

"It's great. Thank you," she said, avoiding his stare.

"You're more than welcome." He lowered his head to look into her face and moved closer. Unconsciously, she took a step back. His hand stretched forward.

"Excuse my rudeness. I'm David. Just started here this week, but I've been working on cars since I was two," he laughed.

Noelle rubbed the back of her neck instead of taking his hand.

"So," he continued, ignoring the cold shoulder, "you're all hooked up to reach your morning classes."

"Who told you I was in school?"

78

BROKEN WITH STAINS

"Oh, Griggs mentioned you'd need your windshield as soon as possible 'cause you did your thing in college - Fordham University, I believe. Said your Neon is how you get there. Your sole transportation and all that. He's real serious about the education thing so - "

"Well it's good that you follow instructions." David's face transformed into a perplexed expression. Noelle knew she was being nastier than necessary. Catching the man you love in bed with another female could make a girl that way. Being bitter was easy. Taking out her frustration on a random man was even easier. She was still grateful for the flawless windshield though. She took her key from the small pocket on his chest and moved past him.

"Hope I didn't offend you," he stated with his arms open to his sides.

"Not at all. I just need to get home. I'm beat."

"I can understand that. You have a good evening."

"Griggs is aware of the payment arrangement, so I'll be around when he gets back." Noelle wasn't sure why she couldn't look him in the face. She wasn't sure either about why she was still standing outside the waiting car fiddling with her keys. David looked precisely like she felt, awkward, smoothing his low cut in a repetitive back and forth motion. *Okay*, Noelle thought as she played with her ponytail, *I guess we're dumb and dumber*. David dared to be the courageous one. "If there's anything else that comes up . . . give me a call . . . if Griggs isn't here. I'll, um . . . be able to assist with whatever you need. With your car I mean."

It had to be the fumes floating out from the garage that made her feel stifled. Noelle adjusted her short-sleeve shirt and scratched a non-existent itch on the tip of her nose.

Give you a call if I need anything? Give me a frigging break. Who are you? The second coming of Christ? Not only do I fix cars, I fix buses, airplanes, and messed up lives too. She was being mean again. Noelle took one foot and stepped on her other. A punishment for trippin'. He'd done nothing but replace her windshield and she was giving the poor guy an unreasonably hard time.

"I'm sure Griggs will be able to help me just fine if I happen to need something." She unlocked the door, plunked down in the driver's seat of her ride, and backed away as David stood there watching. He gave her a slight wave goodbye. It wouldn't have cost anything to wave or honk her horn back, but she wasn't in the mood. Noelle looked both ways before entering the street, mashed the gas pedal, oblivious to the fact that she couldn't feel the throbbing in her flats anymore.

14 sienna

"No. Uh-uh. She cursed you out for trying to help her?"

Sienna placed a slender hand on Marni's leg. "Yes. And not only that - she ran after him scared he'd never talk to her again. I was so . . . so . . ."

"Yeah," Eve said, blowing a stream of cigarette smoke at Sienna. "And her foolery is so much different from the way you run after Marcus when he dogs you out."

Sienna's eyes bulged. "Eve . . . Come. On. Marcus has *never* beat the day lights out of me. And I did not run after him whenever we were having problems. You know that."

"Granted, he might not have been whooping your behind physically, but he sure did a superb job screwing you up mentally and emotionally. You took that, didn't you?"

Sienna's hurt immediately registered on her face. Marni jumped to keep the peace. "Now you know we're talking about two different things, Eve."

Eve smirked, "Are we really though?" She picked up her television remote, flipping channels as she continued, "Women allow themselves to be abused by men in a bunch of different ways. Getting the crap beat out of you is just one."

Sienna leaned forward and sat on the edge of the plush mint-green sofa, "He didn't screw me up. I don't know where you get that from. We aren't together anymore anyway. If I was so screwed up, I wouldn't have been able to move on."

Eve put two fingers up in the shape of an L. "So you say. Ya'll play that little game all the time. Next week your face'll be all crumpled up from something he did to you again."

"Not at all," Sienna protested. "And I can't believe you'd say that. How can you sit there and imply that I was an abused woman?"

"Sea, all I'm saying is, your actions might not be so different from that silly girl in the bathroom."

"Oh. Is that how you really feel?"

Marni felt the rising tension and knew she had to tame it quickly. She dropped her book on the floor, whipped her dreads to the side, and stretched herself out on the loveseat before turning to Eve.

"The girl is only fifteen. Nowhere near ready for a relationship. It's two different situations." She pointed to Sienna. "Let her mother know about this. She could end up dead behind this little boy."

Sienna thought back to the scene in the bathroom. "At the rate she's going, she will."

Marni continued, "Every time I get another call where me and Miguel ends up putting another battered woman on a stretcher, it kills me inside. Sad to say, it's a common thing we see all the time when we get emergency calls. At least three times a month I'm putting a beat-up wife or girlfriend in the back of my ambulance. Remember my aunt that I told you got shot by one of her ex-boyfriends? She hasn't even fully recovered from that incident yet. Shot three times with a bullet still lodged in her hip."

"That's the worst case scenario," Sienna said, massaging the goose bumps on her arms. "I just wish she'd let me help her. She's so young and vulnerable."

Eve snuffed her cigarette out in the souvenir astray Sienna had given her when she'd last come back from Mexico with Marcus. "That little Tandi isn't the only one in this world with a touch of vulnerability."

She threw the remote in Sienna's lap, walked over to the coat closet, and put her shoes on. "I'm going to the corner store. Ya'll want anything?"

Marni and Sienna exchanged irritated looks and spoke in unison, "No."

"Cool."

BROKEN WITH STAINS

Sienna sat miffed as she watched Eve close the door behind her. The chick was wrong. If anything, Eve should've applauded her for finally deciding to give Marcus the boot for good.

Marni rolled her eyes and coiled her dreads with an elastic band. "Don't mind her, Sea. Obviously she has a bug stuck up her butt . . . again."

Maybe so. Yet, the accusation still troubled her. "I'm not as vulnerable as Tandi, am I?" Sienna asked.

Marni flipped onto her back and stared at the ceiling before giving her answer.

"Of course not . . . well, at least not in the same way."

"So you're saying in a similar way, I am."

"No. That's not what I'm saying. What I mean is, as females, we all get a little vulnerable at some point. Just depends on the circumstances."

Sienna processed the words. The pained expression on her best friend's face prompted Marni to clarify herself. "You and Marcus have had your ups and downs for a while. You could've parted ways a long time ago, but you have a love in your heart for him that is hard to let go of. It's natural. Women love hard."

"Truth is," Sienna chuckled, "the harder we love, the harder we fall."

"But if you fall, you get up, and keep going. It's not the end of the road. But a girl like Tandi needs a crutch to keep her moving."

"Shoot. If Tandi needs a crutch, then ask Eve, I'm sure she'll tell you I need one too."

"That's Eve. What can I say? You know Ms. Thang got issues of her own. Daniel took a chunk outta her when he was around. That's our girl, but sometimes you just have to block her out."

"I wish it were that easy. Her mouth is a bull horn, echoing in my head long after she's gone. I don't know —

maybe I'm being too sensitive."

"Don't dwell on Eve or else the girl will drive you crazy."

"You're right. I've told him it's over. I've made up my mind. No more stress. I'm done."

Sienna looked at Marni whose head was turned to the television.

"You don't believe me, do you?" she asked, monitoring her friend's unfazed stare.

"Girl, why would you - "

"You think I'm full of crap, just like Eve."

"Stop it. You're my best friend. Of course I have faith that you'll always do the right thing when you're ready to. You're ready to leave Marcus and I believe you're going to follow through." Sienna paused to see if Marni's reassurance was real. When she felt comfortable that it was, she ran her fingers through her hair, leaned back in the over-sized sofa, and crossed her legs.

Switching the channel to BET, an LL Cool J throwback video greeted her as she sighed. "Good. I'm going to need all the support I can get to purge myself of this man."

Marni looked at Sienna. "Cheer up girl, I got ya back. Now let's figure out how I can find a man as fine as LL."

15 joy

"**G**ood choice, good choice, good choice." Joy praised Luce as they sat in the Caribbean restaurant, Negril. She bit her bottom lip and teased him with a mischievous smile. "I see you gettin' them brownie points up. Two for you."

Luce used his thumb to brush a stray hair away from her eye. "I'm a grown man sweetheart - I don't strive for points."

"So you strive for what?"

"Nothing."

She reflected on their romp last night. It was well worth the wait on both their parts. She had practically attacked him after coming home from the 40/40 Club, but his fervor matched hers without skipping a beat. Joy had two hundred dollars in her hands at the end of the night. The dollars were going down, not up as she expected. Joy knew she was doing everything right. The trusty three step plan had never let her down before. But her gut told her that somehow, the man sitting across from her was digging for something more.

"All men do what they do for some goal they want to achieve," she told him.

Of course she wasn't a man, but her own mission was to pay the thousand dollar rent that was due in a couple weeks. She'd checked her account this morning – only two hundred pathetic dollars left.

He smiled, locking eyes with the light brown ones that doubted him. "I'm not all men. I'm an individual at all times."

She sipped her apple martini. "And I'm real at all times. You ain't wining and dining me and handing over cash for your health."

"And it's wrong for a man to want to take a woman out for a good meal? Or even for a nice stroll in the park? Maybe to a great Broadway show?"

"Hold your horses, buddy," Joy said putting up a hand, " 'cause if you're thinking about taking me to a play, telling you right now – it's not gonna happen. I'd fall asleep faster than you could blink your eyes."

Luce laughed while Joy stared back at him as serious as death.

"Don't knock Broadway. There's Chicago, The Color Purple, Rent - you don't know what you're missing," he said.

"I doubt it's much. I've seen a lot, done a lot. But, what else do you think I'm missing since you know me so well?"

Silence settled across the table. He diverted his attention to the curry goat and rice and peas on his plate. Scooped a substantial portion into his mouth and chewed, savoring each bite. Joy wouldn't let him get away that easily.

"Cat got your tongue? What else am I missing from my life?"

Luce placed his fork to the side of his plate and looked directly into her cat-like eyes. "If I told you, you'd be mad at me."

Joy's interest peaked. She shook her hair and fluffed the long, subtle waves around her shoulders.

"Try me."

She watched him think for a minute as he looked down at his hands, a smile curving the corners of his mouth. Pushing the unfinished plate to the left, Luce crossed his arms and leaned forward on his elbows at the table. His eyes burned into Joy's as he gave into the challenge.

"You could benefit from love in your life. I see a need to be loved the proper way because you've never experienced a real, unconditional, unadulterated love. And I'm not necessarily talking about romantic love. I'm talking about a love that will heal all of your wounds and melt that façade you're so intent on maintaining. Because that is what it is, isn't it? I mean, Joy O'Brien isn't always the ice queen, the high class slash round-the-way bitch, she likes to put on, is she?"

He intertwined his long fingers and grinned.

"I bet you watch romantic comedies, fantasize about being a real princess, and sleep with your arms around a cute, fluffy teddy bear at night. A real hug could help you out a lot. Think about it. Someone to squeeze you tight and let you know it's okay to be soft and pink and leave it that way?

A dose of church and a good King James Bible would do you some good too. Humph, Good Lord. The way you worked me over last night was nothing short of ungodly. But who am I to talk?"

He stroked the ends of her hair with his fingers. "Really though . . . if I could snap my fingers and make all your pain go away, I would. But I can only do so much. You need to get that healing balm and lather yourself up in it. That's what you're missing."

First she felt a twinge of shock, then followed a pang of embarrassment, and finally, a flush of anger. She wanted to prove Luce wrong, so she kept the last feeling in check.

"I don't mean to - "

"It's all good," she snapped as she grabbed her drink and drained it. "That's your little opinion anyway."

Joy motioned to the waiter for a refresher. The lump lodged in her throat needed to be washed down. No one had ever read her like that before. She was mad that he took it upon himself to be the first. How dare he rattle on about things that weren't true. What Joy really wanted to do was spit in his face and walk away, but she wouldn't be tempted to expose how she truly felt. She allowed no one to see her sweat and since he expected her to be upset, the topic was switched instead.

"Opinions aside, I'm missing some facts here. I've let you take me out all over this damn city and I don't even know what you do for a living, Mr. Know-It-All. See, you know it all but I don't."

Luce laughed, sensing her bruised ego. "I'm a business

man."

"That tells me nothing."
"I own multiple establishments around the U.S."
"Like where?"
"New York, Miami, Atlanta, D.C., L.A., Chi-town, Vegas."

Seven cities, she thought doing a mental calculation. *That must mean you have cash coming in hand over fist. Now that's what I'm talking about. Money – not you running your stupid mouth.*

"And what kind of establishments are these?" Joy asked.

"I own clubs. People come. Have a good time. Go home happy. I make a good living from that."

"You own the club I met you in too?"

"No sweets. I don't own that one. My clubs are . . . exclusive."

Joy stirred her drink and wondered what that meant.

"Sounds like top secret information, but I'ma be nosey and ask anyway: How exclusive are they?"

"Extremely exclusive. For those who can afford to pay to play," he answered.

Joy stopped stirring. What kind of clubs were these? Thumping sound systems and velvet ropes were what she originally had in mind. But he wouldn't even give her the name, so her assumption had to be out of the question.

She dug further, curiosity killing her softly, "Am I that much of a stranger that I can't get a better answer than that?"

"Wouldn't say you're a stranger. Yet, the success of my clubs depends on keeping them low key. But I can absolutely guarantee your sexy self that you'll learn all about it soon enough. That look of curiosity looks real good on you though - you're beautiful. Don't worry. I'll tell you everything in due time. Too gorgeous for me to keep much from you."

His eyes penetrated hers. She met his gaze head on. Almost. There was a smoldering sensation that suddenly ignited her cheeks. For a moment it made Joy shift her eyes to the couple a table over.

"Go ahead, charm your way out of answering my questions," she said, turning her focus back to Luce.

"No, for real. Your sex appeal is amazing to me. I know women who could learn a thing or two from you. They have the tools, but not the know-how. You have the whole package when it comes to serving up sexuality. I look at you and lust, desire, craving comes to mind. Sometimes I wonder how it would all translate when it came down to something bigger than chump change."

Translate? Something bigger? Chump change? Joy's head spun as she tried to figure out what he was getting at. She opened her mouth to ask him, but suddenly she realized she was at risk of sounding incredibly naïve. She pulled her words back and changed them to, "Then consider yourself blessed to be in my company."

Luce centered his plate back in front of him, displayed unblemished teeth in a knowing smile, and answered, "Yes, you are the fifty million dollar prize."

She had no idea what he was talking about, just had the feeling there was a message she was missing. Watching him voraciously suck the marrow out of the goat's bone, Joy raised her glass and signaled the waiter for her third drink.

* * *

"What you doing home so early?" Poochie asked as she flipped through a Vibe magazine.

Joy put her suede clutch on the table by the front door and shook her head at her friend's white-crusted feet propped up on the coffee table.

"Your joints need lotion. Get'em off my glass."

Poochie raised her feet at Joy and squeezed them tight until they produced a popping sound. "Ahhhh – that felt so good," she said. "The ash gives it that extra snap, crackle, pop."

"You disgust me," Joy laughed as her top lip curved upward.

"I do my best. But anyway, I thought you'd be out longer. The way you got all decked out, I figured it would be a to-the-break-of-dawn type of thing."

"We called it a night. Luce had a business trip to North Carolina he had to fly out to."

"Is that right? I guess Luce got you on lock now."

"Hold up, rewind." Joy looked away to fiddle with her CDs on the entertainment center. "Nobody said nothing about me being on lock."

"Ho, who you think you fooling? You been out basically every day since you two met. Sounds like he got you in a headlock to me," Poochie said, giving her friend's back quizzing eyes.

Joy saw the look through the glass reflection of the entertainment center's door. She pretended not to notice and smoothed the hump of hair at the front of her head. She raked her fingers through the rest of the long waves that hung around her exposed shoulders and answered, "Bite me. Ain't no headlocks over here. We cool and that's it."

"Just cool, huh? I know you kicked Yaz to the curb, but what happened to Raheem, Cash, Bobby . . . um . . . Amir . . . John-John?"

Joy raised an index finger, "I know I told you I got tired of them a long time ago. Can't deal with the 'where were yous' and 'why you got that ons'. I don't need no dude getting that familiar with me. Just give me the loot. If we can't keep the transactions simple, I'll find another jumpoff who will."

"Well, you usually have a few of them piled up. So how come Luce is the only one I've been hearing about?"

" 'Cause there's nobody else worth talking about. That's why. Luce is big business for me. A real business man. Not a hustler. Not a married piece of shit with a wife and kids to support, still trying to squeeze out his last dime to keep a smile on my face. Getting tired of that anyway. I need real money. Luce money. Plus, he's cool peoples. And it doesn't hurt that he looks good and lays it down when it's time to lay it down too. That works for me."

Poochie threw the magazine to the side. "Business man? What he do? Pimp hoes?" she hollered, slapping her leg like it was the funniest thing in the world.

She stopped when Joy didn't join in. "What? You mad 'cause I'm messing with you?"

"Please."

"Then what's the mean-mugging about?"

She shrugged her shoulders. "He never exactly said what type of business he owns."

Poochie's mind went into overdrive. "You been seeing him all this time and you don't even know what he does? He could sell body parts. Or smuggle in illegal immigrants. Oooh, maybe he's a hit man. I was watching this show the other - "

"No, Poochie. Fall back. He owns clubs, but I'm not sure the name or what kind. Like if it's a dance club, lounge, what kind of crowd comes by. None of that."

"Luce didn't tell you?"

"He was acting real secretive about it."

"I wonder why. Hmph. That's crazy. Maybe it's a strip club."

"A strip club? He don't seem like the type. Probably visit one, but own them . . . nah."

Poochie laughed, "You better hope it's not. I never told you, but . . . my moms used to get down on a pole. Even brought me to the club with her sometimes. God, I hated it there. My skin still crawls every time I think about it. I would sneak out when she was on stage and peek through the side of the curtain. Them old, greasy, stank men was nasty."

"I can't picture your mother spinning on a pole."

"When she had Taji, she quit. I was mad happy when I

never had to go back there anymore. If Luce owns strip clubs, I bet you'd ask him if you could get up on stage to dance."

"Well he did tell me I had the whole package. Sex appeal, all that. Then he said something about it translating into something bigger than chump change."

"Chump change? What? And what you say to that?"

"Girl, I didn't say a thing. I didn't know what the hell he was talking about. But that's not a bad idea you got there. Putting all this luciousness up on a stage and dropping it like it's hot? I do get up on tables at the club. Wouldn't be much different." Joy dropped one time, giving Poochie a good laugh. "Girl, let me tell you - it don't get no better than this."

"Look at you," Poochie said wiping tears of laughter from her eyes. "Looking like the The Predator with that hump on your head."

"Yes, honey. Look at what God gave me. You can't be mad at me for that, boo."

"Goodnight," Poochie said, getting up to gather her belongings.

"Take it easy when you dream about my beauty tonight. I don't want you having seizures or nothing like that." Poochie laughed her way out the door.

Joy flipped on her CD player once her friend left. She listened to the melodic sounds of Mary J. inviting someone to share her world. Joy thought about the part of Luce's world he'd been reluctant to share. There was something about him. His words, his touch, his laid-back demeanor. Their conversation at Negril's wouldn't leave her alone. His eyes had dared her to go where she had never gone before. Somewhere where things were bigger than chump change. Her brain still couldn't grasp what that meant.

16 paul

"Yeah, she's real cool," Paul remembered his buddy Brock saying through a hefty cloud of weed smoke.

The beauty, sporting a small afro, wasn't even aware of the power she held when her lean, graceful body entered the apartment. Paul thought of a million other things she was too. Gorgeous. Classy. Angelic. Divine, to name a few.

Paul's spirit lifted. What a natural beauty she was. No lipstick. No eyeshadow. No foundation. Just the chill of winter flushed across her nose and cheeks. He wanted to reach out and touch her coffee-colored skin. Thought about putting his lips against the facial features that reminded him of Cleopatra Jones. Even her pinkie finger cocked in the air looked elegant when she stripped herself of the brocade jacket she wore. If only he didn't have to wait much longer to see what was hidden underneath the teal wrap dress and tan knee-length boots. But it was only a matter of time.

The first handshake accompanied by her sweet smile was the defining moment in Brock's furnitureless living room. Paul wanted her. Promised himself she'd give in to his request to get comfortable. His arms would become the place she would never want to leave.

That music-filled December of 1981, was just the beginning of his mission to embrace Ms. Annette Burgess. Brock's house party in Brooklyn was where Paul sat sipping a bottle of Guiness, watching her lips move as she explained who she was. Paul listened to the nineteen year-old college student whose interest was in finance. She proudly declared herself a native of the island he'd never visited and didn't know much about.

"St. Andrew, Jamaica is where I'm from. I need to go

back soon – it's been three years since I left. I'm sooo homesick," she told him.

Her soothing accent was a delicacy to his ears as she told him she'd love to take new pictures to send back home. She had looked over to the large black and white photo of Brock in the center wall of the living room. A picture Paul had taken two months earlier of Brock plucking away at his guitar, a skinny, rolled-up spliff tucked neatly behind his left ear. Paul believed it to be his best work to date. Definitely was, if Annette wanted him to take her photograph based on that alone. When her eyes turned back to his face, Paul couldn't think of anything to say.

"Well, tell me some more things about you," she said.

His answer, "Not much to tell. All I do is take pictures. I don't have a wife or kids."

* * *

Annette was all business. Two days after they'd met at the house party, she wasted no time setting up a studio session. Over the phone, she gave Paul a checklist. Day. Time. Number of outfit changes. Music to be played. Also warned that his studio better be warm. Little did she know, it was where he lived, so the radiator worked great or very little depending on if he paid his rent on time. This month, as expected, it frequently chipped out. Luckily, it was in full swing when he photographed Annette in awe. Her uncanny ability to transform herself was out of this world. Gone was the soft Jamaican princess and out came her seductive alter-ego. For a second, he thought he felt his hands trembling as he determined not to miss one move. Soon after, he dropped his camera on the concrete floor. Paul never mishandled his prized possession. The leather-trimmed tool was his life, his livelihood, and so far this month, he hadn't raked in enough cash to stock his refrigerator for the next two weeks or pay next month's rent. This wasn't like him. He never lost his cool. So why were his palms sweating and his heart beating like he'd just finished a twenty mile marathon?

"Do I make you nervous?" she chuckled.

Paul looked up from inspecting the camera. "What do you think?"

"I think I make you a little nervous," Annette said, approaching him.

"Just a little. I almost broke my baby because of you."

The light shined in her eyes as she smiled at him, then touched his hand as she peered down at the camera. "Thank God you didn't. I feel bad. Is your 'baby' okay?"

"She'll be all right."

"She? What's her name?"

He paused. "I haven't come up with one yet. Maybe you could help me name her."

"Hmmm," she pondered with her finger to her chin. "How about Sienna? I've always loved that name."

"A camera named Sienna?" he asked with his eyebrows raised.

"Wait a minute – you didn't say it was a camera. You said it was your baby. A she. I think that's a nice name for a baby girl."

He looked into the innocent eyes embedded in the heart-shaped face. The deep brown pools were beckoning him to dive in. Paul took the invitation and jumped right to it.

* * *

It was seven months to the day of that first photo shoot. On the uncomfortable twin-sized bed they relaxed naked and staid, tangled in each other's arms. She lived with her uncle who was gone for the week. It was the first time Paul had ever been inside the dreary two-bedroom apartment. Her room could double as a shoebox. It was sweltering even as he stared up at the rotating ceiling fan. There wasn't any humidity in the air, though it was the height of New York's summer. He undoubtedly attributed the heat covering his person to the familiar tingling underneath his skin.

Annette's slim piano fingers repeatedly stroked his mustache. It was her favorite habit since she and Paul had become inseparable. She stroked away and hummed along to the Stylistics 'Betcha By Golly, Wow', the noise from behind her closed lips, rising and falling in perfect rhythm. Paul felt her heart thumping as she lay draped across his chest.

She hummed. He counted her heart beats.

She stroked. He noticed their heart rhythms were out of sync.

The song ended. He closed his eyes.

She cleared her throat. His tingling became stronger.

"Paul . . . I'm pregnant."

His eyes flew open immediately. Never had he heard those words before.

"I'm three months pregnant."

Paul said nothing.

"Aren't you going to say something?"

He closed his eyes again as she sat up to look into his face. Enraged by his silence, she viciously slapped his bare chest.

"Annette," he said firmly, holding her hand before she could give him another one.

She leaned back and looked at him. "That's what you have to say? Nothing?"

His conscience got the best of him. "Just a little shocked that's all."

Annette examined him closely. "And?"

"And . . . I'm not ready for kids."

"Damn it, Paul, I'm twenty years-old - neither am I."

"I know."

"You know? My uncle's gonna kill me when I tell him.

BROKEN WITH STAINS

My mother sent me up here to go to school and I end up pregnant. And now you talking about you're not ready for kids? Since when?"

Annette shook in her place on the bed. She shrunk into herself, gripping her hair with her fingers like she wanted to crawl into a hole and die. Paul was numb. Even if he wanted to put his arms around her, his fear wouldn't let him move. All he could see was fire and flowers and caskets. All he could hear was organs and chatter and crying. Paul came to when he felt her dragging the sheets from his body.

She shook her head in disbelief while she moved to the bottom edge of the bed. Annette drew her knees to her chest and wrapped her arms around them. She was too nauseous to look at him. Sure of herself that she hadn't heard right.

"Paul I'm three months pregnant and there's nothing we can do about that now. Face that fact."

"I'm trying to." He knew that wasn't the case because he'd already plotted his next step.

Paul picked up his jeans from the floor and took out a joint. He lit it with sweaty fingers, settled himself against a deflated pillow, and let it burn slow. Mutely, he watched as Annette's shoulders began to shudder. The sobs escaping her throat were tugging at his heart, but it was her news that kept him in place. Nothing could move him on that subject. He almost choked when the thought hit. Why didn't it dawn on him before? He should've left her before it reached this point. Hurting her had never been his intention.

The smoke swirled around him as he finalized the decision in his mind. She could keep her back to him right now if she wanted to. He'd met her as a striking vision of endless possibilities. Tonight he'd leave her and never look back.

17 noelle

The sun shooting through the bedroom window rudely awoke Noelle from her usual uncomfortable sleep. Usual because for the past few weeks, it had become a task for her not to wake up several times during the night. She'd struggled because sleep hadn't been her friend since the afternoon she'd walked in on Chris. Lack of sleep held no mercy for her schedule. It was another reason she felt it would be okay to hunt Chris down and kill him. Bump darts – she'd use something bigger and sharper this time.

In order for her to focus in class, she needed her eight hours of peaceful sleep. The most she'd gotten for the past three weeks: four hours per night. Last night had to be the worst. She figured it was six in the morning when she finally drifted to sleep. The last numbers she recalled seeing on the neon-lit alarm clock were five forty-seven.

Luckily it was Saturday. Her eyes were pushed open by the sun's intruding light at eight thirty a.m. Today would have been her and Chris' two-year anniversary.

* * *

Waffles and peaches with pecan syrup. Noelle was amazed that the breakfast on her plate was almost completely gone. She couldn't remember the last time a clean plate had occurred. The homemade waffles were left by her mother with a note: *Don't make me come home and see these in the garbage like them collards greens and ham last night.*

How Sharon had managed to whip up waffles from scratch at six in the morning before heading off to Soul Divine Restaurant to cook for ten hours, was beyond Noelle's comprehension. As she swallowed the last bite, Noelle was

BROKEN WITH STAINS

belly-full with appreciation that her mom had found the time and energy. But hearing the sound of the doorbell, she didn't see how she'd ever wobble up out of her seat to answer it.

"What's wrong with you?" Noelle turned her back to Candace and patted her stomach on her way to the livingroom. "I'm full. Can't you see me busting at the seams?"

"Oh. So Chris has you overeating too?" Candace asked as she fell back into the nearest seat.

Noelle collapsed on the brown sofa with her hands behind her head. She didn't want to hear her best friend's mouth right now. "Shut your hole," she spat.

Candace ignored the smart comment. "Whatever. Look at you. When's the last time you ran a comb through that bush on top of your head? Looking like pure crazy. And I know that's not crust I see in the corner of your eyes. Where's my belt? I need to whoop your behind 'cause you slipping something awful."

Noelle threw a striped pillow at her best friend's head. "Didn't I tell you to shut that hole?"

Candace stood, grabbed Noelle's arm, and proceeded to pull her up from the sofa. "Come on, we're going someplace fun." The left foot of Noelle's orange socks slipped off as she struggled against Candace's strength. Candace overpowered.

"Keep it up. You may be tall, but I'm an inch taller and about thirty pounds heavier. Do yourself a solid and cooperate." She sucked her teeth as she continued to resist.

"Someplace fun where, Candace? It's eleven o'clock in the flippin' morning."

Now she had Noelle by the seat of her gray sweatpants.

"Someplace away from The Bronx. Far away from Depression Headquarters," she teased. "Going to the mall and then to the movies and then we gonna eat some finger-licking-good soul food at Soul Divine's."

"Mall for what? I don't have any money."

"Then I'll buy you something pretty. You got a ten

dollar limit, so fix yourself up so we can get out this house."

Noelle's sweatshirt was half off now. Candace tugged and pulled, gladly the reason behind that fashion statement.

"Nah son, you can do all that by yourself or go with CJ. I don't feel like going anywhere. Not today."

"Noelle, we haven't been anywhere lately. You need to shake this funk off. The pity-party is over. Chris is not the best thing since sliced bread. How're you going to meet any body else if you sit in the house pouting all the time? Get your behind up and get dressed."

Candace was finally out of breath as she crumpled to the floor.

"Can't believe I have to get a workout just to get you up out this house."

"Nobody told you to come in here and start acting all buckwild and stuff."

"Well, being your best friend makes me that way."

Noelle threw another pillow at Candace's head. It fell short and hit her in the nose.

"I'm not Chris, big-head," she said rubbing the wounded spot. "Don't go throwing foreign objects at me."

They fell into a fit of laughter.

"If I had aimed a bit to the left, I could've gotten a dart between his eyes."

"You're an evil broad." Their cackling enveloped the entire room.

Candace rose to her feet and danced in place. "Now throw on something cute so we can have our girls' day out."

* * *

Noelle felt refreshed. Her bestie had come at the right time. Every woman needed an angel like her - someone who'd reach out and grab a strong hold when they saw their friend slipping. Many years strong, Candace never let her down. Over the past few weeks, her presence was needed more than ever before. She'd been a willing ear to listen and a support system of comfort whenever Noelle had gotten the urge to call. Twelve o'clock, one o'clock, two o'clock in the morning – Candace always picked up the phone. Always called throughout the day to make sure Noelle was feeling okay. It didn't matter that she was studying to be a nurse, had two jobs, a son, and a boyfriend she had to make time for. Candace did her best to never let Noelle feel alone for one minute of the day. Her girl always had something funny on tap to cheer her up and she'd come through once again.

Noelle's breath was short from laughter the entire eventful day. Watching Candace slip and bust her butt in the roller skating rink had set off a day of hysterical giggling. She was finally back home after their last stop, a hearty meal at Soul Divine's. Her mother had stuck her head out from the kitchen in back to say hi for a quick minute. She then disappeared again and sent out piled plates for her and Candace with extra helpings of fried chicken, mashed potatoes, and corn muffins.

She just needed to lay her head on a pillow. Candace had invited her to go play pool with her and CJ later that evening, but she didn't feel like watching them suck face all night. After a shower and a cup of cinnamon spice tea, Noelle fell back into her usual glum mood. A state of being she'd become accustomed to.

It was a Saturday night. She was home alone with nowhere to go. Noelle laid on her bed and played with the decorative netting dangling from the hook on the ceiling. Loneliness was creeping and crawling all over her skin. Noelle looked over at her cell phone. It started to reach its peak, a headache was there to greet her.

Call him. Maybe he didn't apologize, but like Hope said – he already knows that he's wrong. The words reverberated in her heart. The phone was right there, all she had to do was pick it up and maybe they could come to a resolution.

Noelle stretched for the phone right before her mind interceded. *No. You'd be crazy if you did that. He was screwing that chick and God knows how many others. Don't give him another chance to drop kick your heart. He can't be trusted.* Her hands gripped the tiny black phone until her palms were covered with sweat. She needed a glass of water. And a couple aspirin to go with it. She dropped the phone on the bed and sat up. She had to get as far away from it as possible.

Noelle considered heading to the theater to see another movie by herself. The mall was another option that ran across her mind. She and Candace never did make it there today. Thought about splurging with the five hundred dollar check she'd received a couple days ago from building a client's website. Then again, she couldn't do that to her student loan fund. Shopping was only a temporary cure anyway. Noelle couldn't make up her mind. But it didn't matter what she was going to do or where she was about to go, she just knew she had to escape to a place where there were people and distractions.

She made up her mind to do just that. And then her cell phone rang. Noelle checked the lit display. The name she'd erased, but the number she still remembered.

Chris was calling.

The phone was pressed to her ear before she could think twice about it. "Hello?" She swallowed hard as she listened for the familiar voice. "Noelle . . . what's good? Hope you not still mad at me."

18 sienna

So she gave in. It was a secret though. Sienna didn't let Marni or her mother know she'd given into the temptation that was Marcus. She especially didn't dare let Eve find out. That would be death in the form of an eye-rolling lecture.

Standing by the bar, she adjusted the fallen spaghetti strap of her satin and lace brown dress. The saucy new number conformed to Sienna's shape exquisitely. Her light makeup sat flawless against her radiant brown skin. She touched the smooth face that had recently been treated to a facial, a gift that came along with a seaweed body wrap and Swedish massage all paid for by Marcus. She glimpsed down at the fresh, pedicured toes looking awesome in her cute high-heeled sandals. Sienna knew her man was pleased - his male co-workers and seemingly every other male at the after-work party had showered her with nods of approval and appreciative glances ever since she'd stepped through the door. Marcus proudly introduced and re-introduced her, pride glistening in his eyes for the beauty of the woman he possessed.

A glass of Hennessy in hand, Sienna surveyed the crowd. She sat alone, trying to avoid the winks and raised glasses in her direction since Marcus had taken a trip to the men's room. Women seemed to be checking for her too. Sienna couldn't help but notice the woman who stood at the other end of the bar watching every move she made. It was obvious that the curly mix of brown and blonde framing her face was a weave. She didn't understand why the female clad in a black tank and leather mini skirt was staring at her so hard. She rebuffed every guy that approached, but gave Sienna her full attention.

She'd never had the urge or the need to swing that way, so Sienna ignored the obtrusive eyes and took in the scene around her. Overall, the atmosphere was cool. She watched a few familiar faces on the dance floor moving to the funky R&B sounds of Ne-Yo. She giggled as she focused on Marcus' co-workers Pebo, Vance, and Pete, act a fool with the ladies they entertained. They definitely knew how to have a good time – free and out of control outside of their daily office environment.

Marcus was different, but she didn't complain. He'd never let loose enough to throw his tie to the side and go for a spin in the middle of a club. He was more the type to grab a glass of rum, puff on a cigar, crack a joke or two, and watch the party unfold. Sure he'd circulate the crowd at least once during the night, but that was to reacquaint himself with those he hadn't seen for a while or to do a little networking. Sienna had grown used to the man she loved and his pattern. It was all the better – her trained eyes could keep tabs to make sure he was behaving.

Sienna looked back over her shoulder and watched Marcus make his way to her post by the bar. Deep down she kicked herself for allowing him to work his way back into her life a week ago. But how could she not? There still wasn't solid proof to verify what Nonda had told her. All she had to go on were a few phone calls and the skanky woman's word.

No way was she giving her man over to an ex-girlfriend who was an obsessed stalker. Sienna took in his sharp, charcoal Kenneth Cole suit and knew she'd made the right decision. He was the supreme combination of style and masculinity, coordinating his coral shirt and multi-colored tie like only a true fashion maven could. The lounge was dark, but the soft lights scattered around the room highlighted his Kenneth Cole shoes. Once he reached her and playfully tapped her nose with his finger, her heart melted when she noticed he had on the gold and diamond cufflinks she'd bought him for his birthday three months ago. "Sunshine, you okay?" Marcus asked. She smiled up at him, tilted up from her stool, and gently kissed his lips.

"I'll take that as a yes," he said. "Let's refill that glass for you."

He ordered her another filler of Hennessey as he ran his fingers through the back of her short hair. "You didn't have to cut your hair," he griped. Sienna sighed and put the drink to her mouth. It had to be the millionth time she'd heard him sing the same song.

"Marcus, I don't have hair down to my behind. Get over it."

He raised an eyebrow at her. "Really? I can't wait 'til we get home. I want to get over it, under it, around it, and in between." She poked him in the side and placed her glass on the bar.

"You are so nasty. Come here let me pinch that nasty butt." She grabbed his tie, pulling him close for another kiss, and squeezed his derriere on the low. They laughed together and for a moment Sienna forgot about all the strife that had existed between them. For the past three weeks they'd been separated, she'd missed his troublesome drawers on a regular basis. As she looked into his eyes and traced his thick eyebrows with her middle finger, she felt relieved to have him near her once again.

They talked and kissed and continued to joke with each other by the bar. Everything was great until Sienna noticed Marcus' eyes darting in one direction over her shoulders. Her words were falling on deaf ears - something more important was stealing his attention. Sienna let her voice fade and slowly turned around to see what the deal was. She zoomed in on the culprit: a woman with double D's dressed in white and glowing like a night light. Her strapless mini dress strained against each and every one of her curves. The busty eye candy slowly swayed her hips from left to right to the flow of the booming beat. She rocked while lifting the long, wavy hair with one hand and cradled a red alcoholic beverage with the other. Sienna recoiled at the sight of gloss on her lips that made them so wet, it looked like she'd just spent the day finishing off buckets of

KFC.

Facing Marcus again, she swept a hand down the back of her bare neck.

"I see Snow White over there has you in a trance."

Marcus refocused his attention back to Sienna's face, blinked a few times, and glanced at the woman again.

"Oh, Fallon? Nah, it's not even like that, sunshine. She's the new receptionist at the architectural firm. Been there two weeks now. She moved up here from Tennessee about a month ago. I . . . we invited her. You know - Me. Vance. Pete. Pebo. Just checking to see if she's comfortable over there by herself."

Sienna spun around to take another look.

"I see one . . . two . . . three . . . four . . . five guys hovering around her like vultures." She faced him. "She looks alright to me."

Marcus smiled and kissed her neck. Sienna took that as his way of calming her down. She decided against turning it into a big deal. Men were visual and it made no sense to nail him to a cross for taking a peek at the tits she was serving up on a platter. There were more pressing things to tend to anyway. Things like getting to a rest room. Her bladder was screaming from the drinks in her system. She let him nibble her earlobe for a second longer than she should have and then excused herself for some relief.

* * *

It felt like she was floating on air. After taking a tinkle and touching up her makeup, Sienna walked back out onto the floor, heading over to reclaim her spot. Unfortunately, the seat was being occupied by a wide man with cornrows. Marcus was nowhere in sight though he was supposed to be guarding it with his life. Her shoes didn't understand the concept of standing up for long periods of time.

BROKEN WITH STAINS

She looked around the dimmed lounge, tip-toeing to see if she could spot him at the edges or in a corner somewhere. He didn't dance, so the gyrating bodies weren't her main priority. He couldn't be in the men's room because he'd been there right before she took her turn.

After five minutes of searching, she began to grow impatient. Just as she made up her mind to stay put in a corner, she spotted him where she least expected. It was a fact that her contacts dried out sometimes, so she blinked twice to make sure it wasn't her man in the middle of the dance floor, grinding his front all up on Snow White's junky trunk.

Nooo . . . couldn't be. She jiggled her eyelids with her fingers, forgetting she'd reapplied her gold eye shadow not too long ago. Sienna took a couple steps closer and watched the woman turn around and whisper something in Marcus' ear. He grinned like she'd just explained the key to life, then held her hands as she wound her hips. Sienna boiled like a pot of acid set to bubble over. She watched Fallon take her time, rolling and slithering before him while Marcus refused to miss a beat. His eyes inspected every nook and cranny of his dance partner's body as every now and again he whispered in her ear. They smiled at each other so much, Sienna wondered if they'd still be as happy if she took a hammer to their teeth.

The thought made her tremble, but she didn't believe in creating scenes in public either. A lady always held her peace until the time was appropriate. For now, she headed straight for the front door.

Stepping into the night's warm air she inhaled deeply and let out the pent-up breath in one powerful stream. Leaning against a car not too far away was the curly-haired woman who'd been scoping her out by the bar. Sienna turned her eyes in the other direction and disregarded the impolite staring. It wasn't long before Tandi's face flashed across her mind. The next face was Eve's, whose words seemed to echo in the space around her.

TAMARA BURKE

"Women allow themselves to be abused my men in various ways. Getting the crap beat out of you is just one . . . Ya'll play that little game all the time. Next week your face will be all crumpled up from something he did to you again . . . Sea, all I'm saying is, your actions might not be so different from that silly girl in the bathroom."

Eve. Sienna chuckled at the thought of her best friend. Maybe there was a golden nugget in the things she'd said, despite the callousness. The girl was like captain Save-a-Ho since surviving her ex-boyfriend Daniel. Now it seemed at every turn, she was wearing a red cape and S on her chest to rescue Sienna from Marcus. As much as she wanted to whip out her cell phone, there was no way Sienna could call and vent to her about what Marcus was up to now. She fanned her eyes, drying the tears before they fell. She looked out at the passing cars and thought about calling a cab to take her home. *And leave him here with that groupie?* Things might've taken a turn for the worse since she'd escaped outside to sulk.

Sienna marched back into the lounge with the look of death on her face. Scoping out the dance floor, her head flew back and forth in search of the two offenders. She needed to get a better look, so she walked around to the side of the bar and squirmed herself in between the crowded bodies. Propelled forward by anger, Sienna was halfway there before a strong hand grabbed her by the arm. She whipped around, ready to pounce on the idiot who failed to see she wasn't in the mood. Marcus' face greeted her instead.

He pulled her to him and his eyes widened at the intense look on her face.

"You okay?"

She yanked her arm away from him. "Let's go," she spat between clenched teeth.

* * *

BROKEN WITH STAINS

Sienna envisioned herself jumping on his back, punching the hell out of the back of his head. "I can't believe you see nothing wrong at all. So typical of you, Marcus. Why should I have expected anything different?"

"I should be asking you that question. When will you ever learn to stop getting all excitable over little shit?" he shouted as he unbuttoned his shirt.

The tightening muscles in her shoulders were provoking her to say another word. She didn't want them to win, so she clamped her mouth shut and stomped out to the kitchen.

She filled a red kettle with water and searched for tea bags to make a cup of tea. There were none in the small round tin. She took a can of Swiss Miss from a cabinet. It had barely a drop of cocoa left inside. Desperately, her eyes scanned the top of the refrigerator for a jar of coffee. Not one ounce of caffeine in sight. That was it. She picked up the kettle and slammed it back down as hard as she could. *If you're going to get on my nerves, the least you could do is have something for me to calm them down with.*

"Are you stupid or just retarded?"

Sienna twisted around to see Marcus and his six-pack staring at her. A perplexed look screwed his handsome face. "I'm talking to you. Don't just stand there looking at me like *I'm* the one who's crazy."

With folded arms across her chest, she walked away from him, lips sealed shut. He followed her back into his bedroom. Sienna grabbed her shoes, sat on his bed, and commenced to putting them on. Marcus' disgusted laugh filled the silent space.

"You know what, Sea? When I met you, I thought I'd found a real woman. Turns out I was wrong, because for the longest time you've been proving you're a little girl. You throw these stupid bitch fits and then walk away until you cool down. Do you need to see a psychiatrist or something? Because

I know a guy -"

"Screw you," she exploded.

"Babe, you already did that."

Her face showed the shock that gripped her insides. Sienna couldn't believe he had flipped and began speaking to her this way. To make things worse, she was so caught off guard by his statement, she couldn't find a good enough comeback to bring him to a halt.

Marcus rubbed his small goatee and continued, "Why do you do this to me Sienna? We can't even go out without you turning it into something ridiculous."

She fought her tongue with all she had within her. It was simply time to go. Slinging her overnight bag and purse over her shoulder, she stepped past Marcus and into the living-room. Sienna glanced over the spotless room with its modern black furniture to make sure she wasn't leaving anything she might have to come back for. Marcus remained on her heels.

"Would it have been better if I banged Fallon right on the dance floor? At least then you could really have the proof you needed to confirm your suspicions. Then you could free up your brain to focus on something intelligent for a change."

She froze just as her hand grasped the doorknob. Tight muscles be damned, she faced him as frustration shot to her mouth. "I'd tell you where you could kiss, but I don't feel like bending over!"

Marcus shrugged and folded his arms across his broad chest, "I'd be doing that right now if you weren't acting like a raging bitch."

Sienna's mouth dropped open. Where was this coming from? He'd never called her that before. Here she was with every right to be livid at his behavior tonight, but conveniently he'd found a way to make it look like she was the one who had the bigger problem.

"Where do you get off calling me a bitch?! I've taken you back the numerous times you've messed me over and now

BROKEN WITH STAINS

I'm a bitch? I'm a little girl, but you're the one who's always calling me, begging me to take you back. And I do. That's the only thing that makes me unintelligent."

"Number one: I never called you a bitch. I said you were acting like one. Number two: Why wouldn't you take me back? I'm the only man who's willing to put up with your craziness. Your mental trips. But I put up with them because I love you."

"You love me. What a funny way to show it. I guess love is just in your mouth and not in your heart too."

"Sienna, you know I've never been one to withhold the truth."

"Is that what you like to call it?"

"The truth hurts, but I tell it because we have that kind of relationship. An honest relationship. You know I love you. I just want you to think about what goes on in that brain of yours."

Sienna couldn't understand why she kept letting him do this to her. She adjusted the bags on her shoulder and looked up at the ceiling. "The manipulation thing is getting old Marcus. This is not about me - it's about you. It's about you and how you disrespect me and lie to me and how you treat our relationship like it means nothing to you. It's not honest. It's a sham and you made it that way. You take everything for granted. Tell me: Why is it so easy for you to do that after all the love I've given you?"

Marcus swiped his hands over his face and walked towards Sienna. They stood less than a breath away. "I'm sorry Sienna. I'm sorry you feel that way. I honestly don't take us for granted for one minute of the day."

She wasn't buying it and turned towards the door. He blocked her exit and gently pulled her body towards him. His large hands reached down and cupped her face. Sienna wanted to move, but didn't as his thumbs coursed over her soft skin.

"Baby, listen to me. I love you so much, it

burns sometimes. Let's not argue anymore. You're my sunshine. These past weeks without you . . . they were hard. Don't walk out of my life like that again. Please. On my life, there are no other women you have to worry about. That stupid dance with Fallon, was just that - a stupid dance. I don't want to lose my sunshine over a stupid dance."

She didn't know what it was about the man that stood before her - his powers expertly massacred her doubts where all instincts were concerned. The guy's knack for making her second-guess herself was utterly astounding and seemed to be the theme of their shifty relationship since they'd started dating. Sienna could feel something jumping around in the pit of her stomach. Could it be her gut signaling her to walk out the door and never look back? Or was it guilt running amuck as a result of her accusations? She needed to take a minute to figure it all out. Needed to remove herself from his apartment so she could think in her own space and time. Couldn't do any of it right now. She was too busy wondering why she was off her feet and in midair.

Before she could form the words to question him, Marcus had her scooped up in his arms and was halfway across the living room.

She found her speech as he walked them into his bedroom. "Put. Me. Down."

"Not until you tell me you love me too."

She twisted in his arms. "Stop it, Marcus. This isn't cute. Put me back on the floor."

He smiled at her. Played like he was about to drop her. Sienna screamed. And then he kissed her cheek. "I could stand like this all night if you'd like. Just tell me you love me."

"I'm not playing with you," she said fanning her feet.

Marcus gripped tighter. Kissed her cheek again and demanded, "Say it."

She knew fighting him was futile. Swallowing her pride, Sienna reluctantly gave up what he wanted. "Okay . . . I love you."

"Say it like you mean it."

"Marcus, put me -" His arms tightened around her. She decided to make things easier on herself. "I love you," she responded with a lift to her voice.

Sienna's feet touched the floor. He held her waist as he spoke, "I just want to put tonight behind us. No more dance floor. No more Fallon. Let's forget about the things that aren't important because I don't want there to be any more problems between us."

She opened her mouth to reply, but he sealed it with a potent kiss. "Sunshine, I don't want to say another word about it as of right now."

He grabbed a remote to turn off the lights, dropped it on his night stand, and drew Sienna into him. Her eyes soon closed as Marcus' tongue swirled in perfect wet circles against her neck. His eager hands fondled all the gems and pearls and beautiful things that made up the treasure chest that was her body. He explored it thoroughly, reaching for all he thought belonged to him.

She tried not to think about her man dancing too close to Fallon earlier that night. While Marcus used his fingers to swiftly pull off Sienna's slip of a dress, she tried not to see him undressing the stacked double D's with his lusting eyes. Right after their naked bodies fell back against his cool black sheets, she made herself turn off the memory of him running his hands over that other woman's hips.

"I love you, Sunshine," he whispered in Sienna's ear.

She ran a hand across his bare back, passed it again over what felt like a long, thin scar. He took her hand from his back and smothered it with kisses. Her warm body shuddered at his delicate touch. A touch that made her utter, "I love you more."

19 joy

I'ma need to scoop up them purple, jeweled six-inchers over there too. Joy pointed to the three shoe boxes on the store's tiled floor, signaling the eager saleswoman to drop them by the register. Next, she drifted over to the decked out stilettoes she'd spotted from across the room. On instinct, she lifted the heel to check out the white sticker on the bottom. *Four hundred and thirty-six dollars.* "Ummm, excuse me," she called to the raven-haired woman. "I'll be adding these to the rest."

Joy was in Miami living it up with Luce by her side and loving it.

Not only did he have buckets of money to go around, he'd told her not to worry about "petty prices" - money wasn't an object. He didn't need to repeat himself twice. The Lamborghini they'd ridden around in all morning wasn't rented, he owned the yellow stunner.

Joy just knew she had to be dreaming. But just in case she wasn't, no store was exited without a brimming shopping bag in hand. Outwardly, she tried to keep her excitement to a minimum, but caught herself slipping when she looked down and realized she'd let Luce lace his fingers through hers. *When did that happen?* she wondered. She came to the conclusion that it must've happened somewhere during the time he whisked her into that mouth-watering jewelry shop a half hour ago to get a closer look at the pink diamonds in the window.

Yup – it was a wrap. She'd certainly given herself over to the excitement of it all. Didn't even feel the urge to pull away from his confident grip. Joy played down the slight heat crawling across her cheeks. Hand holding in public wasn't her forte, but she let the walking bank indulge to show a small token of her appreciation. Besides, he was starting to actually feel like a little something more than a good time. And truthfully, she kinda liked it.

She looked over at him, chill as a late November breeze, in a Ralph Lauren short-sleeve polo and simple khaki shorts. His beautiful, dark skin unexpectedly incited a quiver within her chest.

She was only nineteen.

She knew she loved shopping. Knew she loved looking at herself in the mirror. But she had never experienced anything more than a loving feeling for a guy's money - not the knucklehead doling it out. For some reason, Luce didn't seem to be the average knucklehead. This baller was the square peg in the round hole. All others were incomparable. How he managed to sober her bit-by-bit lately, was nothing short of a mystery. She went to sleep at night with Luce on her mind and woke up with it just the same. A trip to Miami was the last thing on her mind when her cell phone rang at six this morning. Luce was on the other end of the phone instructing Joy to get dressed and pack light. She was a second away from telling him he was bugging, but when he told her he wanted to spend the day chillin' with her in Miami, she hung up and was ready before the phone was able to cool down.

It was a whirlwind once they touched down in the Sunshine State later that morning. His friend met them with Luce's Lamborghini. They rode off with the top down as the beautiful sun kissed their faces. After dropping the friend off, they headed straight to the shops to stock up on all he'd made her leave home. Spending had no end. He more than made up for the lack of money in her paltry bank account.

Joy revved up the leather platforms on her feet and became an enthusiastic spender. It all started with the metallic gold Guiseppe Zanotti heels with feathers in an array of colors. The turquoise Chloe dress was next on her radar. It was too adorable. So much so, in fact, that after exiting the boutique, Joy backtracked and made him buy her the purple one too. When she spotted the over-sized Missoni shades, it nearly caused her to suffer a seizure. Those were thrust into the stack of purchases, immediately. Thanking God for her keen sense of smell, she subtly sniffed the leather of a phenomenal brown and purple Lanvin bag. She knew it would be a crime to walk away and leave it, so she snapped it up quicker than Olympic competitor at the sound of a horn.

Shopping was just the start. After a few hours of buying out Miami's hottest boutiques, the pair ate a late lunch at the Brazilian steakhouse, Porcao. From there it was off to the beach just before the sun began to set. Relishing the sand between her toes, Joy strut her stuff like a supermodel, showing off her new, embroidered bikini. She wanted to offer cups to the men who stood on the sidelines drooling. As they held hands, strolling down the crowded beach, her eyes told Luce his drool was the only one that mattered.

They left the beach, checked into their hotel suite, took showers, and headed straight to the hotel's spa. Hot stones ignited the skin of her back as she welcomed the sweet pain while slowly slipping into sleep. The last thing she remembered before she succumbed to euphoria, was Luce face down receiving his own massage, mentioning something about tonight.

* * *

Luce made a right turn once they hit a big intersection between a strip of restaurants and clubs. After what seemed like a thousand turns, he pulled the car up to large white gates. The solid barriers were so high and wide, Joy couldn't see what was hidden behind them. A stone wall of equal height was erected around the perimeter. Removing a white card from his wallet, Luce inserted it into the slit of a black box next to his window. It took a short time before it spit the card back out. As soon as it did, she impatiently watched the enormous gates slowly separate.

BROKEN WITH STAINS

He drove up to the circular driveway. It was paved in stone and complemented the white, expansive three story Spanish-style mansion that seemed to have no lights on inside. The only lights on the premises lit up the fountain in the center of the circle and each side of the walk way leading up to the front door.

Valets dressed in all black approached the car. One opened Joy's door and helped her out, while the other opened Luce's door, took his keys, and sat in the driver's seat. As the Lamborghini pulled off, Joy looked around at the spacious manicured lawn in the surrounding area and then became mesmerized by the huge, rotating S and D in the middle of the fountain. Water spewed out from the top of the letters into a round pool with dark pink lights illuminating it from below. Luce placed a hand on Joy's waist and guided her in front of him towards the front door.

A third man greeted them. His slicked-back hair made Joy think he'd recently dipped it in the fountain's water. "Good night Mr. Lucien," the large olive-skinned man greeted him. "Leo," Luce responded as the man opened the door. Leo said a goodnight to Joy. She responded with an, "I'm sure it will be."

"Go 'head babe," Luce said as he followed close behind.

The shut front door left them enveloped in a long hallway highlighted by black lights. Joy looked around with lips parted. Felt for Luce's arm, just as his warm breath crept along the back of her neck. "We're almost there," he said. Joy stepped lightly, pulling down the strapless, fuchsia baby-doll dress that landed just under her rear end - a number he'd especially picked out.

They approached two more men standing on each side of the double-doors. All she could see were glowing teeth, the whites of their eyes, and the radiant ties uncovered by their suit jackets. "Mr. Lucien," they said together and then nodded in Joy's direction. "Isaac, Roderick. This is my beautiful lady-friend," Luce said turning to Joy. "Let's open these doors so I can show her around." The two doormen smiled broadly. Joy was so eager to see what would be revealed, she almost reached out and slapped them for opening the doors in slow motion.

Her eyes widened when she stepped into an immaculate, extra long white hall saturated in round white lights beaming down from high ceiling. Pure white. White so bright it rivaled fresh fallen snow. There were three doors spaced far apart on each side of the hall. "This is my pride and joy. Welcome to The Six Doors Social Club," Luce said with a glint in his eyes. Joy noticed a set of double doors all the way at the end. "We'll get there," Luce reassured her. "But first let me show you what's behind door numero uno."

"What you know about Heaven?" Luce asked as he opened the first white door to the right. Joy's eyes swept the large room in astonishment. It was unlike anything she'd ever seen before. She took it in all at once and then once more to make sure it was real. The surreal room was as dazzling as the hallway. There was one female per male. At least a dozen of the bodacious black women were scantily clad in white and draped across their partner's laps. The women came in every shade of brown. From vanilla to damn near onyx, they practically glowed from corner to corner. They even glowed as they sat suspended in rings hanging from the ceiling. With the biggest and most gorgeous angel's wings Joy had ever seen, they made music on white violins. Sparkling white floors reflected the white circles of light that crashed through ballooned clouds of tulle draped completely over the ceiling. Lights that also made the white leather walls give off a luminous sheen. The men wore the room's color scheme too. Low glass tables in the shape of cubes were stationed in front of their white leather seats. Most had their heads bent over a white powdery substance on see-through glass plates. Joy took a double-take when she noticed the famous football player who lifted a female with a sheer white body suit from his lap and encourage her to dance on top of his cube.

Luce took hold of her hand and pulled Joy back so he could close the door.

She faced him. "What in the - "

Putting a finger to his lips, he silenced her. "That's only the first one," he grinned.

Her eyebrows reached their maximum height. She was dying to see what could be more extreme than that. Easing open the door directly across from the one they just left, Joy placed a hand on his back and peeked around his shoulder.

"I like to call this one Gold Rush," he stated proudly.

Gold rush was an understatement. Joy looked at the varying lengths of the strands of gold beads that fell from above. They could double as Mardi Gras beads, but these were of a much higher quality. Metallic gold body paint coated every inch of the shapely figures of all the women in the room. Their matching high-heel sandals perfectly blended in with their skin. Some were perched on the laps of the men sitting at large gold poker tables. Others walked back and forth to the gold fondue fountains spread out around the room. Those women, returned with chocolate-covered strawberries to feed to their designated men. As they pranced around, the strawberry-fetchers kicked up pieces from the crusted gold metallic floor. It was odd, yet stunning. Joy couldn't tell if the metallic wonder on the walls and floor was paint or some sort of expensive paper. Her eyes moved back to the three massive octagon tables. Eight men tossing gold poker chips were stationed at each one. Those who weren't gulping down their glass flutes of champagne were puffing on long, brown cigars. "Those are cigars I imported from Cuba. The finest if I do say so myself," Luce mentioned.

Joy could care less about the cigars, she just wanted to figure out how much money all the men in the room were worth. Wealth exuded from their pores as they flipped their concentration from the game to the women and back.

Luce tapped Joy on the butt so they could exit the decadent space.

"Who . . . what the . . . how do you do this . . . stuff?" she asked.

"Questions already? The tour's not even over yet."

He left her standing in front of Gold Rush's closed door and opened the second door on the right. An unnaturally bright blue light spewed out. Joy hesitantly left her questions behind and hustled to see what was inside. The overpowering light almost blinded her as soon as she stepped into the room that was just as large as the previous ones. Glass block walls and floors with royal blue lights glowing behind them, inundated everyone there.

"The Submarine," she heard Luce say from far away. Her eyes zoomed in on the large square-shaped in ground Jacuzzi that was in the middle of the room. The water in the tub glowed the same color as well. Joy stood amazed at the sight of the steaming pool. There had to be at least ten more striking black women in and around the water, with long, wet hair cascading down their backs. "Them broads on the cover of King got nothing on these chicks," Joy mumbled to herself. She looked at the flawless, dripping bodies that donned g-string bikinis completely studded in crystals. They were mannequin-like, shining beyond measure from the water and light bouncing off the glittery stones. Joy touched her waist, hating to admit she felt a tad self-conscious. She resisted the impulse to reach out and touch them in order to confirm they were made of flesh and blood. Were they really real or had Luce created them in a lab somewhere? She wouldn't put it past him. It looked like Silicon Valley when looking at their chests. And the mayor of the valley? Clearly, the honey-complected hottie with an armful of silver bangles and crystal-rimmed sunglasses on. Her rack made Pamela Anderson look like she wore a training bra.

Shaking the sight off, Joy focused her attention

elsewhere. She was unable to tell if the men in the Jacuzzi were
naked or not, but thought she saw the crack of a few behinds as
some of them played with the bikini-clad lady of their choice.
Two male waiters walked around with sterling silver trays. Luce
leaned over and whispered in her ear, "Caviar flown in from
France. And I had to get octopus as well – it tastes absolutely
delicious . . . especially with hot sauce."

The next thing Joy knew, her body was outside a closed
door once again. She was getting tired of Luce pulling her out
of rooms before she was able to let each scene marinate.

"Yo! I need more than a couple seconds to check this
stuff out. Seriously, I don't know how you pull this mess off,
but it sure don't look like a dollar store operation. Just chill
and give a ho a minute to count the money on the walls."

Luce laughed and kissed Joy on the forehead. "Relax
and be patient. I need you to trust me, baby. I'd never give
you more than you can handle at one time. Plus, there's so
much more to see." His eyes told her that her cooperation was
mandatory in order to continue. She let her shoulders fall
slightly as she attempted to loosen up. Sure she'd given in to
his encouragement, he took her cool hand and slowly made his
way over to the second door on the left. The cool touch of her
fingers were dishonest about how she felt on the inside. Her
stomach burned as if the energy from behind the door had
seeped through her skin and electrified it. Luce's hand gripped
the round knob and pushed. Black patent leather walls
screamed at Joy on the other side.

"I love rock music, that was the inspiration for what I
like to call The Dungeon," he whisper-shouted in her ear.

All bass and electric guitars, Joy cringed at the
deafening heavy metal music that rained down from above.
Eight high-back chrome chairs faced the walls, forming a big
circle. It kind of looked like they were playing a dirty game of
musical chairs, but instead of the men walking around before
the music cut off, they sat in the stiff seating – each had a long

chrome pole five feet in front of them that ran from the ceiling to the floor. A girl was on each pole. Four were costumed in skimpy, black patent leather. The other four were covered in silver chains that clanged against the poles as they viciously climbed. When the women smiled, Joy saw diamond-studded grills in their mouths. She looked at a super-tall light-skinned girl with a jet black mohawk, her leg reaching to the sky. Next to her was a shorter girl with breathtaking ebony skin and super-round rear end. She was bald as Mr. Clean, a silver chain hanging from her nose connected to her ear. She had a baby face, but a domineering attitude as she put her metal spiked heel against an Indian man's chest and forcefully pushed him backward, flipping him over in the chair. Joy took a step further inside, accidentally sliding a bit on the super slick floors beneath her. She looked down at the black floor that was so shiny it could double as a mirror. She took another step, carefully. Luce was behind her again, tugging at her dress. She backed out of the room hoping to catch a glimpse of what the outrageous girl would do next as she stood over the cowering man. But of course, the party pooper wouldn't allow it, locking her out of the patent leather fantasy world. Joy followed him as he walked to the last door on the right.

She was beyond guessing at this point. Couldn't even begin to dream up what craziness Luce had tricked out behind the final door on this side of the hall. When it was revealed, she saw a room full of men and women. Or so it seemed, until she squinted her eyes and took a closer look. It was actually wall-to-wall mirrors. Floor and ceiling too. Six women who looked like they could give Naomi and Tyra a run for their money, sat erect in the middle of the room, elegantly decked out in floor-length, flesh-tone beaded gowns that sparkled under the large sphere of soft brown light emitting from the ceiling. An audible gasp escaped at the sight of small blinged-out tiaras adorning their neat updos.

Joy had to ask. "Are those - "

BROKEN WITH STAINS

"Yes," Luce interjected. "Those are real diamonds. Twenty carats apiece set in platinum."

She stared at them sitting posh and luminous on what looked like mahogany wood-trimmed thrones. The seats were made of tan raw silk. Each woman was elevated on a high, rectangular platform made of mirrors. Legs crossed, they each sat with a suited man down on bended knee kissing their naked feet. Joy laughed when she saw the intensity in which the men worshiped and smooched the delicate soles and toes.

"You'd be amazed to find out the number of men who have serious foot fetishes. That's why I had to create it – the Palace of Pedi Pleasure."

It felt like she'd only been in there for thirty seconds before it was time to leave. She wanted to protest and tell Luce to shut the door and leave her in there alone. But there was only one more door on the left to go, so she kept quiet, and followed him there. Standing next to him, she shut her eyes for a moment, deciding, just for the heck of it she would try to think up what she would see next. Joy's lids flew open when a high-pitched scream hit her ears.

"And at last we have Hell," Luce said.

She took a step backward as she looked around the wildest and most crowded room of them all.

"Whoa," she uttered with a hand to her stomach. The entire untamed attraction was drowned completely in vivid red paint and siren-red lights that whirled about. Mists of smoke filtered down from vents above the writhing bodies on the floor. The women wore red masks with distorted smiles and odd heels that made it look as if they were standing on the tip of their toes. Their bodies were covered only in oil. Joy's eyes bulged at the blindfolded men, with hands tied behind their backs, laying face down on their stomachs. The women walked around them with black whips, lashing the torture gluttons who screamed out in pain. Joy realized she hadn't heard them outside because the room was completely sound-proofed.

What had possessed him to create something like this? "So you put Heaven at the top of the hall and Hell at the bottom?" she asked in disbelief. He put an arm around her shoulder and answered, "With all the excess in between."

The other rooms were something to behold, but this one was overwhelming to every single one of her senses. Her pupils throbbed as she strained to see all that was unfolding. It was hard to concentrate, when the crack of the whips against flesh caused her to jump every time they landed. Swallowing the vanilla-scented smoke that had begun to seep into the back of her dry throat, Joy made an effort to look closer. Viewing the scene all over the floor made goose bumps crop up on her arms even though fire licked up to the top of huge black fireplaces inserted against each wall.

Luce backed out of the room and pulled Joy's hand. She could barely rip her eyes from the sadistic group.

In a daze, Joy looked around the unbelievably pure white hall. The contrast to what she'd just stepped out of was so tremendous it left her speechless.

Luce grinned at the look on her face. "And those are the six doors of The Six Door Social Club," he said. She rubbed the pimples still on her arm and tried to bring her racing pulse to a halt. "So what's that?" she asked, nodding her head towards the large double doors at the very end of the hall. "Wouldn't that be the seventh door?"

"No. That's The Grand Ballroom."

They walked the rest of the hallway's length. A small tremble was slowly taking over her hands. She breathed through her nose as discreetly as possible and talked to the heartbeat that had started to stutter. *This ain't nothing. Stop being a punk.*

Luce placed his hands on the curved door handles. "Ready?"

The anticipation was off the meter right now. But as the thumping in her chest quickly sped up, she firmly admonished herself to keep a brave front on. Joy clenched her toes in her sparkling heels and commanded, "Open the damn door."

A gasp escaping from the base of her throat almost caused her to choke. She never knew rooms this beautiful existed. Even the rooms in the large home of Blue's millionaire dulled in comparison.

Bold, fuchsia lights flooded the patterned walls. Joy shielded her eyes at the blinding chandeliers hanging down from various areas across the ceiling. Three brilliant poles covered in Swarovski crystals were erected in the middle of the colossal room. They were anchored from the ceiling to the platform stage and had women expertly spinning around on them. More women were suspended on swings with ropes covered in what Luce told her were ostrich feathers. The flat seats they sat on were covered in the same crystals as the poles.

Tables swathed in fuchsia, iridescent tablecloths held an abundance of food and drink. Candles of various shapes and sizing burned in the center amongst overflowing plates of steaks, calamari, roasted duck, crabs, grapes, cheeses and bottles of Courvoisier and Veuve Clicquot. Luce led Joy further into the room. She watched seductive women in dark pink satin and diamond necklaces dance in front of the men as they ate with satisfied looks on their faces.

Everyone knew Luce. The nods and handshakes seemed never-ending as they made their way to a large, elegant table in the back. Joy wanted a closer view of the stage, but backed off from making a big issue. It felt great just to be at the side of the baller who owned this grand design. *Cha-ching-ching-ching,* she thought to herself. If only Blue could see her now, it would be the sweetest icing on top of the cake.

After downing her second glass of Courvoisier, Joy began to snap her fingers and move along to the pounding beat of the latest hip-hop banger. Luce smiled at her energized sway and took the tight body in with a sweeping glance.

"Why don't you get up out that chair and show me a little something." Joy continued to rock in her seat as she lip-synced the words to the rap song.

"I know my Joy ain't shy, so why you playing that seat so close." She threw her hands up in the air and popped her bare shoulders to the music.

"Don't tell me my girls got you shook. They're all beautiful, but I didn't know they were going to intimidate you like that."

Intimidate? Luce had to be out of his wretched mind. This was Joy Boogie he was talking to.

She slid her chair back and gyrated her hips up out of the padded seat. Moving her way in front of Luce, she straddled him, popping her booty to the thumping bass line. Her eyes seared into his. Joy licked her lips as she positioned her cleavage in front of his face. She lifted herself from her place on his lap, turned around, and gave him a back view. A second later, she was bent over and touching her toes. After, shaking what her mama gave her, she wound her way around to face him yet again. By then, she had caught a few men not too far away, looking hungry for her to hit them off with their very own lap dance. She looked down at herself, realizing her dress was the same color as the other girls' outfits.

Joy wore the sweat beads on her forehead with pride. She was happy to see the look of satisfaction on Luce's face, just as the song faded and another one took its place.

She took a seat and fanned herself with her hand. "That's how I look when I'm intimidated. Real shook, right?"

He laughed at her comment, "Aight, aight, you got me. I take it back. I love the way you wiggle that beautiful round brown . . . since that night I first spotted you in the club."

"Bet I had you dreaming about it that night too," she teased.

"And wishing to take a bite of it," he added. Joy flushed hot.

BROKEN WITH STAINS

"I've always admired the way you handle your body. In the club. In the streets. In the bed . . . and now in my domain. You sure are something special my pretty cinnamon skin."

As simple as they were, his words were like the bread and water she needed to survive. She swallowed them whole, her heart feasting on his adoration.

Luce gave her thigh a gentle squeeze, saying, "Dance for me."

Joy tuned out everything in The Grand Ballroom, except for him and the music. As she seductively moved about, giving Luce his second lap dance for the night, she made up her mind that she'd dance for him all night if he wanted her to. She'd dance in slow motion. She'd dance on the table. She'd dance hard until four in the morning. She'd dance forever and a day until he said stop.

20 paul

Maureen came along one fine spring day when Paul was photographing everyday life on Manhattan's South Street Pier. The eclectic flight attendant was all big hair and shoulder pads, but her silky, long legs made Paul's interest soar. He liked her from the get-go. How she owned her addiction to fast cars, funky Prince records, fish net stockings and pink sapphires galore. For five amazing days, Paul was caught up, having more fun than he'd had in a while. And then, one Sunday afternoon over brunch, Maureen's plump lips announced her parents were flying in from Cali. He swallowed a piece of scrambled egg down the wrong way when she suggested a tie should be worn when he met them at six the next evening. The self-satisfied smile on her face made Paul's stomach sway something awful. She'd continued by informing him "your in-laws sure can't wait to see you face-to-face". He honestly didn't know if she was joking or not. Even so, he wasn't taking chances by sticking around to find out. An hour later, with a crooked smile painted across his face, he kissed her goodbye for the last time and hastily flew from the air hostess's front door.

Free-spirited Jocelyn soon grabbed his attention. An afrocentric sista with pretty little feet and an outline of The Mother Land tattooed on her chest, Paul knew he could get used to the activist and her growing collection of lace garter belts. He later discovered he was wrong when she showed up at his studio unannounced and demanded he attend one of her demonstrations. Where did the down-to-earth, free spirit go? Paul considered her antics proof that the little soldier had no idea he had no problem standing on his own. Proof also, that she was passing her place a bit too fast. Though he'd miss seeing that tattoo jiggle when she African-danced in her fancy underwear, he'd always been a firm believer that all good things must come to an end. After pulling that bumrushing stunt as if she were the Queen of Sheba, Paul removed the royal pain, cutting her off without a second thought.

Zolida, on the other hand, was a Brooklyn-bred bombshell who could tie a cherry stem with the tip of her tongue. He blonde bob and warm honey skin caught him by surprise in line at the Manhattan post office. He'd only wanted to pay some bills, but instead crashed into this brickhouse and her sexy gap-toothed smile. It would be insane to let this fine specimen slip through his fingers, The receptionist by day couldn't get through a night without a bubble bath, a glass of rum and Coke, and a yoga session in the buff. Everything seemed to be shaping up nicely, so it didn't make sense when she started bringing up engagement rings each time they were together. The third time she mentioned her penchant for princess cuts, Paul couldn't understand why she felt blindsided when he pulled the plug on their three months.

And then there was Sharon Caldwell.

Pure. Simple. And beyond serious. None of the aforementioned could compare.

Paul sat alone and hungry in the diner. Seeing her made him yearn for something more than a greasy cheese burger and fries.

Her light brown hair was pulled back into a low bun. The oval face unsmiling and focused on her small yellow pad. He made it a point to read the name on the blue badge when the pretty waitress approached his table. She didn't make eye contact, all she wanted was to take his order. The sexy southern-laced voice soothed all the frayed edges of his nerves. Looking at the woman before him, he wished the dowdy gray uniform that covered her baby-soft peach skin could be replaced by whip cream instead. Her shape was more than easy on the eyes. It burned him to know where this one had been hiding.

TAMARA BURKE

She was nothing short of angelic. His twenty-six years had exposed him to many types of women, but not since he'd first met Annette had he ever wanted a woman as bad as he now did Sharon. Paul watched her every move from his seat at the diner. He was amazed at the never-ending length of her legs, but his awe didn't stop there. When taking his order, her puckered pink lips reached out to him for a kiss. At least in Paul's eyes, that's what they seemed to be doing. And the scenery from the back. When she walked away from him, he knew it would have been possible to rest his plate on her blessed behind, if only she would let him. He wanted to know where she came from. Wanted to take her somewhere and keep her there locked inside a glass box. Any man could see that a lady as rare as she was best to be cherished.

Much to his surprise, Paul left the diner without her number that afternoon. The challenge only fueled him. He sought Ms. Hard-To-Get at any opportunity he could manage. Eating at the same spot for two weeks straight was no big deal. His patience finally paid off when Sharon finally cracked a smile on her sweet face and agreed to give him the time of day.

It was May 14th, 1985. They sat enjoying each other and a small picnic in Central Park. The bun was gone and the long, soft curls licked across her face. Her butter-yellow sweater and ankle-grazing denim skirt, a demure, yet welcomed change from the minis and halters he was used to. She was refreshing. Inspiring even as he thought of plenty ways her softness could materialize on film. Paul loved the tiny dimples in her cheeks. Adored how her nose tilted downward, the small nostrils that had a tendency to take on a life of their own. His ears welcomed the drawl that rode on the light breeze. He laughed every time she started a new sentence. She blushed, saying it wasn't something she could help.

"I love it just the way it is. When did you move to New York?" he asked.

Athens, Georgia was her place of birth. She and her

sister, Rinelda, moved up to the Bronx only a year before. They'd come up alone, determined to conquer the world. She gushed about her love for cooking and said the only reason she was a waitress at the diner, and not a cook, was because she was so nervous her first day, she accidentally set a cloth on fire at the restaurant stoves. Waitressing wasn't too bad though, but she hoped to one day own a soul food restaurant. If the fried chicken and biscuits she'd made for their picnic was any indication, Paul knew any restaurant of hers would be a success.

A couple dates later, Paul got the feeling she was in love. She never mentioned meeting parents or engagement rings and never unexpectedly showed up at his front door. It was the little things: falling asleep against his shoulder as she held his hand, the way she let her fingers dance on his arm just because, feeling her heart beat wildly every time he held her close. His mission was accomplished and ego bigger than the Brooklyn Bridge. But that pomposity came to an end once he met "Regal Rinni" Bass at Sharon's abode.

Paul figured he'd meet a slightly older version of his shy Sharon. He soon found out he was as wrong as sweatpants in ninety degree heat. The sisters were from the same mother, different father, but still he was amazed by the differences that were too huge to be denied. It wasn't only in the physical sense - Rinelda was at least two inches taller, a shade darker, and just around thirty pounds thinner than Sharon - their personalities were in contrast as well. Where Sharon was quiet, Rinni was loud. Where Sharon sat to the side, Rinni sat square in your face. Where Sharon bit her tongue, Rinni equipped hers with a bullhorn. Where Sharon stood completely still, Rinni charged full speed ahead. The differences rubbed Paul the wrong way. Didn't like the way she talked nor the chip on her boney shoulder. Couldn't stand the way she looked at him when they were in the same room. Cold looks that warned him that she'd looked over his head and peeped all the cards he had in his hand. Most certainly, he could do without her regal behind in the picture. Paul abided nevertheless - he wanted to keep his Georgia peach by his side.

Paul and Sharon stayed strong and maintained a cozy relationship as they fell into a comfort zone. And just when he'd relaxed into contentment, tragedy shattered his world. Brock was dead. September of 1985, his life ended when he unexpectedly died of heart failure. At the age of only thirty, his friend of eleven years was gone in a flash. Loss was not something Paul dealt with well, but Sharon helped him find a way.

She commenced to being his rock. Allowed him to cry in her arms - something he'd never been able to do with any other woman before. The warmth Paul grew to depend on was there at the funeral holding his hand and every painful day after. She was his savior during that crucial time. When memories from the past floated back into his life with its flashes of fire and screams and the people who'd disappeared. Brock was with them now. On nights that sleep ran away with peace-of-mind, Sharon was at his side massaging away the tension in Paul's shoulders. Waiting until he could find rest in her arms. Their bond became solidified. Until, of course, she told him something to melt away what she thought was strong.

A little more than two months after Brock's untimely death, they celebrated Sharon's twenty-second birthday. While candlelight flickered across the table as they held hands in the small Thai restaurant, Paul's thoughts were preoccupied with how it was too warm with everyone and everything way too close in the intimate room. It took an enormous amount of effort to simply focus on the lady he had before him.

She quietly reeled him in when her soft voice crept across the table.

"Paul I thought today would be the perfect day to tell you that we're going to have a baby." He could feel his muscles shrivel a touch, pulling tight from all ends. Paul was about to ask if she was pulling his leg, but thought better of it when he saw the elated look on her face.

Was it the first month or the second? It could've been somewhere in between, but Paul was sure he'd told Sharon kids weren't something he wanted at this point in his life. Eight months they'd been together. How did she forget that valuable piece of information? The smile took up a major portion of her face now as she waited for his enthusiastic response. It was her birthday. The excited eyes were telling Paul that he couldn't disappoint.

"Wow, baby . . . wow. We're . . . having a . . . baby."

He smiled outwardly, but his stomach was threatening to throw back up the spicy food he'd just consumed.

* * *

Seven months later, Noelle Paulette slept silently in his arms. He was there this time to actually hold his child; he'd never laid eyes on the firstborn Sharon knew nothing about.

Sure he hadn't made it to the actual delivery of Noelle, but he came to take his daughter and her mother home after two days in the hospital. Rinni had been on standby in case he didn't show. But when he graced the three of them with his presence, she refused to let him take her sister and niece past the hospital's exit. Rinni didn't drive, but she was prepared to pay a taxi whatever she had to for her sister's sake.

Weak and sore, Sharon insisted that Rinni calm down and let Paul drive them all to their apartment. She didn't want to upset Sharon during a time that was supposed to be joyous in her life, so Rinni decided to clamp her mouth and give it a rest.

Paul didn't last one month. From the moment Sharon revealed she was pregnant, that ever-growing itch taunted him day and night. He needed to get away and fast. Had been pulling away slowly since that very minute the news hit him in the gut on her birthday. Sometimes he swore he could still taste the spices he'd ingested that night. But he knew what the real deal was. The itch had reached its peak. The last time he saw Sharon, her tears made him aware that she knew it too.

Silent rivers ran down the red face all night as he watched his child's fragile mother in her apartment. He chose to play stupid, continually asking about the reason for the tears. Sharon withered before him in silence, moving around the apartment with Noelle pressed against her chest. Knowing was in every jerky move she made. They both knew it was the end, though neither chose to speak it aloud. Rinni would be home at any minute. Still he approached Sharon one more time, trying to make her understand by the solemn look in his eyes, he wasn't cut out for this type of life.

Her back was what Paul received as she walked over to the apartment window to look out at nothing in particular. Noelle's chest rose and fell with every sleeping breath she took. Her mother's tears washed her in a flood. The tiny body stirred and for a second Paul questioned what he was about to do.

"Go on," Sharon croaked out, "but just make sure you don't come back." He wanted to apologize. Wanted to kiss his daughter's mass of curly hair one last time. Sharon didn't understand that it wasn't that he didn't care. It crossed his mind to try to explain why he couldn't stay, instead, he calmly bowed out and walked away.

21 noelle

I wonder how many channels she gets with that big satellite dish?
Noelle chuckled to herself. The woman two benches in front
of her had a hat on that was so big, she hadn't peeped the
preacher's face since he walked up to the pulpit.

Noelle glanced around Hope's church and saw about
twenty more hats like the one blocking her view of the man
delivering the Word. She'd come because she needed it.
Something, anything, to help her get herself together. He was
full-fledged under her skin. Noelle hoped if she let some
encouraging words seep into her thoughts, they could drive out
the demons that were keeping her in bondage. Those demons
equaled Chris. Trying didn't help, she just couldn't shake him.

Focusing on the pastor's words was nothing short of a
task. Dozens of distractions were running through her head
and all of them had to do with how she should kill him, when
she should kill, where she'd hide the body, and variations of the
like.

Last night when he'd called and made it known that he
wanted to see her, it was a battle and a half to keep from giving
in. The aching and lonely side of her wanted to say yes . . .
along with "I'll be over in five minutes with strawberries and
fried chicken, no undies, a bottle of Nuvo, some DVDs, and
no grudge against you." And that was just the edited version.
But waking up in her own bed this morning, she felt good
about her decision to keep her butt put.

Even so, the voice she loved and hated at the same
time, wouldn't stop reverberating against the walls of her head.
She'd listened to him try to explain himself to her, saying
everything he thought she wanted to hear. *It's game, all game,*
she repeated inwardly. But for a moment, she allowed herself

to envision resting her stressed-out heart in his familiar arms. That was as far as she dared to venture. After the call ended with her abrupt "No" and a click, she was wracked with guilt, feeling she'd betrayed herself. Couldn't believe, as much as she tried not to, she'd sucked up his every word, secretly contemplating a future with each one.

Noelle gripped the wood bench and closed her eyes to squeeze away the haunting. The knives were creeping up again. Threatening to stab away at what was left of her mutilated soul. He was on top when Noelle walked in. Back sweating like he was a slave in the field., sowing his seed to the best of his ability, the girl's big feet planted in the air. Her untamed weave were like a scattering of weeds. Those big eyes and below average face coated with a look off shock. Noelle still angered up at the thought. He was no good - she knew this - yet, she couldn't let go of the way things used to be. The new Chris wasn't the old Chris. The one she'd given license to convince her he was nothing but the best.

"Let's pray."

Noelle snapped out of her troubling thoughts and watched as the whole congregation stood up for the final prayer at the urging of the preacher. Church was over and she still hadn't heard a word, much less gathered a quote for courage.

She raised her right hand when the pastor followed with the benediction, shutting down any hope for a solution to her problem.

* * *

The crowd was overwhelming. It was a small space with huge hats, strong perfume, cheek-kissing, and a bunch of pushing. Hope and Candace were lost in the confusion. All Noelle wanted to do was make it to the front door. She almost did, but then she spotted him.

He was looking straight at her, seeming unsure of whether he should make a move to speak. Noelle was poised to walk right past him when he pushed out a hand. "Hello, Noelle. It's good to see you again."

There was no chance of escaping now. "Hi David," she said, deciding it was best to ignore how handsome he looked in his suit and tie. A pause settled between them. Her gaze shifted left, then right.

"You look nice," he said stepping back to take her all in.

"Thank you."

"No - thank you for being so beautiful."

Her eyes fell to the floor as if her next words could be found amongst the bustling feet. "Yeah, ummm . . . thanks . . . it's a new dress I got . . . like, ummm . . . three days ago."

She wanted to slap herself, but decided against it and settled for a stern talking-to, *Stop the mumbling foolishness and get it together. Acting like you seen Bob Marley rise up from the dead . . .* "Well it looks great on you," he responded, interrupting the scolding session. "Thank you." She kept it safe this time.

"It's a small world. I can't believe we ran into each other. I came because I was invited by my cousin and his wife. Normally, I'm at my own church every Sunday. Deliverance Faith Tabernacle over on 219th."

"Yeah? I'm here with my best friend and her mother. They've been inviting me for a while now, but I've been so busy.

He refused to take his eyes from hers, no matter which way she chose to direct them. "Seems like God has something up his sleeve today." Noelle caught his drift. Couldn't be sure if she wanted to drop it either. It was enough to make her do something quick.

"David I think I see my friend over there, so . . . I'm gonna get going."

TAMARA BURKE

"Okay. I don't know when I'll see you again, so I guess I should ask you now: Can I take you out for some ice cream?"

Noelle laughed, looking at him briefly enough to catch a glimpse of the scar above his eye. Never in her twenty-one years had she been invited out for ice cream. David smiled back at her as he waited for a yes.

"You can get chocolate, vanilla - anything you want."

"What if I told you I was lactose intolerant?"

Slap. *Why'd I have to go say that?* Her fist twitched to connect with her mouth. "Then I'd ask you what you wanted instead and I'd take you to go get that." Though she wanted to, she couldn't find one good reason to turn him down. "I . . . I can't." Her head was screaming yes, so she couldn't understand why her mouth was saying no.

"I'm a man offering you anything you want. Are you really going to turn that down?" His smile made her want to stuff him in her purse and skip all the way home. There was no way she could fight the fight any longer. "Well . . . I do like peach grape nut. I don't know. I guess maybe one day we can do that."

After exchanging numbers, the two went their separate ways. David with his shoulders further back than before. Noelle oblivious to the teeth stretched out across her face as she walked over to Hope standing by the door.

"Mmm-hmmm. I invite you to church for spiritual nourishment and you're here hypnotizing all the men." Noelle stared back at Hope, blinking like a deer caught in headlights. Arm-in-arm, they folded into a fit of laughter and exited the church.

If only you knew, she thought to herself as she glanced back over her shoulder at David shaking a man's hand. *God definitely sent a word up in here for me today. I'll be sure to meditate on it too.*

22 sienna

Sienna was so hungry she wanted to eat the chalkboard. Skipping breakfast this morning had not been the brightest idea. The hunger pains currently slicing through her gut were sharp enough to convince her there was a knife floating around somewhere in stomach. With a lunch break right around the corner, she thanked God that there were only five minutes left before she shooed her students out the room for the day. But before she'd finally be able to ease her roaring stomach, there was something important she had to knock out the way first.

Her eyes zoomed in on Tandi. The grumpy target with attitude splashed across her face, sat to the left of the classroom barely working on a group assignment. *Is that a black shadow under her right eye?* Sienna wasn't sure, but she'd find out in exactly 3.5 minutes. She needed to get a hold of the confused girl to reason with her. Make her listen and understand. This was only the second time Sienna had seen her in class since the bathroom incident. The first time, she'd slipped out like Whodini before Sienna could approach her. There would be no way she let her stubborn student get away this time – her hunger would have to wait.

The blaring bell sounded, inciting a mad dash of bodies hustling to get out the room's door. Sienna slid from behind the dark wood desk as if roller skates were attached to her flats. "Tandi . . . please . . . I'd like to talk to you for a second."

One foot through the door, Ms. Attitude stopped dead in her tracks. The last two stragglers squeezed passed the stiff frame with a hand lazily planted on its hip. Sienna stared at Tandi's back as she debated whether to acknowledge the pleading request or join her rowdy peers quickly crowding the halls.

"Just a quick minute," Sienna reassured her.

Tandi shifted from one foot to the other, slowly turned around, and walked over with hesitation lodged in every step. Sienna sat down in one of the students' seats and gestured at a desk close by for Tandi to join her.

"So, how's everything going?"

She looked everywhere except in Sienna's eyes. "I'm aight."

"You haven't been showing up to my classes. Do you have an explanation for that?"

"I was out sick."

"Would you be able to provide me with a doctor's note? That way I'll allow you to make up the two quizzes you missed."

Tandi shrugged. "I guess I just can't take them then. I didn't go to the doctor."

"So you don't care that you've missed two important quizzes? You're carrying a D average in this class. How would your mother feel about that?"

Tandi lifted her head and gave Sienna a piercing look.

"My moms'll be aight."

The creased forehead and grimace on her face let Sienna know she needed to walk carefully on this thin line.

"Could this . . . relationship you're involved in . . . be the reason you're doing so poorly in my class?"

The thin mouth maneuvered in circles, tense jaw muscles vented out her discontent. "How'd I know you'd find a way to bring that up?"

"I only brought -"

"Didn't I already tell you to mind your damn business?"

This was going to be even harder than Sienna originally thought. "Tandi you can't -"

"I don't need you telling me how to live my life."

"Just listen to me for a second. I'm not trying to tell you how to live your life. I just want to help you. Let you know that I'm here if you need to talk."

Tandi scoffed at Sienna and rolled her neck as she spoke for good measure. "And what would I need to talk to you for? You're my teacher, not my friend."

Sienna looked down at her pastel pink nails and searched for a semblance of composure. She'd prepared herself for Tandi's abrasiveness, but her friendly approach was falling on deaf ears. *She's young and she thinks she's in love. You know how that goes, so don't give up.* Sienna decided to take another route, made herself pull from the times she'd practiced what she'd say.

"I'm your teacher and I care about you. I care about all of my students. Right now it just seems that you're caught up in a situation that is proving very detrimental to you. A situation I want to help you get out of. That's all I'm trying to do."

Suddenly, Tandi stood up, pushed the desk backward, violently banging it against the one behind.

"You need to play your position and keep away from situations that don't concern you. Me and my man are fine now. It was just one stupid argument that got out of hand. Don't be trying to make stories up, 'cause believe me, I'm good without your help."

Sienna stiffened back against her chair, unsure whether she should stay put or take flight. Tandi huffed in a fury, looking like she was set to draw back and punch the wind out of her chest.

She tried to tell herself to let it go for the sake of her own safety, but Sienna had to try one more time. "Tandi, that makeup is barely covering up that bruise above your eye. How long are you going to allow him to beat you like that? You're young. You're beautiful. Don't you think that you deserve better for yourself?"

"You don't know shit. I burned myself with a curling iron this morning."

A curling iron? Sienna felt an overpowering urge to grab the battered young girl and shake her.

"Don't do that. Don't make excuses for him when he treats you like trash."

Tandi moved swiftly toward Sienna and stood in her face.

"Keep talking that mess and I'll knock them teeth straight out your mouth."

Sienna stood frozen and remained that way as she watched Tandi collect her books and exit the classroom door, slamming it shut.

* * *

Food never tasted so good. Sienna took healthy bites of her chicken parmesan and promised to never skip breakfast and lunch ever again regardless of the circumstances. After her battling it out with Tandi this afternoon, food had completely slipped her mind. The girl had threatened to knock the teeth right out of her mouth. Sienna had never been in a physical confrontation in her whole life. Her only assumption was that Tandi could grind her behind into mere dust. The girl was rough despite her five foot four status. Sienna cringed at the memory from earlier today. While grubbing it up with Marni and Eve, thoughts of her collision with Tandi competed with Eve rambling off at the mouth.

"I'm so disappointed with you, Sea. I mean really. How could you take his foul behind back? I knew you'd go sniffing behind him."

Sienna tried to smile off Eve's comment. "I stayed away for a few weeks didn't I? I tried Eve. Believe me, I tried."

"Well heffa, you didn't try hard enough."

"Pass the butter Eve and leave it alone." She handed the butter to Marni who sat directly across from her. Sienna sat next to Marni and reached a hand over to her horror-struck friend.

"I hope you still love me. We're still friends right?"

Eve smacked the outstretched hand to the side.

"I don't know. I don't know if I can be friends with a weak woman who doesn't love herself first."

"So what do you want me to do Eve? Apologize for loving my man? If loving him makes me weak, then I guess I'm weak. How about that?"

Eve slurped from her glass of iced tea and burped across the table at Sienna. "Right. And you talk about Tandi," she said, bringing the glass back up to her lips.

Sienna struggled to keep her patience in check.

"That was disgusting," Marni cut in. "And both of ya'll need to stop. Can't we just enjoy one decent meal without all the bickering back and forth?"

"I'm not bickering, Marni, just letting her know I love my man. And Marcus is not beating me, Eve. I wish you would stop mentioning me and Tandi in the same breath."

"Face it," Eve answered, loudly crunching the ice in her mouth. "Those who live in glass houses shouldn't throw stones."

Marni kicked her under the table.

"What?" Eve asked, looking at the source of the brutal foot. "Tell me I'm wrong."

"How is you being nasty helping her?"

"I'm being a friend. Friends tell the truth. Friends give it raw, not sugarcoated and honey-dipped. Wouldn't be called a friend if I didn't point out the error of her ways."

"A friend hands out constructive criticism, not tear down their supposed friend every chance they get."

Eve let her hands fly in the air and crash-land down to her lap as she sighed. "And what constructive criticism would you give, dear?"

She mocked her friend's unnecessary hand display and responded with her own sigh. "I'd tell her that she should think about the stress he put her through and then decide if it's all worth it. See whether the negatives outweigh the positives. Make the right decision once that's done. And I've told her that."

"Hooray for you. Friends like you deserve a platinum and ice doggy biscuit. Give me a break. I tell her what she needs to hear. Not some 'ole sit around and make a checklist of negatives and positives. Screw the bullcrap. She needs to call a spade a spade. And Marcus is what he is: a dog."

"Why you always gotta be so stank, Eve? I know for a fact you've had some missteps with men in your past. Don't forget the biggest one – Daniel," Marni reminded her.

"Yeah, Daniel was a black period in my life. But I did let go and move on. I wasn't sitting there trying to milk a dead situation."

"Well, we all have our black periods. If this is Sea's period she'll handle her business when she's ready."

"And in the mean time, we should just sit back and watch him ruin our girl. How advanced is your brain?"

"Bite me."

"I would, but unfortunately I'm straight."

"Whatever. You just need to chill sometimes. Obviously, your rude words aren't making her leave Marcus any quicker. Right, Sienna?"

Marni and Eve looked over at Sienna for a response. It was obvious that she had tuned them out a while ago.

Eve rolled her eyes as Sienna typed away on her Blackberry. Wholeheartedly, she concentrated on the message before. As usual, the girl had not been listening. It was the reason why she was in the sad predicament she was in now.

Eve turned her attention back to Marni and asked Sienna a question she already knew the answer to. "There's only one person you text when you're out with us. Let me guess, that's Marcus right?"

She didn't even pull her eyes away from the small

screen. "Huh? Oh – I'm sorry guys. I was just, ummm, seeing what he's up to. All this talk and I just realized I haven't heard from him all day."

Eve looked out the restaurant's large window behind Marni and Sienna as she chewed and simmered in abhorence at her friend's spineless behavior. She was momentarily distracted when she saw a stylishly dressed man walk by with his head thrown back in laughter. He wasn't alone as he walked past the window. His hands were firmly placed around the waist of a woman with deep brown skin and long wavy hair. He was around five foot eleven and dressed in a sleek black suit. Thrown back shoulders were only a part of the swagger he had to him. Eve stopped chewing when the man faced the woman on his arm to give her a kiss on the cheek. She almost gagged on the fettuccini in her mouth when it registered that Marcus was the man on the other side of the glass. And if Sienna was sitting in front of her, then who was that snuggled under his arm?

Eve snuck a quick look at Sienna. She was done writing messages like a complete fool and was working on the last of her chicken parmesan. Eve looked over at the window again, but Marcus and the woman were gone.

Sienna pulled her Blackberry back out of her purse and knit her brows at the blue gadget. "I wonder where he is. It's past seven. He can't still be at the office right now."

Eve glanced over at Marni, who also sat unaware of all that just went down. *Now ain't that something. The lying punk just walked right by this idiot with some tramp on his arm and she was too wrapped up in her own ignorance to witness it. But of course, if I said something right now, I'd be the insensitive friend who don't know when to shut up.*

She looked at Sienna floating on her cloud of bliss. Eve smirked and brought her glass up to her lips. *What will it take to save you from yourself dummy?* Talking wouldn't do it. Sitting back without a serious plan of action wasn't going to make the girl leave him either. Something drastic would have to be done. Something she didn't want to do, but knew was her only way to get through to the silly girl across from her. Eve had hoped it wouldn't have to come to this, but now it was time to put a stop to the foolishness. Daniel number two would be out of the picture once and for all . . . and maybe she'd even have a little fun in the process.

23 joy

"**G**et your hands off me you dumb, big-for-nothing pig!" The young black girl who looked mixed with Asian, kicked the air and elbowed the tall, burly man who carried her in his unrelenting grip.

Joy slowly moved inside the back door, standing a few feet from the action. Her short denim skirt did little to cover the red g-string that was exposed as the girl cursed, screamed, and fought with the big guy steadily moving forward. The platinum-blonde hair flew everywhere as she thrashed about like a wayward child who'd been denied a bag of candy. In no time, the man who never once changed his demeanor, disposed his problem outside on the concrete through a set of side doors. He came back in with the girl hot on his heels. She was stopped in her tracks by two more big men who roughly grabbed her arms and legs and then disappeared through the doors.

"Pardon the scene."

Joy turned towards the voice that seemed to come out of thin air.

"Cinnamon, right? Luce told me you were coming."

She took her time answering. "Nah. I'm Jewelz."

"Well gorgeous, you're Cinnamon now. You've been christened by Luce, so don't shoot the messenger. I'm Rocki - the manager here at The Six Doors Social Club of Westchester." Joy did a once-over of the man with a headpiece over his S-curl and an obscenely thin mustache. His pants were too tight and the black button-down had a few too many extra buttons open at the top. She took note of the man-sandals on his feet, looked back to his wide face and back down to the clear nail polish on his toes.

"And when did Luce decide this, uh, Rocki?"

"The moment you signed up to be one of his dancers. He owns you now - get used to it." He handed her a piece of paper. "Here's your locker combination. Your outfit's hanging there. Follow me."

Joy grilled the back of his head with a stink look as she followed him to a room in the back. Luce was crazy if he thought she would answer to a name like Cinammon. The stage name Jewelz is what she had come up with for herself. And that's what she told him last night on their way home from Atlantic City. Yeah, she agreed to dance for Luce, but damn, did he have to go and pick her name too?

She put her annoyance on pause once she walked into the fuchsia room covered in mirrors, lockers, breasts, and behinds. Her eyes floated around the dressing room and caught everything it passed. The girl in the orange thong as she bent over stuffing an oversized Gucci bag. A fly buzzing around the huge flat screen plasma television hanging on the wall. Some overturned nail polish dripping onto the floor. A short-haired girl in the corner hunched over a text book. Nothing escaped her.

"Ladies, listen up. I'd like to introduce you to SD's newest dancer, Cinnamon." Joy rolled her eyes when he said the name. "She'll be performing with you tonight. Don't be shy, get acquainted and welcome her to the crew. Jaguar, Luce wants you to show her the ropes, so I'll need to speak with you out in the hallway after this group session is done. Lonnie and the rest of Makeup will be in to beat your faces soon. I want you gorgeous and fierce and ready to turn it out. We got a few special men coming in tonight. I already spoke to the girls in Heaven, Hell, The Submarine, Gold Rush, and so on. I need you ladies to be on point. Don't make me have to send another Karma out the back door. It's not about you when the curtains go up. You're here to please the client; if their not happy, we don't get fed. Now get them knees and elbows oiled up, walk out there tonight, and make it do what it do." With that, Rocki was gone with Jaguar by his side.

Joy stood in the middle of the room with her Louis duffel in hand and returned the mean faces that stared her way. Discomfort was not the name of her game. No way was she about to shrink back into a corner somewhere if none of the girls wanted to step forward and welcome her into the fold. She wasn't here for friends anyway. She was here for Luce and the thousand dollars he'd promised she'd collect at the end of the night. This morning her bank balance told her fifty dollars was all she had. The rent was over due by ten days. Money was all that mattered. Everything else was of no importance if it wasn't mean green. Well . . . everything besides Luce. He needed her there and had even told her last night she could bring the extra spice that had lately been missing from the Westchester branch of his club.

Her man would be happy because she'd get the job done. After witnessing the excitement in Miami, there was no doubt she could rock with the best of them and more than likely rock it better. Luce convinced her she was the showstopper needed to make things really jump off. It was understandable why these other uptight broads were acting stuck-up and completely anti-social. They were good-looking females, but still very dispensable - kinda like the screaming chick that got dumped on the curb.

Joy hoisted her duffle up on her shoulder, moved to retrieve her clothes and shoes from the locker. She touched the silver heels and pink satin get-up that were similar to the ones she'd seen on the Grand Ballroom girls in Miami. Wondering where her diamonds were, she walked over to an empty chair facing the long, lighted mirrors against the left wall. She ignored the row of girls that sat primping and preparing. Checking her watch, Joy noted a quarter to seven. As she unpacked the contents of her bag, she felt a little disturbed by the fact that she hadn't heard from Luce all day.

The last time she'd spoken to him was at around nine

last night. She could still feel the fiery kiss she gave him after he said, "It's a privilege to be chosen as a Six Doors girl. Don't ever forget that. Took me three years to build an amazing team to go out and scout the hottest black women from all over the world. I got six hundred and thirty SD girls in seven states. From Compton to Brazil, we've scouted the best of the best and every one of them have showed and proved. We'll celebrate tomorrow night with a bottle of Dom P. All you need to do is make sure you do the damn thing when you hit the stage . . . just like you did with that lace number when I first met you in the club."

She could taste the champagne on her tongue right now.

Still, his promises for later on didn't excuse him from the disappearing act today. She was going to make sure she voiced her beef with him as soon as the night was over. Until then, she was determined to beautify herself and give the men in the audience a show they'd never forget.

Joy stripped down to her sheer black bra and thong. She attributed the envious stares shooting back at her through the mirror, to the banging reflection she saw. Her C-cups, tiny waist, and round hips usually had that effect. Even without a touch of makeup on, she considered herself better looking than the two average-looking chicks whispering together as they threw glances her way. Joy eyed them through the mirror as she rubbed oil into her hands. The one with the short, white robe and pony tail had a five-head that needed to be hid by a bang. Her nonexistent breasts looked like it lacked nourishment too. An iron board for a chest was not a good look. At least her friend was decent in that area. Too bad that was her strongest point. Fire-engine-red hair made her look like a clown. Big teeth made her look like a chipmunk. Ample thighs made her look one biscuit away from Jenny Craig.

Joy plugged in her curling iron and retouched the loose curls that framed her face. Standing to her feet, she brushed them out a little for maximum volume, dipped her head forward, and brought it back up with a shake. They could all hate on that if they wanted to, her strands were real, not the product of a ten dollar pack of 1B. She propped a foot up on the metal chair in front of her and bent over. Joy oiled her legs once more as she gave them an all-access view to her thonged behind.

Yeah, tricks, she thought, *the baddest chick is taking over your area.* "Look at this one," she heard one of the dancers say. Joy brushed her shoulders off at the comment and began to bounce her booty while still in the same position. A smart remark was all she needed to make her sing out loud a few bars by her girl Remy Ma:

> "My thong showin', but it's cool, my shoes go wit' it
> Now all I need is a room wit a pole in it
> See I look good and I'm knowin' it
> And I was never too proud to be showin' it . . . I'm
> conceited, I got a reason."

* * *

It had been a long night.

Joy's feet ached, but even now, little spurts of energy shot through her body. She pressed the elevator's buttons to take her up to her apartment. After getting inside, she closed her eyes and smiled at the thought of her first night's work and the two-thousand dollars in her pocket. Not one thousand as Luce had promised, but two thousand luscious dollars. The anticipation for day two filled her up instantly.

Day one had been a breeze. There were dimes all around, that she couldn't deny. However, Joy felt she was a more like a quarter, better than a dime any day of the week. She had to be. Too many men had been looking in her direction instead of paying attention to the girls they had in front of

them. The three main men she entertained for the night: a heart
surgeon visiting from Texas, a music producer from New York
City, and an investment banker from South Africa.

The makeup artist had hooked up her makeup. Her hair
was re-curled and brushed to bouncy perfection by a member
of the hair team. The wardrobe stylist finished off Joy's
spectacular look when she placed a mouth-dropping diamond
necklace around her neck. Looking so fly made it easy for her
to step into the Grand Ballroom without any fears. It
practically looked identical to the Ballroom she'd visited with
Luce. And though she wanted to master the crystal pole, Rocki
told her she couldn't because it was only her first day. It was no
sweat. Joy knew she'd be swinging from them in no time as
soon as she made her request known to Luce.

At eight-thirty p.m. on the dot, she began her first
dance with the surgeon. While the DJ blasted the fast-paced
R&B song, she rolled her body as if it were liquid. In the midst
of all the seduction her body fed the balding man, Joy hoped
Luce was there to see it all. She was making money for both
herself and him tonight.

Every swivel of her hip, jerk of her backside, and lift of
her legs brought the man one step closer to euphoria. He
couldn't even touch the feast of lamb chops, and seasoned rice
on his table. The sweat on his forehead increased by the minute
and all Joy had allowed him to touch was her elbows. She
continued to tease him with the rest. Made his eyes and lips beg
for the pieces she dipped and swayed out of his reach. The
same followed with the other two men she danced for.

Never had she been in the midst of a room with so
many men with money craving a taste of her body and time.
Joy was high off the memory. So high, the opened elevator
doors almost closed on her, before she realized it had stopped
on her floor. Her Pumas padded down the hallway as she
blinked back a sudden wave of sleep.

She would've been able to hop in the bed sooner than

the current seven a.m. hour, but champagne, lobster, and Luce had kept her going once she left the club at four a.m. He'd come through as promised and all the anger she'd held onto earlier in the evening vanished once he approached her in the parking lot hidden behind Six Doors.

He made her leave her car and drive with him. Turns out he'd been watching her the entire night, pleased with how she represented in the Ballroom. If she remembered correctly, his exact words were: "I officially crown you Six Doors' reigning queen."

That was all she needed to hear.

His pleasure was becoming increasingly important. Her man deserved all his wealth and a girl like her to share it with. *My man,* Joy mused to herself, *Imagine that. Joy O'Brien's actually claiming somebody as her man.* She couldn't help but feel a rush of pride take over her body as she slipped her key into the apartment door.

The morning light that blasted through the living room's windows was a startling surprise. She always kept the blinds down in that room. Not for any special reason - that's just the way it was. But when she moved her attention away from the window and over to the black leather sofa by the stereo, she realized something else wasn't right.

"Blue, what the hell are *you* doing here?"

Her mother looked at her and offered up a fake smile.

"I can't choose to visit my own daughter? My only daughter?"

Joy crossed the room and threw her bag on the sofa opposite Blue.

"You never visit your only daughter and you're here now at seven in the morning? What are you doing? Hiding from Tom?"

"Joy, I visit you . . . just not often. I mean, it's hard with Tom traveling to his various meetings, benefits, and events all over. It was just two nights ago we were in California

TAMARA BURKE

having dinner with Robert DeNiro and - " Her voice faded
once she spotted the annoyed look on her daughter's face.
"Anyway, it gets hard keeping up with you. You're busy too
and Tom wants me everywhere with him."

Joy shook her head, tempted to drag her mother across
the room's floor and out the front door.

"Whatever. Tom doesn't have a meeting or any oh-so
important event up in this apartment, so I still don't understand
. . . why are you here?"

She watched her mother adjust the collar of the
starched white blouse she had on. Some designer label no
doubt. Probably the only other thing besides good looks she'd
inherited from her mother – the unshakeable love of an
expensive name brand. Clearing her throat, Blue proceeded to
study the wall beyond Joy's no-nonsense stance.

"I don't know how else to say this, so I'm just going to
come out and say it."

Joy waited. Ten seconds went by and Blue had yet to
say "it".

"I need to take a shower. You can show yourself out
'cause -"

"Your father wants to see you."

Joy felt the world shift beneath her feet. She looked at
the eight carat, pear-shaped engagement ring on her mother's
finger and did a mental rewind. The yellow rock reminded her
of the time she was eight years-old, hugging her favorite yellow
stuffed dinosaur under her chin. *Your father's not here. Get that
through your thick skull. I want you lay there and shut up. Don't
mention one more word about him or else I'll slap you to kingdom come.*
She'd never forgotten Blue's screaming demands on the last
night she dared to ask about her dad. Sitting up in bed, she
fought back tears as her mother stood with her finger on the
light switch, prepared to envelope her in darkness. Today,
eleven years later, that same woman sat in Joy's apartment
telling her what the man she couldn't ask about now wanted.

BROKEN WITH STAINS

"Get out of my apartment! Get out right now," Joy yelled.

Blue's face stiffened. "I'm still your mother. I know you hate me - though I don't know why - but you *will* hear me out on this."

"On what? Me seeing some stranger I know nothing about? What does Tom really have you smoking when ya'll be traveling 'cross the world?"

"Don't say things like that, Joy - I'm your mother."

She laughed. "My mother, my mother, my mother! You keep saying that, but how come you've never been one to me, huh, ma? How come you come up in here telling me my pops wants to see me, but for so many years you never even let me ask you one question about him? Answer that, mommy dearest."

Blue swallowed.

"No, I didn't allow you to mention your father back then because he disappeared before you were born. But he recently contacted me and . . . and he sounds like a changed man. I think it could be good if you two saw each other."

"Oh, I get it. This is your way to get some of grandma's money. You're making this much effort now? I thought Tom had enough for the both of you."

"This has absolutely nothing to do with the money that your grandmother left for you."

"Stop lying, greedy. It's really sad. Your own mother died and left you nothing. Nada. Zero. It's almost a year later and you're still coming to sniff around for what she gave to me. I ain't giving you a damn thing."

Joy knew there was nothing to give even if she wanted to. But she'd never let her mother know the seven hundred and fifty thousand was done.

"And I'm glad she left it for you. I never expected anything from her anyway. You know the witch and I never had any kind of relationship. She gave the money to you just to spite me."

"Heard it all before. And you know what? I don't blame her if she did."

"Fine by me, Joy. You don't know the half of what I went through with that woman when I was growing up, but that's besides the point. The only reason I'm here right now is to let you know your father would like to get in contact with you."

"What happened to that angry woman I used to know? You couldn't stand the man for all these years and now you're his number one fan. On the real Blue, you're what I like to call a joke."

The pale skin of Blue's face grew completely red as she sat with her head tilted to the side, an index finger incessantly tapping the top of her purse.

"Look, you little wench. I'm here to help *you* out," she said, with the same index finger now pointing at Joy.

"Wench?"

"Wench is correct, you ungrateful little wench."

"Oh, it's time for you to get the hell up outta here."

"I raised you by myself. Your father was nothing more than a sperm donor for your information. You forget that I struggled to make sure you had everything you needed. You forget that I did it all alone. Your shit of a father was nowhere to be found when I needed money to take care of you."

"Yes, I know. And that's why you've never been too much into black men after him. His trifling black behind left you and the rest, dipping in and out of your bedroom, were just the same. No need to remind me - you've been drilling it into my head since I was a baby."

"I think I need to because you seem to forget that I was the one who was there for you."

"You and your pedophile boyfriends you mean."

Blue put a hand to her forehead and took a couple deep breaths. "That was only one incident Joy," she said, letting her hand fall back to her lap. "One I knew nothing about until you snapped. The rest of those men you keep bringing up, helped maintain a roof over your head and food in your nasty little mouth. It's easy for you to ignore that part, isn't it?"

"You kept your boyfriends around for you - not me. Don't front like you were handling your business for my sake - I was never a priority on your to-do list, Blue. You will never receive a World's Best Mom award. There's no need to fake it."

Finally, Blue stood. Hurriedly, she snatched her black purse from the chair and sternly strut her way to the door. She paused for second, turned to her daughter to let off a few last thoughts. "Yeah, well, you're going to believe what you want to believe - that's your business and there's nothing I can do to persuade you otherwise."

"Glad you know that," Joy said, completely through with this tired conversation.

Blue opened the door, stepped through, and turned to face the stubborn woman-child for the last time. "I'll leave you alone, Joy, but the facts still remain the same. Your father was out of your life back then. He wanted me to ask you to let him in now. Do what you want with that, my love. The choice is yours."

24 paul

Blue O'Brien wore the bold color very well.

Paul supposed that's why the designer had chosen her to model his entire collection of red. Paul was sold. It took a special kind of woman to pull off a red floor-length dress with a six foot train. There was an unquestionable passion behind her gray eyes. The tall woman could've worn a potato sack covered in cow dung and still would've looked just as magnificent.

His trigger finger snapped shot after shot of the trophy woman he focused on. She was that type. The type of woman who could walk into a room full of people and disturb the equilibrium just by simply standing there.

"Gorgeous, sweetheart. Put your chin down a little . . . that's it." He directed the delicious woman he focused on, testing her boundaries to see if she could give him more sizzle than the shot before. "Turn a little to the left. Hold that right there. Beautiful."

She took direction well, moving with the grace of a goddess. Her confidence was magnetic, pulling him in with every slight move of a hand or shoulder. Paul intended to get to know her better after the lengthy shoot. Unfortunately, the designer engulfed him in unwanted conversation. A conversation Paul could barely concentrate on as he tried to monitor every move Blue made before she said bye and walked out the door. He regretted not saying much to the beauty during the shoot, but he was so enraptured in her body language, it was as if she were speaking to him in another form.

Reviewing the photos in his hands, a few days later, Paul studied Blue and wondered why she'd been given that name at birth.

Blue she was not. She was light and strength when

she'd stood before him in the red creations. If anything, she should have been named Violet. Much more suiting was that royal hue.

Paul went over her thin nose with his finger and tried to place her nationality. The voice had made him assume she was American, but the light, cool complexion didn't quite have a red or a yellow undertone. Were her parents from Spain, Puerto Rico, or another Spanish-speaking country? Maybe she was Middle-Eastern. The short, soft, onyx hair made that a possibility too.

Her gray eyes staring back at him were to be considered also. The longer he looked into them, the deeper he fell in. The depth seemed immeasurable. He wanted to find out what lay behind them.

Without a way to contact her, Paul felt lost. She was his client's model - he couldn't just call and ask the designer for Blue's contact information.

He wanted her though. Bad enough to find another way to get her in his possession. Thankfully, she'd mentioned something he could use to his advantage. Paul remembered overhearing her mention to the designer that she was dying to check out the new African artifact exhibition at the Metropolitan Museum of Art in Manhattan. "I'm definitely going next Monday," she'd said. "It's the only time I have in my schedule to see it. I can walk around and take my time before my doctor's appointment at three."

He'd been to The Met a few times - it wasn't hard for him to get there at all. It was a large museum, but he knew she was going to head straight for what she wanted to see. The doctor's appointment pretty much guaranteed she'd stick to a strict schedule. Paul was hell-bent on making sure he wouldn't miss Blue, one of God's superior works of art.

* * *

His memory had never failed him yet. That day at The Met, he'd strategically placed himself by an ebony statue in the center of an amazing room filled with treasures straight from Africa.

He smelled the patchouli scent before he had the chance to spot her.

"Paul. I'm glad you came."

He turned towards the voice, his eyebrows raised in surprise. Blue looked resplendent in a lilac top with butterfly sleeves and a high-waisted white skirt that showed off her legs.

"Really," she smiled. "You're right on time too."

Blue laughed and clapped her hands together lightly as she beamed at him. "You can wipe that look off your face now."

Paul tried desperately to come up with something cool to say. "Uh . . . good to see you, Blue."

"Sorry. I don't mean to laugh at you. It's just that I wasn't sure if you'd caught my hints at the photo shoot."

"I, uh . . ."

"I'm a professional before anything else - I couldn't just make a date while I was on the job," she said.

Paul was dumbfounded. He thought he'd been the brains behind the operation. Now he felt like he was caught with his hand in the cookie jar.

"You take direction well, I take hints well . . . what can I say?"

They laughed and went on to enjoy the exhibit together.

After ending the tour at a quarter past three, Paul stopped Blue in her tracks as they headed to find a restaurant for an early dinner. "Your doctor's appointment at three . . . we got so involved -"

She fell into a fit of giggles and covered her hand with her mouth before saying, "I made that up too. Boy, you really were paying attention to everything I said. Come on you big stalker you." Blue grabbed his hand and pulled him to continue

BROKEN WITH STAINS

walking. "My tummy's talking to me and I'm sure yours is too."

* * *

Passionate and bold, Paul observed Blue through his lens. This time, sans clothing. There was no red. No designer. Just the elongated body spread bare on his studio's floor.

He'd asked and she'd agreed to a nude black and white photo story on "The Exposition of a Pearl". It was a story he'd always wanted to do, but never found the right woman to encapsulate all he wanted to say.

Blue fit the bill.

A natural pearl. It was a precious gem with a luster created by its many layers. Light reflected from those layers. But a pearl could only be appreciated once it found its way out from inside a shell. Paul photographed his vision of a pearl thoughtfully. Her luster under the umbrella's lights captivated him because he knew there were even more layers she had yet to expose. The ones Blue shared with him over the past week made him aspire to get closer and closer. Her outward appearance was phenomenal, but the inward beauty exuded from her pores. It was so palpable in every frame he took, he could almost reach out and touch it. Paul tried to extract from her every drop he could get.

"Exactly - just let it all flow out. Give me all of what you're feeling inside. You're terrific, baby."

She curved her body and angled her face upward towards the camera.

"Amazing. You're beautiful. Just let it pour out. I want to see you - all there is to Blue. Just let it all out."

She shifted her position, brought her hands up to the back of her head as she sat upright.

"That's what I'm talking about. Look deep into the camera. Chin up. There you go gorgeous. You're perfect just like that."

She brought her arms down and looked to the left. "You're immaculate. There it is. Amazing . . . amazing." Blue looked directly into his focus.

"Terrific. I like that intensity. Keep giving that to me."

She abruptly turned away and brought a hand up to her chin.

"You're so beautiful, so beaut -"

He stopped in his pursuit of more as she covered her nose with both hands. Paul watched the tears begin to stream down the contours of her face.

Cautiously, he approached, knelt down, and gently wiped away the growing wetness on her cheeks.

"Babe, what's wrong? Is it something I did?"

She shook her head to assure him that wasn't it.

"Then, why the tears? You're too beautiful for that -"

She put a palm on his chest, stopping him.

"That's it. That's it right there."

He didn't understand what Blue was referring to. He'd said nothing to make her cry. Complete sadness now replaced the light he'd become used to.

"You, calling me beautiful and gorgeous and perfect and all of those things," she continued.

He was still at a loss.

"You probably think I'm crazy," she chuckled. "Thing is . . . growing up, my mother never ever told me those things. She'd tell me everything opposite. Called me stupid. Said I was weird-looking. Told me my hair was too nappy. I was everything but perfect." She pinched her nose and sighed before finishing. "It must be because I'm here before you completely naked. Just feels like you can see every inch of me - all my imperfections. The flaws that woman never let me live down. Here you are telling me I'm beautiful . . . something my own mother refused to say."

He scoured her light eyes and began to finally see the blue past behind them. "Why would your mother not tell you how beautiful you are?"

She gulped and looked towards a window by his desk.

"My mother's white . . . she was raped by a black man. Instead of giving me up for adoption or something, she kept me. And hated me. Called herself being a devout Catholic, therefore abortion or abandonment wasn't an option. She never married either, so I guess that made her strange decision easier too. Heffa was forty-three when she gave birth to me. Never knew she could even get pregnant 'cause the doctors told her different. Ironic, huh? To get pregnant when she was raped and by a black man at that?" She ran a hand along the rising hairs on her arm. "Somehow that disgrace was all my fault. She put me through hell and at the end of the day still called herself an honest Catholic."

Paul hadn't seen that coming. He scratched his goatee as he tried to think of comforting words to say.

"Regardless of what your mother told you, you don't come off as someone who's let that affect you."

"Until now, right?" Blue turned her eyes to his. "It took a lot, Paul. But after a while, my low self-esteem started turning into thick skin. When I left my mother's house for good at eighteen, I looked in the mirror right before I walked out the door and told myself the devil is a liar. That's what's driven me to move on with my head held high."

She wiped a tear with the back of a hand. He grabbed the same hand and put it to his lips. After kissing her palm, he looked down at the pink lines running to and fro.

"Blue, to me . . . you're a wonderful person. To have been through what you say you've experienced, you're unbelievably strong, courageous, and extraordinary to me. I can't begin to understand all you've been through with your mother, but I will say that everything happens for a reason. No matter how you came into this world, your beauty can't be destroyed because of it. It's more than what's on the outside. I see that beauty on the inside too. You're special, sweetheart and

I hope that you never forget that."

The last tear creeping down Blue's face fell onto her thigh. They both watched it dampen her skin. His hand impulsively wiped to make it go away. What happened next came naturally. Whether it was the need he felt to comfort her, her need to be comforted, or both, neither one knew for sure. At that point, it failed to matter. Blue let him in to connect with more layers, temporarily leaving the past where it was meant to be. Touching as many as he could, Paul aimed to make sure she experienced a brighter future. Both took it slow and easy as they explored each other right there on the studio's floor.

* * *

He didn't want to fight about it anymore. It was time to be done with the argument. What part of "Get an abortion" didn't she understand?

Blue was a four-letter word away from taking her foot to his behind.

"You must be out of your damn mind if you think I'd do that to my child. Our child. You're a sorry excuse for a man. You need to be castrated, and even then, never allowed to roam the streets again."

It had been five years since Annette had announced she was pregnant with the first baby he didn't want. And even though he didn't visit her, he knew that in a few months his baby with Sharon would be turning two. Paul didn't want to go through this for the third time. Hadn't he run enough? Blue was supposed to be on the pill anyway. An unexpected pregnancy was not cool by any means.

"Blue, I'm not ready for anoth- I'm not ready for a baby. Parenthood is not something I'm trying to mess with right now."

They sat at a stoplight in his new '87 Toyota Tercel. December's tiny snowflakes swirled about the windshield. The white dots drifting about were such a pretty sight. At the moment, Blue wished her life looked the same way too.

"You really want me to kill our baby?" she asked, looking at the monster she'd never known.

"You don't have to make it sound like that, babe."

"Babe my ass. That's what abortion is – killing a child. You really want me to kill our baby?"

He looked at her with pleading eyes.

"You are the scum of the very earth."

Without warning, she threw open the car door, jumping out just as the light changed to green. Paul quickly pulled over to the curb to appease the honking drivers behind him. He threw the car into park and jumped out to follow the mother of his unborn child.

"Come on, get back in the car. It's cold out here. All we have to do is take a little time to talk -"

"Me and my baby will be fine. My house is only three blocks away."

Paul caught the wide-eyed stares of an elderly couple sharing the same sidewalk. He ran to catch up to Blue's swift pace and lowered his voice in an attempt to get her to do the same.

"It doesn't have to be like this. Just get the abortion and everything can go back to the way it was."

She balled her fists at her sides and moved faster. "Get away from me before I hurt you, Paul," she yelled ignoring his tactic of getting her to tone it down.

He grabbed her hand. She shoved him away. Blue was almost running now, speeding ahead to get away from what she didn't want to hear. Paul looked before him and saw two little girls approaching. The older one put an arm around the shoulder of the younger and drew her close. Hesitant looks covered their faces as they prepared to walk by the quarreling couple. He lowered his voice more.

"You knew I didn't want any children, baby. Why

would you put me in this position? Listen, let's just do what's best for the both of us."

She ignored his pursuit and drew her unzipped wool coat tighter around her body.

"Blue, I don't want to lose you. I'm willing to work on what we have if you'd compromise a little. Maybe in the future we can have some little ones running around, but it's no good for me at this point in time. Get the abortion and we can pick up where we left off. I'll give you the money."

Suddenly, she flung her body around to face him. Blue shoved Paul's chest with both hands causing him to stumble backwards over a trash can.

"I already had an abortion, damnit!" she screamed as spit flew from her mouth. "I was raped!"

He took a step back, both shocked and scared of her next move at the same time.

She took a step towards him.

"I didn't know the dog who raped me, so I had an abortion. But how could you, the father of my child, the man I love, tell me to have an abortion? How could you possibly do that to me, Paul?"

He didn't see any tears, but he could make out the excruciating pain embossed into every square inch of her face.

Unsettled by the sadness that clawed at her eyes, Paul wanted to look away. Her mother was raped, he knew, but Blue had never told him she'd suffered the same fate too. Paul saw something different in her face when he refocused his vision from the falling snow to the woman pregnant with his third child. The death behind her steely eyes, was something he knew would stick with him for years to come.

"If I have this baby, you're gonna just turn and walk away?" Blue stepped as close to his face as she could get, making an extra effort to be sure he smelled the fearlessness on her breath. "Then do it, jackass . . . run."

25 noelle

It just wasn't a good time right now. The ice cream date with David had been cancelled after she called to let him know she had too much on her plate.

What other lie would have been better than that? Was she supposed to just come out and say "My ex - who you know nothing about - called me up and even though he cheated on me, I decided to give him another chance"?

Too much on her plate sounded like a better deal, so she took that excuse and ran with it.

As she sat waiting for Chris to come back from the kitchen, the call that got her here was all she could think about. The vow not to talk to him fell by the wayside when Chris dialed her number at an opportune time. The craving for him had recently started growing her stronger and stronger each day. It had been a little over a week since she and Chris had briefly spoken before Noelle cut the conversation short. When he took it upon himself to call again last night, he made an extra effort to sound so sincere, so apologetic, so in need of everything he said he missed from her.

Now they sat face-to-face.

"I miss you, Noelle. Please . . . we gotta try to work something out. I was wrong and I'll do anything to make things better."

She'd waited patiently to hear those words. Cried day and night, all the time wishing they would soon grace her ears. Now that they were here, she fumbled with them in her hands. It took a moment to figure out the appropriate response.

"Chris, you hurt me so much. Why wasn't I enough? What did I do to make you bring that girl into your bed?"

He sighed and hesitated before his response.

"It's not about anything you did. I'm human - I messed

up."

She would've laughed if she wasn't frustrated enough to cry. "I'm human too, but I never messed up and landed in another dude's bed. Come better than that. Respect me with the truth."

"It is the truth. That chick wasn't nothing to me, I just got caught up."

"And how long did you know this girl before it just happened between the two of you?"

Eyes darting to the left then back alerted her to his mouth ready to give birth to a lie.

"A couple days."

Her unbelieving glance said it all.

"Chris, why you lying to me? We're not together anymore, you don't have to lie."

"I'm being real with you, Noe. It was only a couple days I knew that chick for."

She decided to let it slide.

"Okay, so you knew her for a couple days. Was she the only chick you were messing with during the time we were together?"

"The only one. I swear."

He couldn't tell the truth even if his life depended on it. She couldn't believe she'd fallen in love with such a liar. This wasn't the guy who she believed in. The one who she could trust to do no wrong. "God is gonna strike you right in your mouth."

"On my life, Noelle. She was the only one I messed with. But I apologize for that and I'm trying to get you to give me one more chance."

Her eyes shifted to Biggie's poster on the wall. If they didn't, she would've reached over to hug Chris' neck and tell him she was willing to give him what he was asking for. She struggled with how much he was both the source of her joy and pain.

BROKEN WITH STAINS

Noelle snapped back to reality when his hands slowly waving in front of her face came into view.

"Don't zone out on me now. I wanna know if we can work this out."

It was time to be serious and get away from this apartment before she made a decision she might regret.

"You can't begin to understand how much you hurt me. Even if I did give you another chance, things would never ever be the same again. I gave you a second chance after we broke up the first time. There's nothing to work out. You made your bed, now it's time to lay in it."

"Things might not be the same, but we could work something out if you trusted me to make things right."

"Trust you so you can crush my heart again," she said with a sigh.

"I'm not gonna crush you, boo. What I gotta do? Get down on my knees to prove I mean it?"

He dropped to his knees before her and held on to her hands.

"This is the best I can do. I don't have Kobe's money so I can't buy you a million dollar ring."

Against Noelle's will, a smile slid onto her face. He always did know how to make her laugh.

"Look at me. I'm on my knees. I'd even kiss your feet and you know I hate toes."

She laughed out loud this time.

"I'll do whatever. Whatever it takes to make you trust me again. All I need is for you to just give me the chance to make it up to you."

Noelle looked down at him, wishing none of the drama had ever happened in the first place. *It was only one time,* she told herself. She couldn't prove otherwise. Plus, he was perfect in every other way. Always there when she needed him. Handy and always willing to give a helping hand. Generous. Affectionate and loving in so many ways. Those details gave her an inkling of a reason to reconsider.

She saw her reflection in his eyes and realized it had been too long since she'd looked squarely into them. Every nerve in her body longed to be able to do that on a regular basis again. Noelle swallowed her anxiety, gathered her thoughts, and parted her lips to say . . .

Knock. Knock. Knock.

The banging at the front door put a halt to the words about to come forth. Who was it disturbing the response she finally had the guts to give?

Knock. Knock. Knock.

Now it would have to wait since this mystery person picked the wrong time to interrupt.

Chris walked over to the door, but before he could reach it, a female's voice came through.

"Chris, it's Nyoka. Why you tryna act like you not there, stupid? I saw your car outside."

He stopped moving mid-stride. Noelle's head tilted to the side when she saw his sudden reaction.

Knock. Knock. Knock.

Nyoka wasn't going away.

"Open it," Noelle demanded. "Or would you like me to come over there and open it for you?"

"Noelle . . . just chill."

"I hear you in there. Who you talking to and why am I still out here?" Nyoka questioned from behind the door.

Noelle walked towards him.

"Fine. I'll open the damn door since you don't want to do it."

He blocked her path and restrained her body when she tried to move past him.

"What?" she yelled. "Why can't she come in, Chris?"

"Calm down," he said, obviously trying to figure out his next step.

"No, move. You acting all shook. I wanna see why."

BROKEN WITH STAINS

She shoved him in the face and reached around his shoulder to unlock the door. Her eyes landed on a slim, light-skinned girl with green contacts and dry burgundy extensions. This was not the chubby girl she'd caught him in bed with. Her teeth gnawed at a piece of gum in her mouth as she loudly asked, "What is *your* ass doing here?"

Noelle furrowed her brows, stunned at the rudeness the unknown girl directed towards her.

"Why is *she* here?" Nyoka asked Chris, pushing her way past Noelle. "I thought you said you were done with chicken?"

Noelle took a step towards the intruder. Her hands jerked at the crass disrespect. "I'll stomp a hole in your chest, bitch."

"Nyoka," Chris said, stepping in front of Noelle. "Why you ain't call first? You can't be just popping up at my crib like that."

She laughed in his face. "That's not what you said last night. Don't be trying to act all brand new just 'cause your ex-girl is here. Pictures sure do make a difference." Looking Noelle up and down, she stated flatly, "She's a five at best."

With a death grip, Noelle knew she'd be able to snatch at least six tracks out of the girl's head in one try. "And who would you be? The one dollar crack-ho he picked up to bust a quick nut?"

Nyoka lunged after her, but Chris grabbed the gangly arms and held on tight.

"You're out-of-control right now. As a matter-of-fact, you're gonna have to raise up."

"You ain't kicking me out for her," Nyoka made clear. "She ain't nobody. I can't even believe you got her over here when you told me ya'll was a done deal."

Hands on hips, Noelle eyed him as she labored not to take her wedge heel upside both of their heads. Chris couldn't even look her in the face.

"And just a minute ago you had the nerve to look at me

and tell me to trust you again."

"Noelle I'm . . . I . . . I - "

"Shut the hell up," she said, turning her back to him. She grabbed her keys from beside the fish tank and continued, "Came here like a fool. So stupid to think you were really sorry. Talking about you love me . . . the only person you love is your damn self."

Noelle bumped Nyoka's shoulder on the way out the door. Paid no attention to the constant noise from the girl's mouth as she continued arguing with Chris. Bypassing the elevator, she ran down the four flights of stairs. By the time she reached her car, the tears were like water from a faucet, running down the contours of her face. They seeped into the cotton of her thin white tee.

The signs were evident when Noelle first walked into his apartment only an hour ago. Truth had comfortably made its home in the details of all that she remembered. And like she'd noticed before, nothing at all had changed. Not the furniture, the fish tank, the poster, or Chris' disloyal ways. As much as she had hoped for change, everything, heartbreakingly, remained the same.

* * *

Noelle had succumbed to numbness.

Blindly, she sat flipping through a magazine awaiting a visit from Rinni. Her aunt called and said, with no questions asked, "I'm on my way over. Don't act like you sleeping when you hear me at the front door." Noelle was not in a state-of-mind to deal with any family or friends. Even Candace had called earlier and tried to get her to come to a mutual friend's barbecue. Noelle declined right away, practically hanging up in her ear. But protesting Rinni would be futile, since her aunt usually didn't pay much attention to what people wanted or didn't.

BROKEN WITH STAINS

The doorbell rang at exactly seven p.m. Noelle let her aunt in and settled back into the seat she'd been occupying in a funk. The television was tuned to MTV as the radio blared an old Deborah Cox song in the background. Electricity burned in every corner of the room – Noelle needed as much distraction as possible.

Rinni surveyed the scene. On the floor, an empty Doritos bag was in an unraveling ball next to a can of Arizona iced tea. She eyed the scattered magazines that decorated the peach carpet. Noted the pile of torn pictures leaning against a pile of tissues on the sofa. By the distant look on her niece's face, Rinni figured this wasn't the best time to disclose the news she'd come to share. Still, it had to be said, even if fire and brimstone started raining from the ceiling. There was simply no way it could wait anymore. She started the only way she knew how.

"Your mama didn't come home from work yet, did she? 'Cause if there's one thing I know about my sister, she'd run out into the streets ball-headed, naked, and screaming before she was okay with all this mayhem. You need to clean this mess up. Kill the waste of electricity and stop looking like you've been munching on a bag of shit. Your father wants to call and speak with you, so you need to get it together before you talk to that man on the phone."

Noelle was immediately awoken from the trance the television had helped her fall into. She looked at her aunt as if she'd just witnessed her body split in two.

"What did you say?"

"I said this place looks like crap. Clean -"

"No, not that. What did you say after that?"

Rinni took her time extracting a cigarette from her purse, put it to her red lips, and concentrated as she lit up.

"Your father," she took a deep drag and exhaled for as long as she could, "he wants to get in contact with you. Said he wants to meet his long lost little girl."

TAMARA BURKE

A new type of anger she'd never experienced before began its ascent from the tip of Noelle's toes. "First of all, I'm not a little girl anymore. And second, I know nothing about him. Why does he want to see me now?"

"He's a photographer. Don't know if you knew that or not, since your mama won't talk about him and all. But, I saw him at a friend's wedding the other day and he was taking pictures. Spoke to him that day and then a few days after. He made some bad choices and I ain't making excuses for him, but he seems to have his life in order now. Wouldn't hurt if you got to know him. 'Least a lil bit."

She could feel the new sensation rolling along her calves. "So it was by chance that he got this change of heart," Noelle said. "He saw you and felt guilty. Now he wants to see me."

"Did you hear me say that? Girl, your father wants to see you because he wants to see you."

"Am I supposed to be excited? Am I supposed to be doing back-flips right now?"

"He's a screw up. I know this. You know this. But you can't hold on to yesterday forever. There comes a point when you have to kick the past in the ass and charge full speed ahead into the future. That's what life is all about."

The anger was now pushing up against the walls of her stomach. There was shortness of breath as Noelle tried to blink back the tears that never seemed to stop flowing. It was a battle to make them go away as her hands feverishly swiped at each escaping drop of water. The knot at the back of her throat took up way too much space.

"My father wants to see me twenty-one years later. Just forget what's going on in my life right now." She cleared her eyes enough to make out the mass of bright, messy curls piled up on top of Rinni's head. "What about what I want? I wanted a father when I was five. I wanted one when I was six. I wanted him when I was seven. I wanted him every day of my life until I stopped wanting him anymore. Where was he before I stopped needing him to be here?"

Rinni watched Noelle's display of raw emotion and thought two decades back to the fatherless baby she'd feared for. Way back then, after coming home to see Sharon a listless heap on the floor, Rinni picked up her crying one-month old niece from beside her sister's unconscious body. It was right after Paul walked out on them both. Sharon had dropped Noelle on her stomach when the last morsel of strength she'd been holding onto, finally left, taking with it chunks of a beautiful spirit. After finding her baby niece red-faced and crying, Rinni never got rid of the fear she harbored. A fear that Noelle would be scarred for life, the trauma of that experience embedded in her young mind. As she grew, everything seemed to be completely fine, but now here she was crying, in part, from a lifted scab. Rinni didn't know what to do.

Emotions of her own had been stifled one time too many – she didn't know how to give them up freely anymore. And then to console a young girl who was obviously suffering the fresh pain of a broken heart as well as a reopened wound from the past, it was a tad too much to handle all at once. Rinni brought the cigarette to her mouth, but couldn't bring herself to take a pull of the nerve-relaxer she needed. There was hurt behind Noelle's eyes that was so deep, there was no other choice but to address it quickly.

She stood up, put her cigarette out on the discarded Doritos bag, and raised her blouse up above her bare breasts. "Look at me." She pointed to the three long, ugly gashes across her chest. Noelle's attention focused on the raised scars. "Your grandmama did this to me. Accused me of stealing a lousy two hundred dollars from her back in '72. Guess what? I did no such thing." Rinni dropped her shirt and sat next to a stunned Noelle.

"My father told her I took that money. Lied on me when it was him stealing from her to spend on his other women. My own mama took a razor to my chest, no questions asked."

Rinni used the back of her hand to wipe away her niece's tears. Her own tears had dried up many moons ago. Yet, she was familiar with the emotional pain of each drop that sprang forth.

"I know how you feel. I know pain too. My own mother sliced me over a petty couple hundred I didn't even take. After I came out of the hospital all stitched up, I had to go live with my grand-aunt over in Louisiana. My mama only stayed in jail for two weeks for what she did to me. Then she was out and back up under my daddy again."

Rinni squeezed Noelle's hand, transferring all the love and strength she could through the hold.

"I never talked to her again after she did that to me. Me and your mother moved to New York two years later. I never looked back to speak to my mother or father. But you know what? When my mama died in '89, I had to go back to Georgia and bury her. She had no one else to do it. No one else wanted to."

She chuckled to herself as she considered the woman who ruled her life with an iron fist.

"She was an evil, callous, and vindictive woman. No one even wanted to come close enough to spit on her grave."

Noelle listened to all she never knew. Her mother had told her little to nothing about her grandparents other than the fact that they were dead.

"I'm telling you this to make you understand that I know hurt, anger, and disappointment too. But I had to take big gulps and swallow it. I had to go back to bury the woman who cut me in my chest three times. The woman who was supposed to be my mother."

Rinni pressed her lips together as she absentmindedly rubbed the scars across her chest. She wrestled with herself trying to avoid that hateful place in her memory.

BROKEN WITH STAINS

"I don't know all the details about what happened between you and Chris, but I can see you're extremely hurt because of it. It's going to be a long, hard road. I'll tell you that flat out. When you hurt deep, deep inside your soul, it's not something you shake a day or two later. You can't kick the depression and sadness as quick as you'd like and that's simply just a fact.

I know it's compounded now that I've told you about your father wanting to see you. You'd like to think you got over not having him there for twenty-one years. Truth is, the feelings have been there all along. Chris may have done whatever to hurt you, but even a blind man can see what they both did to you is not so different."

Noelle listened to her aunt. It was the first time she'd really found someone who could understand and clarify the different feelings that had taken residence inside.

"All I can tell you is that you gotta be strong as you can be and then be even stronger. It wasn't easy for me. Believe me, I wasn't always this tough. Your mother . . . she always was different. Scared-like when it came to our mama. She didn't want to go back and stare into that evil woman's face. And we had two different daddies. Your mama didn't care for mine and I didn't either. Was nothing but a womanizer and a wino that didn't have two nickels to rub together. It was my money, my energy, my time that buried that woman. But I couldn't do it unless I forgave her first. In my heart, I had to let go of the past and forgive what I couldn't forget."

Noelle cleared her throat as she sat back in the sofa and plucked at the slip cover. "Can't believe your mother did that to you. I would've never imagined something like that happened in your life. No wonder you're so strong, Aunt Rinni. Can't imagine what I'd do if I was in your position. How can you get over something like that?"

Rinni gripped Noelle's hand tighter. "Life is a bitch, honey bunch. You gotta fight back every single day and kick it in the face. And when you look in the mirror and see all the bruises she left you with, you don't let that stop you from moving forward. Those bruises have to heal eventually. That's only if you let them. Don't pick at'em - you just gotta push forward anyway. Make life see you victorious for moving on and ultimately winning the fight."

Noelle sighed, "Why does that sound easier said than done?"

"Your 'ole Aunt Rinni's living proof, honey, crazy blonde hair and all." She took a hand and brought Noelle's chin up. "Never allow life to see you as a loser. So what if Chris screwed up and so what if your father missed out on so many of your important moments. It's their loss. But don't you lose out on a future filled with joy, Noelle. Just know you have to forgive in order to make it there."

26 sienna

No answer. It was the fifth time Sienna had tried to contact Marcus by calling him on his cell or typing him a message since seven o'clock this morning.

She told herself to wait for a call back after her third attempt at trying to reach him, but now her fingers were having convulsions. Sienna gripped her Blackberry tried to decide how long to wait before calling again. Using her cell while driving wasn't something she made a habit of. Distractions. That's what her mother told her caused people to lose control of the wheel and end up in a gully by the side of the road.

Well Ma, I haven't heard from him since yesterday afternoon and this isn't Jamaica anyway. There aren't gullies in Princeton, New Jersey.

No sense in trying to fight the feeling. She'd tell herself anything to convince her subconscious she had every right call him for the sixth time. And that she did. Waited and waited and waited for . . . still . . . no answer.

Sienna threw the device down on the passenger's side seat and gave the gas petal a bit more pressure. Her foot pressed harder as soon as she remembered the curly-haired woman she could've sworn was following her around earlier. Upon taking a closer look, it seemed to be the same brown and blonde mop-headed pest who'd been staring her down at Marcus' after work party a week ago. Sienna thought it quite strange that when she'd begun to head out of the Bronx, the woman followed behind her for at least eight turns. It was only when she reached the highway, that the Honda Accord the woman drove disappeared from view. It was enough to make Sienna look in her rearview mirror every five seconds the rest of the way to her mother's house. Enough to make her call Marcus a couple more times.

Sienna pulled into her mother's driveway and decided against parking inside the two-car garage. Pouting as she made her way to the front door of the slate blue colonial house, she looked around the quiet neighborhood of similar homes. It was a great area, but Sienna still thought her mother had moved too far. She used her own key to let herself in, stepped out of her slides in the hardwood foyer, and headed straight for where she knew she would find Annette.

"Hi mother," she breathed out as she kissed her on the cheek. The spacious, nautical-themed den was filled with Annette's sweet aroma. Sienna's nostrils welcomed it along with the faint smell of escovitch fish and okra that lingered in the room.

"Hey, sweetie," Annette said, placing her romance novel to the side to exchange kisses with her daughter.

As usual, the television was tuned to CNN. Sienna found it amusing that even when her mother was supposedly relaxing, she always kept one eye on business. Being the CEO of a brokerage firm was Annette's life. There were only two times she escaped that life: when she was sleeping and when she spent time with Sienna.

"How was the drive over? Did it start raining yet?"

"It was fine. No traffic. No rain either."

Annette removed her reading glasses and hooked them inside her heather-gray tank top. "There must be some reason you look so annoyed."

Sienna walked over to her mother's silver lap top computer and logged on. It was worth a try sending just one more e-mail to his inbox.

"No, I'm not. Well . . . not really. Just that, I've been trying to reach Marcus and he's not picking up. I'm starting to get a little worried."

Annette looked at her daughter and sighed, "Maybe he doesn't want to be reached."

Sienna's fingers stopped mid-type as she switched her eyes from the screen to her mother. "Mom, why would you say something like that? What's that supposed to mean?"

BROKEN WITH STAINS

"Exactly what it sounds like it meant."

"He could be in a ditch somewhere. Why do you assume he's purposely ignoring my calls?"

"Because he's Marcus and I wouldn't put it past him. Get rid of the loser, Sienna. How many times do I have to tell you that I don't like him for you?"

She cracked her tightening knuckles and resumed the message she'd been typing.

"We had a talk. I'm telling you mom, things are a lot different between us now. Don't you trust my judgment?"

"Of course I trust your judgment. Just not when it comes to Marcus."

"He's not perfect, but he's not that bad," Sienna tried to persuade.

"He hurts my baby," Annette answered as she switched off the television. "Never will I be okay with that. As your mother, I own the right to be concerned. I didn't break my back to raise a beautiful, educated, successful child just so she could be devoured by a dog."

Sienna's eyes bulged as she clicked send.

"A little overboard, don't you think? He's not a dog, so just stop it. I know you didn't ask me to come over so you could insult Marcus all day long."

Annette moved from the recliner and leaned against the large oak desk her daughter sat behind.

"As much as I'd like to convince you to get rid of that dead weight, no, I did not call you over here for that."

"Well, what is it? I'm hungry. I thought maybe we could get something to eat at the Cheesecake Factory. I'm dying for a slice of cheesecake. You -"

Annette removed a small black and white photo from her pocket and pushed it across the desk towards Sienna.

"What is this?" she asked staring down at the photo of her mother sitting on the lap of an unknown man. Annette's mini afro was attractively sculpted to suit her young face. Her smile beamed like the sun. The brown eyes filled with hope. Whoever the man was in the picture, his look was handsome and strong. The mustache gave his face an edge. Oddly, he looked timid yet sure of himself at the same time.

"Who is that?" Sienna asked, pulling her eyes away from the picture. Annette wiped invisible sweat from her brow and turned her attention away from the picture of a life she'd wanted more than anything so long ago.

"That's me back in 1982 with . . . your father."

Sienna's eyes floated back to the photo.

"My who? I thought you said you didn't have any pics of him. You told me that when I was younger. How long before his death did you two take this picture?"

Annette's gaze momentarily strayed from Sienna's questioning face.

"I told you a couple of things that weren't completely true. That's actually the only picture I own of him. The rest I got rid of back when we first broke up. And . . . and your father . . . he's not dead." Annette winced as she let the words out. She could tell by Sienna's grim expression, there had better be a good reason she'd never shared that information before. "I know I shouldn't have kept it from you," she continued. "There are no excuses. I've lied for so long and that was totally wrong. I am so, so very sorry, Sienna. I sincerely just wanted to protect you from the harsh truth."

In the minute that Sienna glared at her mother, the feelings of anger and betrayal hit her in the torso with a one-two punch. She bit down on her tongue, blocking herself from saying a few choice words she had in mind. Words like, *What kind of mother are you?* But, she couldn't say that because Annette had been nothing short of the best. *Has it ever crossed your mind that maybe I had needs greater than yours and you could've put your selfishness to the side so I'd know I had a father out there?* That wouldn't be right either; her mother had provided everything she ever had need for. She'd never been without. *I don't want anything to do with you, mom, because I can never bring myself to trust you again.* Completely impossible to utter those words - she loved her mother to death and could never imagine life without her.

"I've always had the picture close by and wanted to tell you about him. Tried so many times, but couldn't bring myself to show you the man who walked out on us – walked out on you. I was young and angry. Felt like your father was dead to me for the way he destroyed my life at the time. Showing you that picture would've been like teasing you with the image of a man who would never be within your reach."

Sienna's myriad of feelings simmered as she thought of the secret her mother had hidden all these years. "So are you trying to say he's not out of my reach anymore? I mean, you're showing me this now, is he not still dead to you after all this time? Sorry if I'm not understanding mom – I can't see through the hurt. I really need to know why you're showing me this picture now."

Annette lifted the photo from the desk and recollected the time and place. Playland Amusement Park. Rye, New York. June 1st, 1982. Sienna was born nine months later. "I asked you to come over because now is the most appropriate time," Annette said as she placed the black and white back down on the desk. "It's twenty-four years overdue, but . . . your father called me. He wants to talk. Your father wants to see you."

Sienna looked back down at the picture. She could see where her button nose came from now. Her wide, thoughtful eyes belonged to the man too.

"So this is Paul Brooks. And he's not dead. Well . . . where is he?"

"He lives in Westchester. Scarsdale. Married out there and living with his wife."

"Does he have any other children?"

"Not that I know of. I didn't ask about that."

"How did he find us?"

"You can pretty much find anyone these days with the

computer. He told me he did a little research online." Sienna tried to be upset with her mother, but she really wanted to know, "How do you feel about this?" Annette thought for a minute and gathered her own feelings about the situation. She tried to figure out how she could sum it all up in two sentences or less. "I wasn't sure if he would, but always thought that if he ever did try to make an entrance into your life, I'd polish off my uncle's old machete and chase him away. But truth be told, when I got the phone call, I was relieved."

Sienna could feel what she meant. Though she wanted to resist it, relief was slowly filling her heart by the minute. "Why relieved?" she asked.

"Because of what meeting him will do for you."

"What it'll do for me? I don't get what you mean by that."

"I've seen the destructive pattern of your past relationships with men. Especially Marcus. He's a big ball of destruction. I believe meeting your father will give you the completion you're looking for. Just feels like I've watched you walk through this world with your body sliced in half. One half roaming around, surviving, the other half missing. I want you to stop searching for that other half to make you complete."

Sienna sat quietly listening to her mother, though she'd rather tune out the parts about her relationship with Marcus.

"You've been looking at Marcus as if he's that other half. No, he isn't. He's just not fitting. It's high time you realize it. And there's no way you can grow if you are walking around incomplete."

She'd wanted once, a long time ago, to meet the other half of herself she never got the chance to know. That want had disappeared without her knowing when or where it went. Sienna had to know if, after keeping her father's existence silent for all these years, her mother was really sure about what she was saying. "You really think seeing my father will help me in some way?" Annette looked her daughter in the eyes. "I do. I so sincerely do. But tell me . . . how do you feel about potentially meeting him?"

Sienna picked up the picture, put it closely to her face, and examined every inch of the couple who were destined for an unhappy ending.

"Yeah, I want to meet him. I need to know why he hurt you. And why he wasn't here to protect me like he should have."

27 joy

She'd come a long way. It had been only four weeks since her first day at Six Doors and Joy was sitting on top of the world. Working her butt off didn't feel like much work at all. Arching her back, tooting her derriere, and supplying fantasies five nights a week was a piece of cake at the high-priced gentleman's club. The men who visited Six Doors were more than good to her and she'd quickly become top-billing. Joy hadn't pulled in less than twenty-six hundred dollars a night since a client requested her for Outerspace on Acid three nights in a row. It was one of the new rooms Luce's off-the-chain interior designer created since he changed the themes behind the six doors every two months.

Joy welcomed the change: a chin-length white wig with bangs, long black mink eyelashes, dusted peach cheeks, and an iridescent silver lip gloss that popped under the room's white lights. Gone were her Grand Ballroom pink and diamond necklace, now all she wore were silver metallic thigh-high boots with skinny six-inch heels, silver booty shorts of the same material, and sequin-metallic pasties that only covered her nipples. She laughed uncontrollably the very first moment Six Doors' resident wardrobe stylist gave her the final crowning touch: a form-hugging silver metallic astronaut's uniform to throw over the tiny outfit. But when she did her thing in the tricked out space room that night, the lawyer she entertained practically lost his mind when she delicately peeled it off.

The club's themes, practices, and events got crazier every day. In the beginning, it took some getting used to when it came to Luce's rules. She almost went off on Rocki the first time he told her there were to be no cell phones on the premises. If that rule was broken, the girls were fined five hundred dollars for the indiscretion. And that was just the start.

BROKEN WITH STAINS

There was no meeting with clients outside of Six Doors. No indulging in any of the cocaine, ecstasy, or weed which was solely for the men's enjoyment. No collecting tips or gifts of any kind. No alcohol intake while on the job. No asking clients for a hook up, whether it be a movie director for a film role or a lawyer to help with a brother in jail. No inquiring about money. And absolutely, positively no discussing Six Doors with acquaintances, family, or friends.

She didn't understand the transaction system either until her fourth day on the job when she asked Luce about it. "It's real simple," he said. "We meet with clients on an individual basis, a week in advance. We take out the black book, let them go through your pictures. They pick whichever one of you they desire for the night. Next, if necessary, we show the client a video preview of what's behind the six doors and the Grand Ballroom. Some clients are already familiar with the rooms. Those who want to step into a supreme fantasy pull out their checkbooks and put four zeroes behind the first number. Those who aren't quite there yet, hit the Ballroom and cut a check for three zeroes instead of four."

No wonder he had all that money to spare, from her time in the Grand Ballroom, there were never less than fifty men all around. Luce never made it clear, but even if he charged three grand per client, he was raking in one hundred and fifty thousand each night. She'd gone over it in her head time-and-time again: the club was open seven days a week, so it meant he was most likely stacking over a million dollars in a single week in the Westchester branch alone.

It was intoxicating to have a man who was a millionaire. She'd never much cared how the guys in her life before Luce made their money, but this time she had to know more. When Joy questioned him further about how he'd come up with the idea for this kind of strip club, he answered, "Get this in your head: Six Doors is not a strip club, it's the illusion of sex in a social club setting."

Right. Joy laughed every time she thought about his summation of the glorified strip club. One of the other new rooms, The Circus, had girls jumping on trampolines in nothing more than clown makeup and big smiles. To her, it was a strip club. But Joy had no qualms whatsoever - she was closing out the month with forty thousand big ones passing through her hands.

Reclining in her sofa, admiring the new platinum bangles she'd purchased at Tiffany's earlier in the day, Joy tried to convince Poochie to jump on the money train.

"You buggin'," Poochie said, looking at Joy as if she were dumb.

"What? You got Ja'Nya to take care of. I can slip a word in to Luce for you. If it's aight, you'd be making close to a thousand on day one. You the one who's buggin' for not seriously thinking about it."

Poochie popped a pretzel into her mouth before asking, "What would I look like stripping?"

"What you mean?" Joy asked incredulously.

"You do what you do. I ain't about to climb up on nobody's stage and spread my butt cheeks for the world to see."

The comment rubbed Joy a little to the left.

"You have a four year-old kid, Poochie. You can't tell me it doesn't cost a grip to take care of Ja'Nya. And how about you still living with your moms? Bartending for a living is not where it's at. It might look like just spreading butt cheeks to you, but it looks like getting crazy paper to me. Is you saying you can't use that money?"

"Man listen, the money sounds right, but stripping ain't for me."

"There's more to it than that. I don't just do it for the money, I do it for Luce too. He needs me there. The last time I spoke to him, he was like, 'You seem to be Ms. Popularity around here. The requests for you have been rolling in.' I mean, it feels good to be able to help my man out. Maybe I'll become more than one of the strippers one day. I could be a scout. Traveling around the world, finding the best looking girls for the club. Hey, why not start with you?"

"On the real Joy, I think Luce just brought you in to make money off of you."

"Oh, so you think he's using me?" Joy questioned, drawing her attention away from the jewelry.

Poochie's eyes bucked. "Yes. Isn't it obvious?"

"How could he be using me if he's taken me out so many times? Shopping, Miami – spent mad dough and I ain't even slept with him but a few times."

"That was in the beginning when you two first met. You've been dancing for four weeks now and from what you told me a few days ago, he hasn't been coming around and big-spending-it that much anymore."

"I know what I said," she replied, growing more peeved by the second. "But just because he hasn't been able to spend time with me over the past month, doesn't mean I forgot he's a business man. He can't be up under me twenty-four seven."

"True, but now that he has you where he wants you, all of a sudden he's become that much busier. Come on Joy - you ain't new to this shit. Game's supposed to recognize game."

"Luce done spent too much money on me to just be tryna run a game." Poochie dusted crumbs from her denim capri pants as she shook her head. "He bought you. You're an investment. You've probably already recouped the money he spent on you if not more."

A chill ran through Joy's spine. Bringing the expensive bangles back up to her face, she told herself that her friend was just another one of the jealous ones.

Poochie wasn't done yet. "If the money makes you feel better about the situation, then screw what I just said and drain them pockets until they run dry."

Joy was done hearing the garbage being spewed at her.

Sitting up in one rapid movement, she placed her elbows on her knees and gave Poochie an aggravated look.

"He's not using me, Poochie. You supposed to be my girl - how you gonna just come out your face and say something like that?"

"You my homie for life; that's a done deal. But I'm Poshonda Elise Carter all day, every day. I'ma keep it gully."

Her throat suddenly went dry. Joy licked her lips, attempted to swallow some spit.

"Keep it gully all you want, just don't knock my hustle in the process."

"Whatever, Joy. It's not that serious. You're gonna do what you want regardless."

"It is that serious because from the very beginning, I bet you been looking down your nose at me like I'm some ho."

Poochie licked the pretzel's flavor from her thumb and rolled her eyes as her own aggravation finally came out. "Nobody said anything about you being a ho. But shit, if it's weighing that heavy on your chest, maybe it is what it is."

With cold eyes, Joy penetrated the girl she'd thought was her friend. Poochie stared back with the same amount of intensity. An iron wall had succeeded in rising up between the two of them. Poochie could care less about how Joy wanted to handle the truth. She hadn't tried to purposely throw salt in her friend's eyes, but Joy was determined to see it that way and there was nothing she could do about that.

Thick skin was never a thing Joy lacked, yet Poochie's words had nicked the surface. There was some pain that came with the scratches and she couldn't tell which hurt more – the sting of Poochie calling her a stupid ho or the possibility that she had in fact allowed Luce to use her under false pretenses. For years she'd made it her mission to always be the one in control. Vowed, ever since she'd stabbed Blue's boyfriend to death, that no man would ever violate her in any way. Poochie was trying to say she'd failed this time around. Joy wanted to smack the smug, self- righteous expression right off her grill. No one was going to disrespect her and lead her to believe she'd been played.

"You're the one who had a baby at fifteen and don't know who your baby daddy is," Joy said. "So, if anybody's a ho, that would be you."

"Excuse me?" Poochie exclaimed as her eyebrows shot up.

"You heard right."

"I'm really thinking you need to chill right now."

"Nah, since you wanna keep it gully. I'm sick of you sitting there acting like you're better than me. I was tryna help you out, tryna get you in on some real dough in your pockets. Instead, you wanna talk greasy when you don't even know the deal between me and Luce."

Poochie's forehead crinkled, her face showing how miffed she was. "I think I'm better? You're the one who brought Ja'Nya and her father up. Yes, I did a lot of wild things back in the day and having Ja'Nya and not being sure who her father is, is one. But that was four years ago and now I'm trying to handle my business like a grown-ass woman. That's a lot more than I can say for you, ho. And yes I'm saying it now – you's a ho."

Joy was ready to dish out an uppercut. If it was any other female who'd got at her that way, there would be no more talking, only knuckles across her face. But this was her girl. Her ace who'd just, point-blank, called her a ho. Joy knew their friendship would be forever damaged if she laid a finger on Poochie. She was her only friend. The only person she'd ever had who even remotely understood her and could put up with her attitude. She willed her fists to calm down.

"Bounce, bitch. And on your way to the door, let it marinate: I'm a forty thousand dollar ho unlike you. Maybe if you were one too, you could afford to move out of your mama's apartment and take care of your kid like a real mother should. For someone who can't name their baby daddy, maybe being a ho isn't such a bad idea. You definitely got experience."

Putting her sneakers on her feet, Poochie looked up with a wild look in her eyes and glared at Joy as if ready to strike.

"No wonder Luce had no problem getting you to take your clothes off for a couple dollars - you're pitiful. It's easy to take a pitiful little girl and get her to believe she's somebody if she strips to her ashy behind," she said and walked to the front door. Joy crossed her arms to cover up her trembling hands.

"Jealousy is not a good look on you boo," she replied.

Poochie opened the door and yelled over her shoulder, "And you being a dumb ho isn't cute either."

* * *

It was a half past eight in the evening and Joy was still doing her best to shake Poochie's voice from her head. Luce hadn't returned her calls all day. She'd called him twice after Poochie's early departure, but obviously he had more important things to do other than return her call.

Now that he has you where he wants you, all of a sudden he's become that much busier.

Joy sucked her teeth and blasted the volume on Hot 97. The station was playing Ne-Yo's new cut and she was all for getting lost in his voice at the moment. Mellowing out only lasted for a minute. Once the commercials started playing, she was back to being antsy and annoyed. She turned the volume down and convinced herself to give it one more try. The endless ringing persisted. But just before she decided to hang up, the familiar "Yo" echoed in her ear. She smiled at the sound.

"Yo? Where you been? I know you seen that I called you," Joy replied as casually as she could.

"Joy, baby, you know I make moves."

BROKEN WITH STAINS

Yes, she knew this. Knew he was a busy man who was in a different city almost every day. But after barely speaking to him for the longest time, she really didn't care.

"I'm saying, I didn't forget that you gotta handle your business, but I was hoping we could chill tonight or something. It's been a minute since we linked up."

His silence lingered in the air a second too long for Joy's comfort.

"Tonight?" he asked, finally.

Joy bit her bottom lip, tried to decipher his tone. "Yeah. Wassup for tonight?"

"Tonight's no good. Got some stuff I have to take care of."

Biting her lip harder, she could feel her face get warm. No more waiting - she wanted to see him now. The longing was getting ugly. It had been too long since she'd felt his body pressed against hers. But how could she get that across to him without sounding desperate?

"Stop playing, Luce. Don't front like you don't miss me. I can see that tear falling from your eye right now," Joy smiled into the phone.

He gave up a slight laugh at her slick sense of humor. "You're something else."

Joy waited for him to say more. Something like, "We can get up at around nine. Put something sexy on, we'll be drinking lovely tonight." But all he said was, "I'ma get at you later. I got something important I need to take care of."

She couldn't believe he was brushing her off again.

"Yeah – later," she said sulking and hung up the phone.

Now that he has you where he wants you, he's become that much busier.

Joy cursed Poochie under her breath, pulled herself from the bed, stripped off her baby blue velour short set, and tossed her red lace underwear to the side. She headed to the bathroom naked and stood in front of the long mirror against the back of the bathroom door. Taking a long, hard look at her body she checked off all the things she loved. No stretch marks. Smooth legs. Perfectly trimmed Brazilian. She couldn't spot any visible scars.

"His ass must be crazy letting all this go to waste. Got something to take care of . . . please. What could be more important than me?"

She turned to view herself from the back. There'd been numerous men who had dropped everything they were doing the moment her number showed up on their phones. She was looking at one of the reasons. No dimples in her behind, just pure, smooth, gorgeous, delightfully plump skin.

"And you Poochie - you jealous hood booger - can kiss every beautiful inch of it," Joy laughed as she smacked her backside.

She moved to the tub and decided she'd treat herself to a bubble bath instead of her routine shower. Inhaling the pear scent as if it were a drug, she watched the tub fill with the soft, white bubbly foam.

A twinge of sadness caught her off guard. Joy didn't know why the running water suddenly made her think of Blue's boyfriend sticking his hand in the shower so long ago. Didn't know why her absent father was the next thought to follow. Why was he making an effort now? Blood was on her hands because he'd never been around to protect her. Why hadn't he rescued her back then? Been there to chase away the savage hands on nights they came to terrorize? It made no sense now for him to swoop down when all the damage had been done. As she sat on the tub's edge and absentmindedly waded her hand through the rising water, she wondered if she'd blindly let Luce pick up where her mother's dead boyfriend left off. She'd peeped the fact that she wasn't high on his priority list right now. Joy figured, after her bath, she could call one of the other dudes she used to mess with on the regular. But in her heart, she didn't feel like being bothered. None of them compared to

BROKEN WITH STAINS

Luce. After being with the top-of-the-top, she wasn't in the mood to regress.

Dipping a foot into the water, the warmness signaled it was time to step in. She eased her body back against the tub's interior, relaxed for a moment, and then, without reason, submerged herself underneath the coating of white foam. Joy counted while she held her breath. And even when her lungs felt as if they would explode, she held the air in just a little bit longer.

On the real Joy, I think Luce just brought you in to make money off of you.

Joy's inflamed lungs weren't enough to make her give up the fight.

He bought you. You're an investment. You've probably already recouped the money he spent on you if not more.

Dizziness was slipping in and she could taste the water seeping into the slightly opened corners of her mouth.

No wonder Luce had no problem getting you to take your clothes off for a couple dollars - you're pitiful . . . And you being a dumb ho isn't cute either.

She knew she was on the verge of passing out, but felt the need to torture herself for a few seconds more. Just a few seconds more. And then a few seconds more of pain to distract her from the mounting sadness she wanted nothing to do with. A few seconds more of submersion to mask the tears that mingled with the cleansing water.

28 paul

Paul could smell the light scent of Camilla's sweet perfume wafting throughout the large kitchen. As hungry as he was at the moment, his wife smelled and looked more appetizing than the plate filled to the brim with the Sunday morning breakfast of omelets, ham, and plantains she'd placed before him.

He loved every part of the woman who stood at the sink. Even as she moved around the sizeable kitchen speaking words of heartfelt encouragement to him, he was having a hard time concentrating on what Camilla said. Paul was utterly in awe of her. Here he was, feeling doomed and defeated that he hadn't heard from any of his girls. And here she was cooking him a huge breakfast and telling him to relax because God had everything under control. Without missing a beat, Camilla moved about the kitchen, cleaning up and reassuring him that his daughters just needed time to let the idea of meeting him settle in.

He felt selfish. Felt that over the past few months he hadn't done enough special things for her. Things such as taking her out to dinner, leaving sweet notes, buying surprise gifts, and other things along those lines. Things he'd always done since the first time they met. Lately, he'd been overwhelmingly consumed with how to reconnect with his daughters and why he hadn't heard from them yet.

"When are you going to do it?" Camilla asked, shaking Paul out of his troubled thoughts.

"Do what?"

She placed a steaming mug of black coffee next to her husband's plate, the soft layers of hair falling around her face as she tilted her head towards him. "You haven't been listening to one word I've said."

BROKEN WITH STAINS

"I'm sorry. Just that my baby looks so good this morning, I started daydreaming as I looked at those curves. When am I going to do what?" Camilla smiled at her man, sat down at the table, and took a sip of her Earl Grey tea. "What time are you coming to photograph the spa today? I told the girls to be there by five, but I know you said you could make it by three or four. I wanted to be sure."

"Should be by at three. At least I'm aiming for three, if not, no later than three-thirty. This is probably the shortest and smallest wedding I've ever had to photograph."

"How small is it?"

"Only fifteen guests. And I gotta be at the park in an hour and a half - it starts at nine. Then they're having a brunch reception at Sadie's restaurant."

"Sadie's the woman whose wedding you photographed a few weeks back, right? Where you ran into your daughter's aunt?"

"Yeah." Paul scratched his small goatee, discomforted at the thought of Rinni's piercing eyes. "They're good friends of Sadie's and so, they're having the reception at her restaurant for a couple hours. I'll be taking some photos there too, which'll be quick 'cause they have to be out of there by two. I should definitely be at the spa by three, three-thirty."

"Alright then. That'll give you enough time to set up before everyone gets there. I think this is only the second time I've opened up the spa on a Sunday since it opened."

"When was the other time?"

"Remember when Joyce threw her sister the surprise party there a couple of years back?"

"Okay."

"Yeah, that was the last time. Today I just hope everything goes smoothly."

"Why wouldn't it?" he asked, sipping from the steaming cup.

"I'm sure it will, but I guess I'm a little excited about

getting the website up and running. The web designer showed me a preliminary mock-up of the site and it's really good. The site's colors are chocolate- brown, a pastel peach, and white. A few green touches here and there. Simple and clean, but modern at the same time. I'm so happy with it."

Paul smiled as he watched his wife talk about the new website being built for her day spa. He loved her attention to detail and how she made the ordinary extraordinary.

"Now all that's missing are the great photos you're going to take this afternoon, but once that's all done, the site will be good to go in a week or so." She beamed a joyful smile at him. "I'm so excited."

"I'm excited for you too, babe," he said reaching over to kiss her cheek. "The spa has come a long way - I'm proud of you. Three years in August, I knew it would be a success."

She stroked the back of his veined hand. "I couldn't have ever done it without you." Paul drained the last bit of coffee and put his mug down on the table. He stared at it as if he were waiting for it to tell him something profound.

"It's only been a few days," Camilla said, taking off the gingham top from over her sleeveless blouse.

"A few days that might as well be an eternity."

"Stop it. Nothing happens overnight. Rome wasn't built in a day, remember?"

"Yeah, I know that. But, I just want to start building something with the girls today. How . . . why did I take so long?"

"You were scared."

"I was a coward."

"Stop beating yourself up. Please stop that mess right now. The important thing is that you're finally taking a step forward."

"A step I should've taken years ago. My girls are grown. I don't have any pictures. If I passed them on the street, I wouldn't even know they were my children."

BROKEN WITH STAINS

Camilla stirred her tea and let her husband sort his way through his agony. As much as she hated to see him be so hard on himself, she figured it was his way of coming to terms with the reality of what he'd done all those years ago.

"You know what Sienna's mother told me on the phone? She told me that Sienna graduated magna cum laude from St. John's University. My daughter walked across the stage at her college graduation three years ago and I was nowhere to be found. I feel like a complete farce even calling her my daughter. Like I had something to do with her success."

Camilla continued to stir and combed her fingers through her thick, shoulder-length hair.

"Joy's mother told me she moved out of her house little more than three years ago. Living on her own and making it in this world by herself since she was sixteen. What could have made her leave home so early, Camilla? Why wasn't I there to take her in if she needed to leave her mother's house that bad?"

Sipping the warm liquid, Camilla studied the afflicted look on Paul's face.

"And Noelle's mother? Put it this way: she'd put gasoline and a match to the phone if she found out I was on the other end ever again. I have to find out about my child through her aunt. The one woman who hated . . . Noelle's aunt is helping me more than I could've imagined. Told me that Noelle's a young woman now, but there's nothing wrong with me introducing myself."

He distractedly circled the rim of his mug with his index finger as he leaned forward on his elbows. "How am I supposed to be a father to three young women after all these years?"

"Trust God to show you," Camilla said, breaking her silence.

Paul looked over at his wife as if he suddenly remembered she was sitting there. She took his mug and went over to the coffee maker to refill it. Paul watched her movements and silently thanked her for the simple reminder. At least one of them had internalized Pastor Fisher's sermons. It was that plain. That concise. It was important to start daily refills of faith if he ever wanted his fear to go away. Paul knew he would have to think of something extra special to show Camilla how much he appreciated her for being his biggest supporter, always pushing him forward.

* * *

"Last shot, last shot." The models sat back in the peach leather spa chairs and smiled with mud-masked faces. They were the picture of relaxation and tranquility as Paul wrapped up the photo shoot. "Thanks, ladies," he said, bringing the session to a close.

The three women smiled at him and went to change out of green robes and into their clothes. Camilla walked over and hugged the man she loved. "Thank you, love. Can't wait to see them up on the website."

"No prob. You know anything for my baby."

"I'm going into my office to find a few papers I need to take home with me. You need anything? Something to drink?"

"No, I'm okay. You go on back and I'll just wrap up things out here." Paul began packing up his equipment. The other spa employees were gone once he'd finished taking their photos earlier. He was almost done getting things together by the time two of the models walked out and said their goodbyes.

A few minutes later, out came the last model, her bouncy natural curls, a fan around her head. "Thank you, Paul. It was fun working with you," she said sweetly. "Do you have a card? I'm getting married in four months and I've yet to find a photographer."

"Congratulations. It was my pleasure working with you too, Ashley. The camera loves you even with mud all over your face, so I know you'll make a very beautiful bride."

BROKEN WITH STAINS

They laughed together as Paul reached for his wallet, pulled out a business card, and handed it to her.

"Thank you. I'm so nervous about the wedding already. All these last minute preparations are driving me nuts."

"Don't worry. Just focus on the joy of the day. Call me and my assistant will set up an appointment for you to come by the studio and go over my portfolio. You can even view some of it online, just visit the address at the bottom of the card."

"I'll be doing that very soon, but from looking at these photos on the walls, I'm pretty sure I want you to photograph my big day." Her eyes scanned the room. "They're really nice."

Paul looked over at the photo closest to him on the wall to his right. He'd taken it, along with all the others, just before Camilla's grand opening of the spa.

They were photos of a stunning variety of black women. Different skin tones, shapes, and sizes holding various flowers in bloom. It was Camilla's idea to showcase the amazing range of women in order to get one simple message across: Women who habitually pampered themselves, transformed into ageless beauties. He was happy that he'd succeeded in capturing that on film.

"Well, in that case, I look forward to working with you soon," Paul answered.

"Definitely. I'll bring my fiancée by so we can discuss prices. He's an accountant, so he's always keeping an eye on the dollar. I wish I could be more like him because I know I spend like nobody's business. Anyway, he gets it from his father. Who knows? Maybe if I grew up with my father he would've taught me not to be such a spender too."

She laughed it off, but Paul wanted to know more. "Oh, so your mom raised you on her own?"

"No, actually my grandmother did. My mom's mom raised me. My mother passed away when I was a year old. My father was young - he didn't know what to do with a kid in diapers. Handed me over to my grandmother and then disappeared." Paul took a closer look at the young woman before him. In her mid to late twenties, her sincere brown eyes held no sadness behind them. He'd heard her say her father disappeared on her. So why did she look so calm, collected, and undisturbed?

"How do you feel about that, if you don't mind me asking?"

"About my father not being around when I was younger?"

"Yeah. I don't mean to intrude -"

"It's fine," she said shrugging his words off. "You're actually the first person who's ever asked me that question, believe it or not. I'll admit it was rough at times. My grandmother was the best, made sure I had everything. Still, there were times I questioned my father's love for me. He sent birthday and Christmas cards and that was it. I would've given anything for him to show up on my doorstep though."

Paul looked down at the floor. He was uncomfortable watching the disappointment that had started to creep into her eyes like storm clouds making their way across the sky. She continued, "I knew he wasn't dead or physically disabled and I think that made it worse. Just to know nothing was physically holding him back and he made no effort to see me . . . it hurt."

He raised his gaze to her again. The way her voice changed at the end prompted him to search her face. There he saw memories. Sad and distant ones that had started to replay in her mind.

"But a couple of years ago, he stepped back into my life. We're making progress every day." She smiled and put a hand to her chest. "I was a little skeptical of him at first, but on the other hand, I can't lie - I was happy that my daddy showed up. No matter what, he's my father. I couldn't fight forgiving him when he apologized for not being there."

Paul cleared his throat. "That's good to hear. Gives me hope."

BROKEN WITH STAINS

Her knitted brows told him she was confused about his comment.

"I, um . . . am in a similar situation as your father. You saying that you've forgiven him definitely lifts my spirit."

Awareness covered her face. "I see. If you don't mind me asking *you* now . . . why'd you leave your child behind?"

"I left children behind. Three daughters. And I did it because . . . because I was scared. Men aren't supposed to be scared, but it took me a while to fess up to myself that I was scared of loss."

"And why is that?"

Paul hardly knew the woman who stood before him and had only told Camilla the true reason as to why he'd been so quick to run. He imagined all three of his daughters standing in Ashley's place before him. She'd lost her father for a time too and Paul was sure his daughters had experienced many of the same emotions.

"I suffered a tragedy when I was nine. It's not something I like to talk about, but it's something that played a major part in the decisions I made throughout my life."

"I'm sorry to hear that," she said, unsure of what she was sorry about. He looked beyond her as if seeing the fire play out against the walls.

"It's hard when you lose all that you know as a child. So, as I got older I was afraid to suffer that kind of loss again. There was always the thought in the back of my mind that I could lose someone I'd gotten close to at any given moment. Was just always easier for me to walk away before things got too deep."

He looked at her face once again. "I regret it, deeply. Missing out on my girls' lives. Wish I could turn back the hands of time, as they say."

Ashley pushed a huge pair of sunglasses further back on her head and sighed, "There's no way you can turn back time, so it's best to look to the future. If your girls are open to a future with you, you can do tons of great things with it. How old are they?"

"The oldest is twenty-four. The other two are twenty-one and nineteen."

"Close in age. So you were with their mother for a while then."

"No," Paul said, pausing before he unveiled the rest. "They're by three different women."

Ashley's eyes quickly darted to the floor then up at him again.

He had to clear things up. "Women were disposable to me. I was young, restless, arrogant, but mostly scared. Even when I didn't want to leave these women, I still told myself that starting over would be easier than hanging on to face an uncertain future. And then I grew up when I met Camilla Marie. Got bit hard by that infamous love bug."

They chuckled, both familiar with how that sucker worked. When their laughter subsided she looked into his eyes and squinted as if trying as best she could to see what hid deep within them. "What do you regret most about being absent from their lives?"

He thought for a moment. There were many things he'd been remorseful of. Numerous things that'd tormented him over the years. Yet, Paul never took the time to consider the number one thing that he regretted most.

The weight on his upper body seemed to grow and he remembered the camera bag on his shoulder. He heaved it up further to shift the weight. That one gesture gave him the answer. "I regret not being able to pick them up when they fell."

She was silent as she listened for him to explain further. "I wasn't able to be a support. A reliable hand they could count on. What's a man if he's not reliable? What's a man if he's not a provider when he's supposed to be? He's not a man at all."

"Well, it takes a man to admit when he's wrong," she

stated matter-of-factly.

For a second he turned that remark over in his head.

"I recently tried to get in contact with my three girls," Paul shared. "I reached out to two of their mothers. One's aunt. Haven't heard back from any of them yet."

"How long ago?"

"About four weeks."

"Give'em some time. It's an adjustment in their minds. You came out of nowhere. My father did the same to me."

"But, you're on the road to recovery."

"Yes indeed. But trust, it wasn't an immediate thing."

"But, it happened."

"It's happening."

"Happening. That's what counts most, right?"

"No, actually it's not."

Paul eyed her thoughtfully and asked the question he felt could be the key to his future.

"If that doesn't count most, what does?"

"The fact that he took the first step. You can't get anywhere in life if you don't take the first step, Paul. Maybe it was late. But it showed me that my daddy cared after all."

29 noelle

Noelle switched the small phone to vibrate. Tired of the incessant India.Arie ringtone, it was her last option since Chris wouldn't stop calling.

She didn't know why he was trying so hard. If he thought she was ever going to answer his calls again, much less welcome him back into her life, he might as well have prepared himself for the day Michael Jackson rose from the dead. Plain and simple, it just wasn't going to happen.

Even so, Noelle kept her phone close by as she waited for a call from a classmate's mother, a jewelry designer, interested in building a website. As much as she wanted to shut the device off, there was no way she was would let Chris' annoying behavior get in the way of her thriving business.

Noelle stared at the computer screen. For the past hour she'd been working on a new website for a business consultant who was one of Hope's friends. In her attempt to block out the ache of being deceived once again, Chris calling every five minutes wasn't helping one bit. She couldn't concentrate. Not now, not an hour ago, not at all today.

She'd went to school this morning, but left after her second class was over. She wanted to be alone. Void of monotonous teachers, loud students, and anyone else who might bring out her crabby side. Her plan had been to come home and work on a couple of websites she was in the process of creating. Instead, she'd grabbed a peach yogurt from the refrigerator and spent most of her time sitting on the livingroom floor spilling thoughts into the journal she rarely used.

Noelle looked over at the baby blue leather notebook next to the keyboard and picked it up, flipping back to what she'd written only hours before. It was all a big blur. She'd

BROKEN WITH STAINS

written at the speed of light, trying to purge herself of what was killing her inside.

The vibrating phone started up, yelling at her to pick up and answer. She knew who it was before she glanced at the number. Checking the screen proved once again, the source of her heartache was in an unbending mood. Noelle clicked a button to make the music stop, gripped her fingers around the journal, and read all she'd scribbled down.

July 29th – Noelle P. Caldwell

Rotten bastard. That's what I called him because that's what he is. I wish I never met Christopher Patrick Bryant. If there was no him, there would be no me crying and hurting and crying and aching and crying and missing - I hate his punk ass. I hate even more, what I've become at his hands. Never in a million years did I think he'd ever do this to me. My heart's so messed up because I gave it to him without a second thought. Thanks love – now I barely eat. Don't function right anymore. Can't sleep at night like I used to. Can't even think straight half the time. I don't see a way to put back all the pieces I'm in. Every day I shatter more and more. The only thing left to do is write a letter to tell him thank you. Thank you for taking the veil off my eyes after years of thinking shit was sweet. It'll say thank you too, for making me lose all hope in what I thought was real. That is what I'll tell the idiot now that he wants to constantly ring my phone. He won't be hearing my voice anymore, not after I've finally realized his "love" for me wasn't real after all.

She wiped the tears that wet her chin and threw the bound book on the crowded desk. Wiping Chris away from her mind wasn't easy, but she was determined to do it. *No more crying*, she told herself, gathering a deep breath and exhaling to release the negative energy. Focusing on the unfinished page on the screen, Noelle tried to decide what area of the consultant's website she would tackle next. Maybe the biography. She reached for her notes, a list of questions she prepared for each client which always provided enough information for the project at hand. She stared at the picture the consultant had attached to the biography questionnaire. Foretta Cane had thick, dark brown shoulder-length hair, slight brown eyes, big cheeks, and a strong, confident smile. She graduated from Cornell University as an undergraduate. Moved on from NYU with a Masters in Business in 1984. Worked in corporate America for seventeen years, eventually rising to Senior Vice President of a small Advertising Agency. Today, she was married with two children.

Noelle looked at the picture once more. She searched the eyes, analyzed the smile. The woman looked happy. Not fake happy. Happy, happy.

She felt the tears start to burn the back of her eyes for the millionth time. What would it take to get to that happy place again? Noelle didn't see any possible way. Her happy place was with Chris. He was the one she knew she would marry. He was the one she visualized being the father of her children. Happiness was in his arms. Now it had vanished in the blink of an eye; no time soon would there be a smile as bright as Foretta Cane's.

It was a rushing tide of hopelessness that swooped in and overwhelmed her at that second. She was drowning as she banged the desk with her fist over and over and over again. Foretta's confident smile and answers hit the floor. Noelle voluntarily joined them.

Her shoulders rose and shook with each cry that escaped her throat. It wasn't natural to feel this way. To feel emotionally raped by someone you loved with all your heart, mind, and soul. She stretched out on the floor, her arm supporting her head. Images of walking in on Chris in bed with the other girl was like a knife in her gut all over again. She gripped her stomach as a new wave engulfed her entire body. She couldn't help but remember many of the good times they'd shared together. From the simple act of shopping for items for his new apartment to the first Thanksgiving they sat side by side eating dinner at his mother's house. Noelle's tears fell harder at the thought of the time it would take to get past the aching and tears.

The task of separating herself from the guy she loved was not something she had prepared herself for. It suddenly made her wonder if this was what her father had done to her mother, the still woman, who neither said or felt much. The one who barely smiled and had refused to be involved with any man who showed his interest. Bitterness was what Noelle saw in the woman who'd raised her alone. She didn't want the same to consume her own life. The continuous waves that threatened to engulf her at this very moment made the future look bleak. As she fought to keep her head above the waves, Noelle grew weaker with each sob she had no power to keep at bay.

* * *

The abrupt buzzing rattled her out of sleep. Noelle looked from side to side, drunk with fatigue, momentarily forgetting how she'd ended up on the floor. Foretta's smile greeted her. She then remembered the frustration, hurt, and waterworks and how it all became too much to handle.

Bzzzzzzzzzz.

It was just above her head. She swiveled her head upward and saw the tiny red light through a slightly crumpled sheet of paper. It was officially time to curse Chris out. Quickly, Noelle grabbed the phone before her voice mail could activate.

"What?! Why do you keep calling me?"

"Hey, Noelle? What's going on?"

Her eyes bulged in horror. "David?"

"Yeah, it's me. Is everything okay? Did I call at the wrong time?"

She rubbed her head to relieve the pressure that

magnified by the moment. "Sorry, David. I'm fine," she sighed. "Wassup with you?"

"Calling to check up on you, make sure you're okay. It's been a while since we spoke"

"I'm . . . hanging in there."

"You sure? That doesn't sound too good."

"No, it's . . . I'm cool. What are you up to today?"

"Right now I'm relaxing at home since I'm off today. Just came back from the gym and picking up some things at the supermarket. What about you?"

"Actually, I just woke up. Went to school earlier and I'd like to go to the supermarket myself later, but I keep hearing this funny noise under the hood of my car, so I'm trying to lay off it a bit," Noelle said, rising up from the floor.

"How long has it being making noises?"

"A couple days now."

"You should get that checked out before it gets worse."

"I'm not trying to spend a lot of money right now - it better not get worse."

David laughed at her speedy reply. "It won't if you let me come over and check it out for you. You cool peoples, so I'll do it free of charge this time."

"Yeah? Just this one time?" Noelle asked, finally breaking out a semi-smile. "If I'm good peoples it should be a lifetime guarantee."

"It could be."

She briefly wondered whether or not she should address that comment, but decided against it. "I don't want you to go out of your way. It's your day off."

"If it was out of my way I wouldn't be offering to help. It's no problem, but that's only if you want me to come over. It's completely up to you."

"Well, I'll take you up on your offer this one time. You know, since I'm good peoples and all."

"Thanks for accepting," he laughed. "I'll see you in an

hour."

* * *

Noelle watched him approach her car in his dark stonewashed jeans and white t-shirt. She felt herself smiling, but quickly faked a cough with her hand over her mouth to cover it up.

"Look at this pretty lady," he said, reaching out his arms to hug her. She was caught off guard by his display of affection, but returned it just the same. It was a great feeling as his arms enveloped her close to him. So close, she inhaled his fragrant cologne and immediately relaxed. The smell alone made her want to stay near for as long as possible.

They separated from the embrace. "What cologne is that?" she asked, still wanting to lean in for another sniff.

"Unforgivable," he said, taking a smell of his shirt.

Noelle almost laughed at the unnecessary move. "Smells good."

"Thanks. Glad you like," David replied, displaying his perfect teeth. *Never had a cavity a day in his life.* She pulled her eyes from his mouth and turned towards her car.

"So, this is the death trap," she said tapping the hood.

"Death trap? I doubt it's that serious. Let's take a look."

He raised the hood of the car. "So what's the problem?"

She stared at his back, watched the muscles in his shoulders rotate and rise as he checked the car parts.

"What problem? I don't have a problem."

He stopped his movements and slowly turned his head to stare up at her. "So, you're not having car trouble?"

"Oh. Yeah, um, there's trouble with the car. I thought you were talking about me personally. Don't mind me. Um, yeah, the car sometimes does this weird vibration thingy when I'm driving. It doesn't happen too often, but it bothers me when it does." She wanted to lift up a corner of the sidewalk and crawl right underneath. Moving closer to the car, she tried not to let her embarrassment show.

"Let me just check it out a little bit," he said turning once again to inspect what was before him. "But, what's the problem?"

Now it was her turn to look at him as if his brain was chemically unbalanced. "I just told you the problem."

"The problem with your car, yes. But now I'm talking about what's bothering you."

"I'm good."

"You wouldn't lie to me, would you?"

"No . . . I mean . . . why wouldn't I be?"

"I don't know - you tell me. Looks like the break fluid is low."

"So, I look like I have a problem?" Noelle asked, trying to rearrange the look on her face.

"I didn't say you look like you have a problem, but you obviously thought I was referring to something else when I questioned you just a minute ago."

"I guess I was daydreaming or something."

"About me? I'm so flattered." He removed himself from under the hood and flashed Noelle a playful smile. "For real though, if there's something on your mind, you can talk to a brotha."

"Even if there was something on my mind, what would you be able to do about it?"

"All you need is a bottle of break fluid. I'll pick up some for you at AutoZone. That's one problem solved. As for the other one, I won't be able to help you unless you tell me the deal."

"David, I'm good. I'm good. Really, I am." She felt it coming, but thought she could be strong enough to fight. It wasn't until the tear slid down her cheek that she realized she should have turned her back sooner.

BROKEN WITH STAINS

Noelle felt his hand on her shoulder. Again he was close. It was something she needed and didn't want at the same time. Now she felt his soothing breath on her ear. "Come here," he whispered.

She swatted at her eyes, ashamed that she'd allowed him to see her this way. Turning to face him, she couldn't look him in the eyes.

"I can't right now."

"I'll give you space if you really need it Noelle, but I'm here for you if you want to sit and talk about whatever it is that's making you cry."

More tears fell as she took a chance and let her eyes meet his. "I've just been going through some things. It's . . . nothing I want to burden you with."

He grabbed her hand and led her to the concrete front steps of her house. Resigned, she took a seat on the top step, resting her back against the railing. David sat next to her, legs spread apart with elbows on his knees. "Talk to me."

Noelle tried to smile. The attempt fell short as thoughts of her situation shrouded her like a cloak. "It's a big mess."

"What?" he asked.

"My life. It's all a mess."

"How did that happen?"

"I -," she paused and swallowed the ball of air that was suddenly making it hard to breathe, "I lost the love of my life. We broke up a little more than a month ago and I've been doing everything in my power to find a way to get over him. It's been too hard though."

"So that's the attitude I couldn't understand."

"Yeah, that's it."

"I'm sorry to hear that."

"Don't be. Don't know why I'm even talking to you about him."

"Why not? If it makes you feel better to get it off your chest, you should."

"Yeah, I guess."

"And, one question."

"What's that?"

"If it's just a breakup with your ex, what's that have to do with your life being a mess?"

"Did you hear what I just said? He was . . . I thought he was the love of my life. He crushed me. Dogged me. And he's not here anymore. As bad as it sounds that I still even care, it's hard for me to just get over someone I deeply loved and put my trust in."

"Well, how did he dog you?"

Noelle thought about whether she should reveal the truth or not. He looked sincere enough, though she was still skeptical. But what was there to lose? She'd already lost the one thing she wanted most. "I caught him in bed with some other chick. He was cheating on me with her and a few others. And all along I was just too blind and stupid to see it."

"Whoa, Noelle. Who are you mad at, him or yourself?"

She stayed silent as she swiped away another tear.

David tried again. "How long were the two of you together?"

"Two years. Two long, wasted years."

"Couldn't have been wasted. Obviously it meant something to you - you're sitting here crying."

She cocked her head as she slapped her thigh in frustration. "Yeah, well thanks for pointing that out."

David grabbed her hand. "Cry Noelle. I'm not downing you for that. It's just one of the ways you have to let the pain out."

"How long do I have to keep letting the pain out? I loved that stupid boy. My feelings were sincere. My love was deep. It's gonna take forever and a day for me to let all of it out."

"And some of that love might always be there. But with time - and prayer - it definitely won't be as strong."

BROKEN WITH STAINS

"Not something I wanna hear when I just want to get over him completely."

"I'm not going to sit here and lie to you, but I don't want you to not look at all the possibilities either."

"I just keep wondering what I did to deserve this. Never in my life have I experienced this much hurt and I don't want even a little bit of love for him to stick around."

"I wish there was something I could do to take that from you."

"I wish there was something you could do too," she said, playing with her hands.

"There's not much I could tell you right now to make you feel better because it seems like you invested your whole heart into your relationship with this dude. When it comes to matters of the heart, healing has to take its course. God works that all out if you ask Him to and believe it will be done." He gently wiped a tear from Noelle's chin as he finished, "What I will say though, is that you're a beautiful woman with a beautiful spirit and what might look like a mess now, is really just a temporary setback. Look at you. You're in school, got a great personality, and like I said before, you're beautiful. Your life isn't a mess, if anything, it's even better now because you don't have a useless nut around anymore to distract you. He didn't deserve you."

"I know he didn't deserve me," she said looking him in the face. "At least now I know. It's just that sometimes I can't help thinking about the good times we had together. All those times we were cool . . . it's like it all meant nothing. When I think about that, it's crushes me every single time."

David's eyes scorched into her own as he said, "You'll create new memories with someone who truly loves you." He looked away before continuing, "I'll keep it real - there's a ton of men out there who are dogs. They're walking the streets unchained and on the prowl every day. But there's a few good men out there and when the time comes for you to meet yours, you'll mos' def know he's the one."

Noelle chuckled. "Yeah, but in the mean time, I sit here and die a slow death."

"In the mean time you stay positive by living your life for you. Don't give no man the power to turn your life into a mess. A dog will always be a dog, but a real man knows when he has a great woman by his side. He knows that a real woman makes him better because the females who lack focus aren't good for more than one thing."

She let his truth seep in and quietly filed it in a safe place.

David gave her some more things to put with it. "I don't know all the details, but it's obvious you felt something special for him. You're human. Don't be so hard on yourself for falling in love. People fall in love every day. Love is a risk and no one is immune to its effects. You just have to take this experience as a lesson and use it to your advantage for times that lay ahead."

"I try to look at it like that," Noelle answered, more relaxed now that the tears had finally stopped. "I'm trying to move on and not let it all affect me, but now, he won't stop calling. It's literally driving me crazy. It's not easy getting over a broken heart and he's not making it any easier. Every time I see his number pop up, it's a reminder all over again of everything this fool did to me. We know some of the same people and I can't even hang out with them like I used to because I'm scared he might come around. Sometimes I just feel screwed on so many levels. But I'm trying to look on the bright side of it all and I know there's a reason I'm going through it right now. There has to be."

"You remind me of myself a few years ago," David said, looking over at the two-way street. "In what way?" Noelle wanted to know.

"Me and my brother," he paused reflecting back on the memories. "Crazy times we had, boy. I was feeling the same way you are now, like my problems would never go away."

"Your brother cheated on you too?"

They shared a laugh at her attempt to lighten the mood.

"My brother stole my identity when I was fifteen. Credit cards were opened, even tried to buy a house in my name."

"Your own brother?"

"My own brother. Since he came out the womb he's been a manipulator, a snake, a con artist, every grimy thing you can think of."

"Damn." First, Aunt Rinni's mother sliced her in the chest. Now, David's brother stole his identity. The people around her had gone through pretty wild stuff.

"Around that time, it all got so crazy," David told her. "We came to blows and I got to the point where I thought I was gonna lose my mind. This was supposed to be my flesh and blood and here he was ruining my name. I had bill collectors calling me, my credit was being murdered, bank account was all messed up. I was to my breaking point when I found out he was behind it."

"We all go through things, huh?" Noelle said, in shock.

"And that's just the half. I went through so much, Noelle, it's draining just thinking about it. But here I am today."

"You seem real good for someone who dealt with so much drama."

"Like I told you before - time and prayer. That's what it took. I had nobody to turn to when I was dealing with this stuff. My parents were dead. My aunt who raised me was on crack. I wanted to kill him, had a nine and everything. The only reason that plan fell through is because, on my way to my brother's apartment, I got into a car accident. My jeep crashed into a guard rail on the highway – whole thing flipped over."

Noelle looked at the long, thin scar above his right eyebrow.

TAMARA BURKE

"So that's where that cut comes from."

"I was in a coma for a week, collapsed lung, all that. But you know what? Even though I had a loaded gun in my car with me at the time of the accident, I was never questioned by the police about it. It wasn't registered, I knew nothing about the guy I got it from. Who knows how many bodies were attached to that piece. But nothing, I came out of the hospital and even now, haven't heard one word about it. God had a plan for my life."

"You are one lucky bastard."

He laughed with a fist to his mouth before answering, "No, it's not luck. I recognized the car accident was nothing but a blessing. Sounds crazy, I know, but I could be locked up behind that split decision. Wasting years behind bars for a brother who has never been family to me. It's beyond a blessing, Noelle. And your situation is a blessing too."

"And I suppose it's also a blessing that my father walked out of my life when I was a baby and now wants to come back."

He looked at her as she examined the cracks in the concrete.

"Every man has a story," he said joining in on the examination. "You don't know why he did what he did. Whatever it is, doesn't make it right. Still, there's always something behind the actions we can't understand. No matter what, he's still your father."

"And what's your definition of a father? Because my definition is telling me I never had one."

"I can't change your feelings. Just remember that he's still here. My father's been dead since I was five. If I could have a piece of him back, I'd take it."

"If you could have a real relationship with your brother, would you take that?"

"Honestly, even after all he's done to me . . . I most likely would . . . I've forgiven him."

BROKEN WITH STAINS

"You're not for real, are you? Because I know I wouldn't. It can't be that easy to forgive."

"Remember I said something about wanting to kill him? That was a couple years of anger pent up inside. It wasn't easy letting it go, but I had to ask myself: Where is this anger getting me? Deep down I knew it wasn't getting me nowhere, so I had no choice but to let it go. I'm not saying I didn't battle the memories and the side effects from the identity theft and all the other stuff he did to me over the years, but I had to forgive him if I wanted to move past it."

Noelle thought about all the sadness Chris had caused her. Thought about all the times she'd longed for a father so that she could be daddy's little girl.

"I was carrying so much hostility inside. The best thing to do was just leave and get my mind right. I got out of the hospital and something told me to get as far away from my brother as I could. After that, I went to stay with a cousin who lived down south.

One night, I was sitting at the kitchen table eating, and out of nowhere, my cousin handed me a Bible and said "Read it, man".

I threw it to the side at first. Then one day, it got to such a crucial point where there was nothing I could think to do and no one else to turn to. My credit was still shot, though my brother was in jail and I had contacted different companies to clear it up. At the same time, my stubborn pride wouldn't let anyone know how bad I was hurting. I was ready to get another gun and put it to my own head. But that Bible thrown down on the floor of my room kept staring up at me. I must've purposely stepped on that thing a million times until finally, I had no choice but to pick it up."

David paused and smiled at the memory. "I started reading and reading and I never stopped. Started going to a church down the block from my cousin's house. My cousin never went with me either. That dude partied, gambled, but I guess he felt that I had more of a need than he did. I thank God for him too, because I walked into that church on the corner and my eyes were opened. I didn't change completely right away; it took me a while to get to where I am now. But look at me," he opened his arms wide. "I'm here telling you how I got through."

Noelle gained a new admiration for the guy she wouldn't even let take her out for ice cream. He didn't look like the same tormented person he'd described in his recollection.

"Was it all worth it?" she asked. "From then to where you are now?"

"When I was going through, I couldn't see it. But I thank God for my obstacles and where I am now."

"Damn," was all she could think to say.

"What?"

"You're trying to tell me I need to forgive those two assholes or else I rot in hell."

He smiled, looked at her, and shook his head. "Noelle, I'm telling you that everything that needs to be overcome has to start with forgiveness. It could be forgiving the people who've wronged you or even yourself. How can you move forward if you don't let go of the past? It's impossible, pretty lady."

She sighed at David's logic with a compliment thrown in for good measure.

"I probably have dried tears plastered all over my face. Yup, I'm a real pretty lady I bet."

"Yes you are," he grinned.

"You really think so?"

"Definitely."

"Well, then it's such a shame."

"And why is that?"

"What good is pretty if it couldn't keep the men I needed the most in my life?"

30 sienna

I have every right. Sienna repeated the same thing to herself five more times, moved the index card closer to the phone, and picked up the receiver to make the call. With Tandi missing from class - three days back-to-back and no reason why - it was time to talk to someone who should be aware of what was going down. That was the right thing to do.

Nevertheless, a bad angel sat comfortably on Sienna's left shoulder. It nagged and spit. Poked and whispered, *You need to mind your own damn business, Burgess. She'll learn on her own.* Sienna looked down at the phone number long and hard. Seeing her hesitation, the good angel whispered something entirely different from the right. *Intervene now before it becomes too late. You're more than her teacher, you're an agent for change.*

Since the crack of dawn, both voices had been playing tug-of-war with her conscience. Her watch currently read a quarter to eleven and now she felt as if her head would explode. Something needed to be done. She looked at the olive telephone sitting on the beat-up wooden desk and reasoned with herself, *It's a matter of life and death - just grab the phone and get it over with.* Sienna let that thought push her closer to the edge of the desk. She looked to the door of the small teacher's lounge. It was third period, the perfect chance for her to do this since she seemed to be the only teacher in the building who didn't have a class at the moment.

On the first ring, her heart skipped a beat. On the second ring, she couldn't tell if she was still breathing. On the third ring, she wondered why she was being ridiculously nervous in the first place. On the fourth ring, she nearly choked on her spit when the familiar voice came through on the other end of the line. "Hello?"

"Ah, yes," Sienna croaked out, "may I speak with Ms.

Black please?"

"Which one? There's more than one in this house."

"Ms. Dershine Black," Sienna said, beating a pencil against her bottom lip.

"She's not here, who's this?"

The moment of truth had arrived. "Uh, Tandi, it's . . . Ms. Burgess . . . I haven't seen you in three days." Sienna cringed as she waited for the reply.

"And? You're calling to what? Snitch on me to my moms?"

"It's not about snitching -"

"You know, I saw the school's number pop up on the caller ID and why am I not surprised it's you up to some mess."

"I'm concerned for you. You and your . . . boyfriend . . . it's not healthy. You're missing school. Isn't your education more important to you than some boy who hurts you?"

"I guess you forgot our last conversation 'cause you're begging to get your ass kicked." Sienna ran cold hands over her thin yellow silk skirt and endeavored to put a little bass in her voice.

"The threats need to stop. I'm your teacher, you lay a finger on me and you'll be arrested."

"Ooooh, I'm so scared," Tandi mocked. "So scared I think I'll reach through the phone and slap your stupid ass right now."

"Tandi -" Sienna tried.

"Don't be calling my house trying to get me in trouble! Who the hell do you think you are? I should have *you* arrested for all this harassment. I'm sick. I have a cold. I don't need you calling my house telling my mother lies about me."

"There hasn't been a call to the school to let your teachers know you've been out sick."

"Oh, so let me find out you've been asking all my other teachers about me too."

BROKEN WITH STAINS

"Yes, I have. They've noticed your absence as well, but I don't think they know the cause. I'm the only one who knows what's really going on and I'm not going to sit here and see you suffer through this by yourself. I have a responsibility as an adult, a teacher, and especially a woman to speak up and let you see how you're allowing this boy to damage your spirit."

"You have a responsibility to kiss my black ass. This is the last time I'ma tell you to stick your head back in them school books you supposed to be teaching from and stay out my business. You obviously have a stick up your behind - call your man and tell him you need a good -"

"Tandi!"

Click.

Sienna didn't realize she was still holding the phone to her ear until the janitor entered the lounge. She was jarred back to life when he commenced to knocking a broom handle against the tin garbage can by the door. "Hi Mr. Parker. I was just um -"

"Daydreaming?" he laughed in his loud, exaggerated way. "It's okay Ms. Burgess, I understand. Dealing with these chir'ren will make ya wanna run away any way ya can. Use ya legs or ya mind. Whateva works for you."

Sienna gave him a polite smile as she stood. "Let me get out of your way."

"No sir. You not in my way a'tall. Sit-sit and rest yaself. The day ain't close to over. Don't move on account'a me, you the one with the bigger job. Relax and rest it up while ya can. All I gotta say is, betta you than me."

Sienna knew he wanted to talk. He was a talker, but right now she needed solitude to recover from Tandi's foul attitude. She needed a moment to rethink her plan on finding a way to help the inflexible girl. "Did you see that mess that went on durn second period?" Mr. Parker asked with a finger digging in his gray and black afro. "Not even half way through the day and them fools tearing up a class room, throwing desks and chairs around like it's World War III. Brawling like wild g'ranimals. Lord, forgive me for calling them what they are. But it's beyond me, as a man, why they feel it necessary to act crazy that early in the mo'nin. And in front of the white people too."

Sienna's mind was too scrambled to process what he was saying. "I have no idea what went on earlier, but I have to go -"

"Oh, you didn't hear it? I thought your class was on the first flo' during second period. Well anyway, dem savages was fighting - a group of'em - over Lord knows what. Took two of us janitors to clean that mess up, had to take me couple aspirins after the chaos. But, heh, you know what?"

"What's that Mr. Parker?" she obliged him as she made her way to the exit.

"It'll happen again tomorrow 'cause that's what they do. Fight. That's what they live and die for. But let'em go on. I ain't attending nobody's funeral."

* * *

She had to make it to the finish line. The sweat beads trickled down her forehead one after the other as she ran a steady pace. A luxury yacht to somewhere far awaited her at the end. She had to get there, had to win, and so she ignored the ache in her legs and purposed herself to go the distance ahead.

Sure the distance was only one mile left on the treadmill. But in Sienna's mind, aching legs and feet aside, an escape on a beautiful yacht was motivation enough to make it happen. There was less than half a mile to go when she spotted a familiar shape in the mirror before her. Not quite sure if it was fatigue setting in, she wiped a trace of sweat threatening the corner of her eye. When the woman flung the long brown weave over her shoulder and turned around, Sienna tripped over her feet and almost fell off the treadmill. The woman laughed at a scrawny guy's joke and again flipped her long weave behind her. She was in white, of course. Skin-tight white. The spandex gym outfit could've doubled as a body cast the way it stuck like glue to every curve of her frame. *That's her alright.* Sienna jumped off the treadmill with fifteen seconds left on the timer. Unfortunately, she didn't get the trip on the yacht, but whatever, another destination was now on her radar.

After patting her face with a towel, she took two gulps from her bottle of water and moseyed on over to the spandex queen. Sienna did her best to keep her movements nonchalant. She busied herself with the hand weights on a rack behind the woman and her goofy admirer, making it there in time to hear one of his corny lines. "You is really an angel from God up above. I know it was a hard one letting you come down here to grace us with your presence." With her back turned to the two, Sienna faked a dry heave. It was time for the tired loser to disappear. Thing was, Sienna wasn't sure if she should say something to the "angel from God up above" or if she should watch from a distance and calmly hold her peace. Even if she did say something, she didn't know what would possibly come out of her mouth. She mulled over a possible starter. *Great workout set you got on there. By the way, I saw you all hugged up with my man on the dance floor the other night. Word-to-the-wise, touch him again and I'll hang you by that atrocious, nappy weave. Now that that's out of the way, where can I find that cute two-piece of yours?*

Just then, the shapely figure turned her back to the annoying admirer. Rolling her eyes, she glided over to the hand weights. Sienna averted her eyes to the floor as if searching for something she'd lost. Her feet took her back across the room to the treadmill where she hopped on and absentmindedly set it for ten miles. She felt like a punk. But then again, she was no Mike Tyson either. She was angry. Still, she knew it was no reason to pick a fight with Marcus' overly friendly dance partner.

The frustration refused to let up as she watched the scrawny guy persist in pushing up on Fallon. Was there a real reason to be upset? Thinking about Marcus' hands on the woman's hips, did a fine job of assuring her there was.

It was getting warmer in the air around Sienna as she jogged at a ferocious pace. She watched Fallon lift the ten pound weights up and down in each hand. *Not much to look at*, she thought. *All horse hair and makeup. We're two different people. My hair might be short, but it's mine all mine. And I may be more conservative in the way I dress, but at least I have Tracy Reese hanging in my closet, not Wet Seal. Humph — obviously only one of our mothers gave tips on how to wear decent makeup: I guess everyone can't be like me with minimal foundation and lips glossed with just a hint of color. Some folks need the full mask. And some don't know that a real lady wears natural, manicured nails, not claws that look like they're competing in an Edward Scissorhands pageant. You, Snow White, can take that hideous rug on your head and burn it along with that 1985 block party outfit you got on. Don't forget to throw your bottle of $3.99 perfume and whore-red lipstick in the fire too. You should be ashamed of yourself, walking around in public like that — a behind that big is not normal and you know it. Marcus could never really want you.*

She shuddered at the vision of Marcus holding Fallon's hand and smiling. Deciding it was all fun, she dismissed the bad taste in her mouth. It was time to go. She'd been at the gym for two hours and needed to get home to ready herself for tomorrow. For the next two days she'd be joining Marcus in Virginia to celebrate his mother's sixtieth birthday. A few errands needed to get done, some packing, and then she'd hop in the bed early tonight in order to wake up on time to hit the road with her man the next morning. Sienna wished she'd headed straight home after work, but since she wasn't going to be able to get to the gym on Saturday due to the road trip, she figured she might as well fit in a quick workout.

Her eyes made their way back over to Fallon. Now, she really wished she'd followed her mind. A couple guys not too far away from her treadmill were salivating at the tacky woman decked out in white. Sienna looked down at her own gym-wear, a light pink cotton track suit. It was cute, yet no one was salivating over her. Snow White's round behind was now tooted in the air as she bent over to pick up one of the weights that had fallen. Sienna glimpsed a couple of heart attacks about to occur as the men took in the view. Against her better judgment, she couldn't help but wonder if that view was what Marcus was subjected to every day. If it was, she knew his reaction was probably the same. Sienna bit the short tips of her manicured nails, checked the timer , saw nine miles left. Though every muscle in her body ached like she'd ran one hundred, Sienna knew keeping up with Marcus was finally taking its toll.

* * *

"You're not going? Why?"

Sienna rubbed her aching legs as she listened to her boyfriend explain why the trip to Virginia was being cancelled. Something about work. A project. A deadline. Whatever. She was looking forward to spending the weekend with her man and his family. She hadn't been to visit his mother in a year, plus just knowing she'd be with him made her wake up with a smile on her face this morning.

"But it's your mother's birthday. Work can wait, can't it?"

"Babe, work pays my bills and keeps diamonds in your ears."

"I'm not talking about diamonds, I'm talking about us celebrating your mom's birthday with her. She only turns sixty once."

He sighed into the phone. "Why are we still discussing this, Sunshine? I just can't make it this time."

"So you're busy all weekend?"

"Um, yeah, babe. It's a pressing thing we got going on at the office. Really gotta tie up these loose ends. But hopefully

I'll be all done by Monday. We can go out to dinner Monday night or something," he said.

Or something. "I'm supposed to not see you all weekend, Marcus? I planned my whole weekend around this trip."

"What do you want me to do? Call my boss and tell him to get the project done himself?"

"No, I -"

"Then what do you want from me, Sienna? Work with me here. We'll do dinner Monday night. Italian, Thai, whatever you want. Just give me the weekend to do what needs to get done. Can you do me that one favor?"

She had no choice but to accept the abrupt cancellation. It was necessary in order to avoid a big blow-up. "Yeah . . . I, um . . . it's fine. Monday then."

"Alright then, Sunshine. Love you. You still love me?"

"Of course."

Sienna could hear him smiling as he said, "That's what I like to hear. Later, babe."

She hung up the phone and looked at her stuffed duffel sitting over by the front door. All packed and nowhere to go, she rubbed her thighs and lower legs. She didn't realize she'd over exerted herself so much the night before. The awful sting in her joints coupled with her irritation with Marcus, made an unbearable mix. Sienna couldn't remember the last time work had become that urgent over the weekend. Something wasn't sitting right in her gut. She thought of Fallon, wondering if she could be the cause of his abrupt change of plans. Just as quickly as the suspicion appeared, Sienna dismissed the possibility. After all, she knew work was important to him. It all boiled down to trust. She had to trust him because that was the only way their relationship would work. It was no use sulking about the situation. After unpacking her bag, she gave her mother a call.

Her mother's business tone greeted her by way of

voicemail. "Mom, it's your lovely daughter," Sienna said after the beep. "Please stop screening your calls."

The phone was picked up instantly. "Yes, my lovely daughter? Who said I was screening my calls?"

They laughed, both knowing Annette's method for answering the phone.

"Okay, it's true, but I'm so busy going over these records, I'm about two seconds away from throwing all the papers in the trash."

"Oh, you too?"

"What do you mean?"

"Marcus. Remember when I told you we were supposed to drive up to Virginia to celebrate his mother's birthday?"

"Yes."

"Well, he cancelled. Said he had a ton of work to do at the office."

"I see," Annette smirked. "Too much work to celebrate his mother's birthday for a couple days?"

"Seems so."

"I can only speak for myself - I actually have work to do. Marcus, on the other hand, Lord only knows what's got him tied up."

"Mom, I'm trying not to think bad thoughts. I don't want to believe he'd cancel so he could be out with some other woman."

"Not only out, he could be in too."

Sienna picked at a loose thread on her jeans.

"But what do I know? I'm just your mother."

"I don't know. My gut is telling me not to trust him. And at the same time, my heart is telling me we just have some things we need to work through. Every relationship has its ups and downs."

"I love you, Sienna. And if I've said it once, I've said it twice - it's about time you start loving you. That's all I'm going to say about this matter for the rest of the day."

She knew her mother was done talking about Marcus, but she still had more to say.

"Have you given any thought to seeing your father?" Annette inquired, changing the subject. "A little," Sienna mumbled.

"Just a little?"

"Yeah. I guess it would be good to see him. But sometimes, I wonder why I should even bother."

"Because he's your father."

"What difference would it make, Mom?"

"You'll never know until you speak to him for yourself. He's a part of you whether you like it or not. It won't kill you to pick up the phone and call him."

"All these years he hasn't been here, why can't he pick up the phone and call me?"

"He doesn't want to intrude on your life, Sienna. You're a big woman now, he knows that. And on top of that, he knows he can't get to you unless he goes through me first."

"Why is that?"

"Respect. After what he did, walking out on us when . . . he just knows better. Still, I'm not going to block you from having a relationship with your father. You know I never knew mine either. I think it's about time he came to his senses. A little late, but better late than never is how I see it."

Sienna didn't understand the cool way her mother was dealing with this. "Why is it so easy for you to say that now? Is it that easy to forget?"

"Easy?" she sucked her teeth. "It's been twenty-four years I've had to get over this. But what good would it have done me to shrivel up and die inside? I'm a damn beautiful and very successful forty-four year-old woman. I have a lot to be grateful for, because the icing on the cake is that I raised an awesome young woman by myself. Bitterness has no place in my life. What he did was wrong, but I became stronger because

BROKEN WITH STAINS

I refused to let it make me crumble. Getting there was hard, but I knew I couldn't let him steal my joy."

Was that what it was? Was it bitterness Sienna felt taking over spirit? Her mother was strong. But how could she be the same with all of the fears and doubts hitting her from every angle?

"Sienna, I'm not angry anymore. I got my life in order and focused on creating a bigger future. It's my hope you do the same."

"I'm not angry at . . ."

"Your father?"

"I don't even know what to call him. And I'm sure it's not anger I feel towards him. I just don't know what to make of his sudden entry into my life. Call it confusion maybe. That could be what I'm feeling."

"Take your time then. You know how I feel, but if you need time to sort it out on your own, I don't want to pressure you. Just know that I'm in your corner whatever you decide."

* * *

Marni licked the fried chicken grease from her fingers and wiped the remainder on the soiled napkin. "I don't have a clue where she is. I tried calling her twice this morning. All I get is her voicemail."

The ache still persisted in the lower part of Sienna's legs. She massaged them slowly and then half-heartedly dipped a french fry into a pile of ketchup.

Marni continued, "The girl has problems. I don't know what's been going on with her lately, but she could at least call to let us know she's still breathing."

Sienna threw the uneaten fry down, sighed, and lifted her eyes to her friend. The geometric prints on Marni's blue, yellow, and green hoodie were making her dizzy. "I have a headache," she said, pushing her can of Sprite to the side.

"I have Bayer and Tylenol in the kitchen, want me to get you some?"

"No, it's okay. Maybe if I just lay down a bit, I'll be fine." She took her barely-touched plate to Marni's cute blue and yellow kitchen. After wrapping up her leftovers and placing it in the refrigerator, she went back into the living room.

"Jeez Louise Marni, is the chicken that good?"

She shook her head to remove the dreads from her face and took another healthy bite of the thigh in her hand. "Believe it," she laughed with a mouth full of meat. "I hope you didn't throw all that food away. I could've finished it for you. You know how I do."

"I bet you would've," Sienna laughed. "And if Eve was here, she'd eat both of our plates if we weren't looking.

Marni cracked up as she nodded in agreement.

"I miss her grumpy butt," Sienna said, shifting into a more comfortable position on the old couch. She faced Marni as she lay on her side. Her head was spinning, but she needed to talk. "I called on Tuesday, twice yesterday, and earlier today, at around eleven this morning. She hasn't called me back once and I know you would've told me if she called you. She probably doesn't like us anymore."

"Seriously, Sea? You know that girl can't live without us. We're her bookends; we keep that chick together."

"What if she's dead or something? Laid out on her bedroom floor?"

"Stop. Do not make me start worrying up in here."

Sienna already knew Marni's next move.

"I'ma call her. Where's my phone?"

Sienna giggled, but soon stopped when her head commenced to throbbing a little harder. She watched her friend search for the cordless phone. A thing she always seemed to misplace.

"Here it is," Marni said finding it under a fringed pillow by her side. "Let me see what's what here."

BROKEN WITH STAINS

She dialed and waited for an answer.

"She's not answering, right?" Sienna asked, already knowing the answer.

Marni threw the phone to the side.

"Told you she doesn't love us anymore."

"Wait 'til I see her."

Sienna rolled her eyes and shifted so she could lie on her back.

"Her birthday is next week. What are we doing for her?"

Marni sucked on a chicken bone as she said, "I thought about that, but nothing really came to me. I wanted us to do something fun. Kinda wanted her input, though. Thought we could maybe buy the chick some flowers, a cake, a bottle of bubbly. What did you have in mind?"

"I thought we could take her to the spa. There's one in Westchester, black-owned and pretty fab from what I've been told. One of my co-workers was telling me about it the other day. We should check out the website."

"That's an option. These old bones need a rubbing down."

"Mine too. I went to the gym last night and I'm tore up from the floor up."

"You work out all the time - what happened?"

"Don't ask."

Marni wiped her mouth and placed the napkin on her plate. She burped, "Mission accomplished here. And yes, I need to know. What happened at the gym?"

Sienna breathed a large stream of air. "That big-breasted girl, Snow White, was there. The one Marcus was grinding on the dance floor."

Marni's eyes popped. "Stop it!"

"So serious, Marni. She was there in white again. I swear she thinks the seven dwarves are going to show up any day now. Anyhow, I was watching her so hard, I wasn't really paying attention to what I was doing on the treadmill. I did too much. That's why I keep rubbing my legs. Feels like two sumo wrestlers sat on each leg for ten hours straight. "

"I hope you didn't say anything to her."

"Nope. But, you better believe I thought about it."

"It would've been dumb if you did."

"I know, that's why I didn't."

"Good. If you talk to anybody, it needs to be Marcus."

"Yeah, well, sometimes it feels like I'm hoping to catch him doing something. I know he loves me. I can't keep on doubting him like this. Fallon is his co-worker. She's not even his type."

"And what about Nonda? Is she his type?"

Sienna grew uncomfortable at the mention of that name. Her mind quickly flashed back to the girl she'd seen a few days ago. Wondered if the bushy-head stalker could be the one claiming to be the mother of Marcus' child. It was the second time she'd popped up out of nowhere, staring and seemingly taunting Sienna once more. Marni and Eve had no idea of Sienna's suspicions. Then again, it was probably a simple coincidence. Justification as to why she should keep her mouth shut concerning the creepy chance encounters.

"I don't believe it," Sienna replied as her head began to pound double-time. "I've come to the conclusion that it's some obsessed ex-girlfriend who's just making a play to get him back. That's the only thing that makes sense to me about this whole situation."

Marni stared at her friend without saying a word.

Sienna stared back. "What?"

"Nothing. Nothing at all. There's nothing I can really say. I mean, it's really up to you and what you think is best for you. If you think it's best to stay with Marcus, there's really nothing I can do or say to make you change your mind."

"You think I'm stupid, don't you? Just like my mother and Eve."

BROKEN WITH STAINS

"I don't think your stupid, Sea. You're in love. Love can make even the smartest women do things they wouldn't normally do. I can't judge you. And I definitely can't make you do anything you don't want to do."

Sienna rubbed her temples and took a deep, cleansing breath.

"You know, I'm like, when is enough going to be enough? I'm constantly thinking about Marcus and these random women, my student Tandi and that boy who's beating the crap out of her, my . . . father who wants to make his grand entrance into my life now – really Marni, I'm sick and tired. I'm not exactly sure what to do about anything anymore."

"All I can do is tell you to pray. Sounds small when you think about it being a four-letter word, but p-r-a-y can yield huge results."

"Yeah, like God is going to listen to me," Sienna laughed. "If you ask me where my Bible is, I'd be ashamed to give you an answer. I haven't picked it up in I don't know how long. I'm sure spiders are crocheting cob webs and doing the running man on it as we speak."

Marni waved away the amusing visual. "Spiders doing the running man, crip walk, or the butterfly don't matter. I'm talking about that mustard seed faith. Just pray, is all I can say."

"I tried that a long time ago. Every night I used to pray to Jesus, Mary, *and* Moses that my father would finally come to his senses and swoop into my life like a knight in shining armor. Can you believe that? Honest to God, I used to fantasize that my father was my knight in shining armor. I remember praying when I was small, hoping that for Christmas I wouldn't receive a Barbie, but instead I'd get a huge box delivered to my house and my father would pop out all of a sudden. Like, bam!" Sienna said widening out her fingers in the air. "That's all I ever wanted."

Marni placed her chin on her knee and watched the look of remembrance wash across her best friend's face. "Hey, you got your Christmas wish now. Celebrate that. It came early this year."

Sienna shook her head. "No, it came late. Many years too late. I can't see that man. I don't know him and he doesn't know me. What would we have to talk about? I'm his blood, but he's just a stranger to me."

"It's not too late. You can't think like that."

"What do *you* know?"

Marni was taken aback my Sienna's sudden sharp tone.

Sienna couldn't help being overcome by a newfound fury. The more she thought about Paul trying to slip back in, the more she wanted to vent her aggravation. "Are you some type of professional on this specific subject matter? You've always had both parents in your life. Your mother stayed home to cook while your father went out and made money to bring home for the family. You've always had a family, so what the heck would you know about anything not being too late?"

"Hold up, hold up, hold up Sienna," she said raising a finger. "First of all, it's true – I did have both parents in the home. Regardless, life wasn't always peaches and cream for me either. We struggled. Okay? You have no freaking idea. Your mother might've been a single mom, but she had resources and support to raise you and she worked hard to grow in her career like she has. You grew up wanting for nothing."

"And that means life was always peaches and cream for me."

"Maybe not, but you should be grateful for your blessings every single day. You should be grateful for the fact that you didn't have to wear hand-me-downs and eat cans of string beans for dinner because there was nothing else to eat. You grew up without a father, but I grew up without many of the luxuries you had as a child -"

"You had a father," Sienna interrupted.

"A wonderful father. But there were no summer camps for me or my brothers and sisters. No birthday parties, brand new Easter dresses, ice cream sandwiches just because, or trips to the hair salon to press out the kinks in my hair. My mom came here from the Dominican Republic and couldn't speak one word of English. She knew three words of it when she met my father, a black man whose only skill was mopping the floors of office buildings.

"He came home at the end of the day," Sienna persisted.

"You think life was all good just because I had a father at home? Try being one of six kids, living on a janitor's salary. You got Barbies, I was lucky if I got one piece of chicken with my rice on Christmas. But let me tell you something: we were taught never to complain. And 'til this day, I don't complain about anything because even though my childhood wasn't perfect, I survived it. I'm here today, blessed. Got my own apartment, stashing away to purchase my first house, got a car, a great job that allows me to help save lives, and I got food taking up every corner of my fridge." She picked up a few limp chicken bones. "Look at that. I ate not one, not two, but three pieces of chicken, Sienna. So life is good. And it's never too late to make it better."

Dead air filled the room. Marni saw the tear slip down Sienna's cheek. She looked down on the chicken bones along with the stains on the paper plate before her. She studied the pieces she'd bitten off, sucked, and spit out on the plate when all the juices had been sucked dry.

Without looking up she continued speaking to her friend, "You have your own experiences and I have mine. I don't know what it's like to not have a father in my life. You don't know what it's like to struggle for basic necessities. But one thing we have in common is a universal thing. We all have stains, we've all been broken. There are only two things we can do with the hand we've been dealt. Choose to make the right move or walk away from the table."

31 joy

It couldn't be right.

The two blue lines on the stick should've actually been a single; the one line that assured Joy she was not pregnant. That's what taking the pill was for - a barrier against morning sickness, swollen feet, losing her flat stomach, and most importantly, unwanted kids.

It couldn't be right. The only guy she'd slept with recently was Luce. The last time she'd slept with him was her first day at the club. That was six weeks ago.

Good thing she'd bought another brand of the test, a trick she'd seen her mother do a couple times when she was a small girl. Just in case one was defective, she could double-test to be extra sure.

The two bottles of Evian water she drank an hour ago, made it easy to pee on the second stick. A little fidgety, she used tweezers to pluck away a few stray eyebrow hairs as she wasted time in the bathroom mirror. After the two minutes had passed, she took the white stick from the edge of the tub and prepared to see one pink line proclaiming her non-pregnancy. But all she saw was the slim blue line boldly as bright as day. For this test, that meant she was 99.9% with child. Both brands sat together, side-by-side, asking her what her next step would be.

Unbelievable, Joy thought as she looked into the mirror again and saw that everything was still the same. There was no way she was ready to be a mother. Nineteen years-old and in her prime, there was no way she wanted to succumb to excess baby weight, cellulite, and droopy breasts any time soon. Joy made up her mind that both tests were wrong – she'd to run to a doctor and make them tell her it wasn't true too. At this point in time, Planned Parenthood would have to do.

BROKEN WITH STAINS

She left the sticks where they sat and went to her room to throw on some clothes. If she was pregnant, did that mean life as she knew it would change? Everything? And would Luce be happy about it or feel like she was tying him down? The questions marched around in the back of her mind. Ignoring them the best she could, she slipped on a black Bob Marley tee she'd redesigned to hang off the shoulder on one side and a pair of black pencil jeans that fit a little tighter than they used to. She went to the hall closet and grabbed the black Gucci stilettos she'd worn to the club the night she met Luce. She didn't know of any pregnant mothers who could look this good. Taking one last stop at the wall mirror by the front door, Joy used her hands to smooth the hair that was combed neatly straight down her mid-back. She'd worry later about what she'd do if the tests turned out to be true. Pushing the oversized black shades up against her face, she confidently sashayed her way out the door.

* * *

Joy closed her eyes for a second as she danced in front of her customer in the Grand Ballroom. He was the ugliest man she'd ever laid eyes on in her entire life. However, she would suffer whatever for the good of the almighty dollar. A second ago, she'd peeped the hundred dollar bill he'd sneakily tucked into the front of her g-string. Obviously, he was trying to get her in trouble. Critical times were upon her, so Joy brushed it off knowing she'd be needing that money now more than ever. All it took was a play of her hand to make it look like she was rubbing herself. Joy moved the folded bill quickly and stashed it in a safer place.

For a man this ugly, the money had better be worth it. The weekend was three days away. Soon she'd get her check so that she could purchase the new Fendi bag and two animal print Roberto Cavalli dresses she'd seen yesterday at Bergdorf's in the city. If she'd calculated everything correctly since checking her balance online two days ago, once the items were paid for in cash, she'd have three thousand left in her account to play with until next week. Thinking about it made ugly man's face easier to bear. Yet, Joy didn't want to overdose.

It was time to give him a back view - the sight of his crooked teeth was beginning to become a little bit much. His hands snuck a feel of her behind when he raised them while dancing in his seat. She was a second away from calling security on Mr. Rule Breaker for thinking he was slick, but just then she noticed a very tall, caramel-toned girl walk through the door with Luce right behind her.

Joy watched the two leisurely making their way from the bar to a table four tables back from where Joy danced. Her hips still moved to the music, but she'd forgotten all about her unattractive client, focusing instead on her man sitting too close to the girl that looked familiar from a few music videos. One thing Joy knew was that, she'd never been in the club before. And as she inattentively changed her body's rhythm to the beat of a new song, a slow, disconcerting sensation began to rumble in the pit of her stomach.

Luce smiled at the girl, making butterflies appear in Joy's stomach. He'd done the same to her many times before. So many times, Joy thought she owned that smile and the man who came with it. Evidently she was wrong . He turned his head in her direction and raised a glass to her in acknowledgement. After the quick gesture, his attention went back to his new friend. His hands stroked her lengthy golden-auburn hair. The dark eyes hardly left her face. It was all Joy could do to prevent herself from flying across the room to slam both of their heads together.

Luce signaled the bartender over and ordered another drink for his friend. He hadn't finished his own and rarely even sipped from the short glass. The girl, on the other hand, drank like she'd never take a sip again. Joy couldn't look anymore. She was possibly pregnant with his child and he thought nothing of sitting in her face and showing complete disrespect. He wasn't aware of the possibility, but how dare he cavort with another girl in the club at a time like this.

Joy averted her eyes from those of the other dancers entertaining men at the same table. Cake was on her face, but she wasn't about to let it show. She turned her attention back to her client and smiled at him like he was the finest man to ever grace planet earth.

"Gorgeous. Absolutely gorgeous," he told her. "You're the gorgeous one. You have beautiful eyes," she said lying the best she could. That comment was rewarded with three more folded hundred dollars bills cleverly slipped into her palms as he took hold of her hands. He winked at her after giving the reward. "You're a beautiful liar too," ugly man said, showing the teeth again. Joy was taken aback.

"A beautiful liar?" she asked, confused.

"I'm an ugly man inside and out. No need to lie to me, baby. But I see you working for that money."

"So you think I'm lying?"

"I know you're lying. I wasn't born yesterday - I'm a grown man. Now shut up and turn around so I can see that gorgeous ass."

She did as she was told. If it was any other day, she would have told him where to go for speaking to her like that. But, there was about four hundred dollars sitting on various places of her body. More was sure to follow, so she made an effort to rock to the beat. Luce was still at the table further back, the video girl's body leaned into him now as she slightly moved in pace to the music. Joy's eyes burned holes into the two of them, but they seemed unconscious of her glare. *This is how you do me, Luce? Always have some business to take care of, but you find time to bring this one out for the night?* Heat escalated through her body when she saw them both stand up hand-in-hand. They made their way over to the exit and left, both looking as coupley and cozy as can be. Joy wasn't a crier, yet she felt the stream of tears making its way up from somewhere where a baby might be. She looked to her right and saw a couple of the dancers looking her way, their self-satisfied smiles telling her she was officially a damn fool. There was no chance of letting even one pending tear fall.

Turning back around to face ugly man, she moved her body in the most hypnotizing ways she could.

* * *

Madou was a Muslim with mad loot. She'd been contemplating her future with Luce, when she nearly drove her BMW through a red stoplight. After backing the car up, she looked over to the next lane when she heard a booming voice say, "You need to let me take you out so I can replace whatever's on your mind." Joy really wasn't interested, but thought twice when she remembered Luce traipsing out of the club with the girl, holding hands. And then she took a closer look at the shiny cream Cadillac Escalade the underwhelming, caesar-cut wearing prospect sat behind and bells went off all around her. She took note of the largest rims she'd ever seen on the road. It was more than inspiring to Joy and so she agreed to go out with him to get a feel of his spending habits. But after leaving the spoken word crap she'd just sat through, it was obvious this would just be a one night thing.

From the start, Joy knew that besides his money, Madou didn't have the characteristics she typically looked for in a guy. Yet, there was something she had to prove. Luce wasn't the only one who could get somebody else. She was young and hotter than the nobody he'd had on his arm two nights ago. Tons of guys hollered at her whenever she exited her front door.

Over a month pregnant and all.

It had been confirmed.

BROKEN WITH STAINS

Nearly two months pregnant she was, but that was just between herself and the doctor. Luce still had no clue. And of course Madou was in the dark too.

"I know what you're thinking."

"What?" Joy asked, abruptly dislodged from her thoughts.

"That last poet, the one whose joint was called 'I Know What You're Thinking' - that piece was tight."

He could take "that piece" and choke on it for all she cared. Having tuned out after the first performer, she'd spent the rest of the night rating their looks on a scale of one to ten. Was the only thing that could prevent her eyelids from shutting down from boredom, before they left for the night. Joy wondered if Madou's feelings would be hurt if she told him the spoken word event sucked. Hoping it would, she said, "I could care less about a spoken word. I was bored to tears. Next."

Surprisingly, he laughed and replied, "Don't be like that, sexy."

"Like what?" she asked, playing dumb.

"It's something different. Don't tell me you would've preferred if I had just invited you over to my crib so we could watch Soul Plane or some shit?"

"Ummm . . . yeah."

"You ain't right. But I enjoyed it."

"Of course you enjoyed it. You had me sitting next to you all night," she smiled at him. "You and that smile," he said. "You're too sexy for your own good."

Afterward, they hit IHOP for a bite to eat. She'd chosen the location without thinking twice – the cravings had already begun and pancakes were like crack to her right now.

He tried his best to make conversation while she concentrated on tuning him out. Naturally, Luce was on the brain since he wanted to be out and about, getting close to sub par video vixens and such. She'd have to accept it; the money was too good to leave the club at this point. Where else could she go to rake in thousands of dollars each week? Wasn't like she had more than a high school diploma. Sure, there were men she could find to buy her nice things and give her a few hundred in cash every other week, but it wouldn't be the same after she'd collected more than seventy-two thousand dollars on her own in six weeks. No man had been able to purchase seventy-two thousand worth of anything for Joy in that amount of time. All the better too – she could spend her own money without having to waste time with chumps like the one in front of her at this table. The only difficult part would be seeing Luce. Strong feelings were now in the mix. Add the fact that she was carrying his baby. Making an attempt to block out the stress was all she could do at the moment.

Easier said than done.

She watched Madou's goatee move in time to the rhythm in which he spoke. Luce had no hair on his face, tried to keep it smooth at all times. Madou spoke with his hands, flipping them everywhere. Luce was a still man, relaxed with each word that flowed from his mouth - very thoughtful about each move he made from the soles of his feet to the tips of his large, sturdy hands. For a quick second, Joy imagined herself kissing his hands. She wanted them near, caressing her body, but knew they were probably all over someone else's right now.

She took a bite of her Rootie Tootie Fresh and Fruity, almost piercing her lips with the fork.

"Where's your parents?" Madou inquired.

Joy eyed him as if ready to stab him with the utensil in her hand.

"Why you asking about my parents?"

"Just conversation, sweetie. I see you're not saying much, but at least you're enjoying the pancakes."

"A sista loves her pancakes. Don't get it twisted," she said calming down enough to cut another slice.

He laughed.

"My mother lives in New York . . . and L.A. and

Europe. She pretty much lives all over the world. My father . . . well, I have none - he was never in my life."

"That's too bad," he said taking a drink of his water. "Him not getting to know you and all."

"Can we change the subject? I'm not too fond of either one."

"My bad. Didn't mean to stir nothing up."

An apology. Funny. If it was Luce, he would've threw his devilish grin her way and continued to press the issue. He never backed down; it was his pleasure to make the air uncomfortable around her. Oddly enough, she liked that about him. He was a challenge to her aggressive nature.

She wanted to kick herself for not being able to stop thinking about him. Madou was cool enough, but lacked that extra something Luce offered. A baby was growing inside of her and yet she still felt empty without Luce close. Madou, his rims, money, and temporary company, wasn't nearly enough to fill that void.

32 paul

The morning held potential. Paul stretched in front of his bedroom window with a blue terrycloth towel wrapped around his waist. His morning shower had done its job well. With water still glistening against his skin, he looked outside the window and admired the sun's ascent to the waiting sky.

He watched his neighbors back out of their driveways. Rich, he knew, was on his way to a job he'd termed "The Plantation". Paul found it funny coming from a man of mixed race - half black, half white. A man who'd married a white woman with skin so pale it almost looked unnatural, had two daughters with hair as blonde as Barbie's, and associated with all white friends, with the exception of Paul. Yet, in Rich's "white world", it was still "The Plantation" once he stepped inside the office. Never mind that he was an Executive Director at a Fortune 500 company. He'd confided in Paul that the money was great, but the subtle racism was something he had to fight through almost every day. His way of fighting: grin and bear it and make as many friends with the Old Boys Club as he could. His reasoning, simple, the paycheck was worth the stress – not to mention the annual bonus.

And then there was Cornelius Moore, the antique collector who lived next door to Rich. Paul watched him pull out in his '89 Volvo to go hunt down more antiques. There was always amusement where Moore was concerned. The man insisted that everyone call him by his last name. His own wife included. It was his wife who'd convinced Moore to move across the street into the four-bedroom house. A fleshy lady with beehive-shaped, shocking-red hair, she was the pusher while her husband insisted on being a miser. The big-spender never hesitated to mention her husband's money every chance she got. More than once, Paul had been out front with Camilla when Mrs. Moore had come by to say hello and casually brag about the new diamond-studded watch she'd gotten Moore to purchase for her birthday or the beach-side property they were thinking of getting out in California. Moore usually kept his distance from his wife whenever possible and shuffled around with white t-shirts, his treasured Vans, and the same black or brown corduroy pants he wore every other day. Paul knew his neighbor was beyond peeved at his wife's excessive spending. During the few times Moore had come over to Paul's front yard to strike up conversation, he'd dropped a few sly remarks about the wife who was on the verge of driving him crazy. One Paul never forgot: "That fatty of a wife I got, boy oh boy, if I could do it all over again . . . let's just say I'd be ten million dollars richer."

    Paul shook his head at the lives the people around him led. He had his own problems to deal with, but a disheartening job wasn't one. Neither was an annoying wife. That thought comforted him. And then he thought about his girls. He'd done it. Made some sort of contact with each girl through the women in their life. The calls hadn't been returned yet, but he had a good feeling brewing inside his soul. His talk with Ashley along with Camilla's support had given him new hope. The extra bonus: Sienna's mom had agreed to meet and talk with him this afternoon. He was ready. Whatever the day had in store for him, he was ready. And as the familiar music of his cell phone began to sound, he turned towards it with a large smile plastered across his face. Camilla had left him in bed and headed for the spa at six a.m. He knew it was her, ready with sweet words to start the promising day he felt was ahead.

    He quickly swiped the phone from his bedside table, anticipating his wife's voice.

    "Hey baby," Paul smiled into the phone.

    "I want you to leave my child alone."

    Paul froze. Unsure who the livid tone belonged to on the other end of the phone, he tried to gather himself as swiftly as possible. Tried to focus and figure out who owned the stern voice.

"Leave . . . her . . . alone."

He couldn't speak as he lowered himself to the edge of the bed.

"I know what you're trying to do. You're not going to come in and ruin our life. The life I built for my baby and me. I want you to stay far away from her. You hear me?"

The lilt in her voice gave it away. It was still soft, but he could hear a forcefulness in it now too. Paul found his speech and worked fast to make it count.

"Sharon, I know I was wrong for leaving the two of you, but Noelle is my baby also. Don't shut me out like this." He paused before continuing, "Believe me, in my heart I've paid for all the wrong I've done."

"Don't want to hear it, Paul. You made your bed twenty-one years ago. Lay in it."

"Sharon, please . . ."

"What did you expect? Me to just hand my daughter over to you like all those memories been washed away? Well, they haven't. They haven't you sorry flake. What you need to do is leave my child alone. I don't want to hear another word about you trying to get in contact with Noelle again. Is that clear enough for you?"

"I . . . I can't do that. She's my child too. And as sorry as I am that things turned out the way they did, I can't run away anymore. I sincerely apologize for not being there, but I missed out on years I can't get back. I don't want to lose anymore."

"Sorry for the way things turned out?" Sharon huffed. "They turned out the way they did because of you! Not me. You. You treated me like trash and you walked away from your responsibilities, so don't tell me that you're sorry for the way things turned out. Things would've turned out differently if you had been a man."

Paul ran a hand over his bowed head and let go an

inaudible sigh. "I know that. This has been a burden on my chest for so long. I realize I wasn't a man back then. Thought I was, but I wasn't. I was dealing with so many things in my mind, I didn't know how to be a father. Deep down, I wanted to be there. I just didn't know how. I experienced a lot of loss when I was growing up - "

"Oh no. I'm not going to let you make this all about you anymore. It was all about you when you walked out on me and Noelle. You wanted to move on with your life because we were a burden."

"That wasn't it at all," he countered.

"You wanted to move on with your life because you'd done your damage and didn't want to get your hands dirty with the consequences."

"I didn't - "

"Well thank you for the tool between your legs it took for me to gain my precious child, but no thank you for the hell you put me through and for the times I couldn't tell my baby why her father wasn't there for her when he should've been."

Paul's throat had run dry. He didn't know what he could pull from his reserve to quench the rage building on the other end of the phone.

"I never knew you, Paul. I thought I knew the man I loved, but I didn't. I wanted to have your child. Green and dumb is what I was, but I wanted the love of my man and my baby. The day I found out I was pregnant was the happiest day of my life . . . and then you left us. How could you?"

He sat on the edge of the bed, shoulders slumped, fingers barely clasping the phone. A collection of sweat had begun to replace the water from this morning's shower. His once ready heart, beating less enthusiastically by the second.

She growled into the phone. "You're not going to come into her life and disappear again. Get one thing straight - I refuse to give you the chance to do that again. We're fine. We've moved on. And I'd advise you to do the same."

TAMARA BURKE

* * *

Paul fought himself the entire day after receiving this morning's call from Noelle's mom. The battle's victory was leaning towards the side of his heart that believed in calling the mission off.

Sitting at the kitchen table, as he mostly stared into his cup of coffee, he spoke to God and waited for an answer. He wanted to know if he should stop or go forth with his effort. Told God he was running out of options. Paul tried to play up the fact that he was being respectful to the mothers first and foremost. Reminded Him that he had acknowledged the wrong he'd done and just wanted to make things right.

Paul listened as he sat at the table. He was supposed to be at his studio an hour earlier, but called to notify his assistant that he'd be late, refusing to move until God spoke back.

Three hours later, he walked into the quiet restaurant fifteen minutes early. Paul followed the waiter to a neatly set table in the middle. If it wasn't for the word from above that came in at the last minute, he would've called and cancelled the meeting with Annette and stayed locked in his studio all day.

He slid his large hands down the thighs of his starched black pants. The pants Camilla had bought for him a week ago – a thoughtful token from her last shopping trip - along with the sharp black button-down he had on. Paul needed his wife there with him, even if it was just in the spirit of his clothing. Camilla knew he was here and he wanted to make her proud. Needed to show that her support and God's grace had gotten him this far.

The fifteen minutes went by faster than expected. One second he was preparing himself for what he would say to the woman he hadn't seen in over twenty years and the next minute Annette was headed towards him, amazingly graceful and gorgeous in a white, tailored linen-suit. This woman was nothing close to the naked twenty year-old he remembered like

BROKEN WITH STAINS

it was yesterday. Making her way towards him, the soft ruffles of the white silk blouse under her structured, open jacket, swayed with the light wind she created with her walk. She still looked like a model, all five foot seven inches of her. The silky, poreless brown skin of her face had hardly changed one bit. The only difference was Annette's sleek hair; no longer a 'fro, it sat textured in a closely-cropped stylish look that complement-ed her beauty. Paul marveled at the strong aura of confidence and accomplishment that surrounded her like a light.

He stood to pull out her chair, but she stopped him with a slightly raised hand and a smile. "It's okay, but thank you, Paul. How are you today?"

He sat back in his seat and attempted to brush aside the awkward moment.

"Good. I umm . . . I'm pretty good. Happy you agreed to meet with me today because honestly, I never thought it would happen." There were no hugs and kisses. No handshakes or even a pat on the back. Paul saw the smile on Annette's face, but couldn't predict how the rest of the meeting would play out.

She let the waiter take their drink order before she replied, "I'm happy I agreed to meet with you too. For the sake of Sienna, I felt it was necessary. Glad you were finally thinking of her and made a move towards becoming a part of her life."

"I had to. I failed miserably, Annette. I wasn't the man I was supposed to be. It took a lot of growth for me to get to this point."

She tilted her head to the side, catching the light against one sizeable diamond stud in her ear. "Growth? How much have you grown?"

It was a question he was well able to answer. "By leaps and bounds. And not overnight either. God had to take me and mold me into what he wanted me to be. This growth is not of me. It's all about what my God has done in me."

The words sounded great, but she wanted to know if

they were real. "Is that a saved man I hear talking?" Annette asked, before sipping her water.

He smiled and suddenly the tension lifted. "It is."

"What did it? What brought you to this point where you can sit across from me and say that God has transformed your whole world?"

"Truth be told . . . it was mostly my wife."

"God bless her heart."

They laugh together and he continued. "She opened a door for me to walk through. And when I walked through that door and saw what was behind it, it was too hard to ignore. My defense mechanisms began to break down and I couldn't run anymore. I had to give my life to Him."

"And isn't He wonderful."

"Amazing."

"Yes, He is."

"And I'm here before you today because He slapped me around and broke me down. I was wrong. I was too selfish to admit it back then, but I really do apologize for any hurt and pain I caused you and Sienna."

"Forgiven," she said, looking directly into his eyes.

He was incredulous. "Do you really?"

"Yes, really." Annette looked down at her hands that rested on the white tablecloth. "After a number of years, I decided to let go of the resentment I had for you and use my energy to build a life for me and Sienna."

"How is she?"

"She's well. She's healthy and smart and beautiful and ambitious and she's all the things a mother wants her child to be. She's the one good thing that came of us and I truly couldn't have asked for a bigger blessing in my life. My career, my home – nothing can compare to the joy Sienna's brought to my life."

Paul's eyes dropped from her face as he thought of so many of the things he'd probably missed. "I'm glad to know that. You look well too. Just beautiful, like you've lived a blessed, fruitful life."

"I have. And Sienna is the crown jewel of that blessed life. I love my child."

He leaned forward and stared into her eyes.

"If she agrees to meet with you, Paul, you *better* be good to my baby. You're her father. You may not have been there all along, but she needs your love nonetheless." She placed a hand on top of his. "Treat her with loving care. I wanted to meet with you today to look you in the eye and tell you that face-to-face. I raised her all by myself and I know all her wants and needs. She needs your love and if you've really made up your mind to be a part of her life, then don't do it with a cheap, reluctant heart - do it with a passion."

The waiter came back with their drinks, took their lunch order, and left them in silence to mull over what they'd say next. Annette's words marinated in the air above their heads. Paul examined the woman he'd once wanted immensely and saw that she was still all business. Her fingers sat firmly intertwined on the round table, shoulders pulled back and erect all at once. He could feel her fighter's spirit alive and kicking. Knew that she was giving him a second chance accompanied with subtle warning.

"For the longest time I was afraid to contact you, thinking to myself, you'd laugh in my face and tell me to go about my business." He paused and leaned in more, resting on his forearms to get as close to Annette as possible. "My heart hasn't been right since the day I left you the way I did. Didn't matter back then 'cause there was no way I could face you and a child with the past I had behind me. And I knew it was unfair that I wasn't upfront with you, but for me it was just easier to leave without saying goodbye. I tried, but there wasn't one day that passed that I didn't think about you and the baby. Brock, before he died, told me you were still living in the Bronx and that you'd had a baby girl. He told me what I was doing was wrong, but I couldn't see any other way."

A vision of Annette's trembling shoulders flashed in his mind, reminding him of her raw pain all those years ago. It seemed so fresh and too real at this very moment. If he could, he would reach back in time and wrap his arms around the girl she once was. He attempted to accomplish that with words.

"Tell her I need her. That I can't make it right without her. Words can't express the regret felt for the disaster I made because of my selfishness. I want to make it right, Annette." She shifted her eyes downward and traced a finger along the back side of her hand the way she used to when she stroked Paul's mustache. He saw a glimpse of the young Annette just then before she blew a slight stream of air and made eye contact again.

She opened her lips to speak, shut them, and proceeded to give it a try for the second time.

"My heart needed those words more than you know," she said, voice trembling a bit. Annette cleared her throat, took a drink from her glass and continued, "Women need a father in their lives. I never met mine . . . and 'til this day, I don't know whether he's dead or alive. It means a lot to know that you care about truly getting to know your daughter."

"With all my heart," Paul added.

Annette thought about Sienna and the problems she'd been going through with Marcus lately before saying, "She's all I have. And she'll always deserve the very best."

"I'm committed to giving her my all," he answered.

"Well then, I'm committed to doing all I can to let her know she has a father who needs her."

* * *

Paul reclined in his leather chair and watched Camilla's delight form a cocoon of happiness around her. "Honey, these pics are awesome! They're gonna look so fabulous on the website. Thanks a mill, pumpkin." She turned and walked over to her husband with the stack of photos in her hand. She placed them on his desk and fell back into his lap, wrapping her arms around him. Crossing her legs, she purred into his ear, "How will I ever repay my big poppa?" He stroked her chin and gave her a gentle kiss on the waiting lips.

"You reward me every morning I wake up beside you. Your promise to be my queen until the very end is all the payment I need."

Camilla let out an "Awwwe . . ." and kissed her man on his forehead. She then planted a firm one on his nose saying, "Gladly, my king. I do it gladly." She rested her head against his as he cradled her in his arms and asked, "How did the meeting with Annette go?" Paul smiled a little when he said, "Better than I expected."

"I prayed for you."

"Thank you, because I needed it." Camilla snuggled even closer to him. "What did she say?" It felt good for him to say, "I have her support."

She sat upright and grinned, making her eyebrows take on a life of their own just the way Paul loved. "It's just a matter of time," she said happily.

"Waaaait, hold up a minute," he said, pulling her from his chest for the sake of eye contact. "The battle's not over yet. Let's hold off on the balloons and champagne."

Camilla raised her hands in the air and shimmied her body with a dance of excitement. "No, uh-uh, we *are* going to celebrate because we gained a victory today. No battle is won in one big swoop. Those little victories are what count most."

"You're right," he said, acknowledging her wisdom. He thought about Sharon and the things she'd told him this morning. Trespassing further would get him killed if she had anything to do with it; that much was clear and true. The battle to meet with Noelle hadn't been won, but Camilla didn't need to know that. She was too joyful to throw a monkey wrench in the midst of her celebration. Besides, if Annette had given him encouragement, maybe Sharon would change her mind somewhere in the future. It's what he hoped for. Having Noelle in his life was just as important as having Sienna and Joy in it too.

Paul looked at his wife goading him, slowly raising her arms again to do a little wave and dance in his lap. Camilla laughed as she reached for his hands to raise them up high with hers. "You don't want to raise'em with me?" she playfully asked. "I could do that little dance my niece always does – what's it called again? The Dougie or something like that? Or if you don't want that, I could take it to the real old school and do the twist. I bet you wouldn't mind that."

He shook his head and said, "Yeah, I'll celebrate, but there's an even better dance you could do for me."

"What's that?" she smiled, readily. "Anything for my baby."

He attacked her with his fingers, tickling her in all the places he knew would get her to squeal the loudest. She did everything she could to escape, but her giggles mixed with the faces she made were too enjoyable to make Paul quit.

Camilla was right a thousand times over – the battle might not have been over yet, but a victory was undeniably worth the celebration.

33 noelle

Her restless nights had grown even more restless. Too many thoughts were colliding in her head and peace-of-mind escaped at every turn she made. Chris. Her father. And now, why did she get that tingling sensation every time David crossed her mind? She needed a break; everything was too great to swallow at one time. She needed time to breathe. Decided she'd make time after her last afternoon class. Maybe go to Bay Plaza theater, pick a flick she could get lost in, and hide herself in a dark corner to the back as she snacked on a bag of Skittles. Just a quick fix, but she needed it. Planned on doing that right after she left school, came home, and finished up the last few paragraphs of her second eight page marketing paper of the semester. No more than forty-five minutes is what it would take to finish off those last two pages. And then she'd get to numb her brain.

Yup – that was the plan.

Why Aunt Rinni felt the need to change that plan, Noelle did not know. She'd come home with the intention of heading straight for the refrigerator to grab a light snack. After dropping her school books on the kitchen table, Noelle virtually suffered a heart attack when the shrill ring of the wall phone cried out unexpectedly. It was Aunt Rinni instructing her to turn her cell phone on and listen to the voicemail she'd forwarded two minutes ago. Following the instructions, she walked over to her shoulder bag and turned on the device she'd forgotten to switch back on after class was over. Voicemail code inserted, Noelle leaned against the door post as she listened to the man's voice echoing in her ears. She hung up. And forgot all about her planned escape. If she could think straight, she would've blamed it on that unexpected voice. Her feet dragged as she made her way up the stairs, feeling as if iron chains were attached to her ankles.

Two hours later, mind numb, Noelle sat frigid as a block of ice in her mother's stuffed bedroom chair. She gripped the cell phone in her hand and pleaded with her fingers to press seven for erase. With just a little force applied, she could erase him. His deep, mellow voice. His interruption. She could make it go away just that quick. But instead, her thumb landed on four. That was repeat message. She chose to believe her finger slipped. Chose to believe what she'd heard three times already was someone else by mistake. She listened again.

Rinelda, it's me . . . Paul Brooks. Calling you again because I haven't heard from Noelle at all. I know you said you spoke to her a few weeks back, but um . . . she hasn't contacted me or anything. Anyway . . . I received a call from Sharon the other day and from what she told me, she'd prefer if I stay to myself. She . . . she has valid reasons for being angry enough to push me away, but . . . I need to speak to my daughter. I need to speak to Noelle. You've helped me so much already, I don't know what else you can do . . . just please try to let Noelle and Sharon know that I don't mean no harm, I just want to build a relationship. I know you already have it, but just in case, my number is 914-526-8512. Please . . . it would be great if I heard something back soon. Thanks.

Noelle didn't think it would've happened this way. Never thought she'd be affected if he ever decided to show up. The fries in her stomach from her afternoon lunch were doing unruly things as her finger swayed in between four and seven. She didn't understand why she was nauseous and why the hand she held the phone with was shaking. He was just a man. One she'd never laid eyes on. A faceless man with only a voice she could attach to him. So why was deleting his message such a daunting task? No, it was a joke. Aunt Rinni had gotten her good. It had to be her boyfriend, Carl, she'd put up to running this game. The voice kind of sounded like his. Noelle listened again to be absolutely sure.

"Take your foot out my chair. What are you doing in

my bedroom anyway?"

Startled, Noelle looked up at her mother. Sharon's face was extra pale with no makeup at all. The edges of her brown hair fell to the floor, wayward and frayed.

"What's wrong with you? Look like you seen a ghost. You not still fussing over that boy is you?"

Noelle gripped the phone in her palm. "Nope. I'm good," she said standing up to leave. "You know I always liked sitting in this chair."

"No. I don't." Her mother busied herself at the antique dresser. She took off her watch and placed it on top – the second thing she always did when she came home, after washing her hands.

Noelle watched her, knowing her mother's next move as she walked to the small closet. The ratted peach bath robe was coming out next. Noelle always wondered why her mother kept the bathrobe in the bedroom's closet and never in the bathroom where it belonged. It was one of the things she never bothered to ask about though. Like the thing heavy on her heart she wanted to ask about now.

"Noelle," Sharon said as she put her arms through the robe's washed out sleeves. "You're making me nervous. Stop standing there like that. I brought you home some ribs and macaroni. It's on the stove."

She took that as a sign that her mother wanted some space to unwind. Noelle exited the room without a word, but didn't get far, only making it halfway down the steps. Turning back around, she made her way back up and re-entered her mother's open room door. Sharon sat on the chair Noelle had previously occupied, removing her nude stockings, and nearly flew out of the chair when Noelle said, "Ma, I got something to tell you."

Her hand flew over her heart. Eyebrows crinkled towards her daughter's voice. "You scared the be-Jesus out of me, girl. God knows I love you, but if you're not telling me you have cancer, I don't know what could be so important right now. Let me just get two seconds to relax."

"Ma, he wants me to call him."

"Who's him?" Sharon asked, letting her long, thick hair loose from its banana clip.

Noelle remembered how deep his voice was. Felt it whispering against her ear.

"My father."

Sharon stopped moving, letting her mouth gradually deepen into a murky frown. She turned her eyes from Noelle's and walked back over to her dresser, searching for what Noelle knew was her small enamel pill box. Reaching for her pill box was something her mother always did whenever she grew uneasy. It had been like that for as long as Noelle could remember, like the time she was five and asked Sharon why she didn't have a daddy like her friends in school.

"Aunt Rinni forwarded me a message on my cell," Noelle continued. "He was talking about how he wanted me to call him so we could talk." She purposely left out the part about him mentioning her mother trying to deter his interest.

Sharon threw an envelope to the side. No pill box under there. "Talk about what?" she asked, acting disinterested.

"I don't know. I guess he wants to see me. Aunt Rinni is trying to fix something up." Sharon mumbled under her breath, "Wait 'til I see that damn Rinni. Hell, I'll kill them both."

"Huh?"

"Nothing."

Noelle knew what she'd said. She stood by the door wondering if she was evil for staring right at the pill box sitting on the window sill while her mother searched like a mad woman for the little white stress relievers. "You wanna hear his message?"

"For what? Girl, erase it. Hear a message for what?"

"I wanna erase it Ma, but, I like . . . don't know if I

should."

Sharon's hair fell forward into her face as she lifted her stack of crocheting books, desperately seeking to find what she needed.

"Tell me if I should or shouldn't," Noelle said, watching her. "You know him better than me. Is it worth it?"

The harried woman abruptly stopped digging through the contents before her and faced Noelle, looking as if her face would explode. She pulled back and tried to remain a semblance of calm.

"It really ain't rocket science, little girl. Do not waste your time - he ain't worth it."

"Why? I'm saying . . . I know he's a dead-beat but, I was sitting here listening to his message before you came and I wondered, what if I did call him? Would it be so bad? It's not like I have nothing to lose. Definitely can't lose him again because I never had him to begin with."

"He doesn't deserve you."

"Maybe not, but -"

"But what? You want that man in your life?"

"I'm not saying -"

Sharon scoffed as she drawled out, "Don't lose yourself and get all impressed that he took a minute out his day to think about you."

Noelle took the blow in stride. "Don't it count for something?"

"You tell me. Is it enough to forget about the years he wasn't in your life?"

"I'm his daughter. It's not like I've completely forgiven him or anything, but we share the same blood, ma."

"And my blood is thicker than his running through your veins because I'm the one who's been here for you."

Frustration started to whip around Noelle's insides. Couldn't her mother step outside of her own misery and try to see things through her eyes for a change?

"I know that," she said as her voice rose at Sharon.

"So, if you know that, erase the message, get out of my face, go downstairs, and go eat your ribs."

"What did he do to you?"

Sharon turned her attention back to the missing pill box. Noelle felt bad for not pointing her towards it, but knew if she did it would be the end of the conversation. Her next steps would be to swallow the pills dry and lock herself in the bathroom. Noelle removed her eyes from the most wanted enamel box in America. Folding her arms across her chest, she looked at Sharon with defiance. It was definitely time for her mother to give some real answers.

"Besides the obvious, why do you hate him so much?"

"Leave me be. I can't take no more questions from you tonight. Where is that damn pill box?"

"I won't ask you anymore questions if you just tell me about you and him. You never talk about him and I don't know why. So, could you answer that one question, please? Then I'll leave you alone."

"I wish you'd make yourself useful and help me look for this thing that's hiding from me. Noelle, baby, look by my night stand for me. But I know, last night, I put that pill box right here on this dresser."

"Why is it so hard?"

Her mother ignored her and kept up the search.

"Ma, I just want to know that one thing."

She waited patiently for a response.

"Ma . . ."

Sharon opened her top drawer and moved her underwear around.

"Why are you so bitter?" Noelle finally blurted out, willing to say anything to get a reaction. The underwear's movement came to a halt as her mother froze where she stood. Her head swirled towards Noelle at a snail's pace, the small eyes narrowed and deadly. "Excuse me?" she hurled out.

BROKEN WITH STAINS

"I said why are you so bitter that you can't even talk to me about my own father? I didn't ask to be here Ma, the least you could do is tell me about the man whose voice is on my phone."

"The *least* I could do? You didn't *ask* to be here? A lot of mouth you got there for a girl who wasn't important in her most precious father's eyes. If your trifling daddy had his way, you would've never seen the light of day, much less stand here questioning me about his no-good behind. Maybe *that's* why I'm so bitter."

Noelle rocked on her feet.

Her mother continued, "Yeah, I'm so bitter because your wonderful father didn't think enough of you to stick around and make sure his daughter grew up well fed, with a roof over her head. Ya know, important things like that."

She pointed a finger towards Noelle and grew louder, "I'm bitter because I had a future. A life I wanted to create for myself and he made promises to me he didn't keep. I threw away my life for that man and look at me now . . . a cook in a restaurant doing all I can to make ends meet. Put myself in debt to purchase this house so you could have a real home, all so you can stand in my face and call me bitter."

Guilt immediately slashed Noelle across the gut. "I'm sorry, I -"

"No, don't be sorry. Keeping it real is what ya'll call it, right? Keep it real then. But you just know one thing: that stank dog who left a message on your phone is the man who broke my heart. The man who shattered my dreams. He killed my spirit. I've had just enough strength left in me to take care of you, Noelle. Look at me," she brushed her unmanicured hands over the front of her clothes – a foot-sweeping gray jersey skirt with pilling and a baggy white t-shirt. "I don't wear nothing fancy. I don't get my hair done. I don't remember the last time I bought a piece of jewelry, all because I take care of you. I live to make sure you're taken care of first. Something he never did."

Noelle was well aware that her mother never indulged in pretty little things. "I'm twenty-one. I make decent money with the website stuff I do. You don't need to break your back for me anymore."

"It's all I've done," Sharon said dropping her palms to her thighs. "He left me and all I had was you. A piece of the man I loved. The only piece I had left. I've only needed to take care of you."

Noelle studied her mother's dim brown eyes. They'd been that way forever, but it was at this moment that she could see how they'd originated. Sharon had always held sadness and mild anger behind her quietness. Love had been mixed and dished out in between it all, but the two had always been present, embossed and consistent in her mother's demeanor. For years Noelle wondered where it all came from. It was the same routine without fanfare. The same routine without a smile hardly ever appearing on her face. The constant quietness and washing of hands. But, Sharon didn't believe in emotion-sharing, just simply walked robotic through life doing only the things she needed to do. She woke up in the morning. Washed her hands. Went to work at the restaurant. Washed her hands. Came home after a long day. Washed her hands. Took a shower to get refreshed. Washed her hands. Ate leftovers she'd brought home. Washed her hands. Went to bed after watching the news. And sometimes woke from sleep to wash her hands too. All the washing was now revealed as a way to wash her hands of everything that was Paul Brooks. She wanted nothing to do with him. That mental vow had translated into a physical act that her mother just couldn't quit.

Noelle knew Sharon cared – she showed it in her own way just like when she'd stayed home from work two days in a row when Noelle was sick with the flu last year. Times like the other day, when she'd woken up early to make homemade waffles for Noelle before heading to her seven a.m. shift at

BROKEN WITH STAINS

Soul Divine's. Then there was the time she'd overhead her mother on the phone with an old friend, proudly stating that her daughter was a marketing major with her own web design business. But, Sharon had always held back in one area. Never would talk about Noelle's father . . . until now.

"Ma, I'm sorry," she said as she watched her mother wipe a tear from her cheek with a tissue. The last time she'd seen her mother cry was about two years ago. Noelle knew her mother thought she was sleeping in her room, but the whimpering that couldn't be stifled, pulled Noelle from her bed to peek through the crack in her mother's bedroom door.

Now, at the sight of her mother before her, Noelle's vision began to blur.

"Nothing's your fault," Sharon said wiping at her red face. "I chose the wrong man, that's all."

Noelle rubbed the back of her neck and stared down at the grey carpet. She didn't want to look at the woman who'd been in pain for far too many years. A tear slid from her eye and hit her big toe as she sought the right thing to say.

Sharon spoke first, "I can't forgive him, Noelle. Haven't found it in my heart to do that just yet."

"I know," she whispered in response. "But I'm stuck between a rock and a hard place. A rock . . . and a very hard place."

* * *

She never got around to finishing the paper. The movies – no longer a viable refuge for her unsettled mind. She could've called up Candace, so she didn't know why exactly she was letting David lead her into his livingroom.

"Talk to me," he said reclining back into a plaid loveseat.

Noelle scrutinized his coffee table which was actually a worn green trunk. On it was a yellow note pad, a pack of gum,

a bobble head figurine of Derek Jeter, and a book – The
Purpose Driven Life.

"What's on your mind?" he asked, following her gaze.

Noelle didn't know where to start and continued her
infatuation with the contents resting on the trunk. She felt a
magnetism drawing her hand to the book to see if the answer
to her purpose in life was hidden somewhere in between those
pages. Right now it felt as if her only purpose had been to bring
heartache into her mother's life. If she'd never been born,
would her mother's attitude be different? Would her father
have stuck around and caused light to shine in the eyes that
were now so bereft and dreary?

"My father really wants to see me, but my mother
doesn't want us to meet."

David rubbed his hands together and waited for her to
make eye contact with him. When she turned her face to his, he
asked, "Do *you* want to see him?"

"I want . . . I want . . . I don't know what I want," she
said, giving up.

"What's stopping you from knowing?"

Noelle pondered the question. "Mainly my mother. I
don't want to hurt her. She's really upset about this mess. And
then, I'm afraid for myself. I don't understand why he left to
begin with. Don't know why he wants to try and get to know
me now either. What if he walks away all over again? What am
I supposed to do then? And how will it affect my mother?"

"It's a risk."

"That I know."

"But you gotta decide if he's worth it."

"You tell me, 'cause I'm confused about everything,"
she said and waited for his response.

"No, I'm gonna let you tell yourself because you know
in your heart what you really want to do."

"I'm telling you I don't."

"And I'm telling you, you do."

BROKEN WITH STAINS

She sighed in exasperation and got up from the sofa. "You know what – I'm just gonna leave. I don't know what made me come over here anyway. I thought you could help me, but obviously -"

"Sit down, Noelle," he commanded.

She gathered her car keys and sunglasses from the sofa and turned to walk to the front door.

"I'm trying to help you," he said getting up to follow her. "You have to help yourself too. Don't just walk away. Face it. Face your fears, your anger, and everything else that's throwing you off balance."

She turned to face him and was startled that he was right there, less than half an inch away, penetrating eyes challenging her to walk out the door. She didn't want to leave him. He was right and he also felt safe. Noelle did know why she'd called him instead of Candace. She needed his sturdy arms to embrace her. They were what she wanted to let her know there was at least one man who cared enough to hold her near. The only one that could assure she was lovable and important.

David reached for her hand. She allowed him to lead her back to her seat on the comfy sofa.

"I want to see him," she admitted. "I've always wanted to see my father. I never talked much with my mother about him because she wouldn't talk about him. But it's not like it ever stopped me from wishing he'd come back."

"Then do it. Your mom is hurt – that's understandable. What he did was foul, but a man can change."

"You really think so?"

"I know so. I'm a living testament," he said, placing his palms on his chest. "God did a great thing in me, 'cause like I told you before, I was angry as hell."

She shook her head and laughed a little. "It was bad enough my father did me so dirty, but then came Chris. He did me the same way, David. I keep telling myself that all men are the same. They can't change. They lie. They hurt. And then there's you telling me that a man doesn't always stay the same. What am I supposed to believe?"

"I can't tell you what to believe."

Noelle leaned back, slouching further into the seat. "I look at you David and I think a good man is possible. But I'm tired. I don't want to hurt anymore. My father came at the wrong time. I'm still dealing with this break up and it's rough for me. Most times, I can't even sleep at night."

"I've been there too. It's not like I'm perfect where I stand now either. You're looking at a man that still has a ton of stuff to work on. I'm only twenty-four - I have a long, long way to go. Had to start somewhere though. And I suggest you start by facing your father. Tell him how you feel. Clear your chest, so you can get your mind at peace."

"If my mother found out I met up with him, she'd hate me."

"See, you have to get that out your mind. Stop thinking like that."

"You didn't see how she blew up at me earlier. Trust me, I know shit would hit the fan if she felt like I betrayed her. I don't want to do that."

"I feel you. But check this: What's gonna happen to you if you decide not to see him?"

That was one question she'd never considered. Still, the answer came immediately. "I'd think about it every day for the rest of my freaking life."

"There you go."

"Dang, David, this is so hard."

"It isn't really."

"What makes you say that?"

"A minute ago you said you've always wanted to see your father. Always is finally right here, right now. Purpose yourself to make it happen. And to start you off on the journey, let's make a toast to the future."

BROKEN WITH STAINS

Noelle looked at the trunk. There were no drinks to toast with.

David stood up and answered her next question before she even had a chance to ask, "Come on – we out. We about to get our toast on with some grape nut ice cream."

* * *

On the way to the Ice Cream Factory, the more advice David gave her, the more she began to feel at ease with the idea that something decent could come out of a meeting with Paul Brooks.

They pulled up to the store and Noelle stayed seated at David's request. In his presence, she wasn't allowed to open her own doors. After helping her out, they headed into the store arm in arm. Surprise replaced the smile still in place when she turned to see Chris looking her way.

Her mind halted as she continued to walk, joining the back of the line with David. Chris stood two people ahead in line. Peering into the glass ice cream case, David scoped out the selection, not at all aware that the infamous ex was there watching them both. Noelle tried to focus her attention on the menu behind the counter, but couldn't help noticing him mean-mugging her every few seconds.

She scooped her hair behind an ear with a finger and repeated the nervous motion as she looked to see if he was there by himself. When it became clear that he was, her heartbeat subsided a pace.

"Know what you want?" David asked, jarring her from the distraction.

"Uh . . . yeah . . . I, uh . . . I'll take a vanilla cone."

"Vanilla, plain? I thought you were Queen Grape Nut," he laughed.

"Um, yeah . . . that's what I meant. A grape nut cone," she answered, completely flustered.

Chris further fried her nerves when he turned around again with brows knitted, forcing a new knot to develop in her stomach.

Then it hit her. She wasn't cheating on anyone. So why was she getting all fidgety and scared at the sight of the liar who'd done her wrong? The smile she'd walked in with crept back onto her face and stayed. She was going to happily use this happenstance to her advantage. After catching Chris with more than one girl, it was time he saw that if he couldn't appreciate her, someone else was willing and able to take his place.

Noelle watched as Chris made his order and waited for the girl to come back with his purchase. She noted the shifting from one foot to the other as he continued to take glances at her then proceed to turn away.

She waited until he shifted his eyes towards her again and took the opportunity to lean into David, gently touching him on his arm. David looked to Noelle with a grin. She whispered a joke in his ear and slightly pressed her chest into his arm as they laughed.

Her hope was that Chris was dying inside. She made sure he got a clear view as she tenderly brushed a piece of lint from David's fresh cut. Looking back at her ex-boyfriend, it satisfied her to see that his eyes were fixed on everything she did. Even from where she stood, she could see the muscled tightening under his skin. Chris didn't even notice the cashier handing him the brown paper bag with his items. The customer next in line alerted him to the bag stretched before him.

Clearly disturbed, he collected his purchase and rocked out of the front door with his chest puffed out as far as it could go. His "big man walk" Noelle supposed. The walk that was supposed to let her know he wasn't tripping over the fact that she was there with another guy.

She clapped inwardly and shrugged. *And I should care about your pouting when I have a much better man by my side?* A pound of weight drifted off her shoulders. Her upper hand felt strong and powerful right now as she basked in the glow of knowing Chris had received a tiny taste of his own medicine.

Noelle was so lost in the moment as she stared into the ice cream case, she didn't even notice when Chris walked back into the shop and came to stand beside her.

"Noelle."

She jumped when she heard the voice say her name. He was back and way too close. She scurried to relax herself, unwilling to let him see her tense.

"What?" she responded with a smirk.

"I need to talk to you outside for a minute."

"For what?"

David squeezed her hand. She turned to him to see jaw muscles slowly clench though his eyes were still calm. "Is everything cool, Noelle?"

Chris grilled David with steely eyes. David let go of Noelle's hand and positioned himself to face his new challenger.

The tension was thick and sour and she didn't like the sudden feeling. "I'm cool," she told David. "This is Chris - my ex. I got this."

"You ain't gotta explain nothing to him. Come outside, I wanna holla at you. Now."

Noelle blinked twice before speaking. "Whatever you have to say, you can say it right here." Chris moved closer.

"Stop playing games, Noelle. Whoever this cat is, I don't want him in my business." He grabbed her arm.

"Man, listen," David said shoving Chris' hand away from Noelle. "It's not about to go down like that."

Noelle's pulse raced as she processed the scene about to take place.

Chris grabbed her arm harder this time and yanked her out of the way. He rushed David, but fumbled when he missed his target. He dodged Chris' move and was now behind the guy who was slightly smaller in build. David quickly grabbed Chris' right arm and twisted it behind his back, pressing his face up against the glass ice cream case. A little girl screamed as the other customers hurried away from the altercation. Noelle watched in disbelief as her ex-boyfriend struggled to free himself from the herculean grip.

"Get off me!" he shouted as spit flew from his twisted lips.

David pushed harder against the glass and tightened his hold. "You tripping real hard right now. If you think you 'gone touch her like that while I'm standing right here, I'ma show you what's really good." He smashed Chris' body against the case once more. "Don't ever put your hands on her like that again or else it'll be a serious problem."

"Son, it's my word, I'ma put a bullet in your face if you don't get your hands off me!" Noelle didn't know what to do or say. Couldn't believe a trip for ice cream had turned into this.

"Threaten me all you want," David said, "but when I let you up, you better think twice before you do something you might regret."

All eyes were on the two men. Eyes wondering what Chris' next move would be when David released his grip. Noelle took a step back and closed her eyes for a second when David let go. Chris regained his balance and briefly shifted his eyes towards Noelle - embarrassment flooded his face. Unfortunately, his eyes showed that he wasn't finished and had his manhood to prove. He took his shirt off and threw it to the ground. The store's manager was on the phone, yelling that he was calling the police to lock some asses up. Half of the stores patrons began to leave, not wanting to find out how far this would escalate, while the other half decided to stick around for the show. Noelle wanted to slip out too, but instead rushed in front of David to block him from Chris' attack.

"Move out the way, Noelle," Chris yelled. "I'ma give

this boy the ass-whipping he's looking for."

"No, you need to knock it off. We're not together anymore so quit making a damn scene. You got the manager on the phone trying to call the cops – this is getting completely out of control."

David touched her shoulders and tried to shift her to the side. "Let him challenge a man," he said. "If he's bad enough to roll up on you, let's see him try to do the same to me."

"Let's do it then," Chris said walking towards them. "Push her out the way and let's make it happen."

With her back pressed against David's chest, Noelle felt his muscles tense and knew he was gearing up to teach Chris a lesson. She pushed back against him and shouted, "Ya'll are not about to fight up in here. You need to leave now, Chris!"

He screwed his face up and took a step closer. "Bitch, move or else I'm gonna move you."

David tried to move her again, but she wasn't about to budge.

"You really have some nerve. If I'm such a bitch, why you doing all this then? If you don't care about me, why are you still trying to ruin my life?"

"You got ten seconds before I move you," he shot back.

"You cheated on me and did all your dirt and that's not enough for you?"

"Five seconds."

"Leave me alone. I don't want nothing to do with your 'ignant ass anymore."

"Get outta my way before I slap you, bitch!"

It was a final stab in the heart that was now pure pulp and mass confusion. Her wrath drove her forward. "I'll show you a freaking bitch." Noelle got right up on him. Mustering all of her strength, she slammed her knee between his legs. There were collective gasps all around her. Chris' eyes widened as big as golf balls while in slow motion he slumped to his knees.

"Who's the bitch now?" she yelled in his face. Mouth open, hands grabbing whatever he had left of himself, he struggled to catch his breath. She stood over him with hands on hips.

"Oh, you can't speak?"

David attempted to pull her away from the paralyzed heap on the floor.

"Noelle," he said. "Let's just go."

She wiggled free from his grasp and move back towards Chris. His face was completely red now, the pain tearing away at him bit by bit.

"No," she said. "He ain't got nothing to say yet. Maybe this will help him out."

She raised her fist and brought it down across the side of her ex's face like Tyson aiming for a knockout. His face flew to the right and he lost his stability. Chris' head hit the floor as his hands remained cupping himself.

Noelle picked up her satchel purse which had fallen to the floor, along with the bag of ice cream Chris dropped during his struggle with David.

"Now we can bounce. We got what we came for."

34 sienna

"I'm nervous for that girl," Sienna finished, after relaying to Marni the frightening phone conversation she'd had with her student over a week ago. As they headed to the hair salon where Eve taught makeup application every Saturday morning, Sienna picked Marni's brain for solutions to her problem.

Maybe now wasn't the best time since they were on their way to surprise their friend for her birthday before the class started, but Sienna was at her ropes end and needed answers quick.

"You got me. I don't know, Sea. She kinda has to want to be helped. If she doesn't, there's not much you can do. These young girls are stubborn these days. Hell, grown women are stubborn these days too."

Sienna pulled at her lower region, adjusting the fabric of the new purchase she had on. "I'm sure I have to be missing something. I've never been in this position before, but I know I'm overlooking an answer to all this drama. Come on, rack your brain, girl. I'll be pulling my hair out in a second if you don't."

"You already said you tried calling her mother and couldn't get through."

"Right."

"Well, what about the principal? Or the police?" Marni asked, making a left at a busy corner.

"I can't call the police," Sienna said as her eyes followed a group of scantily dressed preteens.

"Why not?"

"If I did, the girl would skin me alive."

Marni gave her friend a helpless look.

Sienna adjusted the waist of the black capris that were

beginning to become a pain in the neck just like this problem. "There has to be some other way. I'll just have to figure it out." "And what if you don't?" "I will. Of that, I'm absolutely, positively sure. I'd die if she ended up in the hospital or something crazy like that." "I hate to say it but, she might. She knows the type of guy she's dealing with. Don't make a difference though 'cause love is blind."

They pulled up to a parking space a block away from the salon which was always crowded on a Saturday morning. Sienna carried with care, the square white box that held a rich chocolate cake with vanilla frosting. They'd stopped at Eve's favorite bakery and squealed with delight when they'd seen how beautiful the pink frosted roses had turned out. "She's going to love, love, love this," Sienna smiled. "I can't wait to see her face, especially since we haven't seen her in two weeks."

Marni and Sienna hopped out of the car and headed to the salon. The shop's blue and white façade was within view when Marni squinted her eyes at something in the distance and focused real hard. "Hey, is it me or does that look like Marcus' car to you?"

"Where?" Sienna asked, craning her neck in the direction of Marni's finger.

"Right where that parking meter is." She sucked her teeth, waved away her suspicion. "Don't mind me, it's probably someone else because what would Marcus be doing over here anyway?"

Sienna laughed. "I spoke to him last night. He said he'd be swamped at the office, drowned under another stack of papers for the weekend. He's probably up to his nose in them now, trying to claw his way out for air."

They were two cars away from the silver Benz that looked so much like his. Both trained their eyes on the back window to see if they could catch a glimpse of the driver. They saw someone in the driver's seat and another person on the passenger's side. Both occupants had their faces pressed together.

"Oh Laaawd," Marni sighed. "Isn't there a hotel down the street from here? I know we passed one on the way." They giggled as they reached the passenger side of the car. They couldn't help but be nosey and sneek a peek into the rolled down window.

The world ceased to rotate for a minute as Sienna tried to register the situation before her. The man and woman had come up for air after their passionate liplock. The man looked like her man, Marcus. The woman looked like her best friend, Eve.

An unidentifiable sound escaped Sienna's lips.

The two bodies whipped around, facing Sienna and Marni in their stunned silence.

"Eve! What the hell . . . ," Marni yelled, face twisted in astonishment. She was the only one who managed to get a word out.

Marcus was next. "Sienna, trust me baby, it's not what it looks like."

"No . . . no . . ." was all she could get out as she dropped the cake box to the pavement. She felt her feet scrambling to the passenger side window, her trembling hands clutching the low glass as she glared in at Eve. "Don't tell me you did this to me, Eve. Don't tell me that you're supposed to be my bestfriend and you're here with my man."

Eve jerked her body forward and stared up at Sienna with boldness as she said, "Is this proof enough for you? I told you about him. I warned you time and time again. You knew what type of dog he was."

"I knew what type of dog he was?" she screamed, flabbergasted. "I'm gonna kill you . . ." Her next succession of movements were random and uncontrolled. She wasn't aware of the moment her hands sprung into massacre-mode. On impulse she opened the passenger-side door, reached in swiftly, and wildly grabbed Eve by her false hair.

Eve's scream pierced the morning air. Sienna heard Marni in the background yelling, "Oh my God, Sienna. Stop!"

She rushed to pry Sienna's hands from Eve's bulk of black strands. There wasn't much she could do - Sienna held a death grip on the hair entangled in her hands. Eve's body was rag doll-like on the concrete as she tried her hardest to maneuver herself. She ripped her black fishnets in the useless struggle to gain footing. "Everything I've been through with him, you knew about," Sienna bellowed. "And then you go and throw our friendship down the drain like this?" Sienna staggered backward a bit as Eve pushed forward and grabbed her legs.

"You stupid fool," she growled. "He never belonged to you. Can't even see that and the proof's in your face." Eve tried again to climb to her feet. Her blue suede heels slipped off in the process. She reached up and tried to grab at the top of Sienna's blouse.

"Do something Marcus," Marni screamed while struggling to pull the two friends apart. A crowd began to form on the street as the brawl continued. Sienna raised a closed fist and smashed it against the top of Eve's head.

Marcus took it as a cue to separate the two women. "Stop, Sienna! Stop!" He picked her up from behind as Marni pried the strong hands from Eve's hair.

Marcus placed Sienna on her feet once they were separated. Standing in front of her, he did all he could to calm her down while gripping her face between his hands. "I'm so sorry baby. I'm so sorry. Look at me. Just let me talk to you."

She shook herself from the human vise, smacked her hand clear across his face, and yelled, "Don't touch me – I hate you! You couldn't stop doing this mess behind my back, could you? Couldn't be satisfied until you took it one step further 'cause it wasn't enough to have your cake and eat it too. Why Eve? You could've messed with any female you wanted to and

BROKEN WITH STAINS

you had to hurt me by choosing the whore I'm closest to?"

Eve was standing now, her hair an unruly jumble of madness about her head. Rushing up behind Marcus, she swung her fist in an attempt to connect with Sienna's face. Marcus promptly whipped around and held Eve's arms behind her back. "He . . . he was never yours . . . you damn fool." She laughed at Sienna at the same time huffing for lack of breath. "He ain't shit . . . and you dumb as hell for stickin' with him. I told your ass . . . to drop him. You wouldn't listen to me so . . . this is what you get!"

Sienna grappled with the urge to take off her shoe and smack Eve with it. She opened and closed her fists by her side instead. "So you became a ho to prove your point?! All the times I confided in you . . . I thought I knew you, but I was wrong."

Eve laughed louder this time. "You're always wrong. You always act like you know everything, but you the dumbest teacher I ever seen. All this time . . . signs in front of your face and you still couldn't see what he was doing to you."

"It was a mistake, Sienna," Marcus said, jockeying for a position to defend himself. "I love you."

"Shut up, you lie! I gave you chance after chance after chance -"

Eve sucked her teeth, "Yeah, you gave him a chance to screw me too."

The words cut into Sienna like a rugged blade to her throat. It took all the oxygen she had left and at the same time fueled her to lunge forward with a pained growl. Her nails glided across the side of Eve's face, she slid, and landed on her knees next to the forgotten cake box.

Eve shrieked, yet continued her rant as Marcus kept his grip tight. "I let him smash me real good. For you, Sienna! I did it just for you! And I'm sure he'd hit it for me nice and proper one more time if I let him."

Sienna's eyes clouded with vengeful tears. The

woman she'd considered a sister, was crushing her deeper into the ground with every word from her mouth. It all felt surreal. Even lifting the cake box from the ground seemed like an outer body experience. Sienna determinedly charged for the same woman she'd told her many secrets to. The woman who she'd shared her worst fears and saddest tears with.

She opened the lid of the box and heaved the cake into the center of Eve's face. Icing and chocolate slid down her contorted expression in chunks.

Marcus released Eve as a load of the confection hit the front of his suit. The stunned figure wiped at her eyes, tried to quickly regain her vision.

"Well, well, well. Look at these asses fighting over Mr. Hot Shot Marcus." The person slowly clapped her hands before finishing. "Doesn't it make you feel proud?"

All eyes rotated to the woman who'd stepped forward from the gathered bystanders all around. Sienna still had unfinished business to handle with Eve, so the person standing with arms folded across her chest didn't register to her at first.

"Nonda, wha . . . what're you doing here?" Marcus asked, struggling to get the sentence out.

Sienna's head swiveled at the name of the female who'd called to harass her numerous times. *It's her,* Sienna screamed within. *All this time, she's really been following me?* Her eyes passed over the rude woman who'd watched her at the after work party and followed behind her car on the way to her mother's house.

"Don't worry about what I'm doing here," she snapped. "Worry about taking care of your son. You not gonna avoid me and think it's all good. No, you got another thing coming if you think ducking and dodging is gonna get rid of me."

Sienna looked over at Marcus. "She's telling the truth, isn't she?"

Marcus avoided Sienna's eyes as his jaw muscles tightened. He looked up to the sky and blew out a long, shaky breath.

"Answer me, damnit! Do you have a child with her?" Sienna's entire body shook as she waited for an answer she didn't want to hear.

He shifted his eyes and looked at Nonda instead.

"Don't look at me, dummy. The heffa asked you a question."

Marcus moved his eyes back to the ground. "It's true," he said. "I'm so sorry. I didn't mean for this to happen."

Nonda chimed in without delay, "The 'this' he's talking about is our two and a half month-old son. The one he's been neglecting lately. The 'this' I'm about to take his ass to court for in a hot minute."

The sunlight suddenly became dim to Sienna. Her legs gave way and she collapsed to the ground. "Sea . . ." Marni said hurrying to grab her friend.

Marcus ran to her and adjusted his hands around her torso to pick her up. On shaky hands, Sienna pedaled in the opposite direction, moving away from him as fast as she could.

"I don't ever want your hands on me again! You ever come near me, I'll get a restraining order against you. That's a promise you disgusting loser."

Marni helped her best friend to her feet. She grabbed Sienna's hand and said, "Sea, don't even stress it. You don't need this crap anymore."

"Sienna, I never meant to hurt you," Marcus tried one last time.

Marni pulled her along. Sienna stumbled over her feet as she moved with her friend's feverish pace. She wanted to let his words go, but also wanted him to know one final thing.

"The sad part is, you gave up a beautiful woman for these trashy hoes. You were nothing but a waste of my time."

* * *

TAMARA BURKE

Sitting in the gray chaise by the shriveling tower of potted plants, Sienna sat with her knees drawn tightly against her chest. She sipped on a mug of peppermint tea and numbly tuned into an old black and white movie that played on TV. Which one, she didn't know. In a trance-like state she watched the fair-haired white damsel fall into the arms of a dark, mysterious fedora-wearing man. Desperately, she held him into herself like he was the one thing in the world she needed to survive. The man in turn, stood stiff and cold as he removed her hands from his tall body.

The scene brought back the chaos from this morning. Images of Marcus devouring her ex-bestfriend flashed through her mind. It killed Sienna to know she'd been clinging to a man who proved so heartless. Sitting in her apartment with the tepid mug unstable in her hands, she was alone in her desolation when she shouldn't have been. However, she needed this time to sit and mourn in her own space. She let Marni know she would be fine and refused her friend's offer to sleep over. Time was needed as well as the opportunity to come to terms with the fact that it was now time to get used to being without the man she loved with every fiber of her being. The tea was doing little to help - Sienna's belly burned at the realization that she'd loved Marcus so much, she'd forgotten to love herself too.

The muscles in her shoulders felt twisted and battered. Pain, both physical and emotional, blazed stronger with each inhale she took. Today's melee was programmed on repeat; a nonstop whirlwind of playback blinking brightly through her brain. Boldy there was Nonda. Marcus had created a child with the stalker. The girl had been sexing her man, gone through nine months of pregnancy, and nursing a child while Marcus said nothing. Not even after she'd confronted him with the truth on more than one occasion. How could she be so dumb? He'd made her look like a fool in front everyone on that Bronx street today.

Tears rolled down Sienna's cheeks in a fervent storm of

anguish. She felt stranded without a life boat in the vast sea of dejection surrounding her.

More tears came as she watched the couple on the TV screen. The feelings of loss and betrayal were a disease that coursed through each joint in her body. Marcus' cruelty was bold and without bounds; his true colors now spread out and undeniable like a palate of sin. He'd not only given the gift of motherhood to someone else, but he took it upon himself to sleep with one of her best friends as well.

Sienna placed the half-empty mug on the carpet and rested her head against the arm of the seat. The drops spilling from her eyes washed the chair's soft leather as she emptied herself of them all until she'd run dry.

* * *

Three knocks sounded against her apartment door, jolting Sienna from her sluggish daze. She looked at the clock. Eight forty-five p.m. She'd been in the same spot for five hours straight.

She prayed it wasn't Marcus because she was in no mood to file a police report tonight.

Dragging her bare feet, Sienna made her way to the front door. She looked through the peephole and was startled to see Tandi standing there.

"Tandi?" she asked, incredulous. "What . . . what are you doing here?"

"Please, Ms. Burgess . . . I . . . I just need someone to talk to."

Unsure of whether to let her in or not, Sienna held the doorknob and realized once she opened it, there was no turning back. She'd already went through enough horror-filled events for the day, she didn't want to take a chance on experiencing one more. Yet, on the other side of the door was the girl that had been extremely difficult to get through to. How could she simply tell her "no" and walk away? Deciding there wasn't anything more that could happen to sour her day, Sienna undid the locks and hoped she was making a smart move.

She swung the door open and gasped when she took a closer look at her student's face. Fierce, purple bruises were spread across it in about four different places as far as she could see.

"What in the world happened to you?! Come inside," she said, dragging the young girl in. Sienna flipped the light switch on and followed Tandi over to the sofa. The teen kept her head down, but Sienna could see the wet lines along the sides of her face.

"He did this to you, didn't he?"

Tandi nodded her head reluctantly.

Sienna reached out to touch the largest bruise, the one sitting right below her left eye. As she used a finger to barely caress the burgeoning lump, Tandi winced from the slight pressure and moved her head out of reach.

"Oh, Tandi," Sienna whispered at the same time her shoulders slumped. "Why . . . I don't get it . . . why'd you let him do this to you?"

Her eyes closed for a brief second before she finally spoke. "I don't know how to leave him, Ms. Burgess. He's been beating on me for so long, I guess I'm just used to it." She wiped the snot running from her nose with the back of her quivering hand and continued. "You're the only one I have to turn to. I know I didn't want to listen to you before, but . . . you're the only one who even seems to care."

Sienna stared at the harsh, open cut across Tandi's top lip. Her heart ached at the sight of the dried blood around it. "Did you tell your mother what's been going on?"

"My moms don't care 'bout shit like this."

"What do you mean? I'm sure she –"

"You don't know her. Trust me – she care about partying every night of the week, she care about her Jack

Daniel's and Alize, she care about my father who will never marry her ass, but she don't care about me getting my ass beat."

Sienna tried another approach. "So what about your father? Couldn't he -"

"My father lives with his other baby mother and her two kids. He comes around every now and then. But he don't come to see me or my brothers. When he's over, it's to lay up in between my mother's legs."

She scoured Tandi's body to see what else he'd done to her. She noticed the scraped knuckles with a bit of hanging skin. Saw the dirty, chipped nails she knew Tandi must've tried to fight him off with.

"Be right back," Sienna said and rose from the sofa. She returned a few seconds later with peroxide, cotton balls, and an ointment.

Tandi protested before Sienna even twisted the lid off the brown plastic bottle.

"It might sting some, but you have to let me put this on it."

"Chill, Ms.Burgess. I can't even take the air brushing up against my skin right now."

Sienna looked at the scared girl sitting on the edge of the sofa as if sitting back in the seat would be too painful to bear. "Those wounds could get infected. You came to me so I could help you, Tandi. Give me the chance to start doing that right now."

She hesitated at first, but eventually relaxed her body and let Sienna bring the damp cotton up to her face. Tandi cringed and let out a moan when the wetness touched her skin. It was no different when Sienna went over each of the deep purple marks, making sure to get the scarred lip too. She applied the ointment to all the areas and put the products on the floor.

"We have to file a police report."

An anxious expression took over Tandi's face.

"No! No police. Ain't nothing they can do anyway."

"Yes, they will do something. They'll put his black behind in jail for what he did to you." She stood up and turned to walk away. "As a matter-of-fact, let me put on some clothes, I'm taking you to the hospital because -"

Tandi bolted from her seat and gripped her teacher's arm. "Wait! No hospitals either. Stop and listen to me for a second. Just this one time, stop and listen to what I gotta say. I need to be heard - no one ever listens to me. I don't want to go anywhere, I'm just asking you to listen. "

The tough girl Sienna always knew fell apart in her arms. She hugged the pleading girl and held her as tight as she could. The abundant tears soaked through Sienna's t-shirt as Tandi's excruciating cries bounced off the walls of the apartment.

They settled back down into the sofa as Sienna cradled her head against her chest. Love was all the girl wanted. She saw it for what it was and could see herself in Tandi's wounded image too. Sienna knew she'd been searching for the same thing all along. It felt freeing to acknowledge her truth as she comforted her student through this storm. She'd willingly given herself up to abuse the same way Tandi had. The only difference: the young girl wrapped in her arms had the physical wounds to prove it.

"It's gonna be okay, sweetie. Everything will be just fine," Sienna consoled while tears fell down her own face in a sweeping cascade. The drops anointed Tandi's sweet-smelling hair while they embraced each other as if to save themselves from drowning.

Tandi made an effort to get her thoughts out. "It didn't . . . He wasn't . . . Things got out of hand so fast. He wasn't always like this," she hiccupped between breaths.

Sienna stroked the crown of her head. "It's okay. Take your time. You can tell me everything."

She shivered at the same time she coughed and after

recovering, she continued, "We've been together since I was thirteen. For two years I've stayed in his corner. I tried to leave him before, but he wouldn't let me go. Told me if I ever left him, he'd kill me. So I stayed and took the beatings. Partly because I was scared, but mostly because I loved him so much."

Sienna rubbed the raised bumps that assembled on Tandi's arm and listened.

"He beats me so, so bad sometimes. I know I should, but I can't walk away. I love him so much, sometimes I cry at the thought of him not being in my life. I know you think I should kick him to the curb . . . I can't though - he's all I have."

"He's not all you have, Tandi. I'm here. And I'll always be here if you need me."

"I can't leave him – you don't understand."

"You have to."

"I- I- I can't," she stuttered. "It's not that easy."

"Things aren't always easy. But you could try," Sienna said, as she continued to let her tears flow.

Tandi fiddled with her ashen fingers. Sienna could feel the girl's heart beating wildly against her chest.

"You ever been in love, Ms. Burgess?"

She paused before answering, feeling a new spring of tears well at the back of her eyes. "Yes. I have."

"So since you been in love, you know how it feels to wanna be with somebody so bad you don't know what you'd do if you couldn't be with that person anymore."

Sienna thought about Marcus. Flashbacks of him admitting that he'd fathered a child with Nonda, created another shattered piece to what remained of her broken heart.

"Unfortunately, I do know what it feels like."

"Then you know what I'm talking about. You know that even if that person kills you inside . . . the love you got will always stay tough 'til the end. Nothing in this world can tear ya'll apart."

35 joy

For the past week Joy had been out of it. Transitions and oddities were taking place within her frame; her body simply did not feel the same, but she tried not to stress over it and went about life as usual.

She figured it was due to the pregnancy, though it still amazed her that there was life growing inside the slight pouch of her once flat stomach. Joy actually began to love the idea of having a full, round belly. Imagined herself still rocking Marc Jacob heels when she was stretched to the limit and ready to pop. More often than not, she smiled at the thought of her and Luce walking down the street pushing a baby carriage, taking turns changing diapers, and picking out the flyest designer newborn clothes.

When she snapped out of her daydreams and back into reality, it seemed like she spent every waking moment at the club. Starting at six p.m. and ending at three in the morning steadily took its toll. The last time Joy had a chance to visit a doctor at the neighborhood health clinic was last week and even though this three days ago she'd begun to feel light-headed and dizzy, she carried on throughout the following days, ignoring the weird feelings becoming increasingly frequent.

Even so, a queasy stomach or even Luce doing dirt in her face was not enough to deter Joy from stacking all the money she could. Sure, she'd been tempted to storm out and never return since Luce had shown up with the same chick numerous times. His disrespect turned up to the highest notch as he was full-on ignoring Joy now. It was as if she never existed. No longer did Luce answer her calls and forget about acknowledging her whenever he entered the club.

None of the dancers were allowed to speak to him at

any time they were on the clock. But even if a break came up, the bouncers were ever-present near Luce's table to make sure the girls and anyone else kept a comfortable distance. The thought of having an abortion crossed her mind a couple of times over the last few days, but she knew she wouldn't follow through. The baby was her last chance at keeping him.

Joy spent every day trying to figure out when things had turned this way. She couldn't pinpoint the moment when he'd stop wanting her and lost interest in her swagger. It was difficult putting on makeup, wigs, and costumes along with her tough façade every day. It was even harder when life was growing inside of her, knowing that her child's father didn't think her important enough to even care. She was carrying the baby of the man she wanted more than anything. Though he didn't know about his child, it was only because she hadn't been given the opportunity to tell him to his face. Luce could continue making moves and brush Joy to the side today, but once he found out she was carrying his child, she was convinced that it would bring about a change of heart.

Thinking of her own father, Joy had come to terms with the fact that he'd left before she was even born. Blue was the reason behind why she'd grown up without a real father in her life. Her mother was a loser.

It was evident the man had realized what a sickening woman she was and hit the road as soon as possible. Luce, on the other hand, was acting up only because enjoyed getting under her skin. Joy had yet to find a reason why, but somehow it made her want him more.

Removing her body from the pile of decorative pillows covering her bed, she mentally prepared herself for the day that lay ahead. She had to be at the club an hour earlier today. After looking at her watch, she put some pep in her step. An hour was all she had to hustle out the door in order to make it to her number one client. Dalton Cartagena – or Yuck Face as she liked to call him – had booked her for one of the more outrageous new rooms Luce had put in. Iceland was a blue and white fantasy of wild proportions – it would take three hours alone to cover her whole body in the ridiculous amount of crystals that would be her costume for the night. From what she'd heard from one of the other dancers, it was the most expensive room to enter at fifty thousand dollars for the evening.

She ran into her room to find the booty-cutting yellow shorts she'd bought a couple days ago. It was nowhere to be found. After searching every inch of her large bedroom, she sat on the edge of her bed to calm another sudden dizzy spell. Joy tried to think, tracing her steps back two days ago. *I know I'm not going crazy*, Joy assured herself as she disregarded the sharp pain that made a quick move through her belly. There was no time to pay attention to that – those shorts were needed now. Joy racked her brain and leapt up from the bed when she remembered she'd put the bag at the top of the closet in the hallway. She flew to the closet, pulled out the four-step ladder., climbed up, and reached into the mass of bags, clothes, hair tools, blankets, and everything else in her search for the silver shopping bag.

It was at the tip of her fingers, but slightly too far back for her to firmly grasp. Joy stood on the tips of her toes, leaning into the shelf as far as she could go. The feeling of nausea rushed in, blind-siding her and she tilted back on the balls of her feet. She swayed a bit to the side. *Damn, I'm 'bout to break my neck. Girl, quit playing and get yourself together.* Joy tried to shake it off when unexpectedly, the smash of a fist descended into her stomach. There was no one else there, but the blow to her mid-section caused her to look down at the culprit.

She held her tiny bump with both hands as her vision became a dull haze. Involuntarily, she leaned on the ladder and reached forward to grab the pole her coats were hung on. The pain hit instantly as her fingers bent backward, sliding off the hangers in her way. Unable to grip the pole, she fell forward slightly, crashing her shoulder against the closet door. The impact sent her over to the left. Joy screamed as her feet slipped off the ladder and she landed, with a thud, against the hard wood floor.

Her stomach took the brunt of the fall. She could feel her back throbbing from the force of it all. Tears stung at the corner of her eyes while she took her time getting up from the floor. Joy flexed her arms, legs, and rolled her neck around to make sure nothing was broken. Everything seemed okay, besides the slight pain in her back. Moving the ladder out of her way, she carefully stepped back into her bedroom.

Joy moved her head from side-to-side and laughed a little at the idea that she'd almost cracked her skull over a pair of shorts. She wasn't about to risk her life again and decided to wear something reachable instead - at this point, a denim skirt would have to do.

Joy slipped on the denim skirt and found a white spaghetti tank with a sheer blouse to go over it. She looked at the clock on her night stand and saw that she had only thirty minutes to spare. Moving to the bathroom, she ran a comb through her straightened hair and applied a peach gloss to her lips.

Something still wasn't right.

The ache in her back seemed to spread around to her chest. From her chest the uneasy sensation firmly settled into the core of her gut.

"Oh shit," she said, reaching out for the edge of the sink.

Sweat sprung from her pores, saturating her brow, neck, and armpits. She was scared, but encouraged herself to calm down. Time was ticking by and there was no way she'd make it to the club on time if she couldn't pull herself together. She figured, whatever was happening to her, was something that came along with being pregnant. She rubbed her belly in small circular motions, went back over to the sink, and threw healthy splashes of cold water on her face. Cupping her hands, Joy drank from it as water ran down the slopes of her arms. The fluffy blue towel fell to the ground when she tugged it from its rack. Without a care, she put it to her face in a rush to dry herself quickly. Joy turned to exit the bathroom, but didn't get one foot out the doorway when she felt the wicked blow for a second time. Doubling over in agony, she shouted, "What the hell", before falling to her knees.

It was at that precise moment she felt the too-thick liquid forcing itself from between her legs. Sitting on the floor, she pulled her panties to her ankles and panicked when she saw the white lace saturated in dark blood. This was not supposed to be happening. Joy pounded the floor with her fist as the next blast of red tore through her open legs. She found the strength to get on her knees, crawled over to the toilet, and lifted its lid. Her blood-covered hands gripped the bowl's rim as she placed her head above the large hole. Lines of blood waywardly ran down the sides of the porcelain, mingling in jagged patterns with the shallow water below.

Joy heaved the contents of her stomach. It took effort to get it all out. Orange-brown vomit erupted from her nose at the same time, making it a task to get the air she needed. She choked on the remainder of what came spewing out.

It came quietly and unsuspected, the thought that crossed her mind. Like a wish riding on a prayer. *Ma, where are you? I need your help right now.* It would be all she needed so that she didn't feel so alone right now.

No sooner had the thought crossed her mind, she began to hate herself for thinking about it to begin with. Joy brushed the wishful thinking to the side, pushed her head further inside the bowl, and let her center purge itself clean.

* * *

BROKEN WITH STAINS

She lay in bed, a fetus curled up in between her white sheets. Two days ago the walls of all she had left had come crumbling down around her. It had been confirmed. After picking herself up and cleaning her baby from the bathroom floor, an hour later she sat numb as the doctor verified she'd suffered a miscarriage. She didn't need him to tell her. Joy knew she'd seen the little eyes, the feet, the mouth crying out for help.

Or maybe she didn't. But it was hard to tell what was real and what wasn't when the blood was so dark, so deep, and there was nothing she could do.

She'd driven straight home after her DNC procedure because there was nothing she wanted to do more than isolate herself from the world. There was no one she wanted to call. No Blue, no Poochie, no Luce – they couldn't make anything better. She fell into bed as soon as she entered her apartment, staying there with the emptiness mocking her dead plans. It was back to ground zero. There was nothing to keep Luce in her life with; no way she could think to get him back.

Three short days came and went. All she could recall eating was the last half of a left-over beef patty and a twenty-five cent bag of chips. Didn't know if that was yesterday or the day before. It didn't matter - there was only one she was eating for now.

Light squeezed through the slight openings of her bedroom blinds. The lids of her eyes tried their best to block out what came in. It would have been easier to place a pillow over her eyes, but Joy's bones were too weak for her to move. The scent wafting from her body alerted her to the fact that she hadn't seen the inside of a tub in a while.

The sudden explosion of banging on her front door nearly jolted her off the bed. They were like bombs going off, yet Joy was too weak and tired to move. She finally did when Luce's voice loudly rumbled through her apartment door. Gathering all the strength her body could manage, she made it to the door in time to hear, "You're not gonna have me standing out here waiting for you all day, Cinnamon. 'Cause if I have to open this door for you, some serious shit is gonna go down."

Joy could feel herself getting angry, but was too worn out to give birth to the feeling. She took her time unlocking the door. "What's the threats for?" she asked, frowning at his demonic face.

Luce stepped into the apartment and headed for the living room. Joy followed, dragging her feet, not caring about her unruly hair and lack of makeup. "What? You don't answer phones no more? Made me come all the way out here to see about my money? There better be a damn good excuse for why you've caused me to lose almost sixty thousand dollars over the past three days."

"Well, good afternoon to you too."

"Don't play with me."

"No - you don't play with me," she slurred, fighting off her fatigue. "You can't be serious coming over here wildin' out when I've been sick like a dog for three days straight."

"Sick? So what that mean? You that sick, you can't commit to a simple job I'm paying your ass good money to do? It's not brain surgery. You come. Play dress up. Take off your clothes. And smile in the client's face at the same time you're doing it. You cost me almost sixty thousand this week."

"Then you should've done it. If sixty thousand meant that much to you, you should've took my place and locked yourself up in one of them rooms with your leg twisted up behind your ear. Don't come up in my crib with that bull -"

"I give you the privilege of working in my club and you gonna stand here and disrespect me?"

"You brought the disrespect to me," she said pointing to her chest. "I've been here buggin' out 'cause I lost our baby and you come in here cursing me out because you lost a few bucks. Screw them sixty g's - I lost something way bigger than that. Something you knew nothing about because *you* don't know how to pick up a phone."

He blinked rapidly. "Baby? What baby?" he asked, looking at her stomach with perplexity marring his handsome features.

"A baby, ass-wipe! Our baby. Three months pregnant and still bringing my behind to the club every night while you dragging that video-ho to pose off in my face."

"Hold up," he cut in, raising a hand to his chest. "What's this 'our baby' crap you talking about? You got me real confused right now."

"I lost our baby, fool. I was pregnant and I lost your baby."

Luce took a minute to comprehend the news Joy had just dropped on him. She watched his reaction as understanding finally registered on his face. He placed a hand on one hip and rubbed his face with the other.

"How'd you make that happen?" he asked with brows taking on a life of their own.

Joy stared at him dumfounded. "You're asking me, how *I* made that happen? So I made the baby by myself?"

"Look . . . you got pregnant. I don't know that that baby was mine. All I know is that you got yourself pregnant. You would've had to have gotten rid of it anyway."

For the first time, Joy was robbed of all speech. Her usual witty comebacks had disappeared as she eyed him with bile steadily rising in her throat.

"And now that I think about it, it's kind of convenient for you to all of a sudden miss work because of some miscarriage. If you were really pregnant, why didn't you say something before?"

"I'm not lying!" she shouted, as an intense fury shook her to the core.

"Watch your tone. You work for me, not the other way around," he said, taking a step towards her.

She took an unbalanced step towards him in return. "Now it's all about me working for you. In the beginning it was trips to Miami and wining and dining. Now all you can talk about is I work for you?"

"You ever heard of a job interview? That's what the trip and all that was about. Don't tell me you really thought that I was trying to make a commitment to you or something stupid like that? Let me guess," he laughed, "you thought I was gonna slip a ring on your finger too." He shook his head and chuckled at the girl before him. "I told you from the very beginning that I'm a business man. No offense, you're good enough to be a Six Doors girl, but . . . nowhere near an option to be my wife." Joy was stone-faced. There were a million and one ways she visualized killing the man with the indifferent gaze breaking her down to the nothing he thought she was.

She lifted a trembling hand towards the closed door at the end of the hall. "I sat on that bathroom floor and bled all over the damn place. Pieces of your child are still on that mop in the corner over there and you're gonna question me like I'm lying? Disrespect me after I took my clothes off to make you money?"

"Don't forget you got a piece of that money too. One thing you can't say is that I don't pay my girls what they're worth. I choose the best of the best," Luce bellowed as his voice seemed to make the walls quake around them. "You were a top dollar ho when I first chose you, but now look at you . . ." His eyes drifted over her ragged appearance. "Hair ain't been combed in days. Gut sticking out under your dirty shirt. You probably been in here high off some mess and you wanna lay a guilt trip on me talking 'bout you had a miscarriage. I'm not buying into that garbage."

"I can't believe I let myself get sidetracked thinking you were somebody I wanted to be with. I'm so happy I never had the kid. Every piece of the pain was worth losing that baby when I did," Joy said as she let a solitary tear slide down face.

BROKEN WITH STAINS

He gave her a disgusted look as he walked over to the front door.

"You get paid to do a job. All this whining and carrying on ain't doing nothing but wasting my time and losing me money. Make sure you're at the club tomorrow night at six p.m. sharp . . . and don't act like you don't need the money."

Joy moved close to him as she let another drop of water find its way down her skin. "Don't get it twisted - you need me. I'm the one you need to make that money. You wouldn't be here right now if that wasn't the case."

"You were on the verge of broke when I met you. Don't think I don't know about you and who you are. You spend big, but you don't have nothing. You live on your own. Who's gonna take care of you if you don't take care of yourself? Be smart for once in your life. See you tomorrow and don't be late."

She stared at the closed door, unable to move herself from where her feet were planted. He had just been there, but that wasn't the Luce she had come to know. The one who only a few days ago, she'd anticipated bringing a child into the world for. Joy fell against the front door. She could hear the screams around her, but didn't realize they were coming from within. Books. Plants. Chairs. Frames. CD's. They were falling and flying and crashing in a tornado around her. And when it all came to a crescendo, she fell in a hush to the floor. Joy crawled to her room soon after, lay on her bed, and let her tears bleed one by one.

Through unclear vision she looked at her cell phone haphazardly thrown on the vanity table. Joy had no energy left, still she dug something up from the hollowness deep within. On her feet of pins and needles, she drifted over to the small rectangle. Picking it up, she dialed, reaching out to the mother she longed to touch.

"Hello?"

Joy closed her eyes and lost the nerve once she heard

the unaffected voice on the other end of the phone. Pressing "End" she walked shakily to the bathroom, sat on the floor, and hugged the mop's fabric, her head buried in the one thing she no longer had left.

36 paul

"**R**emember, God said that David was a man after His own heart. He murdered a man and God still considered him one of his own."

Paul reflected on the words Pastor Fisher had shared with him earlier that morning. He'd placed his story on the shoulders of the white-haired man, seeking to find a last word from the leader of the congregation. The tall man was as honest as they came, but had a youthful, vibrant approach to life that made it easy for Paul to share his fears. Direction was what he'd come for and so, Paul poured out his past indiscretions and fears so he could be advised as to what his next and final step should be. He told the Pastor of how he'd left the mothers of his children and what he'd done to warrant their hate and anger. Paul told of the years of distance. Shame. The trauma at the root of all he'd done. All he'd become.

He'd been ashamed to share the truth for far too long. But now he was past the stage of shying away from judgment. It was now or never. Do it all or do no more. This was the last place he could find encouragement or a word to hold off.

Annette and Blue had given him the go ahead, but Sharon was another story altogether. Now more than ever, a desperate need was tugging at the corners of his soul, but he wanted to be respectful. Figuring out how not to overstep his boundaries was a challenge.

"You can't change what happened in the past, Paul. What matters is what you do with the future ahead of you. Take note of what God did with David's."

When all was said and done, Pastor Fisher had made it clear. "Do you believe Jesus Christ is Lord?"

"I know He is," Paul answered.

The Pastor nodded his head and chuckled as he sat

forward across the table. "Well then, do you really think what you've done is so great, the Lord himself can't mend the situation if you let him take over?"

Paul let the question linger in the air.

"Take a chance on God," were Pastor Fisher's final words.

That was the fuel he'd come for. Paul shut the studio down today. He sat in his office chair and looked solemnly at the three numbers set before him, whispering to himself, "Take a chance on God."

He'd face the fire, the screams, the hurt, the pain, and the destruction head on – the running was now over.

37 noelle

Noelle sat with her back against the trunk of a tree and watched as Central Park became the scene of what had to be one of the most amazing things she'd ever witnessed. Her text book was open across her lap, but the sweet distraction made the words on the page nothing more than a second thought.

She found it funny that the couple that looked as ancient as time could still be that deeply in love after so many years. Sitting across from her, they kissed and held aged hands under the multi-colored umbrella shielding them from the harshness of the sun's rays. The silver-haired woman with a straw hat tight against her head, held onto her lover's boney arm, her hands thin and fragile, yet strong enough to hold firm. The frail man moved his veined foot with effort, but lifted it high enough to shoo away the low-reaching mosquitoes that threatened to make a feast of his lady love.

The display of affection made Noelle smile. After what she'd been through along with seeing the effects of the things her mother had experienced, it was good to see that someone's love had stood the test of time.

When her phone rang, only then did she pull her eyes from the romantic twosome. Her heart skipped a beat when she saw who was calling.

Paul Brooks.

She was scared and thought about not answering the urgent ring. And then she took another peek at the couple across from her once more.

They were laughing at each other's jokes, making the best of the numbered days they had left.

That image alone inspired Noelle to do just the same. "Hello?"

Paul cleared his throat on his end and spoke. "Hi . . . Noelle. It's Paul Brooks. Your father."

"I know," she said, soaking in the texture of his voice.

"Your Aunt Rinni gave me your number and I didn't know whether I should call you directly or not."

It was really him. She wanted to touch his face through the phone. "It's okay. You called and I'm fine with that."

"Good. I just want to make sure this isn't a bad time for you."

Noelle could hear the hesitation in his voice. "Really, it's cool. I'm in the city. Trying to study for school."

"Yeah, your aunt told me you were in school, taking summer classes. I've been wanting to talk to you for a while now. But if you need to study, I don't -"

"Aunt Rinni told me I should talk to you. Said she ran into you at a friend's wedding."

"We saw each other. I was surprised because I hadn't seen her in years."

Noelle didn't know if her next question would turn him off. Yet, it was something she had to ask so she'd get it off her chest. "Was it guilt that made you want to talk to me?"

Paul's breathing came in clearly over the phone.

She knew he was choosing his words carefully and waited patiently for him to get them out. "I wouldn't say it was guilt. Actually, I've really wanted to take this step for a very long time. I just couldn't figure out how you would react. It was fear that blocked me more than anything else."

"You don't have fear anymore? Or is it that Aunt Rinni made you do it?"

"Your aunt tried to make me take care of you when you were just born. I was stupid. I left. I'm here now because I'm strong enough to be here. I wish back then I could've been who I am today."

She didn't know what to say to that.

"How's your mother doing?" he asked.

"She's . . . okay."

"I feel weird about reaching out to you like this because I know she's not comfortable with the idea of us speaking."

"She told you that?"

He didn't want to stir up any friction. "My actions are inexcusable. I've fought with myself every day for years at the thought of walking away from you and your mother. I want you to know that I thought about you all the time."

"And you've been in New York the whole time?"

"Yes. I live in Scarsdale. In Westchester."

"How's everything over there?"

"Pretty good. I live with my wife, Camilla."

She had a step-mother.

"We've been married for seven years now."

That was when she was fourteen. She wondered if her mother knew about it.

"Ma never talked about you. I asked, but she never told me where you lived or anything like that."

"I moved around a bit. Finally landed in Scarsdale when I got married. We bought a house out here."

"So, what else don't I know about you?"

"I'm a professional photographer. Run my own studio in White Plains. To go back further, my parents both passed away when I was younger. They came from St. Louis where I was born. And . . ."

She waited as he held onto to his words.

"I have two other daughters. Your sisters."

Sisters? Sisters. What are their names? How old are they?

"Do they live with you?"

"No. I . . . uh . . . haven't met them either."

There were two more out there just like her.

"You have two other daughters besides me that you've never met?"

"One was born before you. The other, after."

This was a new twist she never expected. Her mother

had to have been withholding this information. "So you haven't spoken to them? Or are you trying to find them too?"

"Yes, I've been trying to get in contact with them also. You're the only one that I've been fortunate enough to speak with so far."

"How old are they?"

"The oldest, Sienna, is twenty-four. Your sister, Joy, is nineteen."

She'd never had a sister or a brother. Always thought she'd be an only child. Now she had sisters. Noelle couldn't decide how she felt about that.

"So, my mother wasn't the only one you did this to?"

"I made some bad decisions. I want you to know that I'm sorry that I wasn't there in your life. I'm sorry I couldn't be there for all three of you. You're twenty-one years old now. And I missed out on all those great years – I deeply regret not seeing you grow up into the beautiful young woman you are now. Rinni showed me a picture. You look just like my mother."

Noelle tried to picture what her deceased grandmother looked like. "I wondered if you ever thought about me."

"I remember holding you in my arms. I thought about you all the time."

She tried to feel the embrace of the man she didn't know. "Never did I think I'd one day be sitting here talking to you. I mean, I wondered if . . . if . . . if maybe you were close by or far away. Wondered if you were reachable or if you passed away. Not only are you here now, I can't believe I have two sisters I've never met too. Even crazier is the fact that you've never met them either."

Paul measured his answer before he spoke. "I'm trying my hardest to contact them and I'd love for you to meet them one day soon."

38 sienna

"So, I have two other sisters that my mother doesn't know about?"

"They were by two women I met after me and your mother broke up. We stopped speaking before you were born, so she had no way of knowing."

She was chin deep. First he wasn't in her life. Now he was there on the other line with two sisters in his back pocket. Sienna couldn't understand and the confusion only rose higher.

"Let me get this straight - it's three daughters you have in total. Not just me?"

"Yes. I've spoken to only one of them so far. Noelle. You're the second one I've been able to contact. And I'm grateful that you've given me this opportunity."

"I didn't know what to think when my mother first told me that you called her. But, I've just been so caught up in my own life over the past few weeks, I didn't know if I was ready to actually sit down and talk to you."

"Like I said, it's been a long time and I should've done this sooner. I sincerely hope I didn't invade your life in any way."

"I don't know you, but . . . you're my father. The words feel funny coming from my mouth. I know that's who you are and I haven't been told the full details about what happened between you and my mother. But . . . I don't see the harm in finding out more about you."

"Your mother - she's a special woman. When I met her she was intelligent, sophisticated, ambitious, caring. All around, everything a man could ask for."

"So what made you leave?" Sienna asked eagerly.

"My own insecurities. My own fears. It was all me. I didn't want to admit to myself back then that what I was doing was dead wrong, but deep down I was hiding, running from my past and afraid it would catch up to me."

"And my mother was a casualty."

"It was never my intention to purposely hurt her or you."

"Or the other two women."

"No. I never wanted things to turn out the way they did. I always had you and your sisters on my mind. You were the first-born. I should've done right by you. I could've avoided a lot of the unnecessary hurt that I caused."

She thought about Marcus, wondering if he could fathom all the hurt he'd caused her too. Maybe she could find the answer in Paul Brooks.

"If she was such a great woman, why was it so easy for you to bring so much pain to her life and never look back?"

Paul's breaths slowed as he thought about the question. "I was selfish. As selfish as a man could be."

"After all this time, have you truly, truly realized the kind of emotional pain that great woman had to endure?"

"I'll never be able to stand in her shoes and say I know exactly all that I put her through. But, from the heart, I'll tell you that I know what she went through wasn't easy. And if I could do it all over again, I'd have treated your mother like the wonderful woman she is. She didn't deserve what I did to her. You didn't deserve it either."

"So where do we go from here? I feel like I'm going to wake up tomorrow and find out this was just a dream or something," she said with a sad smile.

Paul's mind wandered back to the last dream that started him off on the journey to find his girls. "I would love if I could meet with you in person. Get you and your sisters together. If it were okay with you, I think it would be nice if you were able to meet them." The hairs on the back of Sienna's neck stood up. It was unnerving to know that a simple "yes" would connect her to two other women who shared the same

BROKEN WITH STAINS

blood and fatherless life.

"What a difference a day makes," she sighed. "Yesterday I didn't have sisters and today I do. I haven't yet come to grasp that, much less the idea of meeting the two."

39 joy

Joy absentmindedly closed the door to the club's hidden away storage closet. Paul Brooks was on the phone telling her she had sisters named Sienna and Noelle. It was a curve ball to her head. One that knocked her dizzy for a few seconds too long.

She flipped on the light switch, sat on a card board box in the corner, and questioned the man like she hadn't heard one word he said.

"Repeat that again."

"You have two sisters. The oldest is Sienna, who's twenty-four, and Noelle, she's twenty-one."

Her foot rapidly tapped against the polished floor.

"Blue don't know about your other daughters. I mean, she never mentioned nothing about them to me."

"No, I haven't told her."

"And they're not by your wife, um . . ."

"Camilla."

"Yeah."

"No. They have two different mothers."

"Wooow." She didn't know what else to say. Joy could hear the heels clicking across the floor above her head. She was sure her name was being called by Rocki somewhere up there. It was minutes until she took off everything she had on. Shivering in the small, cool space, she hurried Paul.

"I don't have much time left," she said into the phone. "I have to get back to work in a minute."

"Oh, okay. Where do you work, if you don't mind me asking?"

"I . . . I work with the disabled. You know, talk to them, help them put their clothes on and take them off – things like that."

BROKEN WITH STAINS

"That's great. That's really good. But I won't keep you since you have to get back -"

"Wait," she rushed in quickly. "I got a minute left. Before you hang up, I got a question for you."

"Okay."

"What was Blue like?"

"As far as . . ."

"You said that you weren't there because of some fear that made you disappear. But, what exactly did Blue do to push you away?"

Paul thought back to the loving woman he knew. The gray-eyed beauty with fight in her heart, unwilling to give up her child. "All Blue did was show me love. She's a strong, strong woman. I don't blame your mother for anything."

"And there was nothing she did that was wrong?"

"Joy, I want to be very clear about this: I'm at fault through and through. There's nothing your mother did to make me neglect my responsibilities. I'm the one who messed up when I ran away."

"You said she was a model and you took pictures of her?"

"I did. We shot a designer's collection and a photo story . . . The Exposition of a Pearl."

"She ain't never shown me any of the pictures you took."

"Well, I'd love to show you those photos of your mom along with some of my other work. You and your sisters. I could show you what I do and you'd be able to meet them at the same time."

"How would that happen? I don't even know anything about them, where they come from, or anything like that."

"They live in the Bronx."

She immediately wanted to know where, but thought it better to keep herself in check. It amazed her that she might've passed one of them on the street or that one might even be her next door neighbor and she had no clue.

"We're all here in the Bronx," she said instead. Paul Brooks surely had been a rolling stone.

"You can think it over. I don't want you to feel like I'm forcing you to make a decision this very minute."

"I can't make any promises."

Paul paused, knowing he'd never made any promises himself in the past. "I respect that. You have my number now. You can call me anytime."

39 paul

Paul sat on something that felt like air in the coffee shop across from Camilla's spa. Having an hour to spare was never the norm, but he'd been too excited to sit in the house that morning. Instead he'd gotten up not even fifteen minutes after Camilla left the house with a trail of water blossom perfume accenting the air behind her.

Sienna. Noelle. And Joy. They were the reasons he was restless and elated beyond belief. If he didn't stand the chance of Rich, Moore, or any of his other neighbors thinking he was crazy, he would've went outside and did backflips up and down the street.

Taking a chance on God had worked tremendously in his favor. His girls had given him a chance in return. The victory electrified every nerve in his body. He smiled all the way through his morning shower. And during the first cup of coffee he'd drank too. Driving to the studio, he hummed a made-up melody. Paul was halfway there before he made a U-turn when he thought of the woman who'd stuck by his side from the very beginning of this bumpy ride.

Paul pulled his car over to a florist he passed every morning and came out with a bursting bouquet filled with the daffodils he knew Camilla would love. He smiled for the hundredth time that morning when he saw the look of surprise and love spread across her beautiful face after he'd entered the glass doors and presented them to her with a kiss. Right after he gave her his last hug, Paul jogged across the street to the quaint coffee shop to get his second mug for the day. Life was better than he ever imagined it would at present. The pieces of the puzzle were fitting together in an unbelievable way.

Thank you, Lord, Paul whispered to himself, eyes closed above the coffee's rising steam.

"Paul, are you okay?"

He opened his eyes to see Ashley standing with her own cup in hand. A tan blouse and hammered, bronze necklace gave an extra glow to her fair skin. Her wild, curly hair bounced back into place easily when she brushed it backward with a flip of her hand.

"Hey, how are you?" he asked, still smiling away.

Her dimples came to life as she giggled. "I'm great. I just saw you over here smiling to yourself with your eyes shut and I said to myself, either he's extremely happy about something or there's a few screws that came loose since the last time I saw him."

He laughed, realizing what she was getting at.

"I can assure you I'm fine. Just giving thanks." He gestured towards the seat across from him. "Please join me. How are the wedding plans coming along?"

"Oh, they're coming slowly, but surely," Ashley said, taking a seat. "I still want you to do the photography. Things have been so hectic lately though. I work forty hours a week. Plus, I'm trying to study for these last tests so I can get my Masters next month. And my father was in a bad car accident recently, so I've been going back and forth to visit him. It's been crazy trying to plan a wedding in between everything."

"Sorry to hear about your father. How bad was the accident?"

"Well, he's still here, so in my book it's not as bad as it could've been. But, he broke his leg and has a couple gashes across his face. Overall he's in one piece. It could've been so much worse since he got a direct hit in the side."

"Oh man. Thank God he's doing well."

"Yeah, I definitely realize how blessed I am that he didn't lose his life. And he knows how blessed he is to be able to see another day. It was such a close call. And to think, we reunited just a little while ago. What if things had been different? If we never reconnected and he got in a car accident and passed away? It's things like that, that really make you sit back and take stock of what's important in life and what isn't. No one's promised tomorrow."

"You're absolutely right."

"But enough about me. How are you? Have you heard anything from your daughters? I thought about you after we spoke at the spa and I really hoped everything would work out on your behalf."

Paul couldn't hold back his smile. "Things have been shaping up nicely." His pulse speed up. "Actually, I was able to speak to all three of my daughters yesterday."

"You're kidding me."

"It was cool. I'm telling you, Ashley, it was a great feeling. A really amazing feeling."

"Congratulations. I can see now why you had that big grin spread across your face."

"What can I say? This is a happy man you're looking at. Trusting God is . . . a hard thing. But I'm the one who was making it hard. All along, it was all I had to do. I finally did it and He blessed me tremendously."

"I can see that."

"I thought about you too. Truth be told, you were an inspiration that day we spoke. I said to myself, if you went through so much with your father in and out of your life and you still found it in your heart to forgive him, then maybe I really have a chance. Maybe my daughters, one if not all, could give an old man a try."

"I'm humbled by you saying that. When I was young, I always had the feeling that I was alone. I didn't think there were other girls like me who felt their father didn't care and would probably never show up to say he did. To just see how things have changed so much and then be able to share my story with you, if anything I said really did inspire you to stick with the pursuit of your daughters, everything I experienced was worth it."

Paul's heart filled as he looked at her warm smile. "You really did inspire me, Ashley. You and my daughters didn't have to go through the questioning and doubting. Being a father is something a man has to be ready for and fully committed to. But, you ladies shouldn't have been cast aside because we didn't feel capable. It's no excuse at all."

She removed the cinnamon stick from her coffee mug and bit a piece off before answering. "What's done is done. And the healing process won't be completed overnight. Hell, it hasn't even begun yet – you all are just hitting the introduction phase. Things can go one of two ways: you guys will come together to see if you can build something or you'll decide to keep things the way they were before. Seems to me though, that since they agreed to speak with you, they're willing to hear what you have to say. Keep your faith strong and things will work themselves out."

"Believe me, my faith is stronger than ever now. I received more than I could ask for. Feel like I'm getting a little greedy already. Been trying to figure out the next time I'll get to speak to them again. I'm trying not to be too forceful. They're adults with lives and I don't want to force my way in."

"I'm sure you'll speak to them soon. I'm rooting for you," Ashley said, sliding her paper cup to the side. She stretched her right hand over the table as she leaned towards him. "My hand is here because I want you to promise you'll do something for me and we're gonna shake hands across this table to make sure the deal is sealed."

Paul knew there was no way he could say no to her request.

"I'm going by my gut. I believe those young ladies will agree to meet with you one day. And when they do, I want you to promise me that you'll look them in the face and tell them your truth. Don't hold back with them, Paul. You've let too many years slip by because you've done just that. Tell your three daughters exactly what it is you've yet to say out loud; the

BROKEN WITH STAINS

littlest thing buried in the deepest part of your soul. Can we shake on that?"

He placed his left hand into the softness of her palm. They shook in agreement, trust and honor melded into the solidity of their grip. Her metal bracelets jingled as loud as the thoughts crashing back and forth in Paul's head. He didn't know how he would get them all out, only knew many difficult things had to be said. Everything had to be revealed.

40 noelle

She let David stroke the back of her head. His fingers had a calming effect. Calm was something more than welcomed right now because she'd been extremely tense since the last time she spoke to the man who ruled her thoughts.

It wasn't Chris who'd been occupying her mind these days. That she was grateful for. Still, her father had taken his place, firing up the stress running through her bones.

Noelle tried to shake Paul from her mind. This was officially her first date with David, she wanted to be here with him, wanted to give him her full attention, wanted to let him know she appreciated him spending his time and effort to treat her. She was impressed that he'd succeeded in putting a smile on her face for most of five hours.

Their day had been an active one together filled with stomach-turning rides and stuffing their faces at Great Adventures. The weather was gorgeous. Her time at the park with David, incredible.

Yet, as they headed to the parking lot, her high continued its descent to a noticeable low. His fingers helped somewhat, but it couldn't make the troubling thoughts disappear from her face.

David peeped the sudden swing in Noelle's mood. He waited until they settled into the car, jumped back on the highway, and headed for home.

"Thinking about your father again?" he asked, turning down the radio.

"Trying not to. But can't help it."

"It's gonna happen. You're gonna think about him. Don't try to fight it."

"It's a lot to deal with – just too much going on. I'm still thinking about Chris' craziness. Then there's school which has me by the balls with all these papers I need to get done. Plus, I have some websites I'm behind on. And then my father calls me up talking about let's meet. Oh, and by the way, meet your sisters too. Really? Been two days since I last spoke to him over the phone and for two days I've been constantly hearing his voice in my head."

"So, have you really thought about it? Meeting your father and your sisters?"

"Well, yeah, I'm curious as hell. I want to throw caution to the wind and see these people I never knew existed, but I want to make a decision with a clear head. Not on some 'ole excitement tip. You feel me?"

"I feel you, though I still feel like you need to just go ahead and give it a chance."

"Right. I still have a mother to answer to. She doesn't even know I spoke to the man. Only person who knows I did are you, Candace, and my aunt."

David focused on the road as Noelle stared at the side of his face and admired his handsome profile. Her mind was preoccupied with the decision she had yet to make, yet here she sat, besieged with the urge to reach over and kiss the stalwart curve of his jaw. She controlled herself by turning her attention to the traffic outside her window. "He sounded so . . . nice over the phone. Can't even imagine him being the cold-hearted man my mother said he was. Then again, there's been twenty-one years of proof to back her up."

Noelle's body tingled when David reached out and squeezed her hand.

"One day at a time, beautiful. Just don't be too fast to close the door on the opportunity to see them. You never know what could come of it."

"I haven't thought that far ahead," she said flatly.

"You haven't? 'Cause your situation has made me do a whole lot of thinking lately. About me and my brother. I haven't seen him in almost two years. And the last meeting wasn't that great. I was just in the beginning stages of learning how to forgive him. But, with everything I've been telling you, I'm starting to see that I need to take my own advice. It's not like I don't know how to contact him or where I'd find him. He'd never go out of his way to reach out to me even though he's the cause of the tension between us. But . . . he's the only brother I got. Maybe if I reach out to him, we can at least try to be cool with each other."

"After all he did to you, that's real deep. You're just gonna knock on his front door and say what? Hi brother. You'll burn in eternal hellfire for what you did to me, but it's all good, I love you anyway?"

David laughed and looked at Noelle.

"Who knows what I'm going to say. I just know that I should do what I just told you to do - go ahead and give it a chance."

"If that's what works for you, fine, more power to you. But like I said, I have a mother to answer to. It's just not that easy for me."

"You can do what you want, Noelle. Be bold. And if there's not a light at the end of the tunnel, at least you weren't afraid to try."

She hated the way he seemed to be brushing her mother off. Didn't he realize this woman was the one who'd always been in her corner? He wasn't comprehending that loyalty was at stake here. She couldn't be the one to wreak havoc in her mother's life all over again.

"I don't need you telling me to be bold when you're not in my position. Your parents are dead. There's no mother and father pulling you back and forth, making you feel guilty because you can't decide who's right and who's wrong."

His face went stiff. Noelle immediately regretted bringing up the fact that his parents were deceased. That was a line she didn't need to cross. All she'd wanted was to try to make him understand.

BROKEN WITH STAINS

She stroked her fingers through her hair the way he'd done during the walk through the parking lot. "My bad; I'm sorry. I know I shouldn't have taken it there."

He continued focusing on the road ahead. His lips were set and sturdy, eyes unblinking with concentration.

"David, forgive me for that one. I can be so stubborn sometimes and I don't want to listen and take advice when I know I should. I'm really sorry."

She saw the corners of his mouth move and was relieved when he finally spoke. "Noelle, I'm only telling you these things because I care about you. We all have different experiences in life, trick is, you gotta pull what you learn from your experience and help others to look at the possibilities they might not be able to see clearly at the moment. That's all I'm trying to do for you. Get you to think clearly about your future."

"I need clear vision because it's insane how my mother has me scared to death. I love her, I really do, but she got me taking some serious baby steps. Wanna keep her in mind before I make my next move."

"I know it's hard on you," he said glancing over at her. "Maybe I shouldn't be telling you what to do. I'll just listen more instead."

"Don't want hold back, David. You've heard me go on and on about Chris and my father – thanks for allowing me to whine in your ear. Even through my stubbornness, I've taken in all your advice." Noelle relaxed deeper into her seat when David smiled and put a hand in her hair for a second round of stroking. She cherished it caressing away the anxiety. Her mind chased the calm making its way through out her body. Soon it caught up, invading her head with peace as she watched the scenery slip by in a blur.

They both remained quiet for the rest of the ride. Both creating scenarios of what the future could possibly have in store.

41 sienna

It didn't make any sense for him to keep trying.
However, common sense obviously wasn't that common. After
a week of throwing away flowers, deleting a thousand messages,
sending back unwanted gifts, and trying to do it all while
resisting the urge to kill him, Sienna was on the verge of a
nervous breakdown.

Ashamed, she called to update her mother on the brawl
that had unfolded in front of the salon. "Ma, I mean it. I'm
getting that restraining order," she stated assuredly. Something
had to give.

It wasn't enough, her mother had told her.

"Let Marcus wear himself out. He didn't cause any
physical harm to you, so the courts are going to ignore your
requests."

Sienna didn't want the assumption confirmed, although
she figured that would be the case from the moment she'd
thought of it as a way to keep him at bay. What other options
did she have?

Expecting the worse, she waited for Annette to tell her
how much of a fool she'd been. How she should've listened
and left a long time ago. Why what happened to her was her
own fault.

"Sea, I never wanted this for you. I'm so sorry things
had to turn out this way."

No scolding there. Still, she waited for the verbal
beating she was due.

"Maybe now you can get on with your life. You are
worth so much more than what he had to give."

The rest of Annette's words followed suit. At the bend
of every response her mother gave, Sienna anticipated an "I
told you so" close behind.

BROKEN WITH STAINS

It never came.

She navigated her car over the wet, slick road, comforted by the fact that Annette was thoughtful enough not to rub it in her face. Tough wasn't enough to describe the time she'd spent dealing with the emotions ravishing her since the morning everything blew up. Countless tears did nothing to wash away the resentment and depression.

The only reprieve from her traumatized state, was hearing from Paul. Speaking to her father temporarily made her forget there was a man she'd loved who stomped her heart to pieces.

In the nick of time, she mused while listening to the unbroken music of the windshield wipers pushing the rain away.

Meeting Paul and the two other daughters he fathered was starting to look like a diversion she could use to free herself from the bondage of grief. Sienna found a space to park and headed for the auditorium of the college's main building. Entering the dark space, she spotted Marni standing in the back.

* * *

After receiving signed copies of their books and taking photos with the author, the two friends made a quick exit through the crowd at the book signing. As they moved past the group of people in the lobby, Sienna noticed Marni's odd behavior. Watched as she skimmed over each person that passed by. It was strange because she'd been behaving that way all evening, including the full hour of the author's Q&A. Sienna thought maybe it was just her, but now, Marni seemed like she was on a top secret mission. "Hey - slow down, speedy. Are you looking for somebody?" she asked, tugging at the back of Marni's shirt.

"Kinda," she responded undeterred.

Suspicion confirmed. For a second she lost her friend in the crowd when four laughing women rudely rushed into her path. Sienna stopped to let them go by, in fear of being trampled. Shaking her head, she breezed through her surroundings to see which way Marni had disappeared to. The pink tips of her dreads caught the corner of Sienna's eye. She maneuvered her way over to ask Marni what the big rush was all about.

Sienna knew she had to be seeing double when she laid eyes on Marni conspiring with the enemy. Marni nervously turned to see Sienna ready to explode.

"Sea, just come here for -"

"I can't believe you!" she shouted, hands on hips.

"Hear me out - she wanted to talk to you. She begged me -"

"I'm not talking to that bitch," Sienna hurled. Those closest to the three of them, immediately twisted their heads to see where the hate-filled words came from.

Sienna bolted to the main doors, not wanting to be the zoo animal locked behind a glass wall. Marni ran to block her path and reached out to grab her hands.

"Listen, please, just listen to me, Sea. Eve called and she asked me to get you two together. She really wants to talk to you. To try and explain her side of the story."

"What side? The side about her going behind my back to sleep with my man?"

Marni pulled at the neck of her orange blouse as if it were choking her. "I don't know what she has to say. All I know is that she called me in tears. She really has some stuff she wants to get off her chest. I don't agree with what she did, but I just couldn't say no."

"Yes, you could have said no! How dare you even tell her to meet us here. If I knew this was going to go down, I swear -"

"She's here, Sea. Maybe I shouldn't have done it like

this, but she begged me to make something happen. What was I supposed to do?"

Sienna held her breath in an attempt to control her temper.

"I don't want you to be mad at me. Just let her say what's on her mind and you never have to speak to her again. One time – that's it."

"I really can't believe this."

"Just five minutes to hear her out."

Sienna avoided eye contact with Marni, staring at nothing in particular.

"Five minutes."

She looked back at the pleading eyes.

"Four minutes then."

Sienna let her breath out, flexed her fingers by her side. "One minute. And then I'm out."

They found an empty classroom nearby and closed the door behind them. Sienna stood by the chalkboard with arms folded. Eve occupied the edge of a small desk.

Marni was the first to speak as she stood directly in between the two. "Eve, you know what you did was dead wrong. And even though I hate how you hurt Sienna, the only reason I agreed to do this is because you need to clear some shit up. Not only that, as little as it may do to make things better, I feel you need to apologize. You were foul and we both can't understand why."

Eve looked up at Sienna and quickly put her gaze back to the classroom floor. Haphazardly, her hair was held together by a rubber band. No makeup sat on the sullen face. A grayish-black puffiness under her eyes gave away the fact that she'd been crying for days. It was as if she had ticks underneath her skin; Eve couldn't stop fidgeting in place.

"At the time . . . at the time I chose to pursue Marcus, I did it because I was trying to save you."

Sienna let out a loathsome chortle. "Give me a break."

"You're not going to believe me, I know, but I was so sick and tired of you putting him up on a pedestal when he did nothing to belong up there. I was sick of seeing him hurt you and not give a damn. Complaining about him was all you did, but nothing ever changed."

"What does that have to do with you laying on your back?"

"I had to show you. Otherwise, he would've hurt you more."

"You helped him destroy me. That's what you did."

"Daniel destroyed me. Marcus was just another version of him. I didn't want to see you continue to suffer the way I did. Tried to make you listen to me when I told you he wasn't the type of man you needed. I didn't know what else to do or say. I didn't mean to hurt you, Sienna."

"Did anybody tell you I needed your help?!" Sienna yelled as tears descended from her eyes. She wiped them away frantically. "No one told you I needed to be saved from him."

Eve yelled back with the same ferocity. "You're my friend! I did my best to warn you! It was like living through Daniel's lies all over again. I couldn't do it anymore. How else was I supposed to make you see?"

"You didn't have to make me see a damn thing and I'm not your friend either! If you could stoop so low to do this to me, I'm not your friend. You did to me what Daniel did to you and it was all to make you feel better about your failed relationship; destroy mine so we'd be on even ground."

"That wasn't it - "

"How long were you sleeping with Marcus?"

Eve swallowed. "Only three weeks."

"*Only* three weeks," Sienna said looking up to the ceiling in disbelief. She looked back at the woman who'd wronged her. "I bet you would've continued with him if I didn't catch the two of you."

"I never wanted to be with him."

BROKEN WITH STAINS

"You've always had something against me, Eve. Your attitude towards me has always been so disgusting, so unnecessary, I wondered what I did to make you come at me that way all the time. Now, I know it's because you were jealous of my relationship with Marcus."

"I hated what you let him do to you."

"Admit it! You hated us being together."

"Yes, I hated you being together, but not for the reason you think."

Speedily, Sienna walked around to the front of the teacher's desk. Marni rushed forward to pull her back as she shouted, "You couldn't stand to see me happy with him because you couldn't find a man of your own."

Eve shook her head back and forth as if she were in a trance. "You were never happy with him, Sienna. He manipulated you and I was fed up. I put myself on the line, put our relationship in jeopardy so you wouldn't be with him. I did it because I looked up to you. I admired you."

"And my man too."

"No – you! I envied you. You being educated and beautiful and having a great mother. I envied those things and couldn't stand to see him bring you down. I wasn't about to let him do it anymore. I wasn't about to see him turn you into nothing. I couldn't save myself, but I was gonna do what I had to for you. I feel bad that I hurt you, but I had to make you see."

Sienna's chest expanded and contracted with each angered breath she took. Marni held on, gripping her friend so tight it was impossible to move.

"Save me, huh? Some kind of friend you are to save me in such a fabulous way. Well, let me tell you something," Sienna said as she brought her voice down a notch. "Marcus may not have been the perfect man. And I might've ignored certain things when I know I shouldn't have. But you, you are nothing more than a worthless piece of trash. The only good thing you accomplished was removing yourself from my life."

* * *

Sienna wiped at the exhaustion clouding her weary eyes. It was time to head home. School had let out an hour ago. She'd spent her time after the last bell, going through her students' essays while at the same time trying to banish Marcus, Eve, Nonda, and the baby, out of her head. She'd barely scratched the surface of the thick stack of papers. Though she should've packed it up and left for the day, a snack craving guided her into the main office where she searched for something decent in the vending machine. After settling for a Snickers bar, she grabbed the mail out of her box in the mailroom and made her way back to the classroom.

Sienna was down to her last bite of chocolate when she remembered the small stack of mail tossed to the right of the text books on her desk. Placing it before her, she lazily brushed aside a teacher's supply catalog and a random piece of junk mail. Her attention heightened when she touched the small lime-green envelope with blue ink displaying her name and the school's address. There was no return info. Curiosity moved her fingers as she opened it quickly, wondering who it was from.

The note was short in fast, smooth strokes:

Sienna,

Since sixteen we've been sisters. We've loved. We've fought. We've had each other's back through thick and thin. Whether you forgive me or not, you'll always be my sister for life. I sacrificed to make you see the light. And to see you at peace, I'd do it all over again.

Love Always,
Eve

BROKEN WITH STAINS

No remorse. That was all Sienna could see. She stared at the small slip of white paper. Eve's ink jumbled into a craziness all her own.

The white shreds landed in the basket next to Sienna's desk. Her fingers had ripped the note apart before she'd even thought to do it.

Sisters since sixteen and yet she had betrayed her in the worst way. Eve had received the opportunity two nights ago to say her piece. As far as Sienna was concerned, there was no mending the way things were between them. Her heart ached deeper when she considered Eve's last line. There wasn't one drop of repentance in the girl's heart if she had the audacity to say she'd repeat her actions again.

Sienna didn't give in to the urge to break down and cry. Instead, she forged ahead to the white envelope turned upside down. Flipping it over, she saw Paul's name perched in the upper left hand corner.

Surprised by her excitement, Sienna ripped it open and stared at the large, yellow happy face with the words 'Just A Hi' settled underneath. Her mood lightened when she read her father's thoughtful words inside the card.

Ms. Sienna Burgess,

Hope you are doing well. I just wanted to let you know that I enjoyed speaking to you over the phone. Thank you for taking the time out to chat with me. It was a blessing just to hear your voice. You've changed my life for the better. Don't hesitate to call. I'm here morning, noon, or night.

,Paul Brooks

There was a change in her heart this time around. He was in the nick of time once more. Maybe it was time; she needed a new beginning. Meeting Paul Brooks could be it.

Maybe losing one sister was just a way for her to make room for two more.

Maybe. Just maybe.

"Maybe you were right, Ms. Burgess."

Sienna's head shot up. Tandi stood by the classroom door.

"Tandi . . ." The girl walked to Sienna's desk, looking slightly better than when she'd shown up to the apartment battered, bruised, and defeated.

"When I came to your apartment, it was because I followed you home one day to find out your address so me and my friends could come back and jump you. We were supposed to do it last Sunday . . . but then Saturday . . . I got into the fight with my boyfriend . . . you were the only one I could turn to. I saw how you were all shocked and everything, but that day, I remember you told me that changing isn't always easy, still you could try to do it anyway."

Sienna looked away to the chalkboard, unsettled at how close she'd come to getting her own beat-down. Looking back at the girl who she only wanted to help, she saw the makeup Tandi tried to use to cover up the discolorations. "Yeah, I did," she answered.

"Well, I know that you meant that I should leave Malik alone. Change my situation by leaving him out my life completely 'cause of what he does and all that. But I thought about change in a different kinda way. Started thinking that it's not too late for him to change. Since change ain't always easy, I could help him make it happen, even if it takes a while."

"Take it from me, Tandi - that's not the way to go. You can't change a man. He has to want to do it for himself."

"He be telling me he wanna change. And I know he does too. He don't mean it when he hits me, 'cause he shows me that he's sorry. We been together so long now, I basically know him by heart. He's a dude, he just gets angry sometimes and all I gotta do is help him work through that." She bit her bottom lip before proceeding. "When you really love somebody, you stick by their side no matter what. My mother been doing it for years. My father won't ever marry her, but my mother's shown me what it means to be loyal. If there's one thing I respect her for, it's that. I love Malik. And I gotta hold him down even through the hard times."

I did it because I was trying to save you.

Eve's voice pleaded in the air around Sienna.

She'd failed to save her from Marcus. Sienna had to make Tandi see she had to love herself first and foremost in order to be saved from the lies of a boy who was dedicated to ruining her life.

"Tandi, loyalty is a thing many people have a hard time with. But you can't put your life at risk just to say you've been loyal. Think about yourself. Think about the fact that Malik might never change. If you're going to be loyal to anyone, be loyal to yourself first before you devote your energy to this boy who's just trying to keep you down."

"You don't get it. There's no way I can just not be in his life. The other night you said you know what it feels like to love somebody more than anything. So much you didn't know what you'd do if that person wasn't there anymore. I don't wanna figure out what I'd do or what would happen to me if Malik wasn't there. I just know I wanna be with him. If I gotta fight him to get his anger all out, that's a choice I gotta manage on my own."

I hated what you let him do to you.

Sienna wanted the voice to go away. It reminded her of the things Marcus had done and what she'd accepted. Just like the naïve girl who spoke with the bruises spread across her face.

"You don't need to fight him. Don't you think you're better than that? Fight to get a good education. Fight to become a better person. But please, Tandi, please do not fight a man to make him love you the right way. It might not be easy to walk away from him if you love him, but at this point, your life depends on it."

"My life depends on him being in it, Ms. Burgess," Tandi said with an emptiness behind her eyes.

"Let me help you. I can help you walk away."

Before Sienna knew it, Tandi's arms were wrapped around her, hugging her neck as tightly as she could.

"I wanted to say thank you. I never got the chance to tell you that when I came over. Don't worry, 'cause I'm good. I got this, he loves me, I know he'll change. You don't have to help me walk away. But thank you for being the only one who's cared enough to try."

I couldn't save myself, but I was gonna do what I had to for you.

Sienna hugged her back tighter.

"I hate that you can't see it right now. Hate it so, so much, but just know one thing: Love is not a struggle, a fight, lies, or manipulation. Love is right when it's real. And it can't be real if it's not right."

43 joy

Her reflection stared back at her from the gold-rimmed mirror. Sitting there applying mascara, Joy felt disconnected from everything going on around her in the lively room. The girls were getting ready as usual. The laughter, the smell of perfume, the stroke of the chilly air brushing against her skin from the vents above, seemed close and far away at the same time.

It was an hour until show time. She didn't need the minutes to tick by any faster. Plain and simple: Here was not where Joy wanted to be. Another day, another dollar. Right now, she felt a half a second away from walking away from whatever amount she'd be receiving for shaking her ass today.

She knew she needed the money. Saving had never been a strong point for her. After all the money she'd made dancing at the club for the last two months, she was now down to under two thousand dollars in her bank account. Joy tossed down the tube of mascara and dug inside the small black makeup bag for her blush. The makeup artist was there, but Joy didn't want anyone touching her tonight. Cranky wasn't the word. If any of her clients even so much as breathed on her, she was going to punch them dead in the throat.

Joy thought back to the day she'd first received the check with seven hundred and fifty thousand written across the front. She remembered the excitement of the moment. How the first thing she'd done was run out and buy the expensive car she'd always wanted. She sucked her teeth and swung completely around, turning her back to the image in the mirror. She was tired of messing up. Tired of being the fool. Tired. Just plain tired of what seemed like her inability to simply be happy.

The metallic-gold stilettos were turned over on the floor along with her large leather tote. She picked up the shoes and noticed the yellow slip of paper. Taking it from the floor, she reviewed the number scribbled across - the one she had conveniently forgotten to call. She let her eyes roam over each of the ten numbers for a moment, torn between throwing it in the trash can and stuffing it back into the bag.

She shrugged and pushed it down in between the rest of the contents of the carry-all. Speaking to Paul the other day had been cool, yet she wasn't about to get all caught up thinking everything was going to be a fairytale from there on out. Things could never be different between them. In keeping with that thought process, it made no sense to get her hopes up.

Joy finished putting her look together. Her sequined, light blue mini dress glistened under the lights of the dressing room. She was still the baddest chick in the room even after a couple months. The other dancers still eyed her, still hated everything she had to offer, but Joy never expected anything less, and quite frankly, she didn't care. Strangely enough, she didn't smile inwardly about it anymore. Presently, she would've preferred to throw on a tee and sweat pants, and follow that up with a deep sleep in her bed at home. There was too much milling about in her mind to worry about what the douches in the room hated about her. She sat and filed her nails to pass the time, avoiding all eye contact.

The sudden low rumble in the room caught her attention. She looked up and focused her attention to where the other girls were drawn.

There stood Rocki with the video girl scantily clad by his side. The same one who'd been attached to Luce's hip for the past few weeks.

"Quiet, quiet. Let me talk to you ladies for a minute." He reached out an arm towards the shapely girl. "This is Heaven. She's our newest at SD and she's starting tonight."

Joy listened, peeved to the bone.

"You girls have been doing great lately. The money's

good. The clients have been booking you ladies for so many private sessions, it's unbelievable. Keep shaking them asses like you do and keep the fire going. I'll need you, Jaguar, to take Ms. Heaven and show her the ropes."

Joy puffed out a fed-up breath, turned her back to the group, and began to shove her things into the leather bag.

Rocki stretched his long neck towards her, "Ummm, Cinnamon . . . is there a problem?"

She ignored him.

"I'm talking. Can you please stop what you're doing and show some respect? I'm not done speaking so I'd like your undivided attention."

She proceeded to slip on a pair of flip-flops and snatched her hair up into a ponytail. Aware of the eyes on her back, she bent over and gave them all something to look at while she picked her bag up from the floor.

"Oh no you're not about to just walk up out this room," he said with a manicured hand placed on his hip. "Where you think you going with forty minutes 'til showtime?"

Joy placed the bag on her shoulder, threw on her shades, and walked past Rocki out of the room.

She could hear him yelling into his headpiece as the door closed behind her. If anyone thought they were going to stop her from leaving, they had a better chance of getting a nun to drink pee out of a vase at two a.m. in the morning. Joy skipped steps as she hustled down the stairs to get to the back door. She entered the first floor of the mansion, made a turn around the first corner, and walked right into Luce's chest.

"Wassup?" he asked, blocking her path.

Rolling her eyes, she moved to walk around him. Luce cut her off and grabbed her arm. "You ain't going nowhere. You're gonna turn back around, go back into that room, get yourself together, and wait 'til those men show up with money in their pockets."

Joy roughly pulled her arm from his clench and stepped

closely to his face. "I ain't doing shit."

She propped the drooping bag back up on her shoulder and tried again to get to the back door. Grabbing her by the throat, Luce shoved her backward.

"Don't play with me little girl. I'm sick of you and your mouth. Now go upstairs and get dressed," he spat as a fire ignited behind his eyes.

Joy touched her throat, bowled over by the way he'd just put his hands on her. The memory of her mother's ex-boyfriend immediately resurrected itself. He didn't know who he was messing with; she'd handle Luce exactly the same way she'd done that fool who'd raped her time and time again. No one would put their hands on her like that and live to tell about it. Joy reached into her bag to retrieve the huge blade she always kept near and dear. Her fingers barely touched the steel handle when Luce ripped the bag from her hold and raised his hand to strike.

"Still a punk after all these years." Luce's fist was still in midair as both he and Joy looked to see where the strong voice came from.

"Go ahead. Hit her, Lucien. Or are you man enough to take on a real man like me?"

Joy stood confused. Her anger was still in full effect and she didn't need anyone to fight her battles, but she'd never seen this man before. She scanned her brain to figure out the ruggedly handsome face, the tall, muscular build, the fascinating energy that filled the room.

"David," Luce said turning to face the man in question. "This is my place of business, man. What I do with my girls in my place of business is none of your concern."

"It is my concern when I'm standing in the same room with you and you're about to hit one of them."

Joy's eyes shifted between the two men as she noted the similarities. She had to know the relation. Needed to find out who this guy was and how he had the power to stop Luce in his tracks.

"Who you?" she asked, enraged in the place she stood.

She watched him walk towards her in his black Ecko tee and blue jeans. Kinda rough, very handsome, with a long scar above his right eyebrow. He took the handbag from Luce's hand and held it out to her.

"I'm David Warren. Luce's brother."

Brother?, she thought to herself. *What brother?* Placing the handbag on her shoulder, she stared him down and rolled her neck as she spoke. "Well, I sure hope you ain't a bitch-ass-punk like your brother. And I hope what you're packing isn't as small as his either." She bumped past Luce and headed for the back exit. The bouncers moved to block her path, but Luce put up a hand - a signal to let her go. She was at the exit, could've pushed the door open, walked out of the club, and never turned back, but she wanted to witness whatever was about to go down.

"What do you want?" Luce asked with his arms folded across his chest.

"Had to come by, big brother. Man to man, there's some things I need to get off my chest."

"Oh yeah? You hate me, remember? What we got to talk about that's so urgent?"

"I don't hate you. You changed your number and I figured I'd find you here so we could catch up with each other, clear some stuff out the way." David looked around the sizeable room. "I see you did some remodeling. Brand new furniture. Marble floors. Looks like sex is really selling 'round here."

"My girls don't sell sex. They sell a fantasy. Now, what exactly do you want from me?" Luce asked, blinking back his temper.

"Believe it or not, I don't want anything from you. Even though you tried to take everything from me by stealing my identity, I'm not here to ask you for anything in return. I'm

TAMARA BURKE

only here because I was thinking the other day and I realized that I'd never told my brother that I forgive him."

"You really think I need your forgiveness?"

"It's not about what you need. It's about what I'm giving to you."

"Man, you can get up outta here with all that."

"Not yet. 'Cause see, I wanted to kill you. Had the nine and everything, set and ready to put three or four holes in your head, but you know what? God had a plan for me."

"Is that right?"

"You just don't know."

"No? Then go 'head. Finish telling me how you planned to murder your big bro?"

"I didn't come here for that. I came here because there was a need to get a weight off my shoulders. But more importantly, I had to let you know that even with the weapons you formed against me, you didn't prosper. I forgive you. And I thank you."

"You thank me?"

"Yes, because if you never brought me to the point where I had murder on my mind, I couldn't have become this changed man that I am today. You were supposed to be family. Supposed to have my back through everything when we was coming up, but instead, you robbed me. Tried to take my life from me."

"Hey, I did what I had to do. This is a cold, cruel world. You was gonna find that out sometime in your life. I was just preparing you."

"And that you did. But what you didn't know was that you were only an accessory in God's plan for my life."

"So Jesus is your homeboy too, huh?" David smiled and let the sarcastic comment slide. "I don't want anything from you, Lucien. Just know this: I might not agree with the things you did to me. I might not agree with the type of business you run. And I might not agree with the way you walk all over people. But you're my brother, the only one I have, and that's not going to change. So we can either live in peace or you can live in a cold world all by yourself. But as for me, I'm gonna put myself out there and let it be known that I'm not mad any more."

"You know . . . before ma died, dad used to always yell at her for babying you too much. I guess that's why you came out so soft."

"So I guess being angry all the time makes you hard?"

"Say what you want, but that's what I always hated about you; you ain't stop drinking breast milk until you were one years-old. And in a way, I don't think you ever stopped. You were always the favorite. Always the one I had to take the beatings for whenever you messed up. But maybe if you'd gotten your ass whipped a time or two, you wouldn't have turned out this dumb. Talkin' about you forgive me - what the hell you think forgiveness is gonna do for a grown man like me?"

"You can do with it whatever you want."

Disgust stained Luce's face as he looked at his brother and said, "You come up in my club, on my time, a few minutes before my clients are coming to drop no less than a few thousand on any one of them fine bitches waiting upstairs, and you wanna talk about forgiveness?"

"Ma never loved one of us more than the other. You've lived with that in your mind all these years and it's never been true."

"It's always been true. And the only thing you can really give me is money for my time you've wasted."

"Man, you need to let that go because it's been eating you up for far too long."

"Son, I already let enough things go for you. Including that prime piece of ass I just let walk out the door. Do you know how much I was gonna make off of her tonight? Do you know how many requests I get for that one broad on a regular basis? Why do you think I do what I do? I'm good at this shit. I know how to pick hoes and make them work for me. I was never good enough for ma, but look at me now . . ." He placed his hands on his chest and narrowed his eyes at David. "These girls need me. They come to my joint you don't approve of and take off their clothes because I'm the one who feeds them. They live through me. You said God had a plan for you. Well, I'm the one who made a plan for these bitches. I'm God when they look at me." David bit the inside of his mouth and looked at his brother's bulging eyes. He found no words to speak except, "I feel sorry for you, man."

"Nah, don't feel sorry for me . . . I'm real good 'cause I got money to keep me company."

David turned and headed for the door as he replied, "You won't be good until you look in the mirror and strip away all the dirt that's blocking you from seeing the truth – money will never save your soul."

* * *

She waited with her eyes to the sky. The sun was disappearing and the night's purple clouds were settling in. The air felt a bit damp as she rocked back and forth on her feet. A noise was heard behind the solid white door and then it opened – Blue elegant and stern in black on black.

"This is a surprise. You didn't call. How'd you know I was here?"

Joy stretched her hand out towards the thin, wheat-haired white woman who stood no more than five feet tall, her hands full with two barking Yorkshire Terriers. "Barbara. I called the house. She said you'd be here. Here I am."

Blue backed away from the door and faced the petite woman who fumbled with the dogs. "Barb, I'll be in the kitchen. I told you about the new dog psychologist I got for Pinkie and Moosa. Her name's Kate, she'll be here sometime soon. Put something cute and frilly on my girls. They need to look good on their first day."

She walked away without waiting for a response from the frazzled handler. Joy followed behind Blue rolling her eyes. *A dog psychologist? Yeah, okay.*

They made it to the kitchen where Tom stood dressed in a navy blazer and khakis, popping grapes into his mouth. His eyebrows arched when he saw Joy. "Hey . . . Joy. Good to see ya - it's been a while."

"Yeah," was all she said.

"Yes indeed. But we're ah . . . looking forward to seeing you at the wedding." He took a quick glance at Blue. "Your mom's gonna make one helluva bride. Really hope you make it."

Joy watched Blue wipe at an invisible spot on the kitchen's island.

His reddening face made it clear that he was uncomfortable. He kissed Blue's cheek, mentioned something about heading for the back yard, and quietly disappeared.

"Can't believe you're gonna marry that man."

"And what is it about 'that man' that you can't believe? Wait, no, don't answer that. Why don't you tell me instead why you could never stand to see me happy?"

"Please."

Blue sighed, pulled up her stool, and commenced to tapping her pen against the papers before her.

"I could care less about whatever loser you choose to marry. I came to talk about your baby daddy, Paul Brooks."

"Look, the wedding is next week. I'm going over this guest list one last time. Are you going to be there or not?" Blue asked.

"Forget your precious guest list for a second. I spoke to him the other day and I want to know the real deal on what went down between you and my father."

"You already know what you need to know.

Things didn't work out. We parted ways. End of story."

Joy sucked her teeth, grabbed the felt-tip pen from her mother's hand, and slammed it down onto the counter.

"No! There's way more to the story and I wanna know now. What did you do to that man?"

Blue flipped to the next page of her list and kept silent.

"He told me about you. Talked about how he didn't walk away, you made him walk away," she lied effortlessly.

"And of course you believe that," Blue said, raising cold eyes to look at her daughter.

Now she was getting somewhere. Joy wanted to see the slight flare of her mother's nostrils. It always made her know when she'd succeeded in sparking a flame underneath that pale skin. She turned up the heat.

"Yup. I believe every single word out his mouth. What he got to lie for? He's not you. Not once have you been real with me about what really made him leave."

"Some things a child should let stay between the adults involved." Blue's attention drifted back down to the list.

"I'm not a child anymore in case you didn't realize."

"You know what, Joy? I don't owe you anything. I'm the mother here. I know I've told you that before."

"It's played now. So sick of hearing that from you, especially since you have yet to show me what's ever been motherly about you."

The delicate nostrils were powerful now. Her mother put an arm up towards the kitchen entrance. "Leave then. This house belongs to me and Tom. You don't have to be here."

"I'll leave when you tell me what made my father go away."

"If I could, I'd have done what your father wanted me to do. I made him leave because he wanted me to have an abortion when I told him I was pregnant with you."

Joy took time to process what she'd just been told.

"You're lying," she laughed. "That's not what Paul told

me."

"Believe it. An abortion. I can see my life being so much better if I'd went and let them suck you out of me instead of dealing with your rude behind. The pain would've been nothing compared to what I've had to suffer because of you all these years."

An abortion? Joy felt as if her heart had stopped. Her father walked away because he didn't want her here. Now he wanted to come back? Blue was reaching. There was no way he would've wanted something like that. Not the man she'd spoken to on the phone.

"Keep lying, Blue. It's exactly what I expected from you anyway. Just like when I killed your stinking pervert and you lied to the police and the doctors when you told them you had no clue that he was raping me."

"Same thing. Always the same 'ole thing," Blue said, unfazed by Joy's words.

"I'll never forget it either. And I'll keep bringing up the same 'ole thing any time I'm good and ready to because you never gave a shit!"

Blue's voice flew to the roof. "I never knew anything was going on. No matter how many times I tell you that, the angry little girl that you are will never believe me. So what do you want me to do? Keep apologizing for the rest of my life? You're nineteen years old. Cry a river, build a bridge, and find a way to get over it. I don't want to hear it anymore."

Joy flexed her fingers as her insides plunged to the bottom of a dark pit. "Just like that? You sit in your big house, with your big rock on your finger, planning your big wedding and tell me to get over it? Well get over this," Joy said, picking up the loose pages of Blue's guest list and ripping them to pieces. She threw the remnants on the floor.

Blue watched in horror, her thin face a twisted mask of terror.

"Get out of my house," she shouted, springing up off

the stool.

"I ain't going nowhere! Not until you start acting like I exist. Like I have feelings. I want to know about my father and I want to know now. I want you to tell me he didn't want you to get a abortion 'cause I know that's not true."

"It's true! Live with it you miserable kid. You need to grow up. Can't handle the truth, you shouldn't have pressed the issue."

"No."

"Yes. So what're you going to do now?" Blue lashed out, her frustration gaining momentum each time she breathed in and out.

"No. I'm not going to believe that," Joy's voice dropped in volume when she took a step back and covered her face with her hands.

Blue still fumed with indignation. Her daughter's sudden tears were slipping through the fingers that shielded her face. The whimpering sounds coming from her were unexpected. Her body was now bent in half, the escaping moans growing louder than the last.

Blue turned her head to the side, attempting to distance herself from the pain that was too much and very familiar. She buckled when a cry came from Joy's throat that was so earsplitting it could've shattered the glass vase resting in the center of the island.

Her daughter was almost down to her knees. She picked the girl up by the shoulders and removed the wet hands from her face.

"Joy, he didn't want you, but I kept you. I didn't do everything a super mom was supposed to do, but I loved you with all I had in me. I did what I needed to do in order to keep food on the table."

Joy reluctantly released herself from her mother's grip. It was the closest she'd been to her in years. It felt good, yet she didn't want to get too comfortable.

BROKEN WITH STAINS

"So why does he want me now? That's what I don't understand."

Blue watched the years of damage fall from her child's eyes. As much as she hated to endure the vile behavior from the girl now falling to pieces in her kitchen, she still couldn't turn away from the baby that Paul had tried to make her flush away. Blue longed to be the mother she knew she hadn't been. The mother who could strip away the iron wall around her heart, releasing herself to love unconditionally. She walked closer to Joy and used a hand to touch her shoulder. "People change sometimes, Joy. Some of us evolve into better selves and decide we need to make amends. I believe he means well. The scars of the past may still be there, but a man always has to live with himself and all of his decisions at the end of the day. He just wants to say he's sorry."

Joy pushed away the hair matted to her face by her tears. "They're all alike. All these boys posing as men . . . they think a pole between their legs make them so big, so manly. They don't even know the definition of the word 'man'. They only serve one purpose . . . all I ever wanted them for was money. Like you."

Swallowing the lump in her throat, Blue reflected on the statement. "It's true . . . at one time in my life, after I left your father, money was what I was all about. But this time it's different. My feelings for Tom are real."

"I had real feelings too."

"I know. We all get them at some -"

"No, Blue . . . I fell . . . in love with a guy. I didn't even know I'd fell . . . until he kicked me when I was down." Icy tears clouded her eyes as she stared at her mother. "You were going to be a grandmother in six months. I had a miscarriage a few days ago. Bleeding by myself, all over the floor. I lost my baby and all the father said was . . . was that I was gonna have to get rid of it anyway."

Overwhelmed with a new cascade of water from her

eyes, Joy continued, "They're just the same. They'd kill their children at the drop of a dime and walk off, leaving you to pick up the pieces without a second thought. What they don't realize is that it hurts. It hurts. It hurts so much and they just don't even care."

Blue wiped the wetness from her own eyes and clasped her arms around her child's body.

"I know it hurts. I know it kills you inside. But, trust me, they can't escape the guilt. It catches up to them one way or the other. Facing it is always inevitable."

"I lost my baby," Joy choked out. "The only one I felt like I had left."

"You should've called me. Sorry you had to go through this all by yourself."

"I didn't think you would care."

"Joy, you're my only child. I get mad, I get frustrated, I say angry things to you I don't even mean sometimes, but you're the baby a man tried to tell me I had to kill. There's no way in this world, I wouldn't drop anything I was doing to be there for you. I've always wanted to be there. Just got tired of you always pushing me away."

"Your boyfriend raped me. You were supposed to protect me, make sure I was safe. My father wasn't there to do it. I thought you knew all about it and didn't want to do nothing."

Blue cupped the tear-stained face with both hands, looked into her daughter's weary eyes. "Joy, I promise you, I didn't know anything about what was going on. We're more alike than you think, because if I'd known, I would've killed him too . . . nobody comes before you."

44 paul

"**S**urprissssse!"

Camilla gaped at the room full of friends and family who were all smiles, gathered together in the hotel's large banquet room.

"How . . . what . . . when . . ." It was impossible for her to get the words out.

Her husband came to her rescue.

"Happy anniversary, baby," Paul said embracing her around the waist.

"Paul . . . I'm going to get you good for this. You said it was a weekend getaway," she said turning from him. "I can't believe you guys are all here."

The room filled with laughter.

"Paul, we have her face on camera for you, man," a short guy in a navy blue suit bellowed.

He smiled. "Thanks, Sam. I'm gonna have to blow it up and frame it on our living room wall. Give your sister something to enjoy for a very long time."

Camilla waved him away with her hand, blushing while everyone stood amused at the teasing.

One by one, the guests approached them, hugging and sharing their well wishes for the two who glowed with love. After mingling for a while, Paul took Camilla's hand and walked her to the front of the room. He poured them both glasses of champagne, handed one to his wife, and announced he'd like to make a toast.

He waited a few seconds for everyone to settle with their own glasses. Seeing that he had everyone's full attention, Paul began.

"I have to make this toast in honor of my lovely wife, Camilla Marie Brooks. She didn't know the kind of trouble she was getting herself into when she decided to give this black man a chance," he said as the audience laughed along with him. "But on a serious note, the progress I've made as a man is in large part do to this great woman standing by my side."

Paul faced Camilla, gazing intently at the smooth contours of her face.

"You have been my rock. You are my rock today. And I know you'll be my rock for many years to come. These seven years we've been together weren't always perfect, but you were patient enough with me to withstand my imperfections. There's no way you'll ever know how much of an honor and a privilege it was for me the day you said 'yes' to being my wife. Thank you for loving a man like me, unconditionally. I still promise to love and to cherish you for all the days of my life." With his thumb, he wiped away a single tear falling down her cheek. She mouthed the words "I love you" before they kissed with the music of hoots and cheers rising in the background.

Paul came up for air and turned back to the tables. "Please everyone, raise your glasses with me in a toast to Mrs. Brooks." Glasses graced the air and the guests drank at Paul's request.

Stepping closer to her husband's side, Camilla took the moment to claim the floor. "Don't drink it all folks, because I got a few words to say about this man of mine."

"Go ahead, tell us all the trouble he done caused you," a female voice shouted from the back.

Camilla craned her neck as she grinned, "Who's that back there? Marsha?"

The room erupted with laughter once again.

"Well girl, no, my man has been a God-sent. Though he might get into a little trouble tonight for telling me we were just taking a three-day retreat, overall he's been everything I've ever hoped and prayed for." She looked into Paul's eyes. "I didn't think it would happen for me. Nine years ago, I thought that was it. A woman is never supposed to tell her age, but I'm comfortable in my skin so I'll tell you that I was thirty-five when Paul came into my world. I wasn't looking for a man because at that point I thought I'd never meet the man who was my other half, but then here came Paul, crashing into my cart at the supermarket one day. Who knew I'd meet the love of my life in the frozen food isle?" She smiled brightly. "We didn't fall in love, we grew in love from that moment forward. A year later we made a vow before God and today I can still say it's one of the best decisions I've ever made."

She clasped her hands in his and looked beyond his faults, his insecurities, and his past. "There is no other man on this earth that I'd rather be with. You're my bestfriend, my confidante, my supporter, my love, and forever my husband. I'll always be your rock no matter what comes our way. I'm so proud of you and all you've accomplished. I know that you're a good man and I respect you for your honesty and for knowing I can rely on you any time, any place. I thank God for sending you to me. When I wasn't even looking, He sent you . . . everything I needed."

The applause shook the room as Paul swelled with happiness at his wife's words of adoration.

He put his hand up to halt all the loved ones cheering them on.

"There's one thing I forgot to say." Camilla's brother came forward from the table where he sat with an aqua square-shaped box wrapped in a white bow. Paul took the package marked Tiffany's and handed it to Camilla.

"Nothing that I buy could ever show my love and appreciation for the miracle you've been to me. But because it's our anniversary, I give you a token."

His wife eyed him and hesitantly unwrapped the box every woman loved to behold in their hands. Looking into the package, she almost fell over at the sight of the sparkling necklace of diamonds that had to be worth the down payment of a mansion.

"What . . . when . . . how," speech escaped her again as she fumbled to get the beauty out of its casing.

Paul helped her undo the clasp and slipped the jewels around her bare neck. He delighted at her expression of awe and utter amazement. His heart was full and it felt good down to the last drop.

Camilla had never judged him. Never ignored him. And always pushed him to keep on going no matter what. He was definitely in debt to his woman. The necklace wasn't enough, but he knew nothing ever would be. Paul was just happy he could add something sweet to her life in return.

He planted a peck on her collarbone. "Anything for you, Mrs. Brooks."

* * *

The surprise had gone over smoothly. Paul was still up, still charged at four o'clock in the morning.

He watched Camilla's chest rise up and down from his vantage point on the balcony. Knocked out on the hotel bed, sleep had finally caught up to the woman who he'd watched bounce around the banquet hall just a few hours earlier.

Paul's future rested on his shoulders. He looked at the empty metal chair beside him, offered the seat to his load, and then sat back, reminding himself that he needed to be content with the progress he'd made. The future could wait for a while. He'd sit back and relax until it was the right time to get up and move into his destiny.

A cup of coffee would calm him down just like it always did. Paul walked back into the cool room and headed over to where the coffee maker sat. He flipped on the tiny lamp, noticing he'd left his cell phone there all evening.

There was only one message. It was late. Daylight would be here in a couple hours, but he listened to it anyway.

Paul, it's Blue.

BROKEN WITH STAINS

He listened to the urgent-sounding message. Blue wanted to meet with him soon. It was "Joy, confused about everything", according to his ex. She made it clear that they had to discuss things. She made it clearer that it had to be now.

* * *

"That's what you bailed out on, Paul. That beautiful child. She was a bad ass growing up, but a beautiful child nonetheless."

The photograph bent with the light breeze that passed between him and Blue. Their heads almost touched as they peered at the tiny little girl in a checker-print blue dress and brown sandals, two curly pig tails puffed out on each side of her head.

"I didn't know what I was doing," was his response.

"Yeah, you didn't. But after all's been said and done, that girl is crying out for help. She needs you to be there."

Blue waited for a noisy public bus to go by before she finished speaking. "Me and Joy's . . . relationship has suffered tremendously. Can't lie to your face and say it was fabulous, because that, it has never been. She's a spit-fire and I have my ways too. Regardless, I gave birth to that girl. I won't say I've been the world's best mother by any means, but I tried my hardest to be all that I thought I was able to be."

Paul sensed there'd been a lot of animosity between mother and daughter. Things said and done to cause ill feelings to abide on both parts.

"I've wrestled with it. Believe you me, I look at this picture and I'm ashamed that I suggested what I did the last time I saw you."

"She knows. I didn't want to tell her, but she knows why we broke up." Paul sighed and rubbed his thumb over the sweet, chubby face. "You didn't have to tell her that, Blue."

"She made me. You don't know your daughter - at least not yet. She's relentless, one thing you'd possibly grow to love about her. She pushes to the limit. Very aggressive, but a woman has to be like that to survive in this day and age."

The tree leaves ruffled above their heads. The bench's dark wood was hard and the only thing unmoving below Paul's feet. He felt his world altering. Going back to the same street, the same sidewalk he'd walked down with Blue, imploring her to get rid of the fetus. Go ahead and kill Joy.

She was nineteen now. A budding young woman. How would he ever get her to understand his thought process back then?

"The past is irreversible," Blue said as if reading Paul's mind. "Our daughter needs both of us now. Above and beyond what all three of us have been through, we are a family. A broken one, but the ties that bind us will always be there."

"Is she and your fiancée close?"

Blue bit her bottom lip and looked away.

"That's a touchy subject. But in short, no, Joy would rather keep her distance. I don't even think she's coming to the wedding. If she did show up, it would be terrific. That's my only child, you know, but she's been on her own for a while. She makes her own decisions and I have to accept whatever she chooses to do."

She scoped out the white gold band on his ring finger.

He examined the brilliant diamond, oversized and ornate, on hers. "Blue, what we had meant a lot to me."

"You don't have to bring that up -"

"I do because I ran away from my own fears. It wasn't you and Joy I was trying to remove myself from. I wanted to tell you why I wasn't ready to be a father. Couldn't do it though. Didn't mean I didn't want to be with you - I was happy. Just wasn't man enough to be honest. You deserved my honesty. But I'm glad you found someone now. I'm hoping he's real good to you."

BROKEN WITH STAINS

She ran the back of her right hand over the large stone decorating her finger and thought about Joy.
"Tom takes real good care of me. I kissed a lot of frogs to get to him, but I got a real jewel in the process."

45 noelle

She couldn't resist the urge to hear his voice one more time before she went to bed. Noelle's tear- shedding for Chris had eased up considerably, but love had no way of fading that fast. She tried hard not to be stupid. Her fingers itched. Then itched more.

Yes, she enjoyed David's company. So why was she swaying, about to fall into a downward spiral over an old dog like Chris? If that L-word popped into her head one more time, she was going to have to beat it out.

Noelle shut her eyes tight, let the waves of missing Chris pass through her body like a rushing tide. It was time for something different. No more feelings of betrayal. No more feelings of depression. She fell back onto her bed, willing herself to sleep. She tossed and turned for about and hour before she reached for the phone, following the voice she'd tried to avoid for more than a week.

He picked up on the second ring.

"Noelle?"

She should've sucked it up and waited until she drifted off to sleep.

"Hello, are you there?"

Sitting up, she answered, "Yeah, I'm here. Hi Paul. It isn't too late, is it?"

"Not at all. Actually, I'm relieved that you called."

"Didn't think I would, huh?"

"Honestly, I didn't know what to think. Everything happened so fast. Our last conversation seems so short now."

"Yeah, I know, right?"

"Yeah." The silence was deafening, both trying to come up with the most meaningful thing to say.

"I was calling because . . . I just wanted to hear your

voice. Sounds childish, I know, but that's what I wanted."

"I don't see it that way. I'm grateful that you think enough of me to pick up the phone to call. I've been wanting to call you again. Didn't want to come on too strong though. Have you given any more thought to meeting some time?"

Her mother's scowling face flickered before her eyes.

"I did think about it."

"If you're not ready -"

"It's not that."

Here was the opportunity to say yes, presenting itself again.

"I've given it a lot of thought. Thinking about the things I need and the things I have to get rid of in my life."

"We're on the same wave length. For a while I've been up to the same."

"I wish I had started doing this for myself sooner. Feel like it's time to do what I have to for me. Gotta get rid of grudges and anger I've been holding on to. And now seems like the perfect time. I want to meet with you and my sisters."

There. She said it. Now following through would be a whole other story.

* * *

Sharon was expressionless as she stirred oatmeal over the old white stove. It was now or never. Noelle pulled out a chair at the kitchen table, sat, and picked at the withering cherries on the plastic tablecloth. Avoided everything she came to say until her mother had no choice but to extend her attention to the table close by.

"Why you sitting there looking pouty like that?"

"Not pouting. Wanted to tell you something."

"What's that?"

"You promise you won't be mad?"

"Girl, what is it?"

"Just be calm when I tell you."

Sharon added more milk to the bubbling pot.

"What I came to tell you is that . . . I spoke to Paul and I'm going to meet him, ma."

"Oh," she responded as an eyebrow flew up.

"Oh? You're not going to say nothing else?"

"What do you expect me to say? You already know how I feel. Go 'head and handle your business."

"You sound so cold about it. I wanted to let you know so you wouldn't find out about it from Aunt Rinni or something. So you couldn't say I was hiding things from you."

"Rinni started this bull. She was always in the middle of something."

"She didn't start anything. They saw each other at a wedding one day, but she said Paul had been thinking about trying to contact me for a while. Don't blame nothing on her."

"What are you? Her bodyguard?"

"I just don't want there to be anything between you and her because of me."

"Everything ain't all about you, Noelle. Get over yourself."

She cocked her head back and waited to see if her mother was serious. Sharon held a small jar of cinnamon and shook it into the pot's contents. Noelle got up, making her way near the stove to lean against the fridge. If she reached out she could touch Sharon, but instead, kept her arms folded across her chest.

"Ma, for real, are you really going to stay mad at me about this? Because if you are, I don't know how you could live with yourself for being upset with me because I want to meet my own father."

"Get out of my face with that," she said, waving Noelle away with a hand. "If you like your life you won't start nothing with me right now."

"It's not fair that you can't see things from my point of

view."

"See something from my point of view then: I'm not forgiving that man for what he did to us. If *you* want to, whatever. But don't try to force anything down my throat and think I'll jump to swallow it."

"I want you to be happy for me. This is big. I never thought I would see him."

"He should have kept it that way."

Noelle knew Sharon's reaction would be bad, but now she was just spitting venom.

"You would really rather I never met him? Even if it made me happy?"

She dropped the long wooden spoon in the oatmeal falling down the sides of the pot. "Yes. I would rather you never met him and he was rotting in the pit of hell too."

46 sienna

Sienna swallowed her mouth full of french toast and replied to her mother's question.

"I guess I'll take a leap. Too stressful picking it apart and wondering if I should. I'll just go ahead and meet with the man. See what he's all about. You've really been pushing me to see him a lot lately. I know you don't hate him, but why do you even care so much?"

Annette sipped from her glass of water. "I'm your mother – I'm supposed to care about anything that involves you."

"But if I do go through with it - meeting the other two daughters as well - what if nothing comes of it? I don't want this to be a waste of time when I could've continued my life without any further disappointment. You know what I mean, Marni?"

Marni wiped her mouth with a napkin. "Life is full of disappointments, Sea. It sucks, but it's true," she replied.

"Thanks for reminding her," Annette chimed in. Sienna sighed and drank from her glass of orange juice.

"I'm torn. I'm so, so torn. One minute I'm feeling it, thinking I should give him a chance. Then the next, I'm scared to get into a situation I might regret."

"There are worse things than meeting your father for the first time," Marni said reaching for a croissant. "Go ahead, take that leap. You'll thank yourself later." The girl had a point. "Maybe," Sienna answered.

"She doesn't get the worrying from me," Annette said, turning to Marni. "I don't remember Paul being much of a worrier either. He was more on the quiet side. Has to be from my mother. Back in Jamaica when I was growing up, my mother worried about e-ver-y-thing. She only had me and my sister and we'd laugh at her all the time. We laugh and we laugh and we laugh 'cause my mother would worry if too many days go by and there's no rain, she worry if we don't eat every lick of food off we plate, she worry if the sky get too black at night, she would worry if she made the water for we tea too hot. Boy I tell you, sometimes Sienna reminds me of her so much."

Sienna pushed her lips up and stared at her mother. "Mother, don't exaggerate. I don't worry that much."

"Not saying that much. I just think that sometimes it's better to let things be. Run when you see certain signals for certain things. But seeing your father shouldn't be a source of stress for you."

"You're not in my shoes. You don't know how I feel."

"I don't know my father either. And if I did hear from him, as much as I resent the fact that he wasn't there, I'd see him. I only have one father. So do you."

"That's what I told you before," Marni interjected.

"I'm not disagreeing with either one of you. Already told you I'm going to see him in person. But I worry about the different outcomes that could potentially take place. It's only natural."

Annette placed her napkin on her finished plate. "Don't take what I said the wrong way. I just want you to be strong in your decision. If you're going to meet with him and your sisters, go prepared for what will happen that day, the next, and every day after that. Makes no sense to go through with it if you're going to worry about each step along the way."

Sienna played in her freshly styled short hair. "Okay. No worrying along every step of the way. I'll write that down, mother - in big red marker across my forehead. That way there's no way I'll forget."

47 joy

With her back facing the door, Blue shimmered in the soft sunlight that filtered in through the open windows in her master bedroom. Joy didn't know what to say. Her mother had always been an undeniable beauty, regardless of how much Joy had despised looking her. But she'd never seen her look this phenomenal. The cream satin dress adorned with crystals and pearls made her statuesque physique so radiant, Joy felt like she was dressed in rags.

The Yorkies jumped for attention at Blue's heeled feet. "Pinkie, Moosa, you know mommy loves you, but not right now, sweeties. Barbara, take them downstairs please."

Barbara quietly did as she was told, picking up the puppies and moving along. "And one more thing. Make sure the waiters are all here. I know that's what I'm paying the wedding planner for, but she's out in the backyard and I'm just being my paranoid self. Nothing can go wrong today," she said, turning around from the woman tending to the front of her dress. "Joy," she said, stunned.

"You look . . . beautiful," Joy replied, finally moving from the doorway towards her mother.

"Thank you." She brushed back the embroidered cornflower blue sash wrapped around her waist. "Reem Acra. I fell in love with it the moment I saw it."

"I can see why."

Blue nodded as she rubbed her palms together.

"I didn't think you were going to come. But I'm glad you decided to."

"Didn't know I was gonna come either. Woke up this morning and something came over me."

Blue continued rubbing. "I love that dress on you," she said, looking at her daughter from head-to-toe. "It's gorgeous against your skin."

It was a coral little something. Not too tight. Not too low-cut. Leaving something for the imagination, but stylish in its own right. She looked down at herself, tugging at the chiffon of the dress she'd purchased at Neiman's last night.

"Thanks."

Blue's eyes sparkled at her daughter. She addressed the woman who'd been fixing her gown and the other six women in the room Joy had never met.

"Ladies, this is my daughter Joy O'Brien. Joy this is Chelsea, my seamstress. Pia, my hairstylist for today. My makeup artist, Venus. Dawn and Luca, my bridesmaids. And my matron of honor, Amelia."

They all exchanged hellos.

"I wanted to call you," Blue continued as the photographer took the opportunity to snap their picture. "These last minute preparations had me so flustered, before I knew it, the big day was here."

"It's cool," Joy said.

"No, no. It's not. I have to learn to do better. But, I wanted to tell you that I met with Paul a couple of days ago. We talked about you."

Joy's neck snapped back. "You did?"

Blue spoke to everyone in the room, "Could you all please excuse me and my daughter for a moment. We need just a few minutes. Thank you."

They quickly left and Blue invited Joy to sit on the massive bed.

"I showed a picture of you. The one where you were in that cute blue and white dress that looked absolutely adorable on you. I remember I was headed for these to-die-for pair of shoes I found in a boutique in Manhattan when I spotted your dress in a window. I said, forget the shoes, my baby's gotta have that dress."

Joy looked down at her hands and gave a wistful smile.

"What did he say when he saw the picture?" she asked, looking back at Blue's face.

"He was sorry. Said he didn't know what he was doing. You should give him a chance, Joy."

She couldn't pull her eyes from her mother's flawless features. Makeup was there, but barely. Her eyelids highlighted in soft shades of pink, her lips delicately sparkling underneath its rosey hue.

"I don't think that'll work. He got a life. I got a life. Feel like it's better we keep our lives separate. Didn't think you would meet up with him and all that. I can't forget how you never would let me talk about him. Ask questions and stuff like that."

Blue raised her hand to show her engagement ring. "Things happen."

She let her hand fall back into her lap. "I won't ever, ever forget what Paul Brooks did to me when he told me he wanted to get rid of you. A piece of my soul died that day. Today, it's almost completely been revived."

She took hold of Joy's hand and squeezed. "I loved your father. I wanted him in both of our lives. But if he didn't want to be there, wasn't anything in this world that would make me force him to do it. My mother taught me a lot. She never wanted me, but she kept me because it was a part of her beliefs.

She was raped by a black man, but somewhere deep down inside of her was something immovable, that wouldn't let her give up even an unwanted child. She taught me that there's some inkling of good, even in the hardest of hearts. I left home when I could manage and I made a vow to myself. I said, Blue O'Brien, whatever happens out here in this cruel, cruel world, don't forget to hold on to that part of you that is steadfast and pure. Your father tried to take that away from me, but I held it close. And now he sees the right in me for not giving in. The good in him, that was always there, is finally coming out."

Joy blinked at the things she was hearing for the first time.

"He knew about the rape and your mother and how she treated you?"

"Paul knew everything."

She looked at her mother. The woman who was at such a different place in her life on this day. Blue was ready to walk down the aisle, a man who truly loved her would be waiting at the end. One who made her every wish his command.

"There's a lesson in dying. And I had to die a little before I rebounded and rose up again," the gorgeous bride said standing up. "I'm guessing your father did the same."

Joy laughed and said, "You landed a damn good rebound."

Blue flashed a smile and put forth her hand.

"I know. And I have my daughter here to celebrate it with me. How about helping me put on my veil."

48 paul

Paul settled down into his favorite recliner after a long night of running back and forth taking photos at the sweet sixteen party for Rich's youngest daughter. The extravaganza proved to be excess at its best. It could've been a wedding if his daughter's gaudy dress wasn't hot pink with green sequins. However, Paul noticed that Rich seemed to be enjoying every last cent of his hard-earned money that had been spent on his baby girl. He admired him for it. He was a man who'd give anything for his kid. A man who worked a job that stressed him, just so he could pay to produce a party that her friends would talk about for weeks.

He wished he could've done the same for Joy, Sienna, and Noelle. Paul would upload over three hundred frames tomorrow. He could already see the birthday girl's smile embossed on every picture taken of her. It was a smile that any real father would work nonstop for to see on his daughter's face.

Paul thought of the many years and celebrations he'd missed out on. Lost. Gone. What would it take for all three of his daughters to give him a chance to create new memories? He would hold on to them and never let go. Be a father for real this time, cherishing each day of their future together.

He kneeled at the foot of his seat. He'd pray until God found it fit to grant the desires of his heart.

Lord, I praise you because you are faithful. And I give you honor because You've never failed me yet. Thank you for all You've done up until now. I know I'm undeserving of the mercy You give to me, but every time I look around You're there, answering my prayers yet again. Providing for me one more time. I feel blessed with Your grace abounding in my life. There's no way I could thank You enough.

BROKEN WITH STAINS

My worship is what I give to You. My worship and trust that you will work everything out according to Your plan. Lord, I want my girls in my life. I've come this far by faith and I'm not letting go until You let me lay eyes on each one of their faces. You know each of their hearts, Lord. Where they've been. What they've had to endure. Why they took the time to speak with me when they did. I pray that You will bless them all and bring us together. I'm believing, Father, that whatever's to come for Noelle, Sienna, Joy, and me will be life-changing and blessed by You. I ask these things in Your most precious name. Amen.

Paul picked himself up, dusting the carpet threads from his brown slacks. Within seconds, contentment fell over him like a cloak. He didn't know when his prayers would ever be answered, but hope was alive and kicking within his spirit.

He yawned as his body acknowledged the fact that it was tired. Paul tried to ignore it, figuring since she still awake, he'd head upstairs to spend some quality time with his wife. He reached just outside the den's door when his cell phone went off in his pocket. Grinding to a halt, he scooped it up.

He couldn't press the 'talk' button fast enough when he saw Sienna's number light up the display screen.

"Hello," he smiled.

"You said you were there morning, noon, or night."

"And I forgot to mention every time in between."

"Well, in that case, that makes me feel even better because then I'm assured you'll always be there whenever I call."

49 noelle

She could hear her mother's footsteps making their way up the creaky steps towards her bedroom. "You look so pretty. Go 'head girl. Show your father the beautiful daughter he's gonna wish he never left. But take this tissue and dab some of that lip gloss off," Candace encouraged, handing a Kleenex over to Noelle. "You meeting daddy, not your boo-boo David." They both laughed at the smart comment.

Noelle pushed her friend out of the way and took a closer look in the long mirror. "I'ma cut you if you don't move out my way. I'm all shaking and buggin' out. Damn, I didn't think I'd be this nervous about meeting him." She smoothed her hair and fidgeted with the silver bangles on her wrist.

"Take a breath. In then out and try a couple more to loosen you the hell up. I feel for you 'cause I'd be a mess too, but if anything, just know that you're looking like the bomb.com, honey. Look at it this way: thing would've been different if you didn't get that perm yesterday. Then you woulda really had something to be nervous about, with your hair looking like Don King. Now your naps are all slicked back and lovely and you have nothing to worry about; you'll be fine."

Noelle gave her friend a sideways glance, indicating she was two seconds away from getting her butt kicked. Soon after, they cackled like two old women at Candace's ability to lighten the mood at a time when Noelle's nerves were on edge. "Girl, you know I love you," Candace said holding her arms out to Noelle. "I hope everything goes well tonight. No, I take that back . . . because I *know* things will." They hugged and pulled apart to see Sharon standing by the doorway. Candace brushed a few hairs from Noelle's blouse. "I'm going downstairs to get something from the car. Be back in a minute."

As she walked across the room, Candace smiled at Sharon. "Your daughter looks good, Ms. Caldwell. I think I'll have to steal that outfit as soon as she's done with it. But, on second thought, I think I gained about fifty pounds from the cheesecake you brought home for us last night. *That* skirt is not gonna fit over *these* thighs. Maaaybe I'll be able to get that cute top past my head, but it's looking kinda iffy at the moment - lately I feel like my head's been getting bigger too. I've always had a dome, but really . . . don't it look a bit swole?"

Noelle watched her mother chuckle at Candace's ridiculous ramblings. "No, Candace. Your head is looking about the same."

"Okay, thanks. Just checking. I'll be back."

She walked out, leaving Noelle with Sharon. "You really did go all out to meet with him and your sisters, didn't you?" her mother asked with arms folded across her chest.

"Ma, not right now. I don't want to hear you -"

"Noelle, I didn't come in here to get on you about your father."

She took a long look at Sharon and then turned back to the mirror to make sure her hair was set in place. "I think you look very nice. And . . . and, I needed to tell you that I was sorry for the way I acted when you told me this meeting was going to take place. I apologize for trying to hold you back. You're an adult. And I need to let go so you can live your life as you see fit."

Noelle answered evenly, "It's okay, ma."

"I've always been a stubborn woman. It took your father about a month of asking me out before I finally agreed to going on a date with him."

"He was really persistent."

"That he was. And once again . . . he got what he wanted."

Noelle stopped combing her hair and forced herself to

face her mother. "I refuse to feel guilty about this. I'm doing what I feel is the right thing for me to do."

"Guilt isn't what I'm trying to lay on you."

"Then what do you mean by he got what he wanted again?"

"What I mean is, your father was never one to back down from anything until he got what he wanted. Like how he made it his business to contact you and make this meeting happen even though I was against it. I'm not mad at you for seeing him. The more I thought about it was the more I realized that I was trying to hold you back because I didn't want him to win. I didn't want to lose my baby to him just because he decided to step back in and claim a spot I didn't think he deserved. But in being truthful with myself, I had to come to terms with the fact that achieving your peace and happiness isn't about pleasing me. After really thinking hard on this, I can say he actually did something right for the second time in his life."

Noelle's heart leaped in her chest as she asked, "And what's the first?"

"Helping me create you." That's all she'd wanted to hear. Something positive. Reassuring. Her mother's acceptance was all that mattered in the world.

"I worried that you wouldn't forgive me for this. Nothing you've done for me has gone unappreciated. Don't ever think I chose sides, 'cause it's not what I intended to do." Noelle tried hard to stifle the tears. "I just wanted to meet him. It's always been something I hoped and prayed for. Who knew that God would hear little 'ole me? Didn't want to mention it to you, knowing how you'd react."

"It was selfish on my part. Shouldn't have deprived you like that. Hurt can make you do the darndest things."

"Oh, I know, ma. I sure do know."

Sharon knew what her daughter was referring to.

"Chris was just like another version of your father, but

one day he'll realize how he messed up too." Noelle smiled and replied, "You ain't telling me nothing I don't know. It's all good though, they both allowed themselves to miss out on the fabulousness of two incredible women."

50 sienna

If there was one thing Sienna hated, it was the fear associated with not knowing. She didn't know what the afternoon had in store. Didn't know what she'd find she liked or didn't like about Paul Brooks. Didn't know if she would get along with Noelle. Didn't know if there was anything she'd have in common with Joy.

She stood in the cool of her air-conditioned apartment, so why was sweat gathering at the nape of her neck? Self-consciousness twirled her about in a flurry of indecision. The mint-green and black patterned dress was gorgeous, yet she questioned whether it was too much. Sienna wished she had a helping hand, but Marni was working and couldn't been there to tell her if she looked like a fool or otherwise and her mother was away on business on the other side of the world.

Sienna raided her closet for something different to wear. She didn't want to do the all black shift that was too plain and more fitting for a funeral. The red pleated skirt might've been an option if the perfect blouse to go with it wasn't at the bottom of the laundry basket. Sienna touched the pink and red dress by her favorite designer, Tracy Reese. Marcus had bought it for her when they'd shopped together a while back. She'd have to throw that one away – it was necessary if she wanted to erase all memories of him that were left behind.

She plopped down on her bed, resigned to sticking with what she had on. She supposed it was good enough with its fuchsia hue, mandarin collar, and length that sat just above her knee. The black leather belt tied around her waist needed adjusting a tad, but for a restaurant setting it was appropriate and comfortable enough. Her black Prada shoes would finish the look off perfectly.

Or why not the black mules she'd bought on sale at

BROKEN WITH STAINS

Macy's last winter?

Perhaps the black mules with the black shift she could throw a bright-colored shrug over.

She closed her eyes and admonished herself to calm down. Joy and Noelle couldn't possibly be nit-picking like this. Sienna guessed the two of them were probably dressed and ready to step out of their front doors right now.

They were dressed and ready to step out of their front doors right now.

The thought scared her to her feet.

She could do this. She was ready. And that's what she'd just keep telling herself.

Sienna grabbed the black Pradas from their position in her closet and let her feet adjust to the pain for beauty. Taking one more sweeping glance in the mirror, she approved herself, grabbed her leather bag and headed for the front door.

She almost made it, before she tripped on the back leg of the sofa and landed on her hands. Her palm slid off a slippery piece of paper as soon as she hit the floor. Settling on her knees, she picked up the glossy 4x6 sheet. It was a picture of her and Marcus on Memorial Day of the previous year. That weekend, it had been just the two of them. No Nonda, no baby, no conniving best friend. Just the two of them and a love she thought was real.

She remembered the stranger they'd selected to take their picture. Remembered the suddenness of Marcus' firm, thick lips planted against her cheek. Her eyes said it all. Shock, joy, peace, satisfaction – life was good right then; she knew nothing could go wrong.

She marveled at the changes from a year ago. There would be no more moments like that shared with the man she still loved. She felt the pang in her chest telling her she would miss him more and more each day. Sienna fanned at her eyes. No way was she about to ruin her makeup at this point in time. Her father was in a restaurant waiting to lay eyes on her for the first time. Today, Marcus would have to take a seat somewhere on a back burner. There'd be more days like this to spend time wallowing in. Days she would cry and hurt and feel every morsel of resentment. But there was still a silver lining on a cloud beyond all that.

Annette Burgess had gone through the same thing. If her mother had the ability to survive, Sienna knew she could too.

She crumpled the picture into a tight ball, picked herself up, grabbed the fallen purse, dusted off her dress, and strutted her way to the door with chin up and shoulders held sky high.

51 joy

Joy frowned at her bank statement. Five hundred and fifty-four dollars. Ninety-five cents. It was all she had to her name.

She knew she had to do some quick thinking over the next couple days. Five hundred dollars was play money in her eyes. She'd spent that in five minutes a dozen times before.

Joy dreaded the thought that she'd have to resort back to Yaz or call up Madou to run game. It was tiring. Draining to be exact. Depending on a man to be the source of her survival, was becoming a chore she no longer had much interest in. She'd just lost a child for one of them she'd made the mistake of depending on. The only one she'd ever really cared about. The one who wanted nothing at all to do with her when all was said and done. She'd paid for it with her body and now only had five hundred and some change to show for it in the end

Joy concluded that there was no point in worrying about it now.

She hadn't placed a foot in the club after Luce's brother stepped between them that night. Wasn't any way in hell she'd have anything more to do with Luce or his Six Doors. Her bank account needed the loot fast, but she hadn't reached the point of desperation just yet. Still, as much as she tried to focus her mind elsewhere, the money woes flooded her brain. How was she supposed to focus on food and catching up when she was practically a dollar away from rooming in a card board box?

The clock shouted eleven a.m.

At twelve she'd be seeing her father for the first time.

Immediately, Joy's heart stuttered in her chest. She forced herself to think about the money instead. That was much easier.

Where did it all go?

She looked at the mass of unopened shopping bags thrown over the shoes at the bottom of her hall closet. Bags that held clothing, shoes, and accessories purchased weeks and weeks ago. Wooden hangers jutted out of the packed closet bulging at the seams with clothes that weren't able to fit inside the closet and dresser drawers already jam-packed in her bedroom.

What good was it all if it was all she had to show for herself?

Joy eyed the three hundred dollar coral dress thrown over the zebra-print chair in the corner of her bedroom. *At least Blue was lucky enough to snag a big fish,* she smiled. Yesterday, they'd just come back from yachting around Europe for their honeymoon.

She reminisced on her mother's spectacular wedding day. Dollar signs were sketched into every detail. The hundreds of white lilies and blue hyacinths. Soaring ice sculptures. A seven-tier cake. Even Pinkie and Moosa styled and profiled in little frilled blue dresses with diamond studded dog tags around their tiny necks.

And though Joy would've sworn on her grandmother's grave that Blue was only in it for the lavish lifestyle, it was obvious that it wasn't what Blue agreed to marry Tom for. There was undeniably something much deeper between the two. Joy would've been lying to herself if she continued to doubt the love both shared.

She wasn't going to hold her breath for it, but maybe it could happen for her too. Witnessing the bond her mom and new step-father had, proved to Joy true love wasn't what she'd felt for Luce. There was a difference between unshakeable love and caring for someone and their money. Love had a pulse. Infatuation was something built on unstable ground that could give way at any time.

She grabbed the leather bag she'd spent way too much

money for from its post on her night stand. After running her fingers through her long, wavy locks, Joy wiggled her body to shake off the jumping nerves.

"Joy, you ain't got one reason to be flippin' out over Paul Brooks. Just chill out and do what Blue said: hold on to that part that's steadfast and pure."

With that jolt of encouragement to herself, she took one last look in the mirror and cosigned her designer wear – a marigold corset and over-priced black blazer with the matching pencil pant. In the name of Gucci, she stepped over her fears, pushed her confidence to the forefront, and left her worries behind.

52 paul

Paul sat at his desk too in awe to do anything. All he could think about was his daughters. The three women he'd shared lunch with yesterday. His beautiful babies who weren't babies anymore.

They arrived one by one. Each coming no more than three minutes apart from the one before her. Sienna was the first to arrive to the small private room in Juliano's restaurant he'd arranged to be decked out with roses in every color imaginable. Blue, yellow, red, pink, white, and orange too - it took five florists to put together the awesome décor of flowers sitting in every direction one could turn.

Sienna was the only one Paul had never seen a photo of. He stood up from the table, felt like he was dreaming all over again. Her luminous smile melted him right away. *How'd I miss out on that all these years?* He questioned himself. Paul met her part way, taking as much of her in at once as he could. She was a woman. A full grown, beautiful black woman.

"Good to see you, Sienna," he said taking her hand with a huge, over-flowing smile gracing his face.

Her father was standing before her. She could hardly find the words to speak.

"Hi . . . I can't believe this."

A hug followed and then the sensation of her shaking in his arms. They pulled apart and Paul examined every inch of his first born's face. "Annette. You're all Annette. Striking just like your mother."

"Thank you," she blushed.

"Did you find the place alright?"

"Yes, it was easy. Your directions were just perfect."

"Good. Wow, my heart is pounding sixty miles an hour," he laughed. "But if I keeled over right now, I'd die a very happy man. Seeing you here is the answer to so many prayers. Man, God really is good."

The door eased open and in walked Noelle. She was taller than Paul expected. About five foot eight, plus three inch heels, her perfect hair bounced with every step she took towards him and her older sister.

"And you're the lovely Noelle."

"Yes," she said, enveloping her arms around the man she never thought she'd meet.

Paul gestured towards Sienna. "Noelle, this is my oldest daughter. Your sister, Sienna." The two sisters smiled at each other and hugged as if it would be the last time. Neither one wanted to be too obvious, but couldn't resist scanning the other from top-to-bottom. Noelle the similar physique Sienna also shared. Sienna saw the same mole she owned, gracing Noelle's chin. Paul compared the two. Where Sienna looked exactly like her mother, Noelle looked exactly like his mother. Her butterscotch skin, a color, somewhere in between him and Sharon's.

"Thank you for being here, Noelle. I was just telling Sienna how fast my heart was beating. I think it just sped up a little more."

Noelle and Sienna looked at each other and giggled at their father.

"It's true," Sienna offered. "But correct me if I'm wrong when I say he's not the only one whose heart is racing right about now. Mine is tap dancing in my chest. And I bet yours is probably doing the same thing too."

Noelle chuckled as she nodded in agreement. "I am kinda nervous too, but I'm glad I'm finally here to meet everyone."

The bustling sound at the front of the room cut into their conversation.

"Hi. Hope I'm not too late."

"You made it right on time," Paul assured his youngest

child. Her walk was one of confidence. Definitely a daughter of Blue. Joy was maybe a half inch shorter than Noelle without her heels. The long, pretty waves of hair flew behind her. Paul knew she'd probably broken many hearts with her sultry looks and magnetizing eyes. He took her into his arms. "Joy, meet your sisters, Sienna and Noelle."

"Hi, ladies," she waved. "We finally meet."

Joy followed suit when she focused closely on their faces and saw the happy tears begin to fall.

* * *

Paul's eyes couldn't take in enough of the women surrounding him at the round dining table. While the foursome feasted on the elaborate lunch before them, their father delighted in all of the little things. He noticed how Sienna's almond-shaped eyes shined an extra bit whenever she became excited. Loved Joy's unconscious penchant for whipping her hair back with her hand and laughing with reckless abandon. Noelle was the most subdued of the three, but always managed to get a laugh with her sharp sense of humor. So different were his daughters, but also the same in so many ways. They were all beautiful. All able to sometimes finish each other's sentences. All in tune, like they'd known each other their whole lives. God had been gracious, granting him the desires of his heart. But there was still more to do, a lot more to say. He'd made a promise to Ashley, but more importantly had to come clean for himself.

"Once again, I have to thank you Joy, Noelle, and Sienna for being here when you didn't have to be. There are a lot of events that led up to this day, but there's one event that started it all."

They looked around the table at each other, wondering if they were the only ones left in the dark about what he was talking about.

BROKEN WITH STAINS

"I don't talk about it. Spent most of my life trying to block it out. I tried to reveal it to all of your mothers at some point in time . . . but for something like this . . . it wasn't so easy."

The thought alone made Paul want to get up from the table and leave. He took his time gathering the courage. Lifted his sorrowful brown eyes to his daughters and let his past go.

"I was nine years-old living in St. Louis with my parents and two younger brothers at the time. My mother sent me to godmother's house one day; my god-mother was moving away to Chicago the following afternoon and wanted me to sleep over since it'd be the last time she saw me in a long while. I was the baby she never had, so she spoiled me rotten. The day we spent together was a blast because she was a kid at heart," he smiled. "We ate corn dogs, the best in the whole state. She took me to the toy store, bought me some cars I wanted. Took a car ride over by the water and fed the birds some bread. Later played dominoes, my favorite game back then. Everything was real cool. Then night came; time for me to go to sleep. Didn't want to sleep though. I played with a flash light on the living room floor around the packed boxes. I guess I wore myself out sometime soon after that, because next thing I know, my god-mother's husband is picking me up in his arms."

Paul lifted the glass of iced tea to his mouth and took a swallow.

"He picked me up and placed me in their bed. I had a hard time falling asleep. My god-mother was screaming in the bathroom the whole time I tried. I was a little scared and just tossed and turned the whole time. Finally, right before I fell asleep, her husband went to the bathroom to try to calm her down.

They took me to Chicago with them the next afternoon. I didn't want to go because . . . I wanted my mama . . . I wanted my daddy. My brothers, my toys, my favorite pack of playing cards. But still, they told me 'no'. I bawled, musta been all the way to Chicago. The whole ride. And they let me.

Once we got there, wasn't until a week after we settled in, they placed a picture of my burned down house in front of my eyes. My god- ma told me, 'They all went to heaven, Paulie. Your mama's there with your daddy and James and Walter' - those were my brothers."

Paul made eye contact with each of his daughters before he continued. "Just that quick. I had nobody. Yeah, I had my god-mother and her husband, but my parents and my baby brothers were dead. Gone in the blink of an eye. A gas explosion blew them right up. Just that quick. And I never got the chance to say goodbye; I was traumatized. After that, I was always checking stoves, checking behind people to see if they put things in the right place, checking the windows to see if they were shut tight at night, looking under random cars to make sure bombs or people with guns weren't hidden underneath them. I didn't want to lose anyone else. Had a deep fear that never stopped building inside of me as the years progressed."

He stepped outside of his body and back in time.

"Before long, I became highly paranoid. Distancing myself from my godmother, her husband, all of the few friends I made. I was subject to lose any one of them unexpectedly at any time of the day. The camera became my one and only best friend when I started developing film full-time during my summer break, before my sophomore year of high school. Photography was it for me. I could capture all the memories a roll of film could hold. Create a story board of life. That way memories would never disappear. Never fade away. To this day, I keep a second print of every photo I take and a copy of my discs in a bank safety deposit box. If my studio just happens to explode one day, my photos are safe and in one piece." Paul repeatedly stroked his beard.

"When I left you girls with your mothers, it wasn't because I didn't want anything to do with you. It was anxiety eating me alive. I was fearful that I would lose you all too. The pregnancies weren't planned. I tried to be careful and when I found out each of your mothers was carrying, I panicked. Went into flight mode. I ran because I couldn't risk losing any body else. If I had stayed and came home to find another burned down house with my baby and her mother in it, I would have simply gone crazy. I didn't want to do that. Couldn't take that chance." He watched their solemn faces. Prayed he'd done his best to make them all understand.

Paul took the weathered photo from his wallet and held it, reading what was written on the back. "May 9, 1966." He passed it to Noelle on his right and continued speaking.

"Everything I knew and loved went up in flames with that house. Not only my entire family, but my innocence, and my peace - they all blew up that night. My godmother, her husband, and I . . . we, um . . . we made the trip back for my brothers funeral two weeks after we arrived in Chicago.

Was a closed casket of course. James and Walter had a double funeral. But my mother and father didn't have their funeral until about a week after that. Funds were low. Nobody really had money to help pay to bury four bodies. We weren't well-off by any means, so there wasn't much money that had been saved up. Anyway, I didn't go to my parents' funeral. After Walter and James were buried, we went back to Chicago. I never did officially get to say goodbye to my mother and father. Bethany Ann and Paul Brooks III. Those are your grandparents."

Paul focused on the picture of the blackened house, now in Joy's hands.

"My experience doesn't make what I did right in no way, shape, or form . . . It's just something that's extremely hard to get over when you feel like you've been scarred for life."

53 noelle

Noelle glanced to her left and watched David hanging on to the pastor's every word. She turned to her right and saw her father doing just the same with a smile stretched across his contented face.

He'd come an extremely long way. Leaving her mother to be a single parent had been totally wrong despite his reasons. But regardless of that fact, healing had taken place in that room of flowers a week ago. She was happy Paul had gained control of his life, deciding to climb up, instead of continuing his downward spiral.

Noelle admired him for it. So much so, the prospect of building a solid relationship with her father excited her more than ever. It charged her with a new reason to get out of bed each morning.

Her eyes roamed the medium-sized church, every seat filled with men, women, and children. They all had stories. Trials. Experiences. Matters of the heart that still needed to be worked out. No one was exempt. Everyone had a problem. Who else in here would be bold enough to confront their issues head on and make a choice to do something about them?

Maybe she does have a faint ache in her heart, but look what God can do. Words of Hope. Her bestfriend's mom had certainly hit the nail on the head.

Noelle turned again to David, who this time drew his focus from the podium, and stared right back. She entwined her arm around his, smiled, and batted her eyelashes a few times. She'd given her love just to get her heart shattered in return, but God had a funny way of bringing sunshine in the darkest hour.

"You don't believe that God is able? Consider what he did for Daniel and Joseph. Visit with the Israelites and ask them what the Lord did in their favor." The pastor mopped his forehead with a white handkerchief and continued. "You wanna know the meaning of unconditional, unyielding, undeniable love, look to Jesus hanging on the cross for your sins. Pained, afflicted, but just so He could make an easier way for you, you, and you," he pointed into the crowd. "Laid down His life for the brokenhearted, the wounded, and the weary."

54 sienna

"We all live our lives, at some point, searching for love in all the wrong places. Well, Jesus said 'Come unto me, all ye that labour and are heavy laden, and I will give you rest'. Isn't it good to know that we can fall into His arms and all the love we've ever sought in life is nothing compared to the love He has for us? The best part is, he's available whenever you need him. Today I say, thank you Jesus! Thank you Lord 'cause I'm blessed, highly favored, and loved by the One who loves me best. And guess what? He loves you just the same."

Sienna let the pastor's words saturate her heart. Marcus never loved her the way she'd sought for him to love her since the first day they met. He showered her with lies. And deceit. But never the one thing she truly wanted all along.

She looked to her father sitting by her side. His indiscretions were committed a long time ago. He was definitely a repentant man. One who deserved a chance because he genuinely wanted to love her like a father should. But even if things didn't turn out to be happily ever after once the freshness of reuniting wore off, she'd be quite okay with that. She'd still have her mother, her bestfriend Marni, and above it all, she had herself. The Sienna Burgess who wanted to love herself, but couldn't do it properly before. The Sienna who was now making strides to fiercely love the woman in the mirror, learning to be content on her own. She was determined to be the best woman she could be. And as the pastor shouted from the pulpit, it felt great to know that Jesus loved her too. She'd take that. Take it and stash it away for the times she forgot that she was deserving of real love - love that was right.

She replayed her mother's phone call from this morning over again in her head. Annette was always a mother first - she'd actually taken a two-minute break from closing an important deal overseas.

"Sweetie, I don't have much time, but I wanted to say hi and tell you that I love you and I'll fly up there to break your father's arms in a heartbeat if he doesn't take care of my baby."

Sienna laughed over the phone. "Ma, get back to work. You are too much."

"You know it's all in love," Annette smiled into the phone. "But really, I hope everything goes well and . . . I'm happy. I'm truly, truly happy to see you this rejuvenated again."

She ached to reach through the lines and give her mother a hug. "I do feel so much better. Content. And I owe so much to you. Love you, mom."

"Love you too, honey bunny . . . always."

55 joy

Joy needed help. Hadn't been in a church since her grandmother's Catholic funeral, more than a year ago. Even then, she didn't feel the need to crack open the large book sitting in its holder on the back of the pew before her. No familiarity with the Bible at all, she hastily flipped to the index on the sly and found out what page the book of Matthew started on. Adjusting the black leather Bible in her lap, Joy shuffled through its thin, white sheets until she landed on the correct page. She looked for the verse the pastor requested they turn to – Matthew 7:6:

Do not give what is holy to the dogs; nor cast your pearls before swine, lest they trample them under their feet, and turn and tear you in pieces.

Amen. That made sense.
Dog: Luce.
Pearls: Her.
Pieces: What was left of her after the fat lady had sung her last chord.

Always the fighter, the cold-hearted one who didn't care for anything a man could give except for his deep pockets, Joy was still dumbfounded by how she'd allowed Luce to slip into her sub-conscience. How he'd made it through the wall she'd spent years carefully erecting. If it could happen to her, it could happen to the best and the rest of them. Her finances were still shaky, but Joy knew she'd figure something out. More than anything, she was simply happy that her father came knocking on her door at the time that he did.

She smiled over at David sitting a couple people down

from her. When she'd watched him walk into the church with Noelle this morning, she'd nearly bit her tongue in half as she chewed her piece of gum. She noticed his double-take when he was first introduced to her by Noelle. Joy respected him to the utmost for playing it off like it was their very first meeting. David had shaken her hand with a polite smile on his face and put his arm back around Noelle's waist. Who knew she'd been linked to one of her sisters all along? Who knew she'd ever see the day she had sisters at all? Sienna and Noelle. She now had sisters. Two other females sharing the same blood that she could talk with and relate to. Joy took a peek over at them. They were just as beautiful. Noelle's long, flawless legs were just like her own. Sienna's effortless chic style so similar their closets could be interchangeable.

Well, maybe I could subtract a few booty-cutters and studded mini dresses. But other than that, we pretty much have the same taste. Shoot, maybe I could even learn a thing or two. Them shoes she got on are sick.

Sienna caught Joy's eyes wandering at her feet. She smiled, leaned into her sister, and whispered, "Michael Kors. Macy's sale. $29.99. We'll take a trip one day - I'll show you."

Joy's eyes perked up. There were shoes that amazing that could be found for thirty bucks? She sat back in the bench and mused to herself. *Hey, shawty really alright with me.*

She tuned back into the pastor as he stepped off the podium and stood at the head of the aisles. "You can't trust anyone to treat you better than they would treat themselves. It's a me, me, me society we live in. A lot of times the people who're most cruel with others turn out to treat themselves even worse. I had a problem myself, years ago when I had just gotten saved. I was high for the Lord, but still didn't know how to love my own self the way I should have. I abused my body, partaking in all sorts of filth. But one day, hallelujah, I said one day, I came to realize that God was not a God of self-hate. If I loved myself, ain't no way I'd willingly give myself over to just anyone so they could tear me to pieces. No way, no way, no way. Today I know that when you make enough room for Jesus in your heart, you're completely changed and freed to love yourself like never before. You're perfectly made whole in Jesus."

Joy turned his words over in her head. Perfectly made whole. Could *she* ever be perfectly made whole?

Nah, I done did so much dirt, I don't see how.

She looked over to her father. The man who'd lost his mother, father, and two brothers at the same time. Same man who ran away from three children out of fear. The smiling man who had for the most part overcome it all.

Took some time, but he did it. Had a wife, a house, a successful career, his daughters, and a large helping of peace of mind.

Someone in the row behind tapped her shoulder. She turned around and followed the pointing finger.

At the door was Blue, radiant in white, waving with a perfect smile, all in one piece.

56 paul

"Camilla, I'm gonna have to come here on Sundays more often," Noelle said taking the last bite of the delicious dessert. "I'm thinking you might not be able to get rid of me. This sweet potato pie is yummy. Ever thought about going into business for yourself? I'd order a couple right now."

"Thanks. It's my aunt's recipe. Created it one night when she said she woke up from a dream that made her write down every single ingredient. I could never go into business selling these though. I already have my hands full at the spa."

Sienna chimed in, "Where's your spa located again?"

"It's in Larchmont."

"I don't know where that is. It's like, if I'm not in the Bronx then I'm in the city and if I'm not in the city then I'm in the Bronx."

"You ladies have to come by the spa sometime then. Really, I would love it if you all got together and stopped by. Turn it into a sisters day of beauty. We do everything from body wraps to stone massages, pedicures, manicures – all that good stuff."

"What if our father wanted to come along too?" Joy asked, smirking as she gestured at Paul. "Put your foot in a little paraffin."

Taking a look at Paul, the women laughed.

"I'd dip my foot in a little paraffin. But I wouldn't want to spoil a day of beauty between sisters, now would I?"

Camilla placed her utensils on her plate. "Yeah, it's better if you left him in the studio. Bring him to the spa and I promise you he'd bring a fluffy pillow and in two seconds flat be knocked out in the steam room." The women cackled at Paul's expense. He sat, loving every minute of it.

His wife continued, "Seriously, I don't know what your

schedules are like, but it would be great if you stopped by soon. It'd be really fun."

"I could use a spa treatment. Sounds good to me," Sienna said.

Noelle and Joy agreed.

"Good. When you come up with a time, let me know. I'll let my staff hook you guys up. Tell'em those beautiful ladies get the works."

"Speaking of works," Paul interrupted. "My receptionist is going to Trinidad for five months. Some family situation she has going on down there, so I'm looking for someone to fill in for her. Would any of you happen to know someone looking for a job? The pay is good, I get a lot of clients so I treat my receptionist more than fair."

Sienna and Noelle tried, but couldn't think of anyone.

"I know somebody who might."

Paul looked at Joy. "You do?"

"Yeah, she's smart even though she never went to college or anything like that. And you're a cool guy, so I'm sure she won't mind working with you."

* * *

They gathered in the den. Shoes were off, a DVD was on, they talked more than they watched the film.

"Look," Noelle pointed at Paul's left foot. "You and Sienna have the same pinky toe."

They all erupted into laughter as Sienna pulled her foot back in an attempt to detract their attention.

"I might have his pinky toe, but you have his long fingers. Take a good look."

They all whipped their heads around to compare.

Paul shook his head at them both. "So ya'll just gonna sit here and pick me apart?"

"Don't worry," Joy replied. "We all look fierce, so that

says a lot." The sisters nodded, agreeing on that observation.

"There's no doubt about that. You're all very beautiful women. So beautiful in fact, why don't we take a picture? Got my camera upstairs. You up for it?" Paul asked.

"I'm cool with it," Joy said.

Sienna grabbed her purse. "Let me put on a little lipstick first."

"Hold up, let me practice my model pose," Noelle joked, standing up with her hands bent above her head.

They howled at her ridiculous poses, telling her to strike another and then the next.

Paul raced upstairs to get his camera and came back down ready to take the first shot. Camilla suggested the sisters take it by the stone fireplace.

"You should get in it with us," Sienna said, signaling Camilla over.

"No, you go ahead -"

Joy walked over to Camilla and took her hand, leading her to their spot by the fireplace. "Well, okay . . . I'll shut my mouth and smile when ready," Camilla chuckled.

Noelle spoke up, unwilling to leave anyone out of the picture. "Put a timer on the camera, daddy. We want you in it too."

Paul stopped fiddling with the buttons for a second, forgetting what adjustments he was trying to make. Noelle had just called him daddy. Daddy. The first time any of them had called him by that title.

Tears suddenly began to sting at the back of his eyes. *Not now, I'll definitely save you guys for later.* He gathered himself, saying, "I can do that. Let me just get this bad boy ready." After timing the camera, he placed it on a level place close by and went to join his wife and daughters.

"Ten seconds 'til it flashes, ladies. Ten, nine, eight, seven, six, five, four, three, two, one . . ."

They smiled together as a whole.

www.ingramcontent.com/pod-product-compliance
Lightning Source LLC
Chambersburg PA
CBHW070358260626
47161CB00001B/185